Donald E. Dambois

"A Vampire Novel"

CHANGING WORLDS

Book 1 of:
The Dharalyn Chronicles

Website: http://www.donalddambois.com

Email: author@donalddambois.com

ISBN: 1466271116

ISBN 13: 9781466271111

DEDICATION

This book is dedicated to my Mother: Lois J. Berchtold
You always believed and had faith in me, even when
I had none in myself.
(We will miss you always.)

And to my children
April & Dustin
You are the very foundation of my heart and soul.

For
Trinity
All the love in the world.

ACKNOWLEDGMENT

I have enjoyed the support of numerous family and friends during the creation of this novel. I especially would like to personally thank those listed below for their heartfelt contributions, patience and understanding.

Barbara Washburn: *My dearest auntie and my most valued proofreader.*
Kimberley Beaulieu: *My very best, dearest friend and staunchest ally who kept pushing and never let me settle for second best.*
Glenn Beaulieu: *Kim's wonderful husband and my friend.*
Shaylyn Dambois: *My exceptional niece and the one for whom I wrote this book.*
Ciara Clark: *My favorite first-draft reader and poet.*
Anne Marie & John Dituro: *For listening to all of my crazy ideas & providing invaluable insight at our Friday lunches.*
Scott Dambois: *For being a tough critic and giving solid advice.*
Keith, Jennifer & Kristen Capolino: *My dearest friends and supporters.*
Kathy Ferdon Peck: *Biggest fan and most loyal friend.*
Terri Paust: *Final test read and assistant editor.*
Valerie Goetz: *My niece and 2nd assistant editor.*

Special thanks to: Mary Beth Daly, Amber Kimiecik-Ritchings, Angela Lempka Ottilo, William Youngman, Fran Bernard, Angela & Derek Jenney, Darlene Scott, Melissa Streeter.

Also, for their helpful feedback:

Brenna, Kaylee, Varvara.

CONTENTS

PROLOGUE

"They're coming!" shouted Abraxis, as he simultaneously unsheathed the Scramsword at his side and brushed his horse's flanks so that she would canter out of harm's way. "Hold the line! Make ready the Portal!" he yelled. Quickly he grabbed Dharalyn by the arm and guided her reluctant figure toward the outer ring of the circular eidolith that marked the periphery of a power circle used by the Cavalithic Priests in their transport ceremonies. "Shosa, how long till the rift is open?" he asked, as he glared at one of the many blue robed priests who were rushing frantically about, preparing the circular construct of finished stone and marble centered by an enormous metallic structure that was the portal's frame. Soon, the pulsing vortex of energy contained within the ancient structure would appear, opening a space-time doorway which could then be used to travel long distances across the surface of the planet.

"Not long, not long," gasped the priest, who appeared to be somewhat winded from the wild, chaotic ride they had just taken from the capital city that lay only a few miles north from their current location. "Just keep them off us for a few moments and we will be ready." Loudly, he shouted clipped orders at the other priests and then just as he began to move off, he felt a strong hand grasp his upper arm.

"Here, use this," barked Abraxis in a commanding tone. Pulling a dark blue destination crystal from an inner pocket, Abraxis handed it over and saw the confused look register in the priest's face as the man examined the six unfamiliar coordinate markings glowing within. "It's been specifically tuned for a very special location, one that must be kept secret at all costs," he explained in hurried, muted tones and then added as the priest started to argue, "please Shosa, I must ask you to trust me on this matter."

A few tense moments passed until finally, somewhat begrudgingly, Shosa nodded and then moved off hurriedly. Only once, he allowed himself a quick, worried glance at the maelstrom gathering in the sky overhead and then he returned his attention to the immediate task at hand. "So much to do, so very much to do and no time to do it properly," he mused, his face etched with concern.

Abraxis turned and shouted a few more hurried commands at the two Malakovani family guardians that were busily grabbing their gear before turning toward his young charge. "Dhara," he said brusquely as he grabbed her by her shoulders and looked into her confused and terrified face, "my apologies, my dear princess, but we haven't the time here for explanations. Ghasta and Sheera will accompany you to the underground family stronghold on Gwendovar Island to protect you and look after your needs. The rest of your retainers will join you as soon as I think it's safe for them to do so," he added, as he impatiently waved for the two guards to join him. "The priests are opening a portal now. As soon as it is attuned, you are to go through and stay there in hiding until I come for you!"

"But Abraxis...." Dharalyn shouted over the surrounding tumult, her bright green eyes filled with concern. Men were shouting, thunder was rumbling in the distance and the sounds of fierce fighting were coming closer and closer. "What about Mother? Isn't she coming with us?"

"I'm very sorry to have to tell you this, Dhara," said Abraxis matter-of-factly and with a peculiar tone to his voice that almost seemed to border on indifference, "but, your mother has been killed by a triumvirate of Praxillari Elite and it is probable that you will be too, if we don't get you out of here. And now!" he added abruptly, as he pulled her unceremoniously toward the waiting priests, who had placed the seven red crystals and the one dark blue in their sconces and begun the attunement ceremony. Worry seethed like a storm-tossed sea within his stomach, the churning sensation oddly mirroring the conflicting emotions playing through his mind. Soon the portal would be open and Dhara would be transported to a faraway location, though not the one that he, in fact, had just told her about. A destination that only a very special group of high-ranking Sedai even knew existed. The tall, commanding form and trusted Captain of the Atrova Guardians who was by blood oath sworn to protect the family Malakovani with his very life, gave a last purposeful glance toward his beloved young charge as suddenly, the periphery all about them exploded with the dark, seething forms of dozens of fighting warriors. Within moments, both Ghasta and Sheera were themselves fighting for their lives as Abraxis propelled Dhara forward, shielding her as best he could with his body. "Now!" he barked sharply at Shosa, as the wild-eyed priest glanced at him. "We need it now!"

"A few more moments!" Shosa shouted back, as with an abrupt look of horror, an arrow shaft exploded from his chest.

Abraxis glanced toward the shimmering portal that had only just then appeared before them, and sensing he had no more time, made the only decision left to him. "Damn Fayeki, tell them to hold back and the damn fools do the exact opposite," he muttered quietly to himself as, grabbing Dharalyn firmly about the shoulders, he lifted and practically threw her into the shining, pulsing red light floating within the circular arch of the energy filled gateway. He watched transfixed, as the pool of light suddenly began to diffuse and surround his young charge, as it should. Above them, the brewing storm which had been building for some time, suddenly released its ferocity upon them. With a bright flash and a tremendous roar, light exploded all about him, rocking the solid flooring beneath as, unbelievably and with incredibly poor timing, a jagged bolt of lightning struck the metallic housing of the circular portal frame. Retina searing light assaulted his senses as a second deafening roar shook the grounds, felling all of the nearby combatants. His ears battered with a roaring cacophony of sound, Abraxis felt himself blown back, as a nearly solid blast of energy surged outward with the crushing force of an unstoppable tidal wave, obliterating both his senses and the fading stream of his consciousness that was reeling with shock. His final moments passed in fragmented bits of sound and light, and then he knew no more as in a barely discernible speck of awareness, he felt himself hit the cold, hard ground.

CHAPTER 1

THE WITCH LIGHT

Danielle Frances Walkerman pulled back on the reins of her horse to slow her as she felt a sudden hitch in the small bay's stride. She had thought she had felt something a bit off awhile back, and now it was becoming increasingly evident that the horse was having an issue. "Daddy!" she hollered as she pulled firmly on the reins, bringing the pretty brown horse to a halt. Jonathan Lee Walkerman, or as the locals called him, Big John, turned in his saddle to glance at his daughter while she continued, "I think Biscuit may have a piece of shale caught in her right shoe," she said, her voice plainly worried. "She's been acting funny ever since we passed through the rock slide a ways back."

Big John nodded once and called back in a voice that tended toward gruff, and yet belied his gentle nature. "We're almost at the camp. Go ahead and walk her the rest of the way honey, and I'll check her when we get there."

Danielle nodded quickly and lifted her right leg from the stirrup, swung it over the horse's back and lightly lowered herself to the ground. As she stepped back, she sensed her brother's horse coming up behind her and then felt his toe as, passing much closer to her than he needed to, he reached his foot out and prodded her none too gently in her back. "Dammit Aaron!" she cursed as he moved past her with what was to her, a wicked little chuckle. "You're such a freekin dweeb!"

Danielle gave a surreptitious glance toward her father's retreating back and sighed. The last thing she needed right now was another speech about her colorful choice of vocabulary. *God, what a little jerk,* she thought angrily to herself, while taking hold of her horse's bridle and stroking and patting her neck. Danielle glanced once toward her brother's retreating form, which was now galloping the remaining distance toward the small lakeside camp that was just a hundred yards or so up the trail. "He is just asking for a serious butt-kicking," Danielle said softly to no one in particular, as she grabbed Biscuit's reins in her hands. Leading the small horse that was now clearly favoring its right front leg, she continued up the well-marked path and over a small rise until she spied their family's cabin, along with its beautiful spring-fed pond laid out before her. It was a sight that only a short year ago would have brought her a bright smile but now only caused her to grimace. It had been one of her mother's favorite spots in the whole world. And why wouldn't it be? The Peaceful Pond, as some family member had christened it, probably her grandmother, was in her opinion one of the most picturesque and serene places you could ever envision. A pretty sandy beach outlined the gentle curve of the nearby water's edge. Along the right side was a wide, flat meadow spotted with jumbled thickets of large leafy bushes. Back in the early spring, those bushes had been adorned with bright yellow flowers. Now however, the bushes were simply green and full and surrounded by broad swathes of blooming purplish and white wildflowers. The far edges of the meadow were bordered by dozens of evenly spaced apple trees, which marked the beginning of a small orchard that had been planted by one of her relatives many years ago. She could see that most were still thick with hanging apples and made a silent plan to get Biscuit some of the fruit while they were here. Her horse just loved fresh apples and Danielle knew that the other two horses did as well. The whole back side of the pond was framed by small to medium sized oaks and some ash, creating a tall green backdrop which rose gently into the hills beyond. And on her far left, a small trickling stream wound its way through the lush undergrowth, taking away the excess water that was generated by the myriad of underground springs which kept the pond filled. Her grandfather had cleared this area some sixty years before to create his own private little getaway, and Walkerman family members had been coming here ever since to fish, swim and just get away from it all. A small reddish, clapboard cabin lay just off the shore on the left side of the little beach, which contained several wooden bunks as well as a rudimentary kitchen, a shower that spewed icy cold water that would cause your teeth to chatter on even the warmest of days, a tiny, second story loft where her brother and she sometimes slept and a working bathroom. This last convenience had been installed by her father many years ago at the behest of her mother, whom, she had learned, had refused to make these regular outings without that small concession, as she had called it, to the amenities of the modern world. A small corral for the horses abutted the back of the building and she could see that presently it was filled with the tall, sweet grass which the horses liked to graze upon. Actually, the grass was growing abundantly all about them at this time of the year and gave the area the appearance of an emerald sea, the wind playfully rippling wave-like through the meadow with every gust of air. Danielle handed her father Biscuit's reins and then stood for a moment, gazing silently toward the far hills, a quiet memory tugging at her consciousness. Momma had loved a certain spot up there. A small clay dig that was full of tiny quartz crystals which they had used to make all types of homemade jewelry. Last summer, about this time, they had walked together to the small excavation site on a quiet afternoon much like this one, and had had one of the best talks ever while digging and screening the clay for the colorful bits of shiny treasure. She'd talked about life, love, lessons learned and the wisdom that comes from living a full and joyful existence. Danielle had laughed as her mother had, for the nth time, described her father's bumbling and very funny attempts to court her mother's affection when they were just a few years older than she was now. Like the time he'd stood outside of her window with his guitar and had sung love songs all evening long, until her father had chased him off with a shotgun. And then, there was the time that he'd driven all the way to her aunt's house in Brazzleton, some three hours away, to hand deliver her a huge bouquet of gorgeous red roses which he'd made for her on Valentine's Day. Roses, her mother had explained while laughing, for which he'd never given an even remotely plausible explanation as to where he had gotten them. "I mean, roses are very expensive, and I know for a fact that he was flat broke!" she had giggled. She and her mother had continued to work in the clay as her mother once again related the story of how Danielle's grandfather had finally relented and allowed the young rapscallion, as he had often described him, to stay for lunch. And then there was the time just last summer, just a few months before Momma had passed....

Danielle brushed away a silent tear and then shook herself sheepishly, realizing that she'd been standing still like some dorkish, disconnected statue. She glanced at her father who had been quietly studying her with those big, gentle eyes of his which sometimes, she thought, saw way more than she liked. "Daddy," she said, and then took a quick breath while absently digging her toe into the ground, "I think I'm gonna go for a little walk. Do you mind?" she asked, and then strode away, not waiting for his answer. A few more tears had begun to make their way down her cheeks and she didn't want him to see her crying or to worry about her as she knew he would.

Big John watched his young daughter move off, his face etched with the grave concern he felt for her deep within his troubled heart. She was now sixteen years old and in fact had just had a birthday a few months ago. But she didn't act like the typical sixteen year old who should be constantly on the phone with her friends, talking about everything under the sun. Including, God forbid, boys. She was only a pale imitation of the girl she should be and had, actually, once been. He couldn't remember the last time she'd spoken on the phone or texted with anyone at all. Ever since that terrible automobile accident last February when her mother and his beloved wife of almost twenty years, Marilyn, had died, she had existed in some kind of half-aware state of mind.

Always kind of a loner, as the months had passed, she had seemed to withdraw more and more deeply within herself, and was becoming increasingly lackluster and despondent. Most days, John had to push her to get her to talk to him at any length, and found himself often barking at her when repeated attempts to get her to interact with the rest of the family received little if any response. John rubbed his jaw thoughtfully and then opened the wooden gate and led Danielle's horse within. Grabbing a small pair of pliers from a leather pouch fastened to his belt, he knelt down and began to examine the horse's hoof. Within moments he spotted the troublesome piece of sharp shale jammed into the soft tissue of the heel and soon had it extracted. "Gonna need a day or two for that to heal up there, old girl," he said, rubbing the horse's leg and then standing with a groan. "Damn back acting up again," he growled and moved back toward the gate, which he quickly closed and fastened with a loop of rope that served as a latch. John gazed wistfully across the pond and up the greensward toward the tree line. She was already out of sight. It didn't take much to guess where she was going. Danielle and Marilyn had spent many hours up there together over the past few years, digging for the bits of quartz crystals they used to make the jewelry they so loved. Some of these were sold at a local flea market, some given as gifts and others, too pretty to part with, adorned walls and knickknack shelves all over the old house. He shook his head silently as he felt himself suddenly choke up, nearly overwhelmed by the flood of memories from those happier times. Even though they couldn't begin to afford it, he thought to himself, if she didn't improve soon he was going to have to seek some professional help for her. His sister Sara, who had lived with them for the past two years and helped take care of Danielle's Gran, worked part time at the local hospital in Pine Tree and could probably get him the name of someone competent. Up until now, he'd held off talking to anyone about it and to be honest, had squashed the conversation whenever Sara had seemed to be hinting at the possibility. He had secretly hoped that Danielle would eventually stop grieving so hard and snap out of the terrible funk which seemed to pervade her very being. But week after week had passed and it had been six, no, seven months and she was still getting worse, much worse. John shook his head sadly and began walking over to where his son was busily trying to start a fire in the open fire pit and made a decision he'd been avoiding for quite some time. He had come out here, taken some time off from work he couldn't really afford to miss, in the hope that he could reach her. If he couldn't, though, if over the next few days she stayed the same as she had been, then maybe it was time. Time to listen to Sara and get Danielle some real help, no matter what the cost. Sighing with the number of burdens that weighed so heavily on his mind, Big John knelt down to help his son, whom he could tell from the way he was progressing was much more likely to catch himself on fire than start the simple campfire which would soon be cooking their dinner.

Danielle brushed aside the last branch of a small copse of trees and walked down the short remainder of the path which ended at the clay dig she and her family had worked for years. There was a broad earthen wall here formed by an up-thrust section of the hill behind, that rose steeply about thirty or so feet above her. A whole row of small pines grew along the lip of the ledge high above which shaded the whole area, except when the sun was directly overhead and gave the dig a kind of secluded, guarded quality. It was as if a mythical giant had reached down and grabbed up a large fistful of dirt, leaving a huge semicircular hole of red and gray clay about thirty feet wide, which cut a swath directly into the hill ahead. It was here that the Walkerman family had found the very best place to search for the clumps of clear and milky crystals, which always seemed to Danielle to be like their own private treasure trove. Gazing about, she soon found a good place to sit near the outer edge of the cutout, a small thicket of grass to relax on so that she wouldn't get dirty. She felt bad for leaving her father and brother down below at the camp. She knew why her father had brought them up here and knew too, how worried he was about her. But she just didn't seem to be able to shake this pervasive feeling of melancholy that suffused her very being. Lately, she seemed to find fault with just about everything, from the ministrations of her Aunt Sara who only wanted to be there for her, to the obvious attempts of her younger brother to cheer her up by bugging the crap out of her, which was just his way, she knew, of showing her that he cared about her. And then there was Gran, who needed all the love and attention Danielle could spare her, since the stroke had confined her to a wheelchair. Her grandmother had always been loving, gentle and kind, and here she was, so miserable and within herself she was unable to give back that love and attention when it was so sorely needed. Danielle hated the way she was, hated the way she was treating everyone. Heck, hated herself most of all. She had stared at herself in the mirror that very morning, and shook her head at the memory. Plain face, bad skin with acne all over her cheeks and forehead, like a rainbow of pimples highlighted by red blotches. Ordinary, long brown hair as straight as a ruler, regular dull brown eyes and skinny arms and legs. And worst of all, a poor excuse of a body that no guy in her school would ever think twice about looking at in a good way. She was sixteen years old, and never got asked out on dates, or had ever even known a guy who liked her in a romantic way. She had what she believed was a pretty lousy personality, had few friends and none whom she could call close. There was no one in her life she could call a best friend, and there probably never would be. Her life completely sucked and there didn't seem to be much she could do about it. Danielle sulked, her bad mood growing darker as she became more dejected by the moment. Deep down, she knew this was an abysmal way to act, and a totally irrational way to treat herself. She had done nothing in the last six months to improve her appearance or her self-esteem, which was poor at best. But, as the sun went down and the shadows began to lengthen, Danielle gave in to the burgeoning fog of depression which wrapped her like a cloak, lowered her face into her hands and began to weep...for the loss of her mother which still ached deep within her heart...for the hopelessness that filled her from an all too honest look at herself. And, most of all, from the growing feeling that life was only bound to get worse; from all of her family's problems, Gran's stroke, her father's worsening health, the family's mounting financial problems that her father tried to hide from her but which she was more than a little aware of, to the bleak personal future which seemed to stretch itself out before her. In another month she would be back at school, and there the prospects of her life were even more depressing. Shabby clothes, little money to buy new ones and an equally shabby appearance, did not make for a future filled with new friends and wide social acceptance. Rather, they paved the way for obscurity and even worse, the derisive remarks and scornful looks from her peers that would let her know all too quickly how much she didn't fit in. How much of a complete outcast, a loner and if she was honest, a loser she was. As her tears continued to fall, Danielle clasped her hands together, closed her eyes tightly and began to pray to her mother, who she believed in her heart must be an angel in heaven, and was most assuredly looking down on her.

"Momma," she whispered, "I hope you can hear me right now. I miss you so much, so very, very much. My world's just been broken since you went away and I don't know what to do to fix it. Please Momma, if you can hear me, help me to find peace within my heart. Help me to stop being such a pain in the butt to Daddy and to be a better person again. A help to both him and Gran. Help me to find myself, to stop feeling so empty inside. I still can't believe you are gone. You are the only one who ever understood me, Momma. How different I am. You never cared that I wasn't popular or beautiful. You always loved me for who I am. Just as I am!" she said with a steely edge to her voice, and then paused for a minute as her surging emotions got the best of her. Danielle rubbed her eyes, took a shuddering breath and then continued. "Remember when we came up here and searched for the pretty pieces of quartz together? And last summer I found that really rare blue stone and you took it from me and said you wanted to keep it. You said it reminded you of me, and how with a little time and polishing it would make the prettiest piece of all. I think about that day all the time now. About how you gave it back to me at Christmas and you had cleaned it and fastened it to a pretty silver necklace.... And you were right. It was the most beautiful thing I'd ever seen. Whenever I look at it now, I can't help but remember how happy you were when you gave it to me and how I felt when you fastened it around my neck. Daddy was jumping around with the camera and kept flashing us in the face, so our eyes wouldn't focus. And then you grabbed me and hugged me so hard and told me that it was a perfect little jewel for a perfect jewel. And I knew you meant me.... That I was your perfect jewel. I wish I could feel like that again. I wish you could be here and hug me, wrap me in your arms and make me feel that way once more. It was the most loved and special I've ever felt. Like maybe I was really more than what I see when I look in the mirror. Momma, I know you're up there with God now. And I know that he doesn't want you all interfering with us down here. Like Daddy says, we're here to be forged in the fire. To learn the life lessons, which can't be taught in Heaven. But if you could please ask God to let you send me a little sign that you are still with us and that you haven't forgotten about me. I know it's asking an awful lot and I know it's probably not normally allowed, but please Momma, ask him if just this once you could send me a sign that you can see me and hear me, and that I am not alone!"

Danielle then paused as at that very moment, a burst of illumination shone suddenly against her eyelids, as if someone was holding a really bright flashlight only inches from her face. Surprised and more than a tad alarmed, she opened her eyes just as a great ball of light and energy appeared from nowhere, hovering in the air just before her in the hollow of the dig. Surprise and shock registered on her face as she stood, stepped back and then in a manner which was for her, par for the course, fell over backwards. Immediately a loud whooshing noise began reverberating all about her and then a sharp, pitched squeal began that rose higher and higher toward a shrieking crescendo, which seemed to blare at her from all sides. With a hysterical fear-filled sob she flailed about, trying to right herself, all the while unable to take her eyes from the wildly pulsing ball of light that had taken form and was now turning bluish-white, growing larger as it rolled and flashed before her. Adrenaline surged within her body as Danielle panicked, scrambled to her feet and jumped over a nearby hillock of grass and dirt, trying to get away as the shrieking racket rose higher and louder. Losing her footing on the slippery, grassy surface of the knoll, she tripped and fell yet again, but this time face forward as the ball of light suddenly and without warning exploded outward, leaving behind a complete and utter silence that contrasted hugely with the ringing in her ears.

Danielle took a quick, frantic breath of air, and then choked and spit out the grass and dirt that she'd somehow managed to get in her mouth. After coughing for what seemed like forever, she gathered herself together and sat up in the grass, gazing about. She listened for a moment and even marveled at how quiet and perfectly still everything had unexpectedly become. It was almost, she thought to herself, as if the entire world and everything in it had suddenly paused in silent expectation, to see what fate had wrought. Carefully, she stood and brushed her hands against her jeans, while surveying the scene around her. It had gotten darker in the past few minutes and deep shadows now lay across everything.

She turned toward where the weird light had been and then froze, stricken in awed disbelief. Before her...directly in front of her, a huge circular cutout of soil had seemingly, unbelievably melted away, and in the walls of the melted, fused clay that remained were hundreds, possibly thousands of tiny crystals which were glowing with a mysterious inner light. Danielle gasped aloud in sheer wonder at the breathtaking and magical scene. She had never seen anything so beautiful or been so astonished in her life. The whole hollow was glowing with an incredible radiance of pure white light which was, unfortunately, slowly and most inevitably fading away. The light was almost gone when Danielle realized that someone was calling her name. Or at least, it sounded a lot like her name. *Yes, there it is again,* she thought and turned her head, so she could listen more intently in the direction from which the sound seemed to be coming. She was about to shout out a response when a quiet moan reached her ears and she turned back toward the hollow, an uneasy shiver creeping up her spine.

"What in the world was that?" she said to herself in a whisper, as she carefully moved forward. With a fair bit of apprehension, caused largely in part by the strangeness of the night's events, Danielle searched the deepening shadows with eyes which were still suffering the effects of the bright lights and were not seeing well into the shadows. She'd already had quite a scare and even the beauty of the past few moments didn't leave her with any false sense of security. What had just happened had been way too weird and had her nerves on edge; way, way, on edge. Suddenly, she heard a second moan, this one a bit louder, and felt her heart hammering in her throat as she imagined all sorts of possible causes for the strange noise. Fueled by what was quickly becoming an overactive imagination, Danielle moved carefully forward a few more paces before stopping, as she spied a dark form lying crumpled on the ground. Her hands shaking a bit, she advanced with no small amount of trepidation, until she was within a foot or so of what she could now plainly see was the body of a small female form, lying on her side with her back facing Danielle. Reaching out, she placed her hand on one shoulder and pulled a bit, until she could better see the features of what was actually a very pretty young girl. A girl, who at a glance, appeared to be about Danielle's size and approximate age. "Oh my God," she exclaimed softly. "How in the world did you get here?" Studying the girl's features and clothing, she realized immediately that there were some things about the appearance of the girl in front of her which were simply odd. *Way odd!* "You're not from around here, are you?" she said thoughtfully, unable to stop staring. In fact, she barely moved a muscle when she heard the nearby voice of her father, calling out her name in what was obviously a state of panic.

"Daddy!" she called out, and soon saw his distraught form approaching at nearly a dead run. "It's okay! I'm okay!" she repeated, as she saw a look of relief cross his frightened features.

"Danielle!" he gasped breathlessly, as he came up to her and placed a protective hand on his daughter's shoulder, while she stood to greet him. "Are you all right, sweetheart? We saw a crazy light from down below and then heard that terrible noise and explosion." Big John, who was more than a little relieved to find his daughter unharmed, was just about to grab her up in his arms when he paused and gazed toward the spot on the ground where she was staring. "Danielle, who in the hell is that?"

Danielle quickly knelt down and placed her hand protectively on the shoulder of the young girl. "She came somehow in the weird light you saw, Daddy. I know it sounds really incredible. But she wasn't here before that, and now she is... here," she said haltingly, glancing up at her father, who looked as confused as she felt. "She seems to be unconscious and I think she may be hurt. Daddy, I really think we should get her out of here and back down to the camp."

John Walkerman hesitated for only a second, glanced in relief once more at his only daughter's beautiful profile, and then leaned down and lifted the strange young girl up in his arms. Seemed like that weird light wasn't going to be the only odd thing they would see this night, he thought to himself. One quick glance at this little stranger had told him that much. The odd looking clothing, the crazy coloring of her hair, or to be more precise, the lack of color since her hair was as white as could be. Hell, even the manner of her completely bizarre appearance way out here in the wilderness. Things couldn't get much more peculiar from this point on; of that he was fairly certain.

CHAPTER 2

OVER THE HILLS
AND VALES

Danielle lay on her side on her sleeping bag which she had placed on the floor in the center of the large main room of the cabin. The area incorporated both a living room and a small kitchenette, separated by a wooden breakfast bar, surrounded by treetop stools her father had made by hand. It was very late, and both her father and her brother had retired hours ago outside by the fire with a stern admonition from Big John that Danielle was to come get him immediately if there was any change in the stranger's condition. Lying next to her on what had been her father's sleeping bag was the still unconscious form of the mysterious girl. She knew she should be sleeping, but Danielle was too keyed up from the evening's events and too filled with questions. Earlier she had lit the small kerosene lamp which she had placed next to her bag and had set it at its lowest setting. Partly because she wanted to keep a close eye on the girl, and partly, because she worried that when and if the girl woke up, she was likely to freak out when she found herself in a strange, dark room with no idea of where she was and who was in here with her. Staring, Danielle marveled at the stranger's appearance, which was definitely striking. She had luminous white hair which was braided into delicate, tight braids that were so numerous and fine Danielle couldn't even begin to imagine someone taking the time to do them all. It would have taken days for her to do braids like that, and even then she didn't think she could do them so perfectly. Why, from what she could tell, there wasn't a single strand of hair out of place. The whole thing was done up in a kind of avant-garde basket weave down her back, interwoven with a thick silver thread which looked stunning. Her brow was framed in a widow's peak, where the hair forms a point in the center of the forehead, which Danielle had always found to be very aristocratic looking. Just below the forward crest of the widow's peak was a tiny, perfectly formed silvery eight-sided star, glowing with a light luminescent shine that Danielle could see appeared to lay just beneath the outermost layer of skin on her forehead. The girl's skin tone was a light brown, as if she were tanned extremely well and her overall appearance from her eyebrows to her nails, was meticulously refined down to the smallest detail.

Apparently she is a big fan of jewelry, Danielle thought with silent wonder, as she gazed at the breathtaking silver necklace that was studded with blue sapphires and a large jeweled pendant which adorned her neck, accented by a pair of jewel encrusted silver bands she wore upon her wrists. The same brilliant blue as the necklace peeked out from her ears and curious, Danielle reached out, pushed the girl's hair back a tiny bit and saw there were actually three jeweled studs adorning the outer edge of her ears. There was even some kind of silvery hand adornment glinting from within her palm that she couldn't fully make out, at least from the angle she had. All this strangeness didn't hold a candle, though, to the girl's clothing. What first appeared to be some kind of loose fitting, dark blue satin slacks and matching top with thin black borders and shiny ebony buttons, were at closer inspection, made out of some kind of shiny metallic fiber. Danielle studied the garment, reminded of something she herself wore, and then it hit her. "I think maybe they're some kind of pajamas," she said quietly.

"What in the world are you doing wearing pajamas out here?" Finely wrought, Danielle guessed that they had been made to be comfortable, though she couldn't tell much else about them. The oddest thing about the outfit, however, Danielle had not noticed until it had gotten really dark. The cloth seemed to glow with a soft inner light. She had thought at first that it might just be a light collecting, phosphorescent material, but it was still glowing steadily and she was beginning to suspect there was more here than met the eye.

Danielle pondered her charge while she lay on her side and stared. *Where on God's green earth did she come from?* She couldn't help but wonder. The manner of her mysterious arrival had Danielle considering all kinds of ridiculous possibilities. She was, after all, the product of modern television. Her father had, on the way back to camp, questioned her repeatedly about the fantastic light she'd witnessed, and seemed to be having a really hard time with the idea that the girl had just suddenly appeared, as if from nowhere. When they had gotten back to the cabin and placed the girl on a sleeping bag, he'd made her tell again, in great detail, everything she had seen.

"So, you didn't actually see her appear from thin air, then?" Big John had asked when she had described finding the girl's body.

"Well, no Dad, but she wasn't there before, I'm sure of it!" Danielle had argued, knowing full well she hadn't really looked all that closely at the particular area where she'd found the girl. This was just something she felt deep inside. A lot of this came from the fact that at the time, she'd been praying, and the whole thing smacked to her somewhat of miraculous overtones, a feeling of destiny, even. She was so emotionally overwrought by the whole situation, that at the moment, she couldn't even put all of her feelings into words. She wasn't entirely sure if God himself was involved here, but some greater power had been. This theory was supported, in her mind at least, by both the peculiar manner of the girl's arrival as well as her rather strange physical appearance.

"I'm just saying, Danielle, it seems much more likely that what we have here is one of those crazy, modern age hippie girls who perhaps went for a walk while looking for, I don't know, mushrooms and stuff, and ended up lost out here. Only to trip on some rock or root and knock herself out, just before you arrived on the spot."

"And what then, Dad? And then a large glowing ball of light suddenly appeared in the exact same location as her and exploded by sheer coincidence?"

"Maybe it was some kind of gas," he said, and shrugged his shoulders noncommittally. "Or, you know, one of those rare atmospheric disturbances that people are always seeing up north. Like those weird lights in the sky they always get up there in Alaska." In Big John's mind there was always a reasonable explanation for everything. People were always trying to find something mystical or miraculous in the phenomena that happened. Whether it be a wet spot on a wall that looked like Jesus, or a strange light flashing across the sky. There were stories all the time in those weird magazines you could pick up at every supermarket, and they always turned out to be some guy in a Bigfoot suit, or some other nonsense which was easily explained by the people who made a living looking into those matters.

"I bet I know who she is, Dad!" said twelve-year-old Aaron who up until that moment had stood by, listening intently to the description of earlier events. He had been interested in hearing his father's and Danielle's opinions of who the strange girl was, but he knew better what was going on here. It was quite plain to him who and what she was, but then, he'd always had a better understanding of certain kinds of things than they had. In fact, he was absolutely certain he had this whole thing figured out and couldn't understand why they didn't see it. It was all quite simple, really, and all the facts he'd heard supported his theory. At least to someone who was a well read, open minded man such as himself. "I'm pretty sure I know who she is, Dad," he said again, in case they hadn't heard him the first time. "I think she's probably an alien," he stated simply, and then folded his arms, daring anyone to contradict him. He'd read all the books. Kept up on all the secret stuff the government had been hiding all these years. The Internet gave plenty of insight to anyone who wanted to know the truth. Stubbornly, he waited for the mockery he knew would be coming his way. Men of knowledge and foresight always had to put up with the uninformed comments of unbelievers. What really shocked him next, though, was that his sister, who rarely missed a chance to ridicule him, seemed instead to take him seriously.

"You know, Dad, he might be right," said Danielle, who grinned at the look of disbelief her brother suddenly gave her. "Although, not in quite the way that Aaron probably means. What if that light was some kind of a doorway. An opening from, oh, I don't know, another dimension or some kind of a parallel universe. There've been a lot of things written in recent years from very learned people who have theorized on the possibility of such things."

"Or maybe it was a teleportation beam," Aaron quipped, trying to give his sister his unequivocal support, only to receive a look that plainly said, *"Stop helping me, Dorkus!"*

Big John shook his head. "Danielle, please, now you are sounding utterly ridiculous. And to make matters worse, you're gonna have your little brother believing all of this crap. I'm telling you right now!" he said adamantly in the tone of voice he used when he had made up his mind and expected no further argument, "When she wakes up, and you've both had a good night's sleep, you're going to find out that I am absolutely right about this, honey. She's probably just some young city girl who was out, drinking and partying in the country, getting back in touch with nature, and lost her way out here. Now, the both of you, let's all turn in and we will sort this thing out in the morning, after we've had a chance to think things through and see reason," he added sternly, as he half-heartedly grinned at his daughter, whom he could see from the stubborn look on her face, was marshaling her arguments and preparing to give it to him.

"Dad!" she said, with a little whine to her voice. She hated when he got like this. He could be so darn stubborn at times!

"Tomorrow, Danielle!" said Big John, as he walked off and turned his mind towards his own thoughts. If nothing else, he contemplated to himself, at least there was one small positive thing to take away from this situation tonight. This was the most animated and alive he'd seen his daughter act in months. "Marilyn," he whispered very softly to himself, so as not to alarm his children; after all, he was speaking to his deceased wife. "Maybe this will be the thing that finally does it for her. Maybe this crazy night will bring our daughter back from the dark place she's dwelled in all these months. I can only hope."

Danielle laid her head on her sleeping bag as a wave of fatigue washed over her. *God, it's been a really long day*, she thought to herself, and then stiffened. A muffled noise coming from the direction of the stranger caused her to sit up, her mind suddenly alert. Carefully, she studied the shadowy form lying only a few feet away. Had she made a noise, or had it only been Danielle's imagination playing tricks on her? As she watched, her guest moved her right hand up as though to touch her face, and then unexpectedly yawned. Danielle caught a brief glimpse of pearly white teeth and what appeared to be... "What the hell!" Danielle whispered to herself, as her heart suddenly began to pound nearly out of her chest. She hadn't really seen that, had she? The girl had just flashed two-inch incisors that looked almost as if she were wearing a Halloween insert for a vampire costume. The girl then yawned again, and Danielle leaned over and studied her face from up close. "Nope, normal. You're losing it, Danielle!" she exclaimed breathlessly, and slowly shook her head from side to side at her own foolish paranoia. God, how freaking tired was she? Now she was having hallucinations! As she gazed down at the girl her thoughts turned back toward the current situation. It seemed the girl was finally coming awake. "Maybe I'd better turn the light up a little so you can see your surroundings, and you don't freak out," she said softly as the gentle face below her suddenly opened her eyes.

Without warning, Danielle suddenly found herself thrown to the side, and then faster than she would have thought possible, the girl was on top of her, straddling her body while her hands grasped chokingly around Danielle's throat.

"Sardeel don espay day nu!" the girl shouted in a commanding tone that was clearly antagonistic in nature.

Danielle, unable to understand what was being said, gazed up into two eyes which blazed brightly with a greenish inner light. It was evident that she was extremely upset about something and though Danielle had no idea at all what the girl was saying to her, she sensed intuitively and with complete self-certainty that she was in serious danger. The girl was obviously very, very upset and from the way she glanced all around, was clearly trying to get her bearings on where she was. While Danielle couldn't imagine what had her so worked up, she immediately sensed that she needed to try and assuage her fears, and fast!

"It's all right," she choked out, as the girl's incredibly strong hands tightened even further on her throat. "Please," she gagged, as her body tried to rise up, fighting off a terrible sense of asphyxiation which was coming on fast. "I...can't...breathe!"

"Sardeel don espay day nu!" the girl yelled again, and stared directly into Danielle's eyes with a look that was strangely feral in nature. The girl's bright green eyes were filled, Danielle could plainly discern, with a fierce and angry gleam. "Javay nu-dah! Javay nu-dah!" she shouted, as she moved her face closer to Danielle's.

Danielle smacked the girl's wrists as she tried to twist and turn beneath her. *My God this bitch is strong!* she thought briefly, as stars began to form before her eyes and she felt herself beginning to pass out. "Help!" she gasped hoarsely and then, as her world began to go dark, Danielle felt the girl's body suddenly wrenched off her.

"Sweetheart, are you all right?" asked Big John, as he grabbed his daughter up and crushed her into his huge arms.

"I'm fine, Daddy," Danielle gasped roughly, her relieved eyes searching about the room until she found the small, terrified form of her attacker huddled against the far wall. The girl stared into Danielle's eyes for a brief moment with a puzzled expression on her face, as if she wasn't sure exactly what it was she was seeing. Then, like a shot, she was on her feet and out the door.

"Daddy, I'm okay, really," said Danielle, as she clambered clumsily and a bit shakily to her feet. As quickly as possible, she slipped her feet into her boots as she labored to catch her breath. She stood for a moment more, pulling a huge lungful of air into her chest and then turned to see her father standing behind her, gazing quizzically at his daughter.

"Honey, where do you think you are going?" he asked, as he followed his daughter out the front door of the tiny cabin.

"I'm going after her," she stated, as she glanced toward her brother who was standing sleepily by the fire. "Did you see where she went, Aaron?" Groggily, he pointed in the direction of the small stream that carried away the overflow from the pond.

"Danielle!" barked Big John, as he reached his daughter's side. Placing one of his large hands on her shoulder to emphasize what he was saying, he turned her to face him. "You will do no such thing, young lady! My God, she just tried to kill you in there!" he said vehemently, and pointed back at the doorway of the cabin. "Now, you march yourself right back in there this minute and you think about this situation and try and use some common sense. There will be no half-assed midnight search for some little..."

Danielle cut him off before he could finish. "Daddy, she was just scared!" she argued, and then, realizing there would be no reasoning with her father when he was in this kind of mood, dropped her explanation and made a decision which left her feeling a little weak inside. "Sorry, Daddy!" she said in a half-apologetic voice, "I have to help her!" Pulling herself from his grip, Danielle turned her back on her father and abruptly took off, running in the direction her brother had just pointed.

"Danielle! You get back here this instant!" shouted Big John, who would normally never speak to his daughter in that tone, but who was beside himself at the moment with his daughter's uncharacteristic and insolent behavior. "Damn it, what the hell does she think she's doing?" he said aloud to no one in particular, as he ran after her for a few steps, stopped, and then retreated back to the fire to get his boots, after stepping on a sharp stone. He had pulled them off hours ago when he had lain down, and he hadn't bothered to put them back on earlier when he'd gone into the cabin to check on the girls, only to find his beloved daughter being nearly strangled to death. A terrible scene for anyone to come across, no less a father who was still silently grieving for a loved one lost and who couldn't even conceive of someone wanting to harm his sweet, gentle daughter. A daughter who was now stubbornly rushing about in the dark wilderness searching for the very one who'd just tried to do her harm. Pulling his boots on, Big John gave a terse command to his son to go into the cabin and lock the door until he returned. Grabbing a lantern, he lit it and strode off into the dark, determined to find and bring back his beloved Danielle.

"Look after our headstrong child, Marilyn," he whispered into the night air. "And woe be to anyone who seeks to do her harm!"

Danielle could see fairly well. *Thank God there's nearly a full moon tonight,* she thought to herself. As her eyes grew more accustomed to the darkness, she could see where the tall grass had been slightly bent from the passage of another person. "At least I hope it was made by a person," she whispered. "My luck it will be something else, like a cougar or a bear." As she went on, she worried that she would lose the trail in spots where the tall grass waned near large trees or deadfalls. But fortunately, she was able to easily pick the path up again, helped by the simple fact that the girl was apparently following the small stream which was just off to her right. "I just hope she doesn't try to cross it, or head in some other direction." Danielle knew her tracking skills were poor at best, and after walking for nearly twenty minutes, she was beginning to suspect that she might be following a false trail after all. "Surely you wouldn't have gone this far out here," she said softly to herself. She was just about to call it quits, and head back with the idea of taking a wide detour which would eventually take her back to the camp, when suddenly, she stopped. Up past the trees ahead, she thought she could hear something. Something that sounded almost like...Danielle paused in the midst of her thought, while dropping to one knee. Still uncertain, she moved forward as quietly as she could manage, until she ended up at the bole of a huge tree with large, overhanging branches. Cautiously, she moved around it, then abruptly stopped and tensed up. *There it is again,* she thought, as she listened carefully for more. A sudden breeze brought the sound to her much more clearly. It was then that recognition kicked in as the sound of utter anguish, a wildly keening cry came to her that raised and then lowered in a kind of undulating tone. "Oh my God," she whispered, her concern growing, "she's in such pain!"

Stealthily, Danielle moved forward, past the boundary of the tree and through a pair of large, leafy bushes, where she spied a small, sandy area bordering the stream. Backlit by a pale ribbon of moonlight, she spied the shadowy outline of the young girl who was there, on her knees, her arms wrapped about herself as she rocked back and forth. The sound that came from her was so deeply laden with grief, so wracked with utter loss that Danielle felt her breath catch and her eyes well up. *So terribly sad!* she thought, *Oh my God, what's happened that could have her so filled with such grief, such terrible anguish?* For grief it was, an overwhelming texture within her voice which strove, however it might, to release the mournful shattering of a broken spirit held within. A heart wrenching sorrow that filled one's very soul to overflowing. Danielle had heard something like it before and blanched as the vivid memory returned. She'd heard it coming from herself, in fact. She had made nearly the exact same sound when she'd gotten the news this past winter. The news that her beloved mother, her heart's confidant, her soul's comforter, had been killed in a car crash. Danielle moved cautiously forward, trying to make as little noise as possible, so as not to disturb the young woman or cause her to flee. When she was within a few feet, however, the girl's head shot up, her eyes suddenly gleaming with an angry, supernaturally green light. Danielle pushed away the sudden surge of fear she felt and knelt on the ground, holding her palms forward in what she hoped was an obvious sign of peaceful intentions. "It's all right," she said softly. "I know what you are going through. I may not know exactly why, but it's obvious to me that you've experienced a great loss." Danielle placed her right palm against her chest. "I know how you feel, I understand the depth of the pain you feel deep within. I, too," she explained in calm gentle tones, as she patted her right palm in a reaffirming gesture against her heart, "have lost someone very, very dear to me. Please let me help you," she said, as she slowly moved closer and closer, until she was kneeling right in front of the mysterious stranger who'd so suddenly come into her life. She didn't know why, but she believed that this fortuitous meeting had happened for a reason. That somehow, someway, this young girl was a kind of answer to the prayer she had offered up earlier. She was certain if she tried to explain to her father or her Aunt Sara, they would both claim that it was all just a self-delusion of hers. But she didn't believe it. Deep in her heart, she just didn't believe the two of them coming together this night was just a matter of circumstance. It was much more than that. She felt it within the deepest places of her soul.

Danielle cautiously reached out and took the stranger's hands in hers, squeezing them with gentle reassurance to illustrate to the stranger the measure of her concern and compassion. Silently to herself, she marveled at how smooth and cool to the touch they were. Then, gazing into her eyes, she gaped momentarily as the curiously bright green eyes faded to a pale emerald color that still smoldered with an inner radiance. "I'm here for you," said Danielle, pulling herself together. "I promise, whatever is wrong, I am here now and we will find the answers together."

Big John strode through the underbrush past a couple of bushes and halted, frozen in quiet disbelief at the unexpected scene which miraculously appeared before his eyes. He felt a huge wave of relief surge through him as he spied the form of his daughter, who, thank the good Lord above, seemed to be quite well and unharmed. As he stood there, staring at the solemn tableau before him, his heart filled with a kind of wonder...a joy of sorts. For Danielle, who'd been emotionally closed off to all of them for so many months, had her arms wrapped protectively around the shoulders of the girl she had come out here to find and was hugging her. The girl, he could see plainly, was crying. And Danielle... his remarkable little Danielle, was singing a sweet song that her mother had made up for her and sung to her nearly every night when she'd been little. His wife had named it simply Danielle's Lullaby, and he knew it oh, so well. Had heard it many nights as he'd stood outside his daughter's door listening, awaiting his turn to go in and kiss her goodnight. As unlike him as it normally was to get emotional, Big John felt himself choke up a little and stood there quietly while his daughter sang, freely giving comfort to another. He had many misgivings about this night's strange events. And, although she had never before disobeyed him, he sensed his daughter would likely have her way about this situation; he knew it as certainly as he knew he loved her.

CHAPTER 3

FIRST DAY IN A NEW WORLD

The next morning, Danielle prepared herself mentally for what she knew was going to be a huge argument between herself and her father. He had told her last night as they made their way back to the camp that the young girl they'd found could stay with them until they got back to the house, but that then he would contact the local authorities and turn her over to them. In her heart, Danielle knew that would never do, but she also realized that the wrong time to get into it would have been last night, while her poor father was so plainly tired and at his wits' end. Better to give him some time to consider things in his own mind and calm all the way down. It had taken a heck of a lot of pleading on her part to even get her father to allow the girl to come back to the camp with them.

"Danielle, she was choking you!" he had said, while keeping a mistrustful eye on the girl. He was not one to forgive easily, notwithstanding the evidence that the stranger was plainly very upset about something. "And I'm not about to take any chances with your safety around what could possibly be a very unstable, mentally unbalanced young woman."

In the end, it had only been her proposal that she sleep out by the fire with her father and brother while the stranger stayed in the cabin that caused him to give in and reluctantly agree to let her return with them to the campsite. Of course, as soon as Big John and Aaron had nodded off, Danielle had grabbed up her sleeping bag and against her father's orders, had gone back into the cabin. She had felt more than a trifle guilty about that, since usually it was completely against her nature to lie to her father. But, in this case, there were extenuating circumstances about the girl that she strongly felt required her attention, her immediate personal attention, and she wasn't going to be able to sleep until she got some answers. Answers about the really weird things that had happened earlier.

It had all started when Danielle had been holding the stranger tightly, their heads together, arms wrapped around one another in an intimate embrace, allowing her to sense through the close contact the physical outpouring of grief coming from the stranger and attempting in some small way to help, if in no other way than to show her that she was not alone. That Danielle was here to give whatever support she could, however inadequate that might be, as a shoulder to cry on and more importantly, so that the girl would know that Danielle understood in some part how she was feeling. The stranger had turned slightly, pressing her head snugly in on Danielle's neck and shoulder, her face buried in her hair, when it had happened. She recalled feeling a slight pinch against her neck, after which images had begun to dance before her tightly closed eyes, a kaleidoscope of half formed imagery that had shocked her to the core, as much by the strangeness of the images as by the pure vividness of them. Initially, a small wave of panic that quickly changed to fear had swept through her body, nearly causing her to pull back and break the girl's hold on her, but then from somewhere deep within she'd found the strength that comes of sudden resolve and with a sense of utter abandon, Danielle mentally threw herself into the imagery. What had come next had very nearly overwhelmed her. Truly intense scenes of utter clarity had danced before her, and slowly, as she allowed herself to be pulled further in, the scenes enveloped her until without warning she found herself in the middle of a lucid dream. It was like being in the center of a 360-degree movie. There had been sights and sounds all around her, full of amazing detail and rich in color. She wasn't afraid though; it was as if a part of her knew that she was completely safe and that what she was seeing was the memories of another. Dharalyn's memories!

That realization too, had momentarily jolted her. How had she known her name? It was almost as if...and then the truth of it had slammed into her with absolute certainty. These weren't just random images she was seeing in another person's mind. She was Dharalyn! Dharalyn Xhikaterina Malakovani of the house of The Malakovani Sakatherian Regency. She knew what that meant as well, and then she saw the scene which was the focus of all of her sorrow. The moment that had her bent over with an overwhelming feeling of despair which was wracking the depths of her very soul. Abraxis was standing before her, while priests and guardians moved with purpose all around them. "Your mother has been killed by a triumvirate of Praxillari Elite," he had said, and then things had gotten hazy. Fighting had broken out and she'd seen the sudden light of the Portal appear. He had grabbed her and suddenly thrown her within the globe of energy. Too soon! Too soon, she knew from experience. It hadn't had time to stabilize and attune. It shouldn't have worked at all, but then something had exploded. Brilliant white light and then a feeling of tremendous, instantaneous speed. *This is wrong,* she thought and then, *Oh mother, what have they done to you!*

And then Danielle had been herself again. And felt the tears come as she remembered the loss of her own mother. Of how the news had left her feeling utterly empty and lost. *She's only just learned this,* she thought as the sudden realization hit her, *just a very little while ago.* And so, together they had cried as they mourned the loss of Dharalyn's mother. And Danielle herself grieved as well for loss anew, and loss once removed; one no less than the other.

All this had happened, of course, the previous night. Now it was morning, and Danielle absently rubbed at a sore spot on her neck while listening to her father moving about outside the cabin. She lay on top of her bag, which she had placed right alongside Dharalyn's and waited for the uproar she was sure would soon be coming. She heard him call out her name once, twice, and then heard his boots stomp over to the cabin door. She closed her eyes and pretended to still be asleep, while she held her breath. A moment later she heard him walk off, grumbling loudly, "Never listens to a damn thing I say. Does she think I just like to hear myself talk, just to hear the sound of...." She couldn't make out much more. Slowly, she breathed a sigh of relief. Apparently, this time at least, she was going to get away with this. As she sat up and gazed about her, making plans in her head as to how to begin her day, Dharalyn sat up as well. "Good morning," Danielle said cautiously and a little shyly, not yet entirely certain what the exact nature of their tenuous relationship was. Last night on the way back to the camp, they had held each other's hands the entire way, but Danielle was still pretty unsure about things. The biggest stumbling block she knew was the fact that Dharalyn spoke an entirely different language, and it was like nothing that Danielle had ever heard before. She was completely confused as to why she had understood everything during the weird mind-link thing that had happened between them, though she suspected it had something to do with an inexplicable sharing of their conscious-ness. She had a couple of other off-the-wall guesses, each one progressively more bizarre than the last, and finally she decided it was probably best not to dwell on it too much. *The truth,* she thought to herself, *is that I will probably never understand what exactly happened.*

"How are you feeling this morning?" said Danielle, pretty sure that Dharalyn hadn't a clue what she was saying. She hoped, though, that the girl could at least sense her concern. It had been a pretty intense and emotional outpouring between them last night, and it had gone on for quite a while.

"Nu-day lo agona prevairae, Danielle," said Dharalyn, as Danielle jumped just a little at hearing her name. The girl had a very sweet sounding voice and had pronounced Danielle's name very clearly.

"I guess you got something out of all that stuff last night, too!" Danielle said, in a voice filled with wonder. "I wish there was some way we could communicate better. I mean, I understood you really well last night when we..." Danielle explained, while placing her hand on the side of her own head and then touching the side of Dharalyn's forehead in the same area. "But it doesn't seem to be helping much now." Danielle glanced quickly out the door and could hear her father and brother talking. "If I'm going to help you," she said, "we really need to figure out something pretty quick. I mean, father doesn't believe even a little that you are from somewhere else. And he would call me crazy, if I told him about what happened between us last night." She reached out again and touched the sides of each of their foreheads, feeling a bit foolish, but trying desperately to make herself understood. She knew her father, knew how he responded to things like this. After they got back to the house, he'd have the local sheriff over to take Dharalyn away and then Danielle would probably never see her again.

Dharalyn nodded her head, placed her hand on Danielle's forehead and smiled, and then placed her hand on her own forehead. "Nu katrie, Danielle, Vae na sukra vienima."

Danielle hadn't a clue what Dharalyn had just said, but the girl was on her knees facing her and she was motioning for Danielle to do the same. Danielle sat as Dharalyn leaned forward and placed her hands on Danielle's face.

"Porokay nu-dah, Danielle, Porokay nu-dah."

Danielle nodded; either she really was nuts, or she thought she might have the gist of things. Dharalyn had something in mind and she was pretty sure the girl had just asked her to trust her. "Okay," she said, "it's your party. Tell me what to do."

Dharalyn leaned forward and pulled Danielle to her until their foreheads met.

"Well, this is weird," said Danielle softly, and she turned her head at the sound of her father calling. "Be there in a few minutes, Dad!" she exclaimed loudly, and then turned her attention back to Dharalyn. "Whatever you're gonna do, you better do it quickly. My father is not a patient man and if we're not out there soon, he'll be in here to see what's going on." Danielle closed her eyes and tried to relax. For a moment, there was nothing and then... Whoa! Danielle tensed and felt Dharalyn's fingers on the side of her head, plainly trying to calm her. *Holy Matrix madness!* she thought, as she suddenly felt again a surge within her mind as if she'd been jolted by an electric shock, and then...she was floating freely in a huge, bright nothingness that faded and at the same time seemed to come into focus.... Suddenly, there were millions of tiny points of light all about her in a kind of fog, throbbing gently, some glowing intensely and then...fading out. *This is definitely high on the weirdness scale,* she thought, and then sensed someone with her. "Wodan, Danielle," said a soft voice beside her.

"I don't really know what Wodan means, or what you want me to say," she said, as she gazed all around in wonder. The lights were blinking more now. Some, far off, were blinking wildly.

She sensed Dharalyn nodding. "Say, Danielle, say."

Danielle thought for a moment, noticing as she did the simultaneous reaction of wildly pulsating lights in the distance. "Okay, I guess what you want is for me to talk. I don't really know what it is I should talk about. I don't know about you, but yesterday was definitely pretty crazy." Danielle then noticed that a whole huge section of the lights a long way off were flashing crazily. And there were lots more of them, maybe thousands, she thought. She felt herself moving, being pulled somehow toward the greatest concentration of the flashing spectacle.

"Danielle, talk!"

Danielle nodded, or at least she thought she did. It was pretty wild here in this place. She really didn't want to dwell too much on where she was. If her suspicion was right, and she thought about it too much, she might freak out a little bit. *Talk about an invasive procedure!* she thought, as she gazed all around, still amazed at the vividness of her bizarre surroundings.

"Danielle!"

The gentle urging broke through her wandering thoughts and she felt someone nudge her shoulder. "Okay, okay, I know! I'll try," she said. "I guess I could always talk to you about my family a little bit. Let's see. Well, my father you've met. His name is John Walkerman, although everyone in the community calls him

Big John. And then there's my little brother Aaron. You may have noticed him last night when we got back to the camp. He just turned twelve years old a few weeks ago and is a bit of a pain sometimes." She halted for a minute, and then amended, "But in actuality, he's a pretty good kid. I guess to be honest, I've been kind of hard on him lately. Kind of been hard on everybody, actually," she said morosely, and then quickly moved the conversation on before she started getting maudlin. "Back at the house is my Aunt Sara; she works as an admissions clerk at a local hospital and moved in with us a while back, to help take care of my Gran. Gran had a mild stroke a few years ago and is partially paralyzed on her right side. She needs a lot of help to take care of herself. We all pitch in and do our part. She is such a wonderful person," she said wistfully, and then paused. They had come to a stop within the center of millions of tiny, winking lights that were now surrounding them in a thick cloud. All about them, too, Danielle could hear, was a delicate thread of music that began softly at first, but was quickly growing stronger and more pronounced. A gestating thread of perfect tone that rose and fell in an indescribably, beautifully rich cacophony of musical notes. Danielle paused in wonder as without warning, a second uniquely distinct tone even richer and more complex than the first unexpectedly joined in, forming an oddly synchronized duet. The pair of tones wove together, forming a rich and joyous harmony, as if they were two halves of a perfect song. The combination was so compelling that she felt herself give in to it, her emotions rising in a blissful crescendo of passion that was gathered within the gorgeous tune like a whirling tornado of sound. All about her, the myriad of lights began to shine and pulse with incredibly vibrant color. The sight was absolutely breathtaking and just as she leaned back to take it all in, she heard from somewhere far off in the distance a loud voice call out her name. Instantly, she found herself back inside the cabin with her head still pressed up against Dharalyn's. She felt a momentary rush of vertigo as if she'd suddenly stood up too fast, and then a wave of nausea hit her as she attempted to readjust herself back to normal surroundings.

"Danielle!" hollered Big John Walkerman, who strode into the cabin and looked at his daughter with a quizzical expression on his face. "Didn't you hear me calling you? And what in God's name is going on here?" John studied the two girls, who were facing each other and only moments ago had been holding each other in what was, to him, a very peculiar and strangely unsettling manner.

"Dad, it's okay," said Danielle, as she raised herself to a standing position and faced her father.

"Danielle!" said John, suspicion brimming in the tone of his voice. Something about all this was not sitting well with him at all. In his mind, the sooner they resolved all of this and got rid of their little problem, the happier he would be. "It sure the hell is not okay! You shouldn't even be in here. I believe I gave you explicit instructions about that last night. Now I find you two in here, doing God knows what together!"

"I was teaching her our language, Dad!" Danielle said exasperatedly. She knew she was reaching, that her father would never accept this rationale, but she was stalling as best she could. Normally very quick-witted, she felt weirdly out-of-sorts and sluggish. She needed a little time to come to terms with what had just happened. And she could see her father building up quite a head of steam. She needed to calm him down, and quickly.

"Teaching her our...what?" Big John sputtered, concern for his daughter's psychological wellbeing and his temper taking an instant turn toward the worse. "Danielle, I don't even know what to say to that. Are you sure you are feeling all right? She didn't make you swallow anything did she, or get you to smoke something?"

"Dad, don't get all mental on me!" said Danielle, as she glanced toward her new friend and then back at her father, pausing at the stern look on his face. Panicked, she started spouting anything that came to mind. "I didn't mean that, I mean, I meant to say that..." She paused, as she realized she was sounding more and more like a blithering idiot.

"I'm very sorry, sir," said a soft, sweet sounding voice. "What Danielle means is that we were just getting to know one another. My name is Dharalyn."

At a loss for words, Danielle gazed in unexpected surprise at this girl, who only a few minutes before had been completely unable to speak in any known language, and who was now speaking perfect English. Making an intuitive leap, Danielle figured that somehow she must have copied her language while they'd been in the bizarre brain sharing thing they'd just experienced together. Shaking her head slowly at the perplexing weirdness of it all, she watched as Dharalyn hesitated, then slowly, as if not too sure about it, stretched out a friendly hand toward her father.

Big John stared curiously at the two of them for a moment and then finally, as Danielle let out a small sigh of relief, stretched out his own hand. "Hello there, young lady, my name is John Walkerman, although most of the folks around here just call me Big John. You, however, should probably just call me John."

"It's very nice to meet you, John."

"Hmmm," said John, as he stroked his chin. "I suppose. So, do you want to tell me what you were doing out here last night, and where exactly you are from?"

Danielle groaned inwardly; it was so like her father to get right to the heart of things. She saw Dharalyn glance at her questioningly, and then jumped in. "Dad! Could you please wait a few minutes with the twenty questions? We were just about to get cleaned up and dressed for the ride back. Why don't you let us talk a bit more first, and then I'll bring you up to speed on things."

John hesitated for just a second, stroking his chin in thought, then nodded and silently left the cabin. He wasn't exactly sure who this girl was that he was seeing at the moment. Not the stranger, he thought to himself, but his daughter. She was being so unlike herself. Her recent self, that is. What he was seeing this morning reminded him more than just a little of the old Danielle, back before the accident. She'd often been willful then, sometimes obstinate, although rarely disrespectful. She'd always been ready to argue semantics with him to get her way, as well as with her mother. They'd raised the roof sometimes, the two of them. It was that way between mothers and daughters, he supposed. Such a deep love, though. They could say anything to each other, but don't jump on one of them when the other was in earshot, oh no! He himself had always been such a pushover, he knew. Marilyn had always teased him about it. "Some help you are!" she had said laughingly, when she'd had Danielle come to him about some expensive item she'd wanted. Some newfangled music thing that fit in your hand and held thousands of songs. He'd stood firm for a whole two minutes or so and then caved, as he so often did. He never could say no to his little girl. Not to something that was really important to her. But then, the accident had happened, and everything had changed practically overnight. No longer the happy, talkative teen so carefree and full of spirit, Danielle had turned inward and changed from the person she'd been to someone completely bereft of her onetime sparkling personality. That was what this camping trip had been all about; a last ditch effort on his part to somehow reach her. And then everything had gotten crazy with that mysterious light last night and this loony new-age girl they had found lost out here. John didn't know why, but even though he was seeing a change in Danielle, one he'd been hoping so badly to see, something inside him was troubled. Deeply troubled. "I just don't trust this new girl," he said aloud to himself. "Something about her just isn't right."

"What, Dad?" said Aaron, who had been watching his father's approach.

"Nothing," said Big John in a surly tone, as he glanced concernedly back toward the cabin door. "Come on, son, help me get the horses ready."

Danielle handed Dharalyn some extra clothes she'd brought with her, a pair of old jeans and a green top. "Here, put these on, they should fit you okay. You can't very well travel in the clothes you have on." She then handed Dharalyn a small bag. "Put your extra stuff in here for safekeeping. I'll gather everything up while you get dressed." Danielle watched as Dharalyn took the clothes and bag and walked to the back of the room. She rolled up the sleeping bags and packed her few things in the roll sack in which she had brought her extra clothes and necessities. As she placed everything by the door, she glanced up as Dharalyn walked over and handed her a bundle. Kneeling, she carefully put Dharalyn's possessions into the pack and stood up. "Well," she said appraisingly, "you look nice." The white-haired stranger certainly filled out her jeans and top better than she ever had. She had removed most of the gaudy costume jewelry, too. "You almost look like one of us now."

Dharalyn smiled. "Thank you Danielle, for everything," she said, and took Danielle's hands in her own.

Danielle suddenly felt very uncomfortable. She'd never been at ease showing her emotions and had only been comfortable with tactile expressions of sentiment with a few of her family members. The tender sharing of feelings, combined with such an intimate embrace which she'd shared with this complete stranger the night before, had been so very unlike her. She had no idea where all of that had come from and had avoided even thinking about it this morning. "It's all right," she said meekly, "it was nothing."

"No, Danielle," said Dharalyn gently, as she placed her right hand under her chin and raised it up until she and Danielle were looking straight into each other's eyes. "Thank you for your gentle compassion, for your understanding and for your kindness. It is a rare and beautiful gift you offered me."

Danielle nodded her head and then felt a light wave of euphoria sweep through her. She should have been uncomfortable, she knew, but as Dharalyn stared into her eyes, she felt a sudden relaxation of her fears and she smiled sheepishly back at the girl. "It was my pleasure," she said softly, trying hard not to choke up. Her emotions running high, Danielle stepped back and suddenly folded her arms, in an abrupt attempt to change the dangerously melancholy mood of the moment that threatened to engulf her and possibly bring with it a flood of tears. "So, tell me Dharalyn, not to change the subject, but where in the heck are you from, anyway?"

Dharalyn stared at her with a strange smile on her face and then suddenly laughed. Grinning and feeling a bit foolish for some reason, Danielle suddenly joined her and they laughed together.

"So, it's direct and right to the point then," said Dharalyn, after the two of them had calmed down.

Danielle shook her head. "My father may believe you are some new-age hippie chick, and Lord knows he doesn't really hold with all this being from another world stuff. But I was there when you arrived and I know better. You are, aren't you? From another world, I mean?" she said, waiting expectantly.

Dharalyn looked thoughtful and then said, "Yes Danielle, at least it seems the best explanation, considering nothing I've seen until now looks like any world I know, though I will have to give this some real thought when I have the time." She paused and gazed around the cabin's interior. "Why don't you tell me, since this is your world, where am I?"

"Well, let's see.... You are on the planet Earth and you just happen to be smack dab in the good old United States of America, in the great state of New York, and only about two hours away from New York City itself, also known as the city of lights, Broadway, and as my father will attest to, home of the greatest baseball team that ever was, the New York Yankees."

"I understand most of the words you are saying, Danielle, and I see the images you assign to them, but some of it makes no sense to me at all." Dharalyn looked thoughtful for a moment and then glanced at Danielle with a confused expression on her face. "Your people have built a huge stadium where they go to watch other people hit a ball with a stick?"

Danielle laughed. "Yes, I'm afraid so."

Dharalyn shook her head and looked perplexed. "I'm sorry, Danielle, but that all sounds a little bit crazy!" Again both girls laughed as if sharing a joke.

"So, Dharalyn, that weird thing we did earlier. You went into my mind and that's how you learned our language, huh?"

Dharalyn nodded. "Very good, Danielle. Yes, I copied your speech patterns and used them to learn your language."

"That is so cool!" said Danielle, and then added, "Listen, Dhara, do you mind if I call you that, by the way?"

"Well, usually only family members call me that, but considering you have no way of knowing any of the proper formalities you should use when addressing me and in view of how we seem to be well on the way to becoming very good friends, I think Dhara will be okay."

Danielle paused for a moment, sensing that she was missing something, but then continued. "Um, Dhara, for now I think you'd better let me do the explaining as to where you are from and all. If I know my father, he will probably call the local sheriff's office as soon as we get back, and I'm going to have to do some creative explaining to get him to let you stay with us."

"You mean lie, Danielle," said Dharalyn, and gave her a disapproving look.

"Listen, you're just going to have to trust me on this for now, Dhara. We will tell him the truth eventually, well, maybe...but if we tell him the truth right now, you'll be packed off as a bad influence as soon as we get back to the house and I will be sitting in some psychiatrist's office come Monday morning." Danielle picked up her pack, handed it off to Dhara and grabbed the two sleeping bags. "Come on, I'm sure he's waiting for us. We can talk more as we ride back."

CHAPTER 4

A STRANGE STORY

The way back to the house took longer than Danielle expected, since her father had her leading her horse Biscuit by the reins, rather than riding her.

"I don't want you putting too much weight on her just yet, and I especially don't want the both of you up on her till her hoof has had a few more days to heal," John had said and then added, "we'll take it slow up ahead while you two follow."

Danielle had nodded in agreement and called Dharalyn over. "I want you to meet someone," she'd said, smiling broadly. "This is my horse, Biscuit. She's been my friend and close companion for many years now."

Dharalyn reached up a hand and gently stroked the horse's long neck. "Hello there, Biscuit," she said in a soothing tone. "My, you are a beautiful animal, and so gentle." The horse responded by lowering her head and nuzzling Dharalyn's side. She then gave a deep throated nicker while shaking her head.

Danielle laughed. "She's saying hello. She likes you!"

"She's sweet. We have animals much like her in my world. Only some small differences from what I can see, like larger ears and a longer mane," Dharalyn said, "but otherwise, mostly the same."

A call from her father made Danielle glance ahead where he motioned for them to begin walking. They had been on the trail for about an hour or so and had been quietly talking when Dharalyn gave her a serious look.

"Danielle, where exactly is it that we are going right now?"

"We're taking you home. Why?"

"Danielle," said Dharalyn, with a note of apprehension, "try to see it from my point of view. I'm not from here and I am a little uneasy about what is going to happen to me when we get to your home. After all, it's quite evident that your father doesn't like me or trust me very much."

Danielle nodded as she glanced at Dharalyn. She hadn't really thought about any of this, herself. She tried to imagine how Dharalyn must be feeling. How lost and alone and probably even worse, scared. She was in a strange world, where she knew no one and where their customs, the way they lived their lives, everything, would be completely alien to her. Oh sure, she had the small advantage that looking into Danielle's mind had given her. But other than that, as far as she was concerned, they were traveling into the complete unknown, where her future was anything but certain and probably more than a little terrifying.

Dharalyn stopped and Danielle halted beside her. "Danielle, maybe I should just stay here. I mean, what if my people are trying to find me? It may be better if I just stay back at your cabin for a few days and wait there, in case they show up looking for me."

"Do you really think they will be able to find you here?" Danielle asked, aware that Dharalyn seemed to be panicking a bit.

"I don't know," said Dharalyn, who was quite conscious of the fact that she was allowing the immensity of what happened the previous night to overwhelm her sensibilities. She began breathing heavily and said, "Nothing like this has ever happened to one of us before. I don't know if anyone even knows if it's possible. I mean, I was supposed to travel through the portal to an island fortress that's been in our family for countless generations. Not here!

Not to a world that no one's ever even heard of before. At least, none of my people. What if they can't find me, Danielle? What if I'm stuck here forever?"

Danielle reached out and took her hand. She saw the look in Dharalyn's eyes and felt her compassion rise. "I understand how you feel, but I don't want you to worry," she said. "You and I will figure this out together, somehow. And don't worry about my father. I can handle him. You will stay with us and we will look out for you."

Dharalyn nodded as she stared at this brown-haired girl who stood so absolutely resolute before her. *There is strength here,* she thought to herself and felt herself calming; *and something more, much more.*

Danielle gently squeezed Dharalyn's hands, trying to reassure her. "I recognize your concerns and I know you are feeling a bit lost and overwhelmed." Danielle paused for a moment, searching for the words that would put her new friend at ease. Finally, she blurted out, "Listen, do you trust me, Dhara?"

Dharalyn looked at Danielle and after a few moments, slowly nodded.

"A lot more happened last night than I think you realize. At least, that's what I believe. I know you will probably think I am crazy, but I honestly think we were brought together for a reason. Call it fate, or destiny if you will, but I believe that what happened to you wasn't just chance. It wasn't just an accident that I happened to be out there last night at the exact same time that you arrived. I believe that there is a reason for all of this, although we may not know what it is yet. And it's up to you and me to follow this through, to whatever providence has in store for us."

Dharalyn stared thoughtfully. It wasn't often that she was impressed, but something in the intensity of Danielle's gaze and the sentiment it embodied reached out and spoke directly to a place deep within her soul. It reminded her, in fact, of something she had once seen in one of the scrolls stored in her family archives, which contained some of the writings left there by Cere Magumentae. A short but meaningful passage she had read in one of the more ancient texts that her aunt had let her see. "*The Creator weaves a subtle brush that is beyond our understanding, but is not without cause. And so, our life's journey may take a meandering path, which has within it the seeds of great purpose.*" Dharalyn looked at this young girl before her and realized in that moment, that she felt something pure in the strange bond that existed between them. Something that she had only felt toward one other person in her life. The memory of her mother suddenly swept through her as she fought to hold back powerful emotions that would overwhelm her if she allowed them to. She squeezed her hands in the manner of a reply. "I do trust you Danielle," she said, "and I think perhaps you are correct; I believe it quite possible that our two lives are intertwined for a greater purpose, though we know not what it is."

Danielle started to smile and then blanched at the grimly recognizable sound pressing inward on her consciousness. Her father was calling. And from the serious tone of his voice, she realized that he'd probably been hollering for some time. "Sorry, Dad," she called out to Big John, who was stopped up on a hill some thirty yards away and waving wildly at them. "We were talking."

"Well, talk less and walk more," he shouted back, then turned and rode up the hill away from them.

From where she was, Danielle could see Aaron sitting on his mount and just staring at them for a long moment, almost as if he were in a trance. A few seconds later, he finally turned and rode off while repeatedly glancing back.

"Your brother keeps staring at us," stated Dharalyn, as they began walking.

Danielle chuckled. "He's not staring at us," she said succinctly. "He's staring at you!"

"Why," said Dharalyn, plainly mystified, "doesn't he like me?"

Danielle laughed again. "Well, from the way his eyes bugged out when you came out of the cabin, I'd say he likes you just fine. In fact, I'd say that baby brother has a little bit of a crush on you."

"A crush...I don't understand. What do you mean?"

"It means he thinks you are pretty. You look way better in those old clothes of mine than I ever did and you certainly fill them out a lot better, and my brother, well...I think maybe we have a case here of puppy love."

Dharalyn looked suddenly uncomfortable and Danielle chuckled at the expression on her face.

"Don't worry," she said, "these things have a way of working themselves out. He'll probably gawk at you for a few days until the next young hottie catches his attention and then you'll be passé. Boys his age are just beginning to discover girls and they go batty over a different one every week." Danielle looked at Dharalyn who still looked a bit discomfited. "Don't guys in your world ever stare at you that way?"

Dharalyn shook her head. "My life does not include close association with males of my own age. Until we pass the Probost and take our place in Sedai society, the only males we come in close contact with are the Atrova Guardians, who are sworn to protect us and members of our immediate family."

"I don't really know what you mean by, *pass the Probost.* What exactly is that?"

Dharalyn looked suddenly taken aback, as if the subject was distasteful to her, or one that she was uneasy about. She looked at Danielle for a long moment and then said, "Danielle, I have never spoken of this to anyone before, so forgive me if I seem hesitant. The Probost is a very important test, which is given to Sedai Novi females when we reach the age of fourteen. Although it is hard to explain to one not of my world, I will try to explain it to you as well as I can. You see, in my world, when we reach the proper age, we are taken to a very sacred place located deep within the bowels of a gigantic ancient coliseum, built a very long time ago by my ancestors. This place was designed to be large enough to contain all of the Sedai Novi at once, and is used for both phases of our testing. The Novi are members of the Sedai aristocracy, of which there are thirty-two ruling families, each of which is represented in council by the Tessera, who is the head of each of the families. The Probost itself is actually just the first phase, that authenticates our spiritual relationship with our Kamanah, which is located within our spiritual center. That center is referred to as our Egana, and it is here that we are first anointed and shown the extent of our blessing by Anon." She paused for a moment. "I'm not explaining this very well, am I?"

Danielle shrugged her shoulders. "Not bad, I'm following it pretty well. So this Probost tests you on the connection with your Egana?"

Dharalyn nodded. "Yes, that's good."

"And then?"

"Well, when the test is given, we go into our Egana and we are shown our relationship with our Kamanah. We see it as a pool of water. The larger the pool, the more powerful the Sedai Novi."

"I see, and what happened when you were given the test?"

Dharalyn glanced at the ground, shame filling her features. "I failed it."

Danielle gazed at her friend. "You failed, you couldn't connect with your Egana?"

"Yes and no; I made the initial connection fine. It's actually quite simple to begin."

"So, what happened then?" asked Danielle, aware that she was touching on memories which, from the expression on Dharalyn's face, were very upsetting.

"I reached deep within and started to descend toward my Egana, excited about the prospect of seeing Anon's blessing and becoming one with my Kamanah. I could sense where I had to go, and at first, I thought it would be easy."

"But," pushed Danielle, sensing that this was a very painful memory, but unable to stop herself. She had to know. She just had to!

"I began to drop within, but soon I became really dizzy and waves of vertigo washed through me as I fell. There was nothing... just...blue emptiness, everywhere, all around in every direction. And then, the energy storm came. A violent tempest that overwhelmed my senses and tossed me about like some child's plaything. Every moment that passed, the fear within me grew as the powerful forces drove me back, beating against my mind and body, until I could stand it no longer. I have never been so absolutely terrified of anything in my life, Danielle, and I never, ever want to feel that way again."

Both girls were silent for many minutes afterward. Danielle, feeling badly about the obvious pain Dharalyn had relived, suddenly took her hand. "So, what happened then, afterwards?"

Dharalyn shook her head. "Well, you have to understand. The Probost is a sacred test that's been given to Sedai Novi females since we were blessed by Anon and ascended to a higher calling, thousands of years ago. Our laws are very clear on what happens to Novi that fail the Probost and it's been our way for thousands of years."

Danielle felt a shiver shoot up her spine. "So what happens?"

"They are immediately put to death. To keep any genetic aberrations from polluting the Novi bloodlines. Blood is life, after all, and blood purity is sacred."

"But you weren't put to death."

"My mother wouldn't allow it. As Tessera of our family, and Khan-Tessera of the Sedai Novi, she was able to hide for a time my disgrace from others, although I'm sure there were plenty of rumors circulating about me."

A half-dozen questions immediately sprang forth in Danielle's mind. "What is a Khan?" she asked, completely caught up in the strangeness of the tale.

"The Khan-Tessera is the Supreme Mother, the council head and leader of all the Novi, who in turn govern our worlds."

Danielle blanched. "Wait, so your mother is like the Queen of all your people. The head of your whole society, of your whole world?"

Dharalyn thought for a moment, and then answered, "Well, yes. Queen, or perhaps, Empress, would be a relatively good analogy using your words. She was the Empress of my world of Asreod, which consists of three principal peoples: the Sedai, the Cascai and the Gunta, as well as Khan over the rest of the Amalgamation Worlds. But Danielle, she is not the Khan anymore. You see, my mother was killed just before I came here."

The aura of extreme sadness surrounding Dharalyn was palpable, as Danielle stared at the young woman walking next to her. So much was suddenly becoming clear to her. After all the tears last night, it was plain that the emotional wounds here were still raw. Though it was also evident that she was even now working hard to suppress and keep them hidden deep within herself. Danielle shook her head slowly. "I'm so sorry, Dhara," she said, as a shared memory suddenly came back to her. "I remember hearing about that now. When I was in your mind, I heard that man tell you about it...I'm really so very sorry."

Dharalyn looked at her. "I know, Danielle. Please, don't let it concern you right now. This is not the time to continue grieving. One day, perhaps, there will be a time for that, but for now there are much more immediate concerns."

Danielle looked at her perplexedly. "I can't believe you would say that. I mean, my mother was killed last winter and I'm still not over it. She was everything to me and I still grieve for her loss. I will always grieve for her!"

Dharalyn stopped and turned toward her friend. "Please try and understand, Danielle. I've been taught since a very young age that my personal needs must always be second to the needs of others. As a Sedai Novi, my first responsibility is to my people and to those under my care. My first responsibility right now, Danielle, is to survive here and find a way to get back home. I have many people there who are depending on me. My personal needs must always be addressed when they don't interfere with my duty."

Danielle shook her head. "But she is your mother, you have a right to grieve for her."

"I grieved last night, Danielle. Were my mother here now, she would likely berate me for wasting time on an emotional outburst that served no purpose. I was just her daughter, and there were many things much more important than our personal relationship."

"I'm sorry, but I will never believe something like that," Danielle said adamantly. "It's so cold. There is nothing wrong with mourning for the loss of someone you love. Someone you were obviously so very close to. I mean, look what she did for you. She hid you away when you failed that stupid test and wouldn't let anyone hurt you. And screw the *thousand-year-old laws*!" she mimicked Dharalyn's tone. "You don't do that for someone who is *just your daughter*," she mimicked again. "You do that for someone who means more to you than anything in the world. Someone who means more to you than your own life! I didn't know her, but I knew someone like her...and I can tell you this. YOU, Dharalyn, were the most important thing in the world to her. Not the Sedai, or the Novi, or the people of Asreod, but you!" Danielle glared at Dharalyn fiercely and then paused, alarm spreading over her features. In front of her, Dharalyn's face had choked up in anguish, huge sobs exploding from her as she began to cry.

"Oh my God! Oh my God!" exclaimed Danielle, as she grabbed Dharalyn in a fierce embrace. The tears were coming faster now as Dhara's body shuddered. "Oh my God, Dharalyn! I'm a terrible person," she said, as her own voice began to crack. Within seconds, her tears flowed as well and the two of them stood together, crying and hugging one another while Biscuit nuzzled both of them.

It seemed like a long while, but eventually the two of them calmed down and pulled back from one another.

"I'm sorry, Dhara," said Danielle, "I can be so callous sometimes."

"No, Danielle, you are right. I think maybe in some way you are one of the wisest people I've ever met. I'm so very glad you were the one to find me here."

"Me, too," smiled Danielle, as she turned toward the sound of a clearing throat. A very loud and disgruntled sound.

Danielle and Dharalyn turned together and gazed in surprise at Big John, who was sitting on his horse only a dozen feet away with a look on his face that defied description. He raised his hand once, started to say something and then paused mid-thought, as something akin to a grunt escaped him. Grabbing his head with both his hands, he then let out an exasperated wheezing noise that seemed to embody a great amount of emotional angst, shook his head as if he could not believe what he had just seen, flung his hands in the air, then turned his horse about and rode away. Faint, grumbling words reached them which Danielle could barely make out. Something about crazy, emotional, daughter, why do I even, and then...nothing. Danielle turned her head toward Dharalyn, who turned toward her at the exact same time. The juxtaposition of her father's concern and his obvious aggravation with them hit them both the same way. Notwithstanding the tears of only a moment ago, the giggles seemed to explode from them both simultaneously, and it was a good long while before either of them was able to stop.

"I think we better get going," remarked Danielle, as she grinned at her companion in mirth. "I believe we've all but exhausted my father's patience. We better not push it anymore."

Dharalyn nodded once and taking up Biscuit's reins, began once again to follow what had now become a clearly marked path, through a growing field of grass. Next to her, she noticed that Danielle suddenly seemed lost in thought. A few minutes later, the girl turned toward her with a questioning look.

"Dhara," she said, "I want to ask you something."

"Okay," she replied.

"Well, I don't want to bring up a subject that is probably hard for you to talk about right now," Danielle paused and looked beseechingly toward Dharalyn. She knew this was a subject she should probably leave alone for now, but she had always been too impulsive. Too stubbornly curious, as her mother had often remarked, and this thing she wanted to ask had her bursting inside.

Dharalyn quietly nodded for her to continue, as she watched Danielle's face.

"If your mother was the Khan of your people, doesn't that make you some kind of a royal princess?" Danielle held her breath, as her mind raced. The whole situation reeked with the adventurous, romantic undertones of the fantasy stories that she had read so voraciously when she'd been younger. Tales of handsome knights rescuing fair young maidens, and stories of fabulous far-away kingdoms and royal intrigue. These days, however, her reading interests tended to lean a little more toward maidens who were capable of rescuing their own damn selves. Like a particularly popular new vampire series she was in the midst of reading. But that didn't stop her from feeling giddy inside with the possibility that Dharalyn's situation paralleled closely the things that had so often stimulated her young female heart. "I mean, aren't you like some kind of royal heir, or something?"

Dharalyn looked thoughtful, as if carefully considering her reply. "I am the Malakovani family heir for the Khan-Tessera, which leads the Sedai Novi and is rightful holder of the Prime Quadraprym Council Seat, should my Egana prove worthy." She saw the confused look on Danielle's face and continued to explain.

"My family name is Malakovani, Danielle. We make up one of the thirty-two ruling families of the Sedai, those who were blessed by Anon. The ruling families are referred to in my culture as Novi. Each of the families of the Novi are headed by one female and it is usually passed down from mother to daughter through the generations. The daughter, though, must prove herself in the second phase of the Probost as being powerfully skilled in Kamanah, proving her worth by being the most powerful head of each of the Novi families."

Danielle nodded, beginning to understand. "And what is this Kamanah you keep mentioning? Is that like, magic, or something?"

Dharalyn slowly nodded. "In a sense...yes. But not quite as you mean it in your cultural definition. Kamanah is the force that intertwines and binds us all. It is the power that sustains our life and culture. It is the gift of Anon that allows us to lift ourselves up and know each other's hearts. It allows us to be aware of that which can't be seen, to be more in tune with that which binds us all together. Oh Danielle, it is so hard to explain in just a few quick words. Those of us who have been so blessed, use it to better the lives of all of the people and help them keep to the principles of honor and truth."

"I see, I think," said Danielle, who was nearly as confused as she'd been before. "Maybe we can talk more about this some other day. When you have more time to explain it better."

Dharalyn grinned and nodded her head. "Perhaps you are right. That discussion would be better served at another time."

Danielle gazed ahead and suddenly pointed. "There, Dhara, that's my house up ahead." From a rise in the land, Danielle could see at the bottom of a wide field the form of a white, two story house decorated with black shutters, topped by a cross gabled metal roof and solitary red brick chimney. The house was surrounded by leafy green bushes of a flowering variety and bordered on two sides by a rather large covered porch. A wide, graveled area separated the house from a long, white barn on the right side, as well as a smaller shed which bordered the field they were currently traversing. A tall windmill stood next to the shed, where it whirled about slowly, helping to provide power to the house, though not nearly enough, as her father so often complained. In the front and to the right of the barn were a series of black, creosoted fences that divided the area into four separate paddocks as well as a fenced off field which provided the horses with plenty of room for running and frolicking, while keeping them safe from harm. In the driveway her father's late model blue Chevy pickup was parked, as well as her little silver Volkswagen Bug. She had worked hard after school and weekends for the last two years to save the money to pay for it and her car insurance, and she was proud of it. She could see, as they got closer, that a green Ford van was also parked in the driveway next to her father's truck. *Oh good,* she thought to herself. *Aunt Jay is home.* She knew her father very well and was deeply worried about what his immediate plans concerning Dharalyn were. Especially after a few of his comments back at the cabin. She sensed that things were likely to get a bit dicey between her and her father soon, and Danielle felt better knowing that in all likelihood, she would probably be able to count on her aunt's support and her rational approach toward all things Big John.

Aunt Sara Jane Walkerman, or Jay, as she was called by friends and family, worked at the local hospital in Pine Tree as an admissions clerk. She had moved in a few years ago to help take care of Danielle's Gran, and was as sweet and nurturing a person as Danielle had ever known.

As they got close to the house, she could see her Aunt Sara come out onto the front porch and give her a friendly wave. Her father and Aaron had brought their horses up to the barn, removed their saddles and bridles, and put them out into the nearest paddock by the time she and Dharalyn walked up leading Biscuit. Big John began to pull the saddle from Danielle's mount, and soon had Aaron leading her off toward the paddock, as well. Aunt Sara walked up and glanced toward Dharalyn, while grabbing Danielle in a huge, welcoming hug.

"What are you guys doing back, already? I didn't expect you here for several days at the very least," Aunt Sara said, as she glanced with obvious curiosity at both Dharalyn and her brother, John. He was fuming about something, she could see that quite plainly. But then, John was often in a poor humor about one thing, or another. Recently, it had been his extreme concern for Danielle's poor state of mind as well as her obvious depression and disassociation from all things family. Something in her manner had changed drastically since they'd left for the camp yesterday, though; Sara had noticed that about her almost immediately, when Danielle had walked up. As much from her niece's improved posture, which was no longer all slumped over, to her general demeanor, which seemed brighter and much more positive than it had in a long time.

Big John finished putting the saddles inside the barn and then hung the rest of the tack outside on some pegs, till he could get to it later. "Had a bit of a situation come up," said John succinctly, as he glanced briefly toward Dharalyn.

"Oh, and would this pretty young lady with the beautiful white hair be the situation that he's referring to?" Sara said to Danielle, completely ignoring the gruff tone of her brother, who could be so unsociable at times.

"Oh Auntie, yes," spluttered Danielle, as she grabbed Dhara's hand. "This is Dharalyn Malakovani; we, uh...we found her out by the campsite, last night."

"My, what a beautiful name. I don't believe I've ever heard it before," said Sara, as she turned and gave Dhara a welcoming hug.

"Don't be going and getting too friendly there, Sara, she's not going to be with us all that long," stated Big John, as he began walking toward the house.

"Dad!" Danielle called out, "I need to talk to you for a minute."

"Not right now, Danielle," said Big John as he continued walking, not even bothering to look back. "Help your brother brush down the horses and get them watered and fed!"

Danielle stammered for a second and turned toward her aunt, sudden anxiety registering in her eyes. "Aunt Sara, I need your help, please! I think he's gonna call the Sheriff to come pick up Dharalyn. Please, help me stop him! Help me to reason with him! There's so much here he doesn't know."

Sara gazed at her niece. She was not normally one to get between Big John and his daughter, especially when John had that serious, peeved look on his face like he had right now.

"Honey, I'm sure your father knows what's best. He wouldn't do that unless he had a good reason to."

"Aunt Sara, please," begged Danielle, as she grabbed her aunt's hands and folded them within her palms. "I need you to trust me here. Please, I know it's asking a lot, but he's making a huge mistake. I won't let them take her away, Aunt Sara. I won't let them.... Please, Auntie, please believe me! He's doing the wrong thing here."

Something in Danielle's beseeching eyes tugged at Sara's heart. She hadn't seen her niece react with this kind of passion in a very long time. And she knew John, knew he tended to react sometimes out of sheer pigheadedness rather than from his heart, knew how deep his stubbornness could go. Instantly she decided, "Oh hell, this is going to be bad. Well, come along, love, let's see if your father can be reasoned with." Sara turned and pulled Danielle behind her. It was going to take both of them, she knew, to get John to listen to any point of view other than his own, and still it was going to be chancy. *Marilyn could have done it,* she mused. Her dear brother had never been able to refuse his beloved wife anything. But she wasn't here anymore. It was up to the two of them to try and reach him. *This is gonna be a tough one,* she thought, as she entered the side door into the kitchen, followed by Danielle.

"Jonathan Lee Walkerman," Sara said sternly, while pointing a firm, unwavering finger directly at his chest. "You put that damn phone down right now and talk to me!"

It was then that Danielle fainted.

CHAPTER 5

THE HOUSEGUEST

Danielle opened her eyes and felt a cold cloth being pressed against her forehead. "What happened?" she whispered. "Where am I?"

"You're on the couch honey, because you blacked out on us," said Aunt Sara, worry in her eyes and concern in her gentle voice. "I guess all of the excitement kind of got to you. Did you eat breakfast this morning, or drink anything?"

"No," answered Danielle, her muddled mind slowly clearing.

"What about dinner last night?"

Danielle tried to shake her head, but immediately it began throbbing with the beginnings of a painful headache. "No, Jay, so much happened, I didn't even think about it."

"Here you go, Sara," said Big John, as he handed her a tall plastic glass of water. His face was etched with worry, as he gazed at his resting child.

Sara put the glass down and grabbed Danielle under her shoulders. "Here, try and sit up, honey. I want you to drink this. You're probably just dehydrated, so the first thing we need to do is get some fluids into you." Sara helped pull Danielle into a seated position and handed her the glass. "Slowly sweetheart," she cautioned. "Don't drink it too fast. Just a little at a time." She watched as Danielle began to drink and then said, "Good, now you just sit here with your friend while I go have a chat with your father. Okay?"

Danielle nodded once as her focus shifted to a point behind her aunt where Dharalyn was standing silently, looking unabashedly out of place, her returning gaze filled with apprehension. As soon as her aunt moved away, Dhara scooted in close to the couch and knelt beside her.

"Are you feeling all right?" she asked in a voice laden with concern, as she took Danielle's hand. "Can I do anything for you?"

"I'm fine," stated Danielle, who was feeling a little embarrassed now that she was beginning to feel like herself again. "I have a terrible headache, though...." She was about to try sitting up when suddenly, she spied movement at the door and saw that her brother was standing there looking, well, a little bit scared. "Hey there," she said. "Aaron, come over here." She patted the couch and pointed by her feet, which she pulled up to give him room. Moments later, he was sitting on the couch, a troubled cast to his features. Danielle smiled to herself, as she caught several little covert glances aimed at Dharalyn. *Oh no*, she thought, smiling to herself, *he really has it bad.*

"You okay?" he mumbled, sounding as if he was feeling both a mixture of concern and nervousness. Concern for her, Danielle supposed; nervous, she sensed, because he was so close to Dharalyn.

Dharalyn turned toward him. "Aaron, your sister's head is hurting her. Do you have something that can help ease her pain?"

Aaron froze and tried to speak, but no sound came out for a few seconds. Feeling foolish, he finally managed to recover himself and said, "Yeah, um... I can get her some aspirin. We have some in the upstairs medicine cabinet, I think."

"That would be wonderful," she said, and smiled warmly at him. "Would you mind getting it for me?"

Aaron nodded, and like a shot he was out the door and up the central staircase, headed on his errand.

Danielle chuckled softly and looked at Dhara, who seemed completely unaware of anything amiss.

"He's a sweet boy," Dharalyn said, "and he's very kind and concerned for you."

Danielle laughed again. "Oh sure, he's sweet, sometimes. But it's not me he's concerned about right now!"

Dharalyn looked puzzled. "What do you mean, Danielle?"

Danielle smiled and shook her head. "Not right now. I'll explain it to you some other time, when my head isn't pounding."

Dharalyn nodded and looked uncertain as to how to respond. "Very well," she said simply.

Out in the kitchen Sara and Big John were faced off against each other, mutual concern registering in both their faces.

"Really, John, no dinner, no breakfast, this is how you take care of your eldest child?"

John shook his head. "I couldn't get her out of the damn cabin, Jay! I mean, you don't know what I went through last night. If she wasn't out running through the woods half the night, she was sneaking into the cabin to be with that girl." He motioned in the direction of the small den and toward the far wall, where an arched doorway marked the entrance to the foyer and living room beyond. They were far enough away that he was pretty sure they couldn't be overheard; although, that was the least of his worries at the moment.

"You don't like this girl very much, do you?"

Big John shrugged his shoulders. "I just don't trust her, Jay. I mean, the first time I saw that damn girl awake, she had her hands around Danielle's throat and was choking her. A scene like that doesn't exactly promote a welcoming first impression."

Sara nodded thoughtfully. "Well, Danielle doesn't seem to hold it against her, so there must be more to it. And from what I can see, she seems to care very much about this girl, John. Do you know where she's from, where her family is?"

Big John slowly shook his head. "That's just it, there's something really weird about this situation with her. I can't wrap my head around it, at all. I mean, there she was, lying out there in the dark all alone and completely unconscious, when we found her.

At first, Danielle told me this absolutely crazy story. Seemed convinced, somehow, that this girl was brought here inside this giant ball of light that we saw up there."

"Ball of light?" Sara asked, looking confused.

John shook his head, as if he were denying an internal thought. "Yes, there was this strange, bright light up there and some kind of an explosion. It must have been a gas pocket, or something. Scared the hell out of me! Anyway, it was up by the old crystal dig. The one Danielle and Marilyn used to go up to all the time. I ran up there and found Danielle standing around, and looking weird as all hell. And next to her, I see this girl Dharalyn, lying unconscious on the ground."

Sara looked at John with an incredulous expression on her face. "What? You mean Danielle thinks this girl appeared out of nowhere, as if by magic, or something?"

"She told me that she'd been praying, Jay, seemed convinced that this girl was some kind of answer to her prayer. I think Marilyn was involved too, somehow. Or at least, Danielle seems convinced of it."

"What do you mean Marilyn was involved?" Sara asked in a half whisper, aware that her natural skepticism concerning these events was slowly causing her voice to take on a slight edge of hysteria. Her dear sister-in-law had died this past winter, and the whole family had had a very bad time coming to terms with their loss. The idea that Danielle felt her mother was somehow involved, from beyond the grave, sent a chill shivering through her body.

John shrugged and shook his head noncommittally. "I don't know. She said she'd been talking to her mother and to God. She didn't make all that much sense at the time. But she seems convinced that this girl is some kind of answer to all of that."

Sara nodded, thinking about her poor sister-in-law and remembering how hard the news had affected them all. Marilyn had been so very dear to all of them. But no one had been affected as much by the news as Danielle, not even John, who had utterly adored his wife. As the months had passed, they had all managed to put their lives back into some small semblance of order. They had slowly come to terms with the loss of her. All of them, that is, except for her beloved niece. As most of them returned to their daily routines, Danielle had continuously resisted any form of comfort and had been slipping slowly and ever deeper into melancholy. So often in the weeks following Marilyn's death, Sara had heard her crying alone in her room, while she'd stood feeling helpless outside her niece's door, her troubled heart breaking with constant worry. She'd tried to console Danielle so many times, tried to talk to her and reach her somehow, but the girl had repeatedly pushed her away. Pushed them all away, in fact. Her father and even her brother, had tried to bring her out of her depressive state, to no avail. Always a happy young teen, she was very intelligent for her age and though she herself would disagree, had a sparkling personality, with a fair bit of sass thrown in for good measure. Sara had always found her sharp wit to be utterly delightful, although Danielle's mother had often warned her daughter about her tendency to speak before thinking. She had often smiled and remarked that Danielle's mouth was bound to get her in a lot of trouble and in point of fact, had done just that, several times since Sara had begun living with the family. Sara had often marveled at Danielle's ability to wheedle and charm her way out of trouble, though. Things that any other teen would have been completely lambasted for, she had escaped easily with a playful tilt to her head, a bright smile and a quick quip. That was the old Danielle, though, the one Sara had known before Marilyn's passing. The girl she'd helped take care of since then was a shadow of her former self. Recently, John had grown so concerned that he'd spoken to her about the possibility of getting Danielle some professional help, which said a lot about how deeply worried he had become. With everything else, the timing couldn't have been worse, though. Their little family was living on the edge of financial disaster, and Sara had been worried that the expense would probably sink them. It had finally come to that point, though, where they needed to make a decision about Danielle, no matter what the cost. She had told John after talking to one of the psychologists associated with the hospital she worked for, that long periods of depression could often lead to substance abuse and even thoughts of suicide. This weekend trip had been John's final attempt to reach out to his daughter, before committing to the next step. Sara had one more thought though, and this one she brought to John's attention.

"You know, John, there's something here that I think you're missing. Something that I think you need to consider very carefully before you make any drastic decisions."

John looked at his older sister and waited; he often valued her advice and something in her tone immediately grabbed his attention.

Sara raised a finger to her forehead, like she always did when she was carefully considering something, and spoke, "Earlier, when I saw you all come in, I realized something right away, that you seem to possibly have missed."

John nodded thoughtfully, not sure where she was going with this. "And what is that, Jay?" He always called her by her pet nickname when they were alone, or speaking frankly.

Sara pursed her lips as she carefully formed her thoughts. "I recognized something in Danielle's general demeanor that I haven't seen in a very long while. I saw a little of the old Danielle, or someone very close to it. She was happy...a little reserved, maybe, for the sake of her new friend, but there was joy and a new buoyancy in her step. Joy like I haven't seen in her in a very, very long time. There's something going on between the two of them, John. Some kind of intangible bond, as impossible as that may seem to you. Whatever the reason, Danielle cares for the well-being of this girl. Cares very, very much."

John nodded slowly. He'd noticed it too, he suddenly realized, but he'd been so distracted by other concerns it was only now, with Sara's assertion, that he gave it some real thought. "This girl, though, we know nothing about her, Jay," he said. "At first, I thought she was some new-age girl lost in the woods, looking for, oh, I don't know, enlightenment or some other garbage. But now, I'm thinking it's more likely that what we have here is just a runaway. And Jay, if that's the case, we have to let the authorities know about her."

Sara shook her head in disagreement. "I don't know, John," she warned. "I think you had better be awfully careful here. Call it woman's intuition, if you will. But if you have her picked up by the locals, you're liable to do irreparable harm to your daughter's fragile mental state."

John was momentarily astounded by Sara's statement. Always the most level-headed of people, it was completely unlike her to go against social norms, which dictated at the very least that they alert the authorities. "What are you saying, Jay, that we keep her here with us?"

Sara nodded. "Well, for now, anyway. I mean, John, what harm can it do? This is a very delicate matter here before us, whether you realize it or not. So, we keep her with us, for now.... At the very least, it will likely do wonders for your daughter's well-being, who, in case you don't recall, was outside before, hollering quite vehemently at you to talk to her. I'm telling you, she is very emotionally invested in this situation and highly concerned about what you are going to do now."

John shook his head stubbornly. "We can't do this, Jay! What if someone is looking for her? What if her family has the police, or someone else, out searching for her? We could get in an awful lot of trouble, if the authorities find out she's been staying here all along and we haven't bothered to inform anyone of her whereabouts."

Sara smiled ruefully. "I never knew Big John Walkerman to be worried about what the police think about anything. And what about Danielle? How is she going to react when the sheriff gets here and takes this girl away? She's going to be inconsolable, and will likely never forgive her father for not considering her feelings on the matter."

John looked down at the floor, anxiety flushing the features of his face. "Oh God, Jay, I can't even think about that. We have enough problems in our life right now, what with the bank breathing down my neck. So what do we do here? What's the best course of action for our family and for Danielle's well-being?"

Sara smiled grimly. "Very simple, my dear. For now, you make a few quiet calls and find out if there are any bulletins, or whatever they call it, for any runaways that meet her description."

John chuckled nervously. "Well, that should be easy enough. Have you even seen hair that color before, in your life? I mean, it's as white as the snow in winter. I've never seen the like."

Sara smiled. "No, can't say I have, either. It's awfully pretty, though I can't for the life of me figure out how she got it to look that way; it's really gorgeous. I wonder where she got it done?"

John grunted disapprovingly. Hair was not his thing and talking about it only made him cringe with boredom. "Well, that's neither here nor there," he said, as he folded his arms and sighed in obvious consternation. "All right. Here's what we will do. I will call sheriff Drawbridge," he said glumly. "Even though he's a bit of an ass these days, we go way back and I should be able to find out if anyone is looking for our little visitor, or someone who matches her description. Meanwhile, you do your best over the next day or so to get to know her. Talk to her, Jay, and find out what you can about her. We'll let this thing simmer for a few days, at the most," he said resolutely, "but then we'll need to decide on how to proceed and what to do with her, long term."

Sara nodded. "That sounds fairly reasonable, my dear brother. I hoped you'd listen to some good sense."

John grunted again in disapproval. He didn't really like this, but he suspected Sara was right. He knew deep down that if he pushed too hard right now and mishandled this matter, that it might be a huge setback to his daughter's delicate state of mind. And in Big John's world, nothing was worth that. In his mind and heart, his daughter Danielle came first and foremost, and always would.

Back in the living room, Danielle was beginning to feel better. She had taken the aspirin her brother had gotten for her and it was finally starting to take effect. Nervously, she glanced in toward the den and beyond where she could see her aunt and her father talking. She couldn't make out what they were saying, but it was clear that whatever it was, it was of a very serious nature. Here in the living room, the three of them sat quietly. In fact, no one was saying anything at all. Danielle could see that Dharalyn was really deep in thought about something, from the look of extreme contemplation residing in her eyes. Nearby, her little brother sat quietly as well, just staring off into space. Normally, that would make her smile and she might tease him a bit, but right now she was too preoccupied. Carefully, she put together the best argument she could. She was pretty sure that Dharalyn's fate was being decided in the kitchen right now and she wanted to be prepared to argue her cause. Although Aunt Sara could be pretty persuasive at times, she knew her father's stubborn nature, had seen how he'd been acting since last night, and had very little hope that her aunt would prevail. She watched for a few more minutes and finally couldn't take it anymore. Slowly, she raised herself from the couch and winced, as a sharp lance of pain shot through her head. Fortunately, the pain was short-lived and soon she was standing. "Aaron," she said softly, "keep Dharalyn company for a few minutes, will you? I need to talk to Dad." Aaron gave her a quick nod and glanced toward Dharalyn, who still appeared to be in her own world. For a moment, Danielle's sympathetic nature kicked in as she thought about the many uncertainties that must be running through Dharalyn's mind, but the harsh realities of the moment forced her to stay her course, as she made herself resist the impulse to kneel down next to the girl and see if she was okay. *First things first, Danielle,* she thought to herself. *Make sure Dad isn't going to have her carted away, and then you can see to her comfort.* Danielle walked across the room and passed through the small foyer. As she entered the den and approached the kitchen, she saw her father, who had apparently finished his conversation, wave her on into the room where he and Aunt Sara were sitting.

"Hey there, sweetheart, are you feeling better?" he asked, his voice soothing and his eyes surprisingly gentle.

"I'm fine, Dad. Listen, we need to talk," she said, her voice suddenly shaking as her resolve momentarily wavered. "Did you call someone about Dharalyn? Are they coming to take her away?"

Danielle heard her aunt chuckle and say, "Yep, that's the spunky girl I used to know. That's my little Danielle."

Danielle shot a small frown toward her aunt, whom she thought might be taking this situation a bit too lightly and then focused her attention back on her father. For the life of her, she didn't understand what in the world her aunt was talking about. Again she started to speak, but her father quickly cut her off, just as she began.

"Just calm down, honey! I know you are worried about your friend, but we haven't decided anything for sure, just yet. Your aunt thinks it might be best if she stayed here for a few days until we sort things out. I'm gonna make a simple call or two and make sure she's not a runaway, and that no one is looking for her."

"She's not," interrupted Danielle, her face lighting up. "And no one is looking for her. Or at least, no one from around here, Dad."

Big John glanced searchingly at his daughter. *She knows more than she's telling,* he thought suddenly, and made up his mind to wait at least a day before he pressed her for more information. "Danielle, I hope you're not keeping something from me that can cause this family a lot of trouble. The way things have been going lately, we certainly don't need any more problems landing on us right now."

"I know, Dad, I know. You can trust me," she said, and then wrapped her arms around her father, giving him the kind of huge hug she used to give him all the time. The kind that made him melt a little inside. "I love you so much. Thank you! Thank you for doing this!" Big John nodded once and then glanced toward Sara, who suddenly had tears in her eyes and was looking away, so as to pretend she didn't see that he had them as well. She knew him all too well, he thought. He had always been bad at this.

"Listen, since we're kind of tight on space right now, you're going to have to put her in with you. Is that okay?"

"Uh huh," she said, still holding on to her father. "I have plenty of room. We can throw out that old TV and put that fold-a-bed by the window." She had been caught completely off guard and was reeling inside by this news. She hadn't expected her father to be so reasonable. This was so unlike him. *I wonder what made him change his mind?* she thought as she released him, gave him a quick kiss on his cheek and smiled to herself. *Aunt Sara must have really come through, after all.*

"Go on," said John, needing a few minutes himself, "go get her settled in. Your aunt and I will fix some lunch, which you will then EAT!" he stated sternly. John saw his daughter's face light up as she turned and left the room, practically jumping for joy. He turned toward Sara, who was beaming at him.

"Now, do you see that! Wasn't that worth it?"

"It will do for now," said John, with a reluctant tone to his voice. "For now, but what happens in a few days when the manure hits the fan?"

"One thing at a time, John. We'll handle that when and if it comes."

"Oh, it'll come, Jay. With our luck, it will most definitely come."

Danielle rushed into the living room and saw Dharalyn raise her head. "Come on," she said, "my Dad's decided. You are staying with us. In fact, you and I are going to be roommates!"

Dharalyn smiled warmly and took Danielle's proffered hand. Within moments, she was following Danielle up the stairs to the bedroom on the second floor, where she would be staying.

"This is my room, now to be OUR room," pronounced Danielle, waving a hand around an L shaped area that housed a queen-sized bed, two dressers, a large bookcase overflowing with books, several posters and many years' worth of accumulated paraphernalia. In an alcove at the back of the room, sat a sturdily made wooden credenza that held a large television set. On the right wall was a desk that sat in front of an open window, which looked out upon a roof, framing a wide field and a winding road beyond.

Dharalyn gazed out into the world displayed outside of the double-wide window and suddenly felt very small. She was so very out of her element, here. Everything was so different and it hit her all of a sudden, how very different it was. Danielle noticed her discomfiture and placed a hand on her shoulder.

"It's okay, Dhara. I know how strange all of this must be to you. I was thinking about it, before. I mean, being from a different world like you are, all of the things I take for granted must be so strange to you. After all, our clothes are different, and our homes and lives are probably strange to you. Even simple things, like the way our doors and windows open may be different. I mean, how they open and all, might be different than how they latch and open in your world."

Dharalyn shook her head slowly. "I've never opened a door before, Danielle," she said softly.

Danielle looked at her in astonishment. Had she just heard that right? "What did you say? You've never opened a door, before? You've got to be kidding me."

Dharalyn turned toward her and shook her head. "No, Danielle, I was never allowed to. Routine tasks were handled by my Cascai servants and Sedai retainers. I was never permitted to do things like that. It was considered to be beneath my station to do such basic things."

Danielle stood in open mouthed disbelief, until after a moment the realization hit her. "Of course, because of who you are. I keep forgetting that you are a big deal back where you come from; I mean, you're like, some kind of a royal princess, and all."

Dharalyn nodded. "Yes Danielle, something like that," she said simply, and grinned mischievously at her new friend.

Danielle grinned back. "Did you just take a jab at me?" she asked.

Dharalyn shrugged and they both giggled. After a few moments passed, Dharalyn said in a more serious tone, "For now, Danielle, you are going to have to teach me. Treat me as you would a student from far away, who knows nothing of your culture and your ways. I will try to learn as fast as I can about how you do things here."

"All right," said Danielle, nodding, "but I'm warning you right now, I'm not gonna open any doors for you," she teased. "You're going to have to learn how to do that for yourself, although," she paused, a mischievous look appearing on her own face, "I'm sure my little brother may be willing to open all the doors you need." Danielle chuckled at the look of confusion that suddenly appeared on Dhara's face. "Sorry, you're not ready for subtle humor yet, I can see."

Dharalyn nodded in agreement. "Yes, many things you say don't always make much sense, but I am learning."

Danielle became attentive as she heard her aunt call from downstairs and grabbed Dharalyn's hand. "Come on, it sounds like lunch is about ready. Here's your chance to eat some completely new cuisine." As they made their way out the door, Danielle spied her brother's form disappearing down the hallway and into his room. *He's been listening to us,* she thought, and tried to recall if any of the things they'd just talked about were of a damning or revealing nature. The truth about Dharalyn was going to have to come out eventually, but she'd rather it came out when she was ready, and in a controlled fashion, so as not to completely freak out her father. She was going to have to have a serious talk with Aaron, and soon. Before he got on his computer, and half the town ended up awash in rumors about the mysterious girl who was living with the Walkerman family. She knew she'd better make it quick, too. Aaron was likely to use any information he overheard to boost his status among his so-called friends, who were his social peers. Like Danielle, Aaron hadn't fared well in the social pecking order at his school. She worried that he might see this as an opportunity to change that. That was the problem when you were a kid. You weren't aware of the ramifications of your actions and just didn't see the big picture.

Danielle entered the kitchen and sat Dharalyn next to her. "I hope there's something here you like," she said, as she began to pour herself and Dhara a glass of water.

Dharalyn looked around the table as the growing unease and distinct awareness that she was missing something important about these people suddenly took shape and became clear in her mind. *They're like the Cascai and the Ghasta,* she thought, as she studied their faces. *I wonder if they even have anyone like me here.* Dharalyn gazed about the table and for some reason she couldn't yet define, began to feel increasingly troubled.

CHAPTER 6

STRONG ANYONE?

"So, where is Dhara this beautiful morning?" asked Aunt Sara, as she handed Danielle a glass of freshly squeezed orange juice.

Danielle pointed towards the ceiling. "I left her sitting at my desk, upstairs. Last I saw, she was leafing through a whole bunch of my books. She seemed really interested in some of them."

Sara nodded. "Which ones? I seem to recall that most of your recent book purchases tend to revolve around your latest obsession with the supernatural."

"Yeah, she's looking through the newer releases. Mostly, she seems interested in the vampire stories. In fact, when we were looking through them last night and I was explaining what some of them were about, she really seemed to perk up when I mentioned vampires."

"So, like you, she's into the bloodsucking stories then?"

Danielle shrugged. "I guess. I don't know. She's been acting kind of funny since she started looking at them."

Her aunt nodded attentively. "What do you mean, acting funny?"

"Well, she seems almost completely fixated on looking through certain types of books. She's been scanning through nearly every book I own that has a vampire or magical theme. Not reading them, but just briefly jumping from chapter to chapter. It's weird," Danielle paused, and gave her Aunt a piercing look. "It's almost as if she's looking for something in particular."

Aunt Sara chewed on a slice of toast while getting up from the table to grab a pot of coffee. "Well, she's certainly been displaying a lot of odd behavior since I first met her yesterday morning. After all, she didn't come down with you for breakfast just now, she excused herself from dinner last night, and the way she acted yesterday at lunch...Danielle, I watched her and she barely touched a thing. She had a couple of small pieces of fruit, and then nearly choked on her water when she took a sip. I'm not trying to speak ill of your friend, honey, but I can kind of see now what your Dad was saying. And after how she reacted when she met Gran, I've gotta say, he's pretty much back to feeling uneasy about her again and trust me, I'm putting that very mildly, for your sake."

Danielle smiled grimly. So far, things were definitely not going well. Dharalyn was acting so very strange, even stranger than Danielle expected her to, considering that she was understandably going through a major period of adjustment. First, there'd been the eating thing. And then yesterday evening, the oddity of Dharalyn's reaction when Gran had come out of her room to spend a little family time with them. Gran had had a stroke a few years back, and it had left her partially paralyzed and wheelchair bound. She often stayed in her room, most days watching her soaps, but usually came out in the cooler evening air to sit with all of them out on the porch, or even sometimes to have dinner with them. Gran was also the reason that Aunt Sara had come to stay with them two years ago. At first, to help her mother with Gran's general care and then later on, after the accident, to take care of her pretty much full time, when she wasn't working. Even paralyzed, Mabel Frances Walkerman still managed to do for herself much of the time, although everyone took turns helping out when Aunt Sara had to be at work. During the school year, sometimes a close friend of her aunt's from in town came and sat with Gran, until either Danielle got home from school, or her father or aunt got home from work. Danielle often sat and talked to her grandmother about all kinds of things. And she knew her Gran appreciated it too, from all the loving gestures and smiles she got from her. She could talk to her about anything, and besides Aunt Sara, was the only other person in the family that had no problem understanding Gran's garbled speech patterns which, because of complications resulting from her stroke, were hard for some people to understand. They had all been out on the porch enjoying the evening air when Gran had, with Aunt Sara's assistance, joined them outside. Danielle had taken Dharalyn over to her grandmother's wheelchair and been about to introduce her, when Dhara had done the oddest thing: she had suddenly bent down on one knee, reached out and taken Gran's left hand in hers, and kissed the back of her hand. Then she had said something in some strange language that sounded exactly like the same lingo she'd spouted to Danielle the first night they'd met, and then, quite unbelievably, she'd begun to sing a sweet little singsong of sorts. The whole family had sat and stared at her in complete amazement, except for Gran, who besides look-ing a tad bewildered at first, had seemed absolutely charmed after-ward by the unusual event, and even more, by Dharalyn herself. She had taken hold of Dharalyn's hand and had held it in hers for the remainder of the evening, while Dhara had inexplicably knelt and made herself comfortable sitting at Gran's feet. Danielle shook her head as she recalled more of the evening's events. She hadn't dared to look at her father while they'd been out there, and could only imagine the thoughts that had gone through his head. *Well, at least she sings awfully pretty,* she thought silently, while finishing up a bowl of sliced fruit. No one could discount that fact. Her voice had been truly amazing, even singing a cappella, and had reminded Danielle of clarion bells or chimes, ringing across a clear blue lake. She'd heard the saying somewhere and had never thought to apply it to anything, but it certainly fit the exquisite sounding voice that had regaled them all last night. Still reflecting, Danielle suddenly glanced up at the sound of her name being called.

"You seem awfully deep in your own thoughts this morning," said Sara, who was smiling wistfully at her niece. "Care to share?"

Danielle grimaced and shook her head. "Just going over some Dharalyn stuff in my head."

Sara was more than a little curious, but didn't push. She still enjoyed seeing her niece act like her old self, albeit someone who seemed in a constant state of worry, and knew she needed some space. "So, what do you have planned for today?"

Danielle shrugged her shoulders. "I thought I would get Dad to help me move some things out of my bedroom, so that I can make room for Dharalyn."

"Your Dad's not home right now, honey. He went on in to work this morning. Said as long as you guys had cut your trip short, he might as well put in some extra hours."

Danielle nodded glumly. She knew her Dad disliked his new job, but knew also that they needed the money. Ever since the time about four years ago, when he'd had to close his small hardware store and he'd gone to work for the big outfit that had put him out of business. One of those mammoth, corporate chain stores that he said were busy ruining the American dream for regular folks.

"I guess that we will do the best we can, on our own. Dharalyn and I should be able to handle most of it ourselves, except for that big old tube TV that doesn't work anymore. That thing weighs a serious ton, and it took both Dad and Uncle Jack to put it up there, so I guess I'll have to find a different spot for her bed till Dad can get some help to take it out."

Aunt Sara nodded. "I can help you with some of your things, if you like."

"No, that's okay. I think we can handle it," said Danielle, as she began to clean up the table. She had other concerns, too. She was going to have to get Dharalyn some clothes and some personal belongings, since all the poor girl had to wear at the moment was some old jeans and the top she had loaned her, and that funny set of shiny clothes they'd found her in. Danielle groaned inwardly. She guessed that her poor savings account, which had been whittled down so fast due to the car and insurance, was about to expire for good. She figured she had just about enough in there to get Dharalyn three or four changes of new clothing if they stayed with the cheaper stores, rather than the designer, fashion outlets. After that, they would have to beg, borrow and plead for the rest. She noticed her aunt staring at her and returned the gaze. "What?" she said, and waited for a response.

Sara shook her head slowly. "I don't know, honey, I guess I'm just concerned, is all. On the one hand, I see some changes in you that I have to say, I'm really glad to see. I suspect that some of that, or at least a large part of it, has to do with Dharalyn's presence here."

"And?" asked Danielle, knowing full well that her aunt hadn't told her what was uppermost in her mind.

"Well, to be very blunt, honey, your friend is more than just a little..." Sara paused, as she searched for a diplomatic term to describe Dharalyn, "different, don't you think?"

Danielle shrugged noncommittally. "You already said something like that a little while ago."

Sara sighed...she felt like a terrible gossip, but ever since last night, she'd had some burning concerns. One in particular: "I guess the best thing here is, to just jump in with both feet and let the dust settle where it will, so here it goes. Last night, she was downstairs looking for you just before bedtime, and I thought I'd let her know how glad I was that she was staying here with us. Anyway, honey, I walked over to her, you know, all nice and friendly and reached out and grabbed her arm, very casual like. When all of a sudden, she pulls her arm away and steps back with this shocked look on her face! You would have thought I had just insulted her, or slapped her, or something. She was definitely upset, though about what, I haven't a clue. I have absolutely no idea what it was I did and so I stood there, well, stunned for a moment. She just glared at me, and then turned and went up the stairs to your room. I don't know, maybe I shouldn't have said anything to you about it. But then, I thought, what if she's escaped from a mental institution or something? Maybe she's not a runaway, Danielle, maybe she's just, you know, crazy."

Danielle stared open-mouthed at her aunt and suddenly, as the realization of how her aunt must perceive Dharalyn's odd behavior hit her, she began to laugh. The laughter continued on unabated for quite some time, before she pulled herself together. It was the absurdity of the situation contrasted, of course, with Dharalyn's unique reactions to what were otherwise normal situations. Danielle, seeing the confounded expression on her aunt's face, forced herself back into a semblance of composure to explain herself. "I'm sorry, Jay," she exclaimed, as she fought to regain control of her runaway emotions. She was never intentionally cruel, and could see from the look on her aunt's face that she had hurt her feelings. "Oh, Auntie, I'm so very sorry about my reaction just now, but, we really need to talk."

Sara's eyes narrowed as she looked at her niece, her face becoming rigid. "I certainly hope so, Danielle. I have to admit, I'm a little surprised at your behavior here. This is a very serious matter."

Danielle nodded; she had always been able to talk to Aunt Sara about anything and her aunt, in the past, had always been very open to new ideas. And it was becoming more and more plain that in the upcoming days, she was going to need a tough and loyal ally, when it came to looking after Dharalyn and dealing with her father.

"Okay, listen," said Danielle, as she took a second to order her thoughts. "In the past, we've talked about some really bizarre things, you know, like psychic and paranormal phenomena and stuff like that, all things that I could never, ever talk to Dad about and so I really, really need you to keep an open mind about what I'm going to tell you."

Sara nodded, her interest plainly piqued, and so Danielle continued on with her explanation. She told her aunt about her prayer to her mother and to God, and relayed in great detail the incredible events of the night Dharalyn had arrived. Sara's eyes had widened when Danielle described the shining globe of light, and how the crystals had glowed magically afterwards. She then told her, and only because she and her aunt had discussed many things that were just as weird, of how Dharalyn had joined their minds, which had allowed her to learn their language. She also told her some of what she had learned of Dharalyn's world, although she held back on most of the more specific details of who, exactly, she was. In all, it took quite a while to get through the complete description of what had occurred, but finally she finished.

"Oh my," said her aunt, "I can certainly see now, why she seems to be so different, in so many little ways."

Danielle nodded and said, "And that's probably why she reacted that way last night, when you touched her arm. I'm just learning some of the essentials now myself, but where she is from, I think that it might be considered bad manners, or maybe something else which in her culture is considered improper. I'll ask her about it later, when I get the chance."

Sara nodded. "Danielle, I'm not exactly sure I believe all of this, just yet. Your father has a completely different view of the situation, but for now, I will certainly try and keep an open mind on the subject."

Danielle smiled. "That's all I ask. Now I guess I'd better go and get her. We have a lot to do today. We need to make room for her in my room and afterwards, I need to take her shopping."

"Shopping!" said Sara, "For what?"

"You know, clothes and stuff. She doesn't have anything, Auntie. No clothing or personal items of any kind, other than what she was wearing when I found her. It's going to clean out my bank account, but I need to get her some things."

Sara nodded and smiled. Inwardly, she thought that the whole thing might be a waste if John found out that she was on the run from somewhere, like he believed, but she also recognized the look on Danielle's face and knew that her niece's mind was made up. John's stubborn nature was easily equaled by that of his daughter, and, in some ways, maybe even surpassed.

Danielle left the kitchen and was passing through the den, when she spied her brother, Aaron, intently looking through the bookcases of the small library that graced the three walls of a small alcove there. They had a collection of some three to four hundred or so volumes of the classics, as well as a good selection of children's books and a variety of more adult themed titles. She had read nearly everything in the family collection years ago, and was mildly surprised to see her brother there now, since normally, getting him to read was an ongoing personal battle between them. She paused for a moment, thinking to inquire about his real reason for being there, when finally, she shook her head and continued on. She had entirely too much to do today, and no time to wonder about Aaron's constantly perplexing behavior.

She arrived at her room to find Dharalyn replacing the last of the books she'd been perusing. "Find what you were looking for?" she asked amusedly, the idea of shopping generally improving her mood.

Dharalyn glanced at her coldly. "I am very worried, Danielle. Your people seem to have a poor view of that which is different from themselves. You seem to view nearly anything that is strange or alien to your way of thinking as bad, or evil."

Danielle felt bewildered. "What are you talking about? Where did you get that idea?"

Dharalyn pointed at some of her books. "These stories; they are of things that happened in your world, correct? They tell of past histories and the lives of your people, do they not?"

Danielle blanched, as she realized what Dharalyn was referring to. "No, Dhara, no. These are just fictional stories. Made up purely for the pleasure of the reader. They aren't actually real!" she said fervently. Danielle grabbed a book from one of the series she was currently reading. "The people in this book, they are only make-believe. The characters and the adventures they have only exist in the reader's mind."

Dharalyn looked confused for a moment and then said, "These books, then, are of untrue stories? Written for their entertainment value, only?"

Danielle nodded enthusiastically. "Yes, that's right. Now you understand."

"Why are the vampires in your books, why are they all so very bad? Are all of the vampire people in your world of an evil nature?"

"Well, yes, for the most part. In some of the newer series, some of them are kind of good, but for the most part, vampires are these evil creatures that go around drinking human blood and killing people, more or less. They kind of represent the darkest side of the human condition, I guess you could say. In most of the books, they kill and ravage the humans, and then the heroes of the stories go out and find them, to seek revenge and provide justice."

Dharalyn nodded her head slowly in understanding. Danielle could tell by the look on her face that she was still deeply bothered by something, though.

"Dhara, I just want to be sure you understand. These books are not about actual people who lived. Vampires are fictional creatures. They don't exist in real life."

Dharalyn took a few steps and then turned. "If, somehow, a vampire was discovered in your world, would your people be welcoming, or would they fear it?"

Danielle stared. "I don't understand why you would ask that. They aren't even real."

"But what if they were?"

Danielle shrugged in exasperation; this bizarre discussion was beginning to get to her. "I don't know... I suppose, if people suddenly discovered they were somehow real, they wouldn't like them very much. After all, throughout history, in many of our different cultures, the mythos of the vampire has always been one of a fearsomely evil persona. I guess if they were discovered, they would be, you know, done away with." Danielle stared perplexedly at her new roommate and then added, "So, do you have any other questions? I mean, we really have a lot to do today."

Dharalyn shook her head. "No, that will do for now," she growled uncharacteristically, crossing her arms in a staunchly outward display of deep irritation and disgust.

Surprised by her friend's reaction, Danielle gazed at her for a moment, lost in quiet contemplation. It was going to be like this, she thought, and for some time to come. There must be so many fundamental, cultural differences for them to learn about that it was probably going to take time and a lot of understanding to make adjustments for them. Suddenly she remembered, "Dhara, I've been meaning to ask you. Why did you pull away and scowl at my aunt last night when she tried to touch your arm?"

Dharalyn pursed her lips and said in a formal sounding tone, "I am of the Sedai Novi, heir Tessera of family Malakovani of the Sakatherian Regency. Any person who touches me without my prior consent does so at their peril. Should such a thing happen within the sight of my family Guardians, the individual would be taken out and flogged for their effrontery."

"But we've touched many times, you and I."

"Special allowances can be made at times of great peril, when my safety or well-being is at stake. You came to my aid and therefore, you were granted special dispensation by me. Besides, there was also the bonding that occurred between us, which makes you Sho-Notoo."

Danielle winced. "What the heck is that? Does it mean we are special friends?"

Dharalyn frowned. "No, Danielle, not just a friend! In my world, Sho-Notoo is a great honor, but more importantly, it is an exceptionally rare occurrence." She paused for a moment, ordering her thoughts and then continued, "You see, within my culture, we have a great many people who serve as honored caregivers of the Sedai Novi. These individuals are carefully selected from the chosen elite from amongst the Sedai, the Cascai and the Gunta and forge a life-long bond. These people are called Tha-Notoo, and are known as the honor bound. The sole purpose of their lives is to serve the Novi in all things. Once in a very long, long while, however, a more significant bond is formed between a Novi and an individual from my world. This person is known as the Sho-Notoo, and I must tell you, it is extremely rare for this type of bond to occur, never happening twice in a century and then only under very special circumstances. It means that you are as a sister to me, you are of the family Malakovani and have all of the rights and privileges of the Sedai Novi to whom you are bound."

Danielle's mouth dropped open. "Are you kidding? So like, in your world I would be like a royal person of some kind?"

Dharalyn nodded sagely. "That is correct, of some kind."

"But why, why would you bestow such an honor on me? What in the world did I do to deserve that?"

Dharalyn reached out and took her chin. "What did you do? In the time of my greatest fear, lost and alone, you forgave my offense against you and risked yourself to find me. In my moment of utmost sorrow, you reached out and offered comfort. In a time when I am far from home, you take me in and protect me. Yesterday in the cabin, when I searched your heart, I found only kindness, purity and empathy, things that are rare even in my world. When I looked into your eyes, I saw myself looking back out at me. I saw my sister, and sensed my Egana rejoicing along with yours. And so, when we forged the bond, I offered the Sho-Notoo which your Egana graciously accepted."

"Huh?" said Danielle. "I don't remember accepting anything."

"I suspect as much," said Dharalyn. "There is much more to you than just this, Danielle," she explained, as she clasped her hands on both sides of Danielle's body. "There is a whole you that you obviously don't even know exists. It lies deep within you and is connected to everyone and everything. Your Egana allows you to sense things and to know things that you are not even aware of in your present state."

"Sounds like some of the stuff my Aunt Sara and I talk about sometimes with Gran. It's pretty deep."

"Yes," said Dharalyn, "don't worry. I will teach you how to become more aware."

Danielle nodded. "Good, okay, and speaking of being more aware, I need you to do something for me."

"Yes."

"I need you to try very hard to tone down the whole high and mighty, I'm-so-very-important-in-my-world arrogance thing you have while you are here."

"Danielle, I don't understand why you would say that about me. I am not arrogant!"

Danielle nodded. "Oh, I'm sure you don't think you are.... But trust me, you are a little! Look, in your world you are this big, important person who commands the respect of your whole family and the millions of people you all rule. But here, you are simply Dhara, Danielle's normal and quite ordinary friend. And as Danielle's friend and sister and roommate, you will try hard to be nice and respectful to the people in this house. Especially to my Aunt Sara, who is going to help us and who is one of the sweetest, nicest people I've ever known. Okay?" she asked and stared, waiting for an answer.

Dharalyn stared back for a long moment and then gave a succinct nod.

Danielle waited a few seconds more, and since there didn't seem to be any other response forthcoming, she decided to let it go for now. "Okay,... then let's get busy. We need to get this place rearranged and organized so that we can make room for my new roommate...you."

Dharalyn looked around the room. She had never been asked to do anything like this before. Move things around, clean and pick up. She was mortified. "Danielle," she said, "I don't usually do things like this."

Danielle smiled with an almost wicked cast to her features. "Oh, I know, roomie. But trust me, it'll be good for you. Help you to build some real character, my father would say. Look, you want to live here, you have to pitch in. House rules."

Dharalyn sighed. "All right, Danielle, I will try."

Danielle smiled broadly and took her around the room, showing her the things they needed to haul to the basement, and the things they would move. "I'm going to put a bed in the alcove for you, but we will have to wait until my Dad has the time to move that old TV. It weighs a veritable ton." Danielle grabbed a box of old books and handed them to Dharalyn. "Here, why don't you take this down to the basement. Oh, wait, you don't know where that is, do you? Tell you what, my aunt's down in the kitchen right now; ask her and she can show you where to take them."

Aunt Sara sighed pensively; it seemed she had Danielle's friend all wrong. The girl had come down a few minutes ago and apologized to her for the previous evening's insult. She had showed the girl where to put the box and then answered a quick question about where to toss that heavy old tube TV of Danielle's. "Oh hon," she had said, "Best place to put that old thing is in the trash hole behind the shed out there," she had informed the girl, while indicating a small building through a nearby window. "But that's way too heavy for you two girls to handle yourselves. I'll see if our neighbor can come by later and give John a hand getting it down." She then watched Dhara head back up the stairs and smiled as she'd gone back into the kitchen to finish chopping up some celery. "I don't know, the more I think about it, I think maybe my little girl's imagination has gotten away from her on this one," she said softly to herself. She was a bit odd, for sure, but Sara had met plenty of people a whole lot nuttier at the hospital. "I think it's probably just all the stress. In a few days or a week, she'll have time to consider things a bit more and is likely to realize that her new friend is just a bit eccentric. A runaway, like John said, or some other reasonable explanation." Sara heard the back door slam closed and walking to a window, looked out into the back yard to see who it was. A moment later, she felt her mouth drop open and her body stiffen, as the shock of what she saw caused momentary paralysis.

Danielle returned to her room, and turned at the sound of someone at the door. "Oh hi, Auntie," she said, immediately discerning the look of consternation on her aunt's face. "Are you all right?"

Sara nodded. "Oh yes, honey, um, by the way, Danielle apologized to me earlier, oh no, I mean, Dharalyn apologized."

Danielle suddenly became concerned as she noticed that her aunt seemed very pale. "Are you sure you're okay? You seem to be a bit bewildered."

"Well, yes, I've just had a bit of an epiphany, is all," she said, and chuckled nervously. "It seems the universe still has a few surprises left in store for me."

"What are you talking about?" asked Danielle, her curiosity rising.

"Well, I just wanted to let you know that I absolutely believe your story about Dharalyn being from, uh, elsewhere.... I believe it completely."

"Really!" said Danielle, excitedly. "What in the world brought you around?"

"Well, Honey. To state it simply. When you see a beautiful, dainty young girl carrying an incredibly heavy television set out to the trash hole; a set, by the way, that took two grown men a whole lot of sweat and muscle to get up here, it forces you to reconsider some things. Like, that maybe that little girl isn't from anywhere around here."

Danielle stood in shock. "Aunt Sara, what in the world are you talking about?" Her aunt pointed toward the back of her bedroom, and so, Danielle turned to see what it was her aunt had noticed as soon as she'd walked in: the sturdy, dust covered stand now sitting empty in the alcove, where the old TV had only minutes ago been sitting.

"She asked me where to put it and I told her in the trash hole. I certainly never expected her to move it, though, let alone by herself."

"The thing weighs, like, hundreds of pounds," stated Danielle, her tone laden with disbelief.

"Almost three hundred, I think."

Both women turned at the sound of someone at the door. Dharalyn stood there, breathing evenly and without the slightest sign of exertion. "What's next, Danielle?" she asked brightly.

CHAPTER 7

A LITTLE SHOPPING

Danielle started her car, and waited impatiently for Dharalyn to join her. Aunt Sara had been working on her for the last thirty minutes or so, getting her ready after Danielle had first tried dying her hair with some hair color she'd had. It had been in her mother's old things and Danielle had remembered seeing it not too long ago in the upstairs bathroom closet, and so had confiscated the unopened box. She had helped her mother dye her hair several times in the past, and figured with her experience, to have little trouble changing Dharalyn's radiantly white hair to something that would be a little less conspicuous. The whole process had been a complete failure, however. Apparently, something in Dharalyn's hair didn't take to coloring. After almost forty-five minutes had passed, when she'd attempted to rinse the dye from Dhara's head, she'd been disheartened to see all of the color wash right out of her hair, without the slightest bit of dye remaining. "So much for that idea," she had said dejectedly, as she ran her fingers through Dharalyn's still shiningly white locks. "I guess we're going to have to come up with another idea for hiding this."

"Danielle, why can't I leave my hair as it is?" Dharalyn had asked, unhappy with the whole process.

"Because, honey," answered Aunt Sara, who had stuck her head in to see how they were coming. "Danielle knows that if you walk around with this gorgeous head of white hair of yours, you are going to be the center of attention when you go to the mall, and I think it might be best if we try and keep you as inconspicuous as possible."

"So, what do we do, Jay?" Danielle had asked her aunt.

"Well," she'd responded, "We could try a wig. I have a couple that might work pretty well for her."

"Can she wear a wig with that long hair of hers?"

"Well, if we decide to go that way permanently, I'll want to cut her hair back a little bit. But for now, I know how to pin her hair back using a little pantyhose over the scalp trick I learned years ago. We wouldn't want to use it every day, but I'm sure we can get her hair in passable enough shape so that you two can go to the mall for the day."

Her Aunt had then taken Dharalyn away, while Danielle had gone into the bathroom to fix her own hair and apply her makeup. While standing in front of the mirror, dreading the commencement of yet another disheartening bout with her ever present nemesis, her terrible acne, Danielle had done a double take when she'd discovered that her face was clearer than it had been in years. She had been dumbfounded, to say the least, and had stared in disbelief at the mirror. On most days, her reflection caused her to wince in self-loathing, as she fought to cover up, with massive amounts of makeup, the terrible pimples that had plagued her since she'd become a teenager. After a few moments of a hopeful, yet cautiously optimistic inspection of her face had passed, Danielle had felt her spirits buoyed as she'd smiled for the first time in ages at the image in the mirror. Actually looking forward to the mall visit now, she impatiently called out to her aunt, only to be told that Dhara would be ready in a few more minutes.

Soon, she spied Dhara exiting the house and headed toward the car, albeit with a slightly different look than she'd had before. Danielle leaned over and opened the passenger door for her, and waited as seconds later she climbed in. "That looks pretty good. Being a brunette works for you."

Dharalyn nodded and smiled miserably.

Suddenly, Danielle paused and gazed at Dharalyn searchingly as a sudden thought hit her. "You know what I just realized!" she exclaimed, as she continued to stare. "The very first night I saw you, you had this bright star in the center of your forehead, and it just now hit me...I haven't seen it since that night."

Dharalyn looked bewildered. "That's impossible, Danielle. You couldn't have seen that."

"But, I'm telling you, I did!" She paused for a moment, recalling the events of two nights past. "It was an eight sided star, a kind of pinkish-white color. I can't believe I didn't notice before this, that it was gone." Danielle gave a wry smile and her attention focused back on Dharalyn, who looked somewhat troubled by her remarks. "Are you okay?"

Dharalyn shook her head adamantly. "No, Danielle, I'm sorry to disagree with you about this, but you must be wrong. If, for some reason, you had seen a star there, if it were even possible, it would have had six points, not eight. But, none of that really matters, because there is no way that you could have seen this thing, like you described."

"But, Dharalyn, I'm pretty certain of this. I know what I saw!"

Dharalyn suddenly became nervous and said heatedly, "Please stop arguing with me about this, Danielle. I'm sorry, but you have to be wrong, you just have to be. You can't have seen a star on my forehead let alone an eight sided one like you keep insisting you saw. It's impossible, so please let's not speak of it any further!"

Danielle was taken aback by the exceedingly serious tone in Dhara's voice. Realizing she must have inadvertently spoken on a subject that for some reason was taboo, or at least by Dharalyn's reaction, of a very sensitive nature, she decided she'd better drop it, lest it cause a rift in their recently formed friendship. "Okay, Dhara," she said simply, and then said no more, as she put her car in drive and headed onto the main road. The drive to the mall in Centertown took about thirty minutes, all of which passed in an uncomfortable silence. She couldn't for the life of her figure out why Dharalyn had reacted the way she had. Although their friend-ship was still very new, Danielle felt strongly about the bond that they seemed to share, a kind of awareness of each other's men-tal state. Last night, she had awakened very early in the morning to the sounds of Dharalyn's quiet sobbing, and had felt not the slightest uncertainty when she'd decided to wrap her arms con-solingly around her new friend. It had been a very personal and tender outpouring of comfort for another, and was completely uncharacteristic of her, prior to meeting Dharalyn. Oh sure, she'd always been fairly close to her immediate family, but except for her mother and her father, she had never been much of a hugger, or involved in openly casual displays of affection. The finer senti-ments had always made her uncomfortably nervous and yet here she was, expressing something for this stranger that one might normally reserve for a mother or sister, or possibly a grandmother, but never a person you'd only known for two days. It didn't make any sense, and yet, she had no misgivings about her compassion-ate displays, where Dharalyn was concerned. That was what was really weird about all of this. How close she felt to this girl, already. Which was why this thing about Dharalyn's star hurt so much. She felt like, considering what they'd shared together, the question about that star should have been no big deal. Especially since she was absolutely positive she wasn't mistaken and that she hadn't been seeing things. It had been there! An eight sided star. *There must be a lot more to all this than I realize,* she thought, as she pulled into the parking lot of the mall.

As she pulled up into an empty spot and switched off the motor, Danielle turned, reached out and took one of Dhara's hands. "Listen, I'm sorry about before. I should have left it alone, since it's obvious that you don't want to talk about it. Maybe after some time passes, when you are ready, we can discuss it again."

Dharalyn shook her head. "There will be no discussing this, Danielle. I will not speak with you about something that you couldn't have seen."

Sensing that the subject was apparently too sensitive to even refer to in passing, Danielle decided to shelve the whole thing, for now. "You're right, absolutely. We won't talk about it again."

"Thank you," said Dharalyn, succinctly.

"That is, until you're ready to," added Danielle, and jumped out her door without waiting for a reply. She watched as Dhara exited the car and then pushed the remote to lock the doors. The walk to the mall took only a few moments, since she'd luckily found a relatively close spot to park, and soon they were inside. Fortunately, it looked like a pretty normal day; there were a scattering of shoppers about, but not the huge numbers that she knew would have been here if it had been a weekend. Danielle reached out and lightly touched Dhara's arm. "We need to stop here for a sec," she said, and pulled her wallet from her purse. Quickly, she ran her bank card through a kiosk and after entering her pin number, removed the remainder of her savings money. "Well, that's that. It should be enough to get you a basic wardrobe, as long as we don't get too fancy." Danielle looked toward Dhara and saw she was staring all around them, as if in awe. "Don't you have places like this where you come from?"

Dharalyn nodded slowly. "Yes, we have places kind of like this, in some ways. I've never actually been to one, though."

Danielle looked perplexed. "Never been to one? How do you buy clothes and other stuff you need?"

"I don't buy them...my clothes are all made for me, Danielle, and anything else that I need is supplied to me by the Shovanei."

"Shovanei, are they like your servants?"

"Well, yes, but not like your word suggests. A Shovan is a highly regarded and sought after position with my people. Many apply and only a very few are selected, to serve the Sedai. In my culture, it brings much honor to the families whose members serve us."

Danielle nodded thoughtfully. "I don't think I would like being a Shovan. It sounds too much like a servant to me."

"Danielle, the word you use is improper. They are more like caregivers and protectors. The Shovanei are made up of only the most eligible of people, the smartest, most talented and gifted individuals who excel in their particular fields."

"Okay, it's plain that I don't really get it. You can explain it all to me again someday, if we ever go there." Suddenly, Danielle halted her diatribe and brought herself up short. The look that abruptly appeared on Dharalyn's face was one of wretched despair. "Oh God, Dhara, I'm sorry. I wasn't thinking," she said, regretfully. They had touched on this subject a bit last night when they'd lain beside each other in the bed and talked. She had told Danielle that the accident that had brought her here was just that, a highly improbable occurrence that had likely marooned her here, for good. It was very unlikely, she said, that any of her people would ever be able to find her here. Especially since here, as far as she knew, was a place they didn't even know existed.

Dharalyn's face slowly relaxed and she tried a grim smile. "Don't concern yourself too much. This is something that I will just have to learn to accept."

Things lightened up soon after, as they began their shopping experience. They found several outfits in the first store Danielle had suggested, and Dharalyn liked them well enough that she even wore one of the new outfits out of the store. "God, you look amazing in that," Danielle had said, when Dhara had first tried on the black sport skirt, which was a combination shorts and skirt for active people, and dark maroon sport top with black pleats on the sides that she had selected for her. Fortunately, the braided sandals Dhara wore worked well with the outfit, although she absolutely refused to wear the fishnet stockings Danielle had showed her. After that, she selected a couple of pairs of jeans and a few more tops, which she had Dhara try on to make sure everything fit. After selecting another sports skirt combination, Danielle turned toward her. "This will have to do for now Dhara. I think this will pretty much clean me out."

Dharalyn nodded. "Thank you for this, Danielle. It will be nice to have some clothes of my own, again." She smiled and gave her a quick hug. "So what shall we do now?"

"Well, I say we put this stuff out in the car, and then walk around the mall for a while. Maybe get something to eat. I'm beginning to feel the need for some sustenance. And you must need something, too. I haven't seen you eat a real meal since we first met. You've got to be starving." Danielle grabbed the bags up, without noticing the peculiar look that Dharalyn gave her and said cheerily, "Wait here for a few, Dhara. I will be back before you can even miss me." Quickly, Danielle whisked the bags out to her car and then re-entered the mall to rejoin her friend. As she approached her, Danielle couldn't help but notice that a couple of guys had spied Dhara and were boldly checking her out. It was pretty plain from the expressions on their faces that they were both completely mesmerized. Shaking her head back and forth with the realization that this would likely be the norm around her new friend, after all, the girl was strikingly beautiful, Danielle walked up with a welcoming grin.

"Okay, I'm back. You ready to walk a bit?"

Dhara smiled and nodded. "Sure, I like mall shopping with you, Danielle."

Danielle chuckled. "I'm afraid we're all done with the shopping, my dear Dharalyn," she said, intentionally mispronouncing her name as *Darling*. "From here on out it's just looking and wishing." Dharalyn tilted her head, giving her a pleasing little smile in response to the word play. For the next hour, the two girls slowly made their way through the mall, stopping to browse whenever the mood hit them. One particular store, called Spencer's, kept them occupied for quite some time as Danielle spent her time explaining the double meanings and subtleties of the sexual jokes and crude humor of the many objects therein. Finally, reaching a point of complete exasperation and in the interest of her own mental self-preservation, she grabbed a boobs-mug out of Dharalyn's curious hands and forcibly pulled her from the store.

"Some of the things your people buy are very strange, Danielle," said Dhara, in a voice that was obviously mystified. "I can't imagine why people would want some of those things."

The comical expression on Dhara's face was so hilarious that Danielle burst out in laughter that continued on for some time, and left her with a broad smile on her face. "Come on," she said, still chuckling and motioning toward some escalators. "Let's go this way." Suddenly, Danielle's maternal senses were heightened, as a recognizable and mildly disconcerting noise reached her ears. Curious, and a little concerned by the whimpering sounds she heard, she grasped Dharalyn once again by the arm and pulled her forward. She propelled her in this fashion until they reached a small corridor which, according to the posted signs, led to a pair of restrooms that divided two stores. There, standing near the entrance was a small, sobbing child with tears streaming down her face. "Hi, are you okay?" she asked concernedly, as she knelt down. The child was dressed in sneakers, jeans and a blue top, and began to sob uncontrollably. "Honey, it's okay, let us help you. Are you lost?" The tiny girl nodded, and looked at Danielle with large eyes full of tears. "Can you tell me your name?"

The small child stared for a moment as her sobbing slowed, and then answered in a stuttering voice, "I'm not supposed to talk to strangers."

Danielle smiled. "I know, honey. And that's a very good rule, too. But, if we are going to help you, we're gonna have to know your name. Here, this is my friend Dharalyn and my name is Danielle. Would you tell me your name, now?"

The child seemed unsure for a moment and then said hesitantly, "It's Susan."

"Can you tell me how old you are, Susan?"

"I'm six years old."

"Did you come here with your mother or your father, or maybe someone else?"

"My mother brought me," said Susan, faintly. "Her name is Grace."

Danielle smiled and turned toward Dharalyn. "I think probably the best thing to do is to take her to the mall office. I'm sure they will know what to do there."

Dharalyn nodded. "Won't her mother be looking for her?"

"I'm sure she will. If it was my mother and I was lost, she'd be frantically looking for me and calling out my name."

Dharalyn nodded and looked thoughtful. "Wait for just a few moments, then, Danielle. Let me see if I can hear her calling."

Danielle gave her a quizzical glance, but then slowly agreed. "Okay, Dhara," she said, and shrugged her shoulders. "It's an awfully big mall though, and with all the noise, I really don't see how you are going to hear anything beyond ten or twenty feet."

Dharalyn squeezed her shoulder and then stepped a few feet out into the mall proper. Closing her eyes, she shifted her spirit and her body into Kquwaya-Set, which was first level battle mode. Her body responded, making the small subtle changes that come forth during this physical exchange. Her eyes brightened, enabling her to see farther and in the dark. Her incisors extended and her hearing became ultra-sensitive. Her sense of smell, too, was heightened dramatically, though it was of less importance at this time. Knowing that her teeth, as well as her eyes, would likely cause a commotion should anyone see them *(her eyes were shining like twin beacons)*, she kept her eyes closed and her lips pressed together. She had learned much about the people she lived among now and knew that her secrets needed to stay just that. *Secret.* Sounds within her immediate vicinity blared forth and she instantly filtered them out, while driving her sensitivity outward. This was all second nature to her. No more difficult than breathing or walking. As her awareness grew, she heard and filtered more of the sounds from all around her, simultaneously touching on and sifting through much of the background noise that she instinctively knew didn't apply to what she was looking for. After a few more moments passed, she finally found what she was searching for: *the sound of a hysterical woman calling out her missing child's name,* and marked the location within her awareness. "Found her, Danielle," she said, as she released Kquwaya-Set and felt her body relax, while turning and flashing a quick smile at Danielle.

Danielle nodded in amazement and then felt a tiny chill run up her spine, as she caught a glimpse of...*no, that couldn't be right.* Once again, she found herself studying Dharalyn's face and then relaxed, as her friend gave her a wide, normal looking smile. *I better get my damn eyes checked,* she thought, and grinned back. "You found something?"

Dharalyn nodded. "On the next floor up, that big store up in front of us."

Taking her by the hand, the two girls escorted Susan up one floor via an escalator, and into the large department store Dhara pointed out. As soon as they entered the store, they made their way through several isles, in the general direction Dharalyn indicated, until they heard the fretful sounds of an anxious mother calling out for her child.

"Mommy!" replied Susan with a joyful shout, as recognition transformed her features from apprehensive and anxious, to those of a beaming, happy child. Quickly, she ran in the direction of her mother's voice until, spying her form, she launched herself into outstretched arms.

"Oh, Susie!" the woman cried with relief, as the two were reunited. "Where in the world have you been, baby?" sobbed the woman, as she hugged her daughter with fervor. "I was nearly out of my mind with worry!"

"I'm sorry, Mommy," said the teary eyed child. "I was lost, but Danielle and Darling found me and brought me back to you."

The woman immediately peered toward the two girls with a suspicious look in her eyes and then frowned. "Thank you," she mumbled half-heartedly, and then stood, grabbed her daughter's hand and quickly led her away. It was evident that though she was glad to have her daughter returned to her, she wasn't all that pleased at the involvement of the two girls. "I thought I told you not to talk to strangers," they heard her faintly scold the child, as they turned a corner and were gone.

Danielle turned toward Dharalyn and grinned at the puzzled expression she saw displayed there. "Well, that's par for the course," she uttered.

"I don't understand. I think that woman was annoyed with us."

Danielle laughed and shook her head woefully. "I'm afraid that in this world, Dhara, our media has done a good job of scaring people to death, by sensationalizing certain types of stories and the illusion of the dangers that exist all around us. All for the sake of entertainment and market share. It has some people so suspicious and scared of their own shadows, that they are afraid to even be civil to one another anymore."

"Are there many bad people here, so many that it keeps your population living in constant fear of one another?"

Danielle shook her head. "No, my Dad says that our society has become so intent on being ultra-careful and defining everything that's potentially bad in our lives, that we've gone too far with it. People in general, have forgotten how to care for one another, look out for one another and lend each other a helping hand. We've forgotten how important it is to extend kindness and understanding, to treat each other with courtesy, dignity and respect. We've become a society of hermits, shutting ourselves off from one another."

Dharalyn nodded. "Many of my people, too, in the past, have been guilty of this. A long, long time ago, they became so fearful and mistrusting of one another that their social structures degenerated, until their lives had become filled with moral ambiguity and suspicious infighting. Antagonistic groups squabbling over their differences, rather than bonding over their common principles of love, understanding, family values and positive social mores and tenets."

"What did they do?"

"Well, after they fought many destructive wars and nearly ruined their worlds, they asked the Sedai to intervene; to oversee their governments and help them to solve their many problems. Over a long period of adjustment, the Sedai eventually resolved many of their greatest issues and brought comparative peace and prosperity throughout the Amalgamation Worlds."

"So, in effect, your people helped create a kind of utopia?"

Dharalyn smiled sadly. "No, not exactly, Danielle. Although I believe all of the people would say that life has become much better, it is far from being a utopia. There are always too many who want just a little bit more, or believe their ideals are a little bit more important, or who simply crave what power can bring them. Like any society, it is an ongoing problem that we work hard to resolve. I fear that a perfect utopia is only a figment of the artist's dream, and cannot exist when people revel in personal glory and extol their own imperfections."

Danielle laughed then. "God, how did we get from the subject of that lady's ungracious reaction to us returning her daughter, to the subject of world issues? This is too deep a topic for me, right now. Besides, I'm starving. Let's get something to eat."

Danielle led the way to the food court, where she located and ordered herself a burger and some fries. She couldn't believe it when Dharalyn shook her head at a food request and so Danielle ordered her a green salad and a bottle of water, anyway. Soon they were at an empty table in the center of the food court, where Danielle immediately began to hungrily consume her order. She watched in silent incredulity as Dharalyn picked at the salad, eating only a few of the miniature tomatoes and cucumber slices, but little else. She was about to comment on it when Dharalyn, who'd been gazing all around them abruptly asked, "Danielle, why are those boys over there staring at us?"

Danielle glanced behind herself, in the direction Dhara had pointed and then turning back, answered, "Well, Dhara, those guys over there are not staring at us!" she pronounced amusedly. "They are, in fact, staring at you! And the reason for that, my dearest Dharalyn, is that, here in this world, you are what the guys refer to as a major hottie. In fact, you haven't been paying much attention, but ever since we left that store earlier, with you wearing that fab new sport skirt and top, you've been having a major effect on every man, boy and lesbian we've passed by."

Dharalyn looked stunned. "Why?"

Danielle laughed. "Don't guys in your world go crazy over the pretty girls?"

Dharalyn looked thoughtful. "I've read books on the subject, but I'm afraid that in my particular situation, I haven't had much personal experience with the phenomenon."

Danielle chuckled again. "Oh, right, because you were brought up in a protected environment."

"Yes, that's pretty much it, I'm afraid."

"Well, you aren't going to have that, here. Something tells me you better get used to it."

"Can't you help me with how best to handle these situations, Danielle? Surely, you know all about these kinds of social interactions. You can advise me on what to do."

Danielle gave her a weak smile. "I don't think I'll be much help on this subject. You see, I personally have never had this particular problem."

Dharalyn peered at Danielle intently, picking up the obvious melancholy tones in her friend's voice. She understood what Danielle was saying, but was at a loss as to why. Danielle had wonderful features and was very pleasing in appearance. Dharalyn tabled the conversation, however, sensing that this was an extremely sensitive subject to her friend. She was beginning to suspect that perhaps Danielle had some issues, here, that needed looking into. She held her tongue though, for now. This was something she would definitely like to help her with. Perhaps, it was one small way that she could help repay some of the kindness which Danielle had shown to her.

Later, as they finished up their mall visit and made their way back to the car, Dharalyn stumbled a bit. Quickly, Danielle, who was walking beside her, grabbed her arm and helped steady her. "You okay, Dhara?" she asked, worriedly.

Dharalyn nodded, as the sudden bout of weakness passed. Things were going to get bad soon, she knew. It hadn't helped, that when she'd phased earlier into Kquwaya-Set, it had taken a lot out of her. She was nearly done in, and she didn't have the slightest idea of what she was going to do about it.

CHAPTER 8

THE SHOCK OF REALITY

By the time the girls got back home, evening had set in. Danielle stood in the kitchen eating a sandwich, while contemplating the day's events. It had been a nice day, full of carefree shopping fun. Danielle smiled when she recalled Dharalyn's reaction to the rude woman. She was pretty sure that her friend would be having many social jolts like that one. Becoming acclimated to the societal mores of this world was likely going to take some time, especially seeing that her previous life had been one of extreme privilege. Danielle could only imagine what her life must have been like, having scads of people waiting on you and seeing to your every need. *It must be awfully tedious,* she thought, *having someone fussing over you every minute of the day.* Danielle turned as her father walked into the kitchen and opened the refrigerator. "Hey, Dad," she mumbled incoherently, as she swallowed the last bite of her food.

Big John arched an eyebrow at his daughter and turned back to peruse the depths of the fridge. "What do you have there?"

"Just some turkey that Jay picked up, earlier today."

"It any good?"

"Yeah, sure. It's really fresh and tender."

He grabbed a jar of pickles and mustard, and grunted, "Well, that sounds pretty good." He carried his items over to the counter and placed them next to the scattered bins and half opened packages Danielle had there. Grabbing three slices of bread, he began to liberally spread mustard on them, to which he added turkey, pickle slices, lettuce, onions, tomatoes, ham and cheese.

Danielle grimaced and remarked, "God, Dad, how can you eat all that stuff together?"

"Hey, don't knock it till you've tried it," he said gruffly, as he finished up his massive creation and began to bite into it. "Mmmmm," he teased, as he chewed noisily.

"Gross, Dad," she said, and was about to comment further, when her Aunt Sara walked in.

"Good Lord, John, there's enough stuff on that sandwich for two people!" Sara stated, laughingly.

"Yeah, you know it!" agreed Danielle, as she made a face. "You watch, he's going to be complaining all evening about a stomachache."

"Ahh, you women just don't know how to live," said John, mockingly. "I'll be out on the porch if anyone needs me." Grabbing his plate and a bottle of his favorite beer, John left without further comment.

"Best place for him," said Sara, as she began to clean up. "He'll be farting up a storm in a little while."

"Jay!" exclaimed Danielle, appalled but not really surprised, at the blatant statement from her aunt. She had a tendency to speak her exact mind, when she was among family.

"Am I wrong?" asked Sara, with a grin.

Danielle chuckled. "No, probably not. I'll bet in about an hour, you won't be able to get anywhere near him."

"Like I said."

"You want some help there?" Danielle asked suddenly, feeling guilty that her aunt was cleaning up hers and her father's mess.

"No, I've got this. I'm sure you've had a long day. Take a load off and relax."

"Well, then, maybe I should go up and check on Dharalyn. She didn't seem to be feeling very well when we got home, and I think she may have gone upstairs."

"Oh, she's in with Gran," stated Sara. "I left the two of them just a few minutes ago."

"She's with Gran?" asked Danielle, a bit puzzled. "Really?"

"Yep, your grandmother just adores her. Dharalyn came in a little while ago and they've been just chatting away. She's been telling Gran all about your shopping trip. You know, Danielle, I have to say, I'm really surprised by how well Dharalyn understands her. With the limitations caused by her stroke, Gran talks in such a way that most people find it very hard to understand her. In fact, I myself have to really listen and give her all my attention, to make out what she is saying sometimes. It really makes the poor dear so frustrated and she tends to clam completely up with strangers. But with Dharalyn, she just talks in that halting way she has and Dhara answers her without any hesitation. I'm telling you, it absolutely amazes me. She understands her quicker and better than I do, and I've been caring for her for a long time."

Danielle nodded in wonder. Her Gran was so dear to her, and it made her so sad and more than a little upset, to see how people sometimes acted in her presence. She tried to be understanding about it. In the past, when Gran talked to someone outside of the immediate family, she or Aunt Sara usually had to tell them what she was saying. It distressed Gran so much when they had to do that, that eventually she stopped talking to anyone else at all. From what her aunt was describing, though, Dharalyn had no problem understanding her. In fact, it sounded like they were having quite a nice conversation. "I need to see this," she said, and started to leave the kitchen. She stopped suddenly, as her aunt gently reached out and restrained her by the arm.

"Honey, don't go in there right now," said Sara. "Give them a little more time together, alone. I haven't seen your Gran this happy in a long time. She is really enjoying her visit with Dharalyn and it's kind of why I left them. So they could talk without an audience."

Danielle nodded slowly, uncertain of why the idea of this should be bothering her.

Mabel Frances Walkerman sat in her comfy pillowback chair and slowly stroked the white hair of their new houseguest, with her one good hand. They had just had the nicest chat about the event filled day that the two girls had had together, and now Dharalyn had her head leaned against Mabel's legs, while Mabel smiled lovingly. Never in her life had she met such a sweet, gentle creature as this girl Dharalyn. There was something completely otherworldly about her, and of course, that was only part of it. Mabel knew all about Dharalyn, or at least, as much as Sara and Danielle knew, anyway. Sara had regaled her earlier in the day with the things that Danielle had told her, and then described the event that had caused her to modify her first opinion and believe, herself. Mabel wasn't the least surprised by the story, and pretty much took in everything she had been told as fact. Simply put, she believed because she had sensed, what was to her, the obvious differences in this girl, the very first time she'd met her. It wasn't just the eyes, though that was the first thing she'd noticed. How bright they were, and how they pierced you deeply when she looked at you. It was her spirit and her overall demeanor, which took one's breath away. Not only had Dharalyn's initial reaction to meeting her been something heartwarmingly uncommon, but the beautiful song she'd sung to her had resonated within her very soul. No child of this earth would have shown an elder, let alone someone who was wheelchair bound and crippled, the outpouring of compassion and respect that this girl had shown her. Mabel's heart had been touched deeply, and even though they'd just met and it was completely irrational, she knew deep within, in that place of inner certainty, that she loved this child from the bottom of her heart. Not to take anything away from Danielle, she amended to herself. Her granddaughter was the absolute joy of her existence and the person she loved most, in all the world. But Dharalyn had certainly earned a special place in her heart, which was one of the reasons she was so concerned. It was becoming increasingly evident to her that something was wrong with Dharalyn. Deeply wrong. Ever since the night before, Mabel had noticed a distinct change within the child's spirit, her positive energy. She was surprised no one else had noticed, but then again, when you were limited, as she was, you had a lot more time on your hands to reflect and notice things others might not. "Child," she said, as Dhara lifted her head and looked toward her, the eyes plainly not nearly as bright as they once were.

"I've enjoyed our talk very much. But now I want you to share something with me. I want you to tell Gran what is wrong!" The words came slowly but she got them out quicker than normal. A lot of that had to do with how much at ease she felt with Dharalyn. No worry that the girl wouldn't be able to understand. She understood every mangled word Mabel spoke, perfectly.

Dharalyn looked at her with quiet eyes. She was surprised at the request. Surprised that Gran had noticed what she fought so hard to conceal. *She would never understand,* she thought silently. The books had shown her that. These people had made monsters out of her kind. They would never accept her, once they knew what she was. Slowly, she shook her head and laid it carefully back down against Mabel's leg, while a comforting hand brushed at her hair.

"Listen," whispered Mabel. She had spoken so much and it took so much effort to speak at all, that she was beginning to lose her voice. "My life has been full of things that most people would never understand. My husband, God rest his soul, would never allow me to speak of it. But for nearly my whole life, I have been aware of things others could not even imagine. When I was young, about your age, I was in a terrible car accident. At first, I'd been knocked out, but when I came to, I found myself standing by the wreckage. Not as you might think, though. Everything was strange, shimmering, as if I were there but not there, somehow. I could see the emergency vehicles all around me, and people rushing to and fro. But none of them paid me the least bit of attention. I realized, then, that something incredible was happening. I watched them load my body into the ambulance and then I rode with them to the hospital, where I watched the doctors work on me. I know this sounds crazy, but ever since that accident, I have been able to leave my body pretty much at will and travel through the spirit world, and even more. While I traveled as such, I saw and learned many strange and new things." Her voice was almost gone, now. She knew her explanation was pretty rushed, but she was trying to get a lot of information into a very brief account of her experiences. "So, you see, if anyone can understand what you need to say," she paused, as Dharalyn turned and looked straight into her eyes, "I can!" she said as forcibly as she could, and with nearly the last of her strength.

"You can trust me, my sweet child," she added, and then placed her hand on Dharalyn's cheek. For a few more moments, Dharalyn stared at her. She could tell the girl was considering her words carefully, the need to share something very personal burning within her. Finally, as if a wall had finally come down, Mabel watched, as with a simple nod of her head, she signified her agreement.

Dharalyn reached out her hand and placed it against Mabel's head. "Close your eyes," she said, softly.

She was a little surprised by this request, but Mabel knew deep within her heart Dharalyn could be trusted, and so she did as she was told. At first, she only felt the warmth of Dharalyn's fingers, but then slowly Mabel began to feel something subtly probing and trickling into her mind. Tendrils of thought tentatively reached out to her, as if waiting for her acceptance. Having experienced many strange things in her life, Mabel relaxed and allowed her mind to open. *It can't be any weirder than some of the things I've seen and experienced before, in the spirit realms,* she thought, vaguely.

She couldn't have been more mistaken....

When it was over, it took a few moments for Mabel to collect herself. She had been seeing some of Dharalyn's memories, of that she had no doubt. What had truly shocked her, though, was how vivid the entire experience had been. She had not only seen, but had heard and smelled the sights and sounds of Dharalyn's home. It had been incredible, and Dharalyn had taken her time, giving Mabel a chance to settle in and get used to her surroundings, as well as get acquainted with the overall strangeness of the place. There were many things that were much like their own world. Tall, ornate buildings, a bustling throng of people coming and going, on their way to doing whatever it was they did in that world. She had shown her a place where she, Dharalyn, had gone to school. At least, she thought it was a school. It was so big, it couldn't have been anything else. Dharalyn was being tutored there and was being trained in the arts and sciences, as well as more physical skills, like self-defense. In another building that Mabel suspected was her home, she saw that there were many people bowing and catering to Dharalyn's every need, and it became quickly evident that her family was very influential and important. Many of the other scenes she was shown, she was sure, were just to give her a little sense of this strange society. Much of it was a mystery and a lot of it was completely outside the scope of her understanding. That's when Dharalyn took her into the heart of the matter which she'd brought her here to see. She saw some people, who must have been members of her immediate family, sitting down to a meal. Had seen strange fruits and vegetables of many kinds, some bearing a close resemblance to those in her own world. It was going quite well, when Dhara began to show her some particulars.

"We eat many of the same things," Mabel heard, within her mind. "But there is one major component we need in our diet which we cannot live without, much as you yourselves require water."

That was when she showed her the basic ingredient that Dharalyn's people required. Mabel briefly watched the process and immediately had felt her gorge rise at the disturbing scene. She was trying to wrap her mind around it, trying to understand, when Dharalyn suddenly broke the link. It had been a few minutes now, and she was still very unsettled by the whole matter. She had known something was terribly wrong with the girl. But nothing could have prepared her for the reality of what Dharalyn had shown her. It was something that was quite normal for her people, perhaps, but no one here would ever be able to accept it. Mabel saw the troubled look in Dharalyn's eyes and knew the girl could sense her distressed state of mind. She felt a deep sadness growing within her, as she realized what this would mean. If they couldn't figure out what to do, Dharalyn would soon get very sick and possibly even die. Just like she or anyone else around here would, if they had no access to water. She shivered as she considered all that she had just witnessed.

"I'm going to go to bed now, Gran," said Dharalyn, softly and standing, made her way to the door.

Moments later, as Mabel was alone with her own thoughts, she found herself wishing for the company of someone very close to her. There was really only one person she felt that she could talk to about any of this, and she was about to go to the intercom and summon Danielle, when suddenly, her dear granddaughter came sauntering in.

"Hey, Gran," she said, gaily. "I thought Dharalyn was in here."

"She went on to bed," said Mabel, and then added, "You really like her, don't you Danielle?"

Danielle smiled and nodded. "Yeah, besides becoming best friends already, I think there's something really special and unique about her."

"Tell me, Danielle, why exactly do you think Dharalyn is here?" Gran asked, pointedly.

The question caught Danielle completely off guard and she knelt down. "Why is she here?"

"Yes, Sara told me her story. But I want to know why you think she's here," said Mabel, her voice shaking a bit from pushing herself and her voice too hard.

Danielle thought for a long while. "Well, it kinda sounds silly, I know. But, I think she is here for a reason. I think maybe...oh, you're going to think I'm crazy, Gran."

Mabel shook her head. "Tell me, Dani."

"I think maybe God is involved, somehow. I think that he heard my prayer, and I believe she is my answer."

Mabel sat silently. She hadn't expected that particular explanation. She wondered more than ever what exactly had happened out there, out where and when these two had met. Apparently, her granddaughter had experienced a life changing event of no small significance. One even more profound than anyone even suspected. Mabel thought about how despondent she had been, only a few, short days ago. How depressed and unreachable she had been. Both she and Sara had been worried that she might do herself harm. And then, Dharalyn had come onto the scene. The change in Danielle had been dramatic, to say the least. *If this girl dies,* Mabel suddenly realized, *we could lose Danielle forever.*

That night, Danielle sat in her bed for a long while and gazed at Dharalyn's sleeping form. She was worried. Dharalyn didn't look very good. Her skin was pale and there was a distinct lack of vitality about her. When they'd first met, she had practically glowed with a kind of charismatic energy that seemed to emanate from nearly every pore. She had been outgoing, personable and socially vibrant. When Danielle had come up to the room before and spoken to her, she'd been lackluster and sickly looking. Danielle laid her head against her pillow and folded her arms resolutely. Dammit, this had to stop. She'd made up her mind. In the morning, she would find out what was going on, and she wouldn't take any more crap from Dharalyn about it. The girl was going to come clean with her about what was wrong, or else. Content with her decision, she closed her eyes and was soon fast asleep.

The next morning, Danielle awoke to find Dharalyn already gone. She got up, grabbed her clothes and made her way to the bathroom. While showering, she decided how best to proceed with this perplexing issue concerning Dharalyn. *I will simply sit her down*, she thought determinedly, *and ask her straight out what the heck is going on. Why her health is so obviously going downhill and just as important, why she won't eat any of our food.* As she finished up, she decided that maybe it might help, too, if she got her Aunt Sara to help. Two is always better than one, and besides, no one was better than Aunt Jay when it came to using guilt to get her way. She had turned it into a kind of art form, a weapon of sorts. In the past, whenever she'd needed Danielle to do something for her, she'd always gotten her way, whether Danielle wanted to do it, or not. Sara simply made Danielle feel like a terrible, thoughtless person, or completely irresponsible and before she knew what was happening, she was doing whatever it was Jay wanted. She stared in the mirror as she put the finishing touches on her makeup and spoke to her reflection. "Yeah, that's a good idea. I'll get Jay involved in this, too. Dharalyn won't know what hit her."

Danielle made her way downstairs and into the kitchen, where Aaron was busy eating cereal for breakfast and her aunt was making him some toast at the counter. "Morning," she called out, and received a muffled response from her brother and a bright, "Morning, sweetie!" from her aunt. Making her way to the counter, she touched her aunt's arm to get her attention. "I need your help with something this morning."

Sara gazed at her with a solemn expression. She could tell from the tone of Danielle's voice that something important was on her niece's mind. "What's up, Dani?" she asked, using Danielle's nickname.

Danielle whispered so that her brother couldn't hear. "I'm really worried about Dharalyn, Aunt Jay. She looks really bad. Downright sickly, in fact. I want you to help me confront her this morning and force her to tell us what's wrong."

"You think she's keeping something from you?"

Danielle nodded. "I know she is, Jay. She's barely eaten a thing since we first met. Yesterday, at the Mall, she picked at a salad, maybe eating a couple of cucumbers and such, and that was all she had. She looks really bad. I think maybe she is beginning to suffer from malnutrition." Danielle got quieter as she saw her brother's attention pick up. He was doing his best to overhear what she was saying. "Will you help me get her to tell us what's going on? Maybe our food here disagrees with her, for some reason. If we know what it is, then perhaps we can help. Please, Auntie, I need you."

Sara's own concern grew markedly as she responded to the quavering, anxiety laden tone of Danielle's voice. The girl was terribly worried about her friend, that much was certainly obvious. "Okay, sweetheart. Let me get your brother taken care of, should only be a minute or so, and then we'll do this together."

Danielle smiled with relief, certain that her aunt would be up to dealing with this matter. "Okay, where is she now? I'll go and hang with her, till you get there."

"I left her in with your grandmother. Funny thing, your Gran asked for her, first thing this morning. Said it was important and that she wanted to see her right away."

"Really!" Danielle said. "That's pretty nice, I guess. They really seem to get along great, don't they?"

"Yes, she really seems to have a special affinity with old people. Your Gran just adores her. You go ahead on back. I'll be there in just a sec."

Danielle nodded her head and left the kitchen. Her Gran's room was on the ground floor, on the other side of the house. She gathered herself for what was to come. She was sure it was going to be a stressful meeting.

As Danielle reached her grandmother's room, she saw the door was ajar and so reached out to push it aside. As she entered the room, she immediately froze, her pulse quickening as she fought to make sense of what she was seeing. Dharalyn was kneeling on the floor in front of Gran and had her lips pressed up against the old woman's wrist, as if she were kissing it. Startled by the sound of her entering, Dharalyn turned her head and that was when Danielle saw the drops of blood on Gran's wrist, and the fangs. *The FANGS!* All the world seemed to pause then, as for a brief moment of time, Danielle felt the room begin to spin and a feeling of lightheadedness washed over her. In a near swoon, the reality of what she was seeing slammed into her consciousness with the impact of a wrecking ball, forcing her back to clarity. She stared, stricken with fear, at Dharalyn, at the creature she'd become. At her ruby lips, colored bright red from the blood smeared on them, to the bright white fangs that jutted in a horrific, inhuman way, inside of Dharalyn's mouth. As if reliving the past few days, Danielle recalled in that instant, the sight of those devilishly white protuberances and realized with a sudden intensity, that she'd seen them before. Once, in the cabin, and then again in the Mall yesterday, when Dharalyn had done her weird listening thing. She'd told herself both times that it had only been a trick of light, some minor hallucination that had caused her to see them. But now, she knew. She knew that they were not her imagination run amuck, at all. They were real! They were the real deal and Dharalyn was not some sweet, lost visitor from another world. She was, in fact, some kind of demonic creature from another dimension. She was a horrible nightmare, come to invade their world with a revolutionary and insane truth. A bizarre change of rational fundamentals that smacked Danielle right across her face, forcing her to reevaluate her most grounded beliefs in the scintilla of a moment. Danielle's heart raced, as she came to terms with her new reality. The girl was a monster, a cold-blooded, blood sucking creature, straight out of a lunatic's imagination.

She was a vampire!

A STINKING EVIL VAMPIRE!

Danielle took all this in, over the space of just a few seconds, and then she screamed. *She SCREAMED!*

A moment later, she came to herself and reaching out, grabbed hold of a picture frame her Gran had on a table near the door. "Get away from her, you freak!" she yelled, brandishing the frame like a weapon. Dharalyn rose up and stood still, her face a mask of shock and alarm.

"Please, Danielle," she said, beseechingly. "Please listen to me."

"Listen, nothing," shouted Danielle, as her aunt and brother arrived at the door. "Get away from my Gran and get the hell out of here, you bitch!"

"Danielle, what's going on?" asked Sara, who was stunned by her niece's violently uncharacteristic outburst.

"She's a God-Damn vampire, Jay. A real life freaking vampire! I caught her just now drinking Gran's blood."

Sara's mouth dropped open, as she stood stunned. "Danielle, no... That's impossible."

"It's not impossible. Look at Gran's wrist."

Sara strode purposefully into the room and carefully took hold of Mabel's arm. The old woman was plainly very agitated and was trying desperately to tell her something, but all she could see were the two fresh puncture marks on the woman's arm, and the tiny smears of blood all around the wound. "Oh, my God!" she exclaimed, as she raised her head in alarm. "It's okay, Mabel," she said, trying to calm the poor woman down. She was still trying to say something, but Sara didn't need to hear it to know what it was she was trying to get out. With fury blazing in her eyes, she turned toward Dharalyn and pointed at her. "You heard my niece. Get the hell out of this house, right now!"

Dharalyn looked toward Danielle with pleading eyes. "Please, Danielle, I would never hurt Gran."

Danielle shook her head adamantly. "Get the hell out of here, Dharalyn. Just get the hell out, before we call the police!"

Just then, Aaron stepped into the room, his eyes filled with tears. "Danielle, what are you doing?" he shouted. "Leave her alone!"

"Aaron, stay out of this. Didn't you hear what I said? Dharalyn's a vampire. An evil thing, that was hurting your poor Gran."

"She's not an evil thing! She's a good vampire. Don't you know anything? You leave her alone!"

Danielle turned away from her brother and faced the person she had once thought of as a friend. "You've done enough harm to this family, Dharalyn. If you have any decency in you at all, please leave, now!" she said, shakily, her voice betraying the emotional war raging within her heart.

Dharalyn lowered her head and walked past Danielle, into the hall. She gave Aaron a sad smile as she passed him, and then she was gone. A moment later Danielle heard the side door slam and peering through the window, she watched with a mixture of relief and sorrow as Dharalyn walked out toward the road. Turning back toward her aunt, she saw her step back, a needle in her hand. "What are you doing?" she asked.

"I gave her a sedative to calm her down," Sara explained. "The shock of all this could cause her to have another stroke. She was so distraught, the poor dear."

Danielle nodded, feeling a wave of melancholy sweep over her. Only a short time ago, she'd felt so positive and upbeat about things, but now everything was bad again. She turned toward her brother, who was scowling at her. "You okay, buddy?" she said, half-heartedly.

"You're a big, stupid jerk!" he shouted, then turned and ran off.

Danielle gazed forlornly after him, her heart broken. "A freaking vampire," she said in a half whisper, to no one in particular. Raising her face toward the ceiling, she said in a petulant tone, "That's just the kind of answer I would get. So much for prayers."

CHAPTER 9

A NEW DAY DAWNS

Dharalyn walked out to the main road that fronted the Walkerman house and turned right, glancing one last time toward the place she'd thought of as home for the past few days. On the porch, a lone figure watched her as she strolled slowly away, her emotions still seething in a turmoil of sorrow, regret and even a touch of fear. She raised a tentative hand in farewell and watched as Aaron slowly returned her wave. She was still in Kquwaya-Set from the feeding, and so her enhanced perceptions allowed her to hear his sobbing, as well as clearly see the tears streaming down his cheeks, tears that echoed her own. She wiped the moisture from her cheeks and turned her attention to the road ahead. He was a good kid and she would miss him, she thought, though she would likely never see him again, or his sister. The errant thought hit her hard and nearly brought on a renewed flood of tears that she'd only just now checked. Her one friend, her best friend of two worlds, had thrown her out after saying those terrible things. Even though she understood, in part, Danielle's reaction, she was still having trouble coming to terms with it. It was the kind of thing that the people in her world could never have even begun to imagine as causing such a passionately negative response, and yet she'd come to recently realize that here in this place, the reaction of these people would most likely be one of abhorrence and fear. The books Danielle had in her room had shown Dharalyn that. This world had such overwhelmingly strange notions and strong prejudices, when it came to the way her people fed. From her way of thinking, it was a mystery as to why anyone should feel this way, and it made their bias toward something she considered so categorically normal, to be completely ridiculous. After all, blood was life and everyone knew that. Even in this world, these people understood that simple concept. So, how was it they were unable to understand that the sharing of blood gave life, as well as sustained it? The notion that these people found the act of receiving blood as utterly repugnant was so alien to her, that she continued a running argument within, trying to understand it from their point of view, and failing to. Dharalyn shook her head dejectedly as she followed the paved blacktop road, which gently wound up into the hills ahead. Farther out, she could see the dark ledges and outcroppings of a mountain range. She had no idea where she was going. No idea what she was going to do. She was lost in a strange land and the inhabitants of this place would not welcome her. At least, not when they came to understand her ways and found out who and what she was. Hopelessness began to creep throughout her spirit, like the vines of a plant that surrounded and covered an object with its groping, leafy tendrils. She felt a chill and shivered a little, as the depth of her solitude began to sink in. She was screwed, to use a term she'd heard once or twice since she'd been here. Dharalyn paused, as a crippling wave of despair suddenly washed over her; she had nowhere to go and no one to turn to for help. So, what now? What in Anon's name should she do? Dharalyn thought hard about her situation, and even though she'd always considered herself to be fairly intelligent and creative, she hadn't the slightest idea of how to proceed. For a brief moment she considered going back to the Walkerman house, to try and talk some sense into Danielle, to somehow appeal to her good nature. But recalling the look on her face when the girl had seen her feeding from Gran, made her choke up. She simply couldn't bear to see Danielle looking at her that way again. To see her friend openly staring at her with a wide-eyed expression, filled with such contempt, disgust and horror. A look that had steadily worsened as her face changed into an image of fury, her twin eyes blazing with unbridled hatred that had practically seared Dharalyn's soul with its intensity. And then, there were the terrible things Danielle had said to her. Dharalyn could happily live the rest of her life without ever hearing those hurtful words shouted at her again. Words that had wounded like a knife's edge and cut her deeply. If there was any chance at all to talk to Danielle, she would have to give her some time to calm down. Maybe in a day or two she could try and reason with her onetime friend. After Danielle had had time to talk to her grandmother, maybe then she would listen to what Dharalyn wanted to say to her. She could explain it so that Danielle would understand. She was fairly sure of it. Dharalyn nodded to herself, as she began to walk briskly forward. She would try in a few days then, when Danielle was being a little more reasonable. With that smidgen of hope lifting her spirits just a little, Dharalyn walked past the last bit of pasture from the ranch, following the road which was becoming thickly lined with trees that grew about thirty feet back on both sides. It was shaded here, in some spots by a few large oaks that grew close to the edge of the road. Dharalyn welcomed the cover of leaves that broke up the light falling from a sun which was beginning to rise high into the sky overhead. She saw a car approaching in the distance, and not wanting to be seen by anyone, she stepped off the road and moved quickly through some scattered underbrush, toward the trees beyond. As soon as she reached the first of the trees, she entered *Kquwaya-Shira,* which was the second of the three battle-stances she knew and "flashed" about thirty yards ahead, so that she would be completely hidden from the approaching car, which she could hear was slowing way down as if the occupant had noticed something and was looking for her. After a few more moments, she sighed in relief as she heard the car speed up and thankfully, drive away. It was cooler here, under the dense canopy of leaves and as she turned back, she immediately withdrew from her battle stance and nearly swooned from the effort it cost her.

Normally, she would have simply relaxed and her body would have naturally pulled out of *Kquwaya-Shira*, and then *Kquwaya-Set* over a period of time, but being impatient she had unwisely used *Ayowei*, the lesser magic that all Sedai carried within them, to speed up the process. Taking a deep breath and steadying herself, Dharalyn slowly moved off into the woods. She would go to the cabin, she decided. The one where she and Danielle had stayed, that very first night. She was fairly certain of the general direction it lay in, and so she walked on into the forest, her stomach grumbling loudly at her. The tiny bit of blood she'd taken from Gran had helped very little, and had only served to whet her appetite. She was pretty bad off and over the next day or so, it was going to get a lot worse. Dharalyn frowned and tried not to think about her predicament. First thing she needed to do was to find shelter. Then, tomorrow she would decide how best to proceed; how long to wait, before appealing to Danielle to somehow see reason.

As the day slowly passed, Dharalyn found herself thinking about her home. She wondered if her people were trying to find her. Although it was very unlikely, considering the strange event that had brought her here, she knew that there were people back home who were extremely knowledgeable about portal operation and might possibly have ways of tracking her of which she was completely unaware. Deep down, she doubted that anyone would ever actually find her, though she stubbornly refused to give up all sense of hope. Why, with who she was and the high regard her mother had engendered within the hearts and minds of the people of Asreod, the very fact that Pharalyn Sarina Malakovani's daughter was missing would doubtless begin an intense and lengthy search for her whereabouts. After all, with her mother gone, she was now the heir to the *Quadraprym Council Seat*, which was her birthright. She was also first in line to assume the position of *Khan-Tessera*, the spiritual leader of the Amalgamation Worlds, should she be found worthy.... She paused in her torrent of thought, as a sudden pang of both guilt and sorrow hit her. She was still grieving for the death of her mother, the thought bringing back the raw pain of it all. The heartache of her loss was only barely kept in check by Dharalyn's ability to push it deep within, until the time came when she could order her thoughts and open her heart to the memories that would surely come, in a time when it was safe to do so and she had time to remember her dear one in fullest measure. And so she pushed back the sudden welling of emotions that threatened to drown her now, and locked them within an inviolable chamber deep within her heart, to await another time and place more suited for dealing with these painful thoughts. But, the other thing was still waiting for her, the thing that had resided deep within her spirit like a festering wound for the past two years. The guilty knowledge that if her people did, in fact, find her, it would be to return to a state of affairs that would only end in abject humiliation for her and dishonor the members of her entire family. Pharalyn Sarina Malakovani had committed a grave sacrilege before Anon, in protecting Dharalyn from her proscribed fate. A fate that still awaited her back home, when they would test her worthiness to assume the position of Khan. A fate that should have been carried out two years ago when she, Dharalyn, had failed her calling. *The first in her family to do so in their entire history, mind you!* She had failed, the greatest and most important test of her worthiness! The test that measured and joined her spirit to Anon's greatest gift to the Sedai. She had failed to see her sacred pool, which rested within her *Egana* and would connect her to the greater power, known to the Sedai as *Kamanah.*

She had failed the Probost!

Like others her age, she had attended a private preparatory school called the Grand Novi Academy of *Synda Prepator* since the age of four, and had studied all manner of things like Language, History, Art, Music and basic Power Studies, as well as the Book of Anon. She had learned to control her inner power, which was called Ayowei, and how to use it wisely and recharge it when the power was nearly depleted. At the age of twelve, she had, along with her classmates, been tested for her ability with Ayowei against the Obelisk of Ovarious. She had passed; although, this also was a source of no small amount of shame for her, since she had gotten the lowest score of the class. Afterward, she had studied the preliminary materials concerning the Greater Power, which was accessed through one's spiritual center, known as the Egana. Here, when the time came, she would channel her 'self' into her Egana, where she would be shown Anon's gift to the Sedai, a sacred pool which was the individual's source of Kamanah. Her mother had described her own experience many times over the years. How she had felt herself falling, slowly, spiraling down within, to find herself standing at the border of a serenely beautiful glade. As she had moved through the emerald ferns and azure flowers that surrounded the periphery, she had halted as the sight of a gorgeous pool of water that shimmered with a golden hue, was made manifest before her. The size of this pool was unique to each individual and gave an indication as to the strength of Anon's blessing to that particular Sedai Adept. Most pools of Kamanah ranged in width from ten to thirty metrans across. Her mother's had been nearly eighty, which the Holy Triad of an Oracle and two Cavalithic Priests, who had been observing the sacred ritual, had pronounced was more the size of a small lake than a pool or pond, and which was considered to be a miraculous thing, since no one had been so blessed in a long, long time. It was why, when her mother had been tested for her council seat years later, she had lit and sustained four towers in the Crystal Coliseum of Light, which had been remarkable in the extreme. In the history of the testing, lighting and sustaining one tower was the normal mark of a Sedai Novi, two was considered exceptional and somewhat uncommon, three was extremely rare. And four, well, that had never been done before, until her mother had tested, that is. It had been an incredible feat, and one that had brought their family great renown and honor, Dharalyn recalled with pride. It had also earned her both admirers and enemies, alike. Each tower that was lit and sustained earned the Sedai Novi one vote in the council. Her mother voted four, and that had made her the envy of many other council members, especially those seeking to further agendas that were contrary to her mother's policies. The reign of Pharalyn Sarina Malakovani had been a difficult one, filled with violent societal upheaval and strife, as the Amalgamation Worlds and their people had clashed in so many controversial areas, mostly centering around the subject of social reform. None of this had been helped by the division within the core of the Sedai Novi, either. In recent years, a new faction had arisen with strongly opposing views and interpretations of the Book of Anon. They called for the Sedai to take what they saw as their rightful and sacred place, as rulers, supreme and ruthless in the application of their tenet. As things were now, the Sedai were arbiters of justice, caretakers helping to mold and guide the passions of the child races as they strove to mature.

Dharalyn's mind wandered again as she stumbled over a jutting root, vaguely aware that she had no idea of where she was going. She herself had been tested in the Probost. Dharalyn remembered seeing her aunt and mother arguing the night before. It had been by accident, and had left her confused and upset. She had gone to her mother's chambers after giving her Guardians the slip. As she had approached the chamber door, which had been left ajar and was mysteriously unguarded, which, given her mother's position was extremely peculiar and against royal protocol, she had heard her Aunt Olmerelda speaking in vehement tones. Her aunt, she knew, who was getting older and because of a few unfortunate lapses in judgment, had become a bit of a pariah among the senior Oracles of her order, would probably know all of the people officiating at the trial. Although it was considered to be extremely bad manners to listen in, Dharalyn had paused and eavesdropped, anyway. Something in the tone of her aunt's voice had worried her. She still remembered the entire conversation, as if it had happened yesterday, so disturbing had it been....

"You must make this a closed, private trial, Pharalyn; I will officiate at the Probost as High Oracle and we will use the priest I have mentioned."

"But why, Olmerelda? This is all highly irregular. The Novi council will never stand for such a thing."

"I don't care what the damn Novi think. My darling Pharalyn, you are Khan Tessera, the Supreme High Regent of the Sedai Novi Council, of the thirty-two ruling families of the Amalgamation Worlds. You vote four votes in the council and are widely considered to be the most powerful Sedai Adept of the last ten generations. Use your position to force this matter, this one time. For the sake of your daughter, who we both know you love more than anything in this world. Your daughter, whom I know you love more than even your own life. Do this tomorrow, or I'm warning you, it is my belief that our little Dharalyn will die!"

"I hear you, Olmé," she had said, using the endearing nick-name she only used when they were alone. Her mother's voice had been consoling and not the least bit worried. Everyone knew that, as sweet as she was, Aunt Olmerelda was getting a bit daft in her old age. "And yes, you know full well that Dharalyn is the very embodiment of love in my heart. I have never made that a secret and I would do anything to protect her. But I do not understand why you ask this of me. Have you seen something? Have you had a vision or prophetic revelation of some kind?"

Olmerelda must have nodded. "Yes! That's what I'm trying to tell you. Two days ago, I had a horrifying vision that left me weak and shaken. An oracular vision, so intensely clear that it could only have been sent down by Anon himself. In all my years, I have never had a revelation of future events to match it. It was the very essence of divine intervention. A truth I felt deep within the very center of my Egana. I was humbled Phara, humbled and left weep-ing by what I saw. All that we hold dear will be lost, if we lose her. You must do what I ask of you, Phara. You must do what I tell you, or the future of many worlds will suffer, including that of a distant world I did not recognize, filled with people I do not know."

"But, why should we lose her, Olmé? Why do you think her life is in jeopardy?" Her mother's voice, which normally remained calm even in the most heated arguments of her profession had taken on a distressed tone, one that Dharalyn could never remem-ber hearing before.

"Because tomorrow she will face the Trial of the Probost, Pharalyn. Think about that. Think about all the ramifications of what it means, should she falter."

There was a brief silence and then her mother had laughed, nervously. "Don't say you think she may fail. No one in the history of family Malakovani has ever failed the Probost! What in Anon's name makes you think that she will not pass the test as a mar-vel and a credit to her family crest, like all of the generations of Malakovani women before her? I think you are quite wrong in this,

Olmé. I think maybe that your mind is perhaps playing tricks on you."

"Then look within my mind and see what I have seen," her aunt had stated, simply. "Look within and let me relay the images I carry within my mind." Moments passed silently and soon stretched into minutes. Then there was a sudden break in the silence...her mother's voice spoke, her tone shaking with barely suppressed hysteria. "By the Great Creator, Olmé! What does this vision mean? Please, answer me!"

Dharalyn hadn't waited around to hear her aunt's answer. The weighty lack of response from her aunt had scared her enough with its implication, as it was.

The next day, she had entered the sacred garden in her ceremonial robes and knelt before the Holy Cavalithic Triad of the Probost: a group which normally consisted of one Oracle, who was represented by her Aunt Olmerelda, a highly irregular breach of official Sedai protocol, since the trial observers were supposed to be completely unbiased, and that meant no direct family members should be involved. And two Cavalithic Priests, of which, at the moment, there was only one present. She didn't recognize him at all, but that at least was as it should be. The last spot was filled as the third priestly observer suddenly arrived. Dharalyn had nearly gasped aloud when she had seen who it was, dressed in the dark blue Cavalithic ceremonial robes. It was none other than her mother. This was such a huge and flagrant violation of trust and procedure that she'd nearly stood and questioned them about what was going on. A sharp look from her mother made her reconsider though, and she had knelt quietly, shaking her head slightly as she considered the strangeness of this spectacle. For one thing, there were no people in the witness gallery. Normally, the gallery which circled overhead would be filled with dozens of family members and close family friends, all ready to bear witness to the proceedings and share in the joyous occasion, while congratulating the young adept when she passed the trial. The trial in which the youth, who had trained years for this moment, would enter her Egana for the first time and receive Anon's blessing. The trial in which she would enter a new life of adulthood and take her place in respected Sedai society as a young adept, sacred servant to the Greater Power. There was no one there, though. The gallery, she had seen, was completely empty. She remembered how her aunt had begun the rites that had been passed down from ancient times. The room had filled with a white mist, as fourteen crystal globes of energy had throbbed with power. The liturgy had progressed, as the oracle and the two priests spoke their respective parts. There should have been singing at the end, but like the missing witnesses, there was no Choir of the Order present either, laying down their harmonious undercurrent of sound that would have ended in joyous exultation at the closing of the trial. She had awaited the passage that had come unexpectedly from her mother, which signified that it was time for her to enter *Memordei*, the spiritual state that would end, if she succeeded, with her connection to her Egana, which was her absolute center. She had felt herself calm as she released all hold on her surroundings, the room had faded, sounds quieted, all thought about the events that were unfolding around her were released, as she slowly approached a state of pure, relaxed, mental tranquility. This was a state that she had practiced many times over the years and she reached it easily and without difficulty. The next part was new, however, and as she had been trained for this day, she released Ayowei, the lesser internal power and felt the magic reach down until she sensed a spark. A spark that she knew was the manifestation of her Egana and the gate to Anon's blessing. Slowly, she allowed the power to grow and send her plummeting toward the spark. Closer it came and she could see it now, see clearly that it was within her reach, as she gently sank through the depths of her awareness. Then, suddenly and without warning, she was falling uncontrollably! All about her a broad expanse of blue hues reached out on all sides. Horror gripped her as a mind-numbing fear reached up into the depths of her body, as she tried to regain her control. Her Ayowei peaked and she reached out with it, searching for a spar or something to grab hold of, something to steady her headlong, rushing descent. There was nothing. Instead, the sense of aloneness and loss grew, and her fear grew with it. Nothing had prepared her for this and she felt something was wrong. Something was terribly wrong! In a panic, she released her Ayowei en masse and pushed away from the rising darkness below. Mentally she reached out, clawing and grasping for an escape from a spiraling madness that threatened to overwhelm and consume her. She felt herself slipping, felt her body convulsing in terror and heard herself begin to scream. She did not want this. Whatever waited for her below could stay there. She heard herself begin to plead. Pleading for her mother to save her and then, for a while, there had been nothing.

She didn't know how long she had lain there. Had sensed someone holding her and stroking her with soothing tones. Tones that were filled with compassion, love and incredible concern. She had lain there, held tightly in loving arms, as her mother had gently spoken her name, over and over again.

It had taken her a long time to get over the personal anguish and effects of the trial, and even longer to accept her failure. Her mother and aunt had somehow kept her out of public scrutiny, and had kept her hidden away. The humiliation of it all had bothered Dharalyn for a long, long time. It had only been her aunt's visit that had kept her from sinking deeper into depression, kept her from going mad with grief and the shame of what she had brought down on her family. She had arrived at the family estate one afternoon and had taken Dharalyn for a walk in one of the many gardens.

"My precious Dharalyn, I know how you must be feeling. But do not despair, my dear one, Anon has yet a great plan laid before you. And you are only beginning to follow a path that his hand alone has put in place." Olmerelda had smiled gently and held Dharalyn's hand, seeing the anguish that rested in her eyes so often these days.

"I don't understand, Olmerelda. Why is my mother doing this? I should have been given over to the Praxillari after my failure at the Probost and executed, as is written in the Book of Anon. I was found unworthy, and I should pay the price as so many others have, in the past."

"Your mother would never let such a thing come to pass. She would sacrifice herself before she would ever allow you to come to harm. Besides, there are many of us who interpret these passages in The Book to mean something entirely different than what is generally believed. I myself have viewed the original transcripts and I believe they are misinterpreted. The passage in The Book is currently interpreted as, *Take the child who has failed the ordeal of spirit and send them to my bosom to be reborn. The grace of my holy spirit shall anoint them.* And so, the Sedai throughout our long history have taken it to mean that we should purge those who fail the Probost and send them back to Anon. I and many others believe that this passage is at its heart, incorrect. The transcript that it was taken from was torn and incomplete. With the help of a few dedicated Oracles, we have managed with the use of an ancient scrying technique, to go back and see parts of the original writing, as was transcribed by Cere Magumentae, a male Sedai who was directed by Anon to produce this particular manuscript, and as you know, who later went mad from the ordeal. New findings and beliefs show the passage actually interprets as, *Take the child who has failed the ordeal of spirit and send them to my bosom to be comforted. For in the fullness of time, the grace of my holy spirit shall anoint them.* You see, my dear, Anon never meant for us to sacrifice our youth who failed the test. He meant for them to be comforted and when they were ready, to try again. The text, as it exists now, lends itself too strongly toward cruelty, and many of us never believed that to be the true spirit of Anon. He calls for comfort and understanding, and for us to love, nurture and seek understanding of one another, not to kill those we see as not good enough!"

The last statement was made with a strong, passionate shake of Olmerelda's fist and Dharalyn could see that she was extremely sure of her own convictions. "Were you one of the Oracles who researched this false interpretation, Auntie?"

Olmerelda smiled. "Of course. Why do you think I have the reputation of being a crazy old loon? There are many out there who despise change, especially when it concerns the axiom of holy writ. It will be a long while, if perhaps ever, before we as a people stop adhering to such a harsh and ridiculous precept. But then, change always comes about slowly, and sometimes at great cost."

Dharalyn had felt a little better after talking to her aunt, but she had one more thing on her mind that bothered her. "What did you mean, by Anon has a plan for me? Did you see something about me in the vision that he sent you?"

Olmerelda had looked at her with a keen expression, then. "You know more than you let on, little one. What are you keeping from me?"

Dharalyn then bluntly told her aunt, without pretense, everything she had overheard. "So you see, I'm really worried. Worried about what it all means."

Her aunt had nodded. "Viewing future events can be tricky," she then said, thoughtfully. "Sometimes making these events known to the parties they involve can change their outcomes drastically, and not always for the best. So, we Oracles have learned to be very circumspect in what we say and to whom we tell it. Anon sent something very special to me, concerning you and one other, but I could feel the caution in it, as well. So I will not tell you everything I saw, but I will give you this. You have a very great purpose set before you, my dear one. And you will share this great purpose with another. A sister in spirit, if not in blood. Your Egana will sing with joy at the union and with that, the Divine Octahedron of the Eight will come to be, manifested by the intercession of the one."

The shock of recalling those words brought Dharalyn to an abrupt halt. At that time, her aunt's statement had seemed whimsical, and a little bit like nonsense. But not now.

"Danielle..." she quietly whispered to herself, as she recalled the Sharing Ritual she had experienced with the girl, in that first day together. She had done it to learn the girl's language, but during the sharing, something strange had occurred. Something she'd never experienced or even heard about before. There had been this incredible music, a swirling of tones that had melded together into a joyful texture of sound. She wondered if it was this to which her aunt had been referring. She suspected that it was.

Dharalyn suddenly realized that she'd been walking for hours, with no clear idea of where she was going. She gazed around, trying to get a sense of where she was, and immediately noticed the strange tracks all around her. They were thin grooves in the ground that had apparently been made by thin, knobby tires of some sort. Walking forward again, she could see these odd tracks followed the curves of the landscape, as if whoever had made them used these same paths over and over again. As she followed one of the paths that seemed to head in a fairly straight pattern, in the same general direction she'd been going, she hiked over a hill where she could see the knobbed tracks had apparently jumped a large area on the underside of the hill. Looking off in the distance toward where the tracks continued, she spied a small stream and began to quickly head toward it. If she was not mistaken, that was the same stream Danielle had found her next to and if she were right, it should lead her to the pond, and the small cabin that lay near it. Overhead, the sun was beginning to fall and Dharalyn knew that all too soon it would start getting dark among these trees. She tried not to think about how weak she was feeling, and for a moment, she was not even sure if she had the strength to walk the rest of the way to the cabin. "Maybe I'd better rest a little when I reach the stream," she said aloud, and then gathering herself, she made her way down into the grassy greensward that bordered the stream and walked through a wide swath of shoulder high brush and cattails. As she broke through the high growth, she found herself walking on a mixture of tiny rocks and sand, that had been formed when the water had been higher. A sudden noise to her right caused her to turn and then freeze, as a large, furry creature growled at her. Behind it were two smaller versions of the same species, who stood on their hind legs and looked quizzically her way. Searching Danielle's memories, which had contained, besides an understanding of her language, many descriptions and relevant pictures, she came away with a name.

Bear!

The bear in question had risen up on its hind legs and seemed very agitated about something. Suddenly, without warning, it began to charge straight at her, gathering speed and baring its teeth in anger.

Dharalyn was at heart a trained warrior, her ancestry full of battles and conflict galore, enough to earn the humble respect of the most seasoned of fighters. In her world, the Sedai unfortunately had a very bloody past, which had done much to remove those with poor fighting skills from their collective, genetic pool, and in that ages-long historical journey they had proved themselves time and time again as warriors of the first magnitude. As their consciousness expanded and their race evolved over the ages, they never forgot their roots. Sedai children trained in the art of battle from a very early age, for the Sedai knew from experience that it is only through fear and the respect that comes of it, that progress and leadership can be maintained. And so, in the seconds before the bear reached her, Dharalyn's body responded in the only way made possible by centuries of war-bred evolution. Her Ayowei flowed as she instantly entered Sedai battle mode, Kquwaya-Set, first level, which gave improved hearing, sight and sense of smell. Her eyes blazed bright green and her hair blazed white. As second level battle mode, Kquwaya-Shira, was manifested, she gained something she called speed-flashing, something she had discovered quite by accident she could do, which gave short bursts of incredible line of sight speed. Her skin went through a transformation too, and shone with faint lines of silver filigree, that twisted and scrolled artistically about her body, making it nearly impervious to all but the sharpest weaponry. She also gained enhanced reflexes and strength in this mode. Lastly, Kquwaya-Maxx, third level battle mode, added a single nuance of ability, the capability to glide and to fly short distances of up to around three hundred yards in length, depending on several limiting factors. A thin silvery skeletal frame burst out from her upper back, unfolding and covered all over with a translucent membrane that shone with a greenish sheen. Within less than a second, the broad span of wings spread out behind her in a magnificent framing of her gloriously imposing figure. Arcing upward, Dharalyn showed her fangs, spread her arms and roared a ferocious greeting at the approaching beast. Slowing only a bit, the bear raised itself up to grab her adversary with its huge arms, as it slammed against her. Milliseconds later, the bear was knocked backwards, as if it had been nearly weightless, rolling several times from shoulder to haunch and finally coming to stop in a dazed, bedraggled lump of fur. Shaking its head several times as if trying to clear her head, the bear glanced once again toward Dharalyn, and then, as if hastily reconsidering her situation, chuffed a few times at her two cubs.

Turning, she lumbered away as fast as she could, up the stream on very shaky legs, putting as much distance as possible between her and this new and powerful predator.

Dharalyn watched the bear run off, felt the very last of her Ayowei fade and then collapsed, unconscious, onto the gravel stream bed, her body quickly changing back into its original form.

CHAPTER 10

COMING TO TERMS

Christopher Christian Miles donned his yellow helmet, kicked the starter with his right foot and gunned his Kawasaki KX100, while shifting it into gear. His younger brother, Blake, had already taken off and he knew he would have to ride hard to catch him. It was early yet and still cool, but regardless, he only wore a simple t-shirt, jeans and sneaks. It would get hot later and he didn't want to be bothered with carting around a jacket or sweater, that in an hour or two he would not need anymore. Shooting down the hill from the garage where they kept their bikes, Christian, as his family and friends called him, kicked the bike through its gears as it whined and picked up speed, satisfactorily. The old shed passed by his left side while he sped onto a hard-packed dirt trail that led in a twisted path, through the forest of oaks and tall pines that made up his family's back yard. Pushing up the acceleration, he made his way toward a wide, hilly area some miles in, that was his and his brother's favorite riding spot. He smiled a wide and happy grin as he recalled the day before, when he'd been driving into town and spied the lone figure of a girl walking toward him. She had seen him, too, and had immediately ducked for cover as he had approached, going into the same woods that he was now traversing with his bike. Normally, he wouldn't have thought anything more about it except he had been intrigued, not only by her actions, but by her incredible hair color. It had been white, gloriously white, like the clouds on a bright sunny day or the new snow glistening on a full moon night. He chuckled to himself and thought, *There I go, again. Mom always says I can't look at anything without getting whimsical, or making some kind of poetic reference.* And why not? He was, after all, driven by his zest for life, which in turn, drove him to search for the things that inspired him most, like art, knowledge and most important of all, the mysteries of the female heart.

Christian ducked his head to avoid a low hanging branch and veered left around the bole of a large tree. He wondered, suddenly, if she might be out here somewhere. Again, he recalled the previous day's sighting and how, at first, he had gunned the accelerator of his little car, then quickly braked to a near stop where she had ducked off the road. Now that had been strange, he recalled. The trees were pretty sparse and thin for a good way in from the road, before they got dense enough to hide someone. And yet, there had been absolutely no sign of her. He remembered gazing into the trees and looking for a glimpse of that white mane, by which he should have marked her easily. There was no way she could have gotten to the forest proper and disappeared within its depths. Even if she'd been running full out, there was no damn way she could have gotten out of his sight by the time he'd pulled up in his car. And yet, there had been no hint of her passage, anywhere. Not a damn hint. Christian didn't know why all this was bothering him so much. "Here it is, a day later, and it's practically all I can think about," he said aloud, with a touch of irritation, while gearing his bike down and coming out on a high granite overlook, which let him look out across a broad area, below. Gazing far ahead, he could see where the trees thinned out, way off in the distance. That was the spot he wanted to go to, and so, he carefully began to thread his bike down a steep decline that was strewn with rocks and debris. It wasn't the safest path he could have chosen, but it cut off a good ten minutes from the regular trail that looped way out to the east and if he hurried, he would be able to get ahead of his brother, which, in the spirit of brotherly competition, would give him bragging rights later.

Soon, he was down on relatively flat ground again and speeding off at a reckless pace, through a copse of bushes and back into a wooded area. The trees were beginning to thin out here and he figured in another twenty minutes or so, he would be almost to the stream where he and Blake always met up, when they got separated. The wind rushed by and he felt exhilarated, as he took a couple of small jumps and got airborne. His thoughts returned again to the white-haired girl. He'd only gotten a quick look at her from a fair distance away, but the sense he had gotten was that she was really pretty. He wondered if maybe she lived somewhere close by and recalled that there was a small ranch, just down the road, where a girl his age lived and now that he thought about it, he supposed that he might just stop by and ask *her*, if she knew who the white-haired girl was. He'd seen her around from time to time and usually said hello when he saw her, though he didn't know very much about her. She'd always been kind of a loner at school and was kind of average looking at best, definitely not a looker, as he and his friends labeled them. *But this girl, yesterday,* he nodded his head as his thoughts continued to dwell on the subject of the mystery girl, *had most definitely been a real looker.*

She sensed brightness all around her and slowly but surely, awareness grew, pierced by an irritating pain that was throbbing in her shoulder. As she slowly opened her eyes, she squinted and her eyes filled with tears, at the bright sunlight that shone directly into her face. Her body felt stiff and she ached all over, as she tried feebly to rise. Slowly and with great difficulty, she finally managed to get herself up onto her knees. Knees that hurt, as they pressed against rocks and sand that were all about her. Her mind was muddled and she felt as if she were floating, her thoughts chaotic and disjointed. She heard a loud, rushing noise come up from behind that startled her, and she spun her head quickly around, only to see the tall green blades of grass growing near the stream bending and weaving from a gust of wind. The sudden movement had cost her dearly, and she moaned, as her head began to throb with pain.

Raising her hands, she pressed them against her temples, covering her eyes from the glaring sun, as she tried to remember who she was. How she had gotten here. She was weak. So terribly weak that, as a wave of ravenous hunger roiled and raged within, she nearly passed out again. Suddenly, she grabbed and pressed her palms against her stomach, as shooting lances of pain arced throughout her abdomen. Tears blinded her eyes and several times, in as many seconds, she cried out, painful convulsions beginning to wrack her body. She began to pant as she realized something was very, very wrong. A chilling thought suddenly came from within the deepest recesses of her mind; a troubled whisper that gave warning, in an ominous voice not unlike her own, telling her that she was dying, that her energy level was becoming critical. Primal instincts within her mind began to promote an aggressive new awareness, one set deep within the core of her DNA and designed, in times of utmost need, to save her life; long forgotten instincts that had lain dormant for eons, as her people had become civilized and elevated themselves to a higher place. Her ancestors had reasoned that it was immoral to take sustenance from another against their will and in so doing, had made decisions that had allowed her people to grow and raise themselves to a higher level of consciousness, a higher level of humanity. Those ideals and sense of higher morality were gone now, swept away like gossamer threads in a battering wind. Her body abruptly responded with its own ancient, primordial instincts, a natural impulse mostly bred out of her kind, centuries ago. Bred out, but not absolutely, it began to awaken and break free, brought forth from a locked and hidden place, by the critical onset of dire need. A brutal force that now forged a reckoning with her consciousness, surging throughout her mind and body like waves over a dam, each successive pulse stronger than the one before. Stronger and becoming increasingly undeniable, eroding and finally obliterating the very foundation of her will, until she was incapable of doing anything, other than give in to that last and final rudimentary act of compulsion: *her need to hunt!* She felt herself tense up inside, felt her body enter Kquwaya-Set as her senses reached out; sight, hearing and more importantly, smell, sharpened and intensified. She listened and heard an approaching sound, much like that of a growling animal, which raised and lowered its distinctive voice in a strange, howling, undulating manner. She sniffed and then sniffed again, her body rising into a crouch as she caught the subtlest hint of something, her incisors extending to their fullest range, as she growled low and deep in her throat. She was a huntress, sending out a guttural challenge, prepared to do what she must to survive. To do what she must to endure, in this distant wilderness that somehow, she sensed, was so far from home. To feed and as a result, live. She sniffed once again and caught a strong whiff of a scent that excited her, as she recognized its source. There was prey about! Quickly and with great stealth, the predator glided forward with purposeful and catlike ease, on the hunt now, as she sought to quench her deep, inescapable thirst. Purposefully, she continued her silent, prowling motion, the intuition of a much more primitive nature controlling her actions. Moving through the brush and picking up speed, she angled toward the approaching noise, her finely tuned predatory instincts outweighing all reason. It was time, and so she shifted into Kquwaya-Shira, to gain strength, speed and reflexes. *Time to feed!*

Christian slowed the bike and soon came to a halt. He gazed around the wide grassy area that was crisscrossed with old bike trails, and cut the bike's motor. He had beaten Blake here and figured he'd just relax a bit while he waited for his younger brother to join him. After all, it wouldn't be as much fun if he couldn't see the look on his face when Blake pulled up and saw him sitting here, all relaxed and carefree. That was one of the main reasons he'd turned off the bike. No sense in giving his bro any prior idea that he'd been beaten, again.... No, better to see his expression when he came around that last big bush that hid him from sight, further back up the trail. Christian removed his helmet, giving careful thought about what would be the best thing to say. He knew his brother, knew that right now he would be gloating and thinking how he would brag at dinner, of how he had finally beaten Christian to the stream. He couldn't wait to see his face, when he arrived in a few minutes. Off to his right, he saw something flash white and as he turned his head, he felt himself yanked violently from his bike. "What the hell!" he shouted, as with uncommonly quick reflexes he managed to roll and come up onto his knees. As he glanced around, trying to see what had hit him, he saw her.

It was only for the briefest instant, because she was lunging at him again. Quickly, he dodged and rolled to his right, but to little avail, as she altered her movement and grabbed him again, pulling him down. *Damn, this girl is strong,* he thought, as his adrenaline kicked in and he whipped his arms around, attempting to fend her off. Suddenly, she grabbed his right arm in a vise-like grip and as he felt pain explode from overwrought tendons, she slammed his arm back and then shoved his body down beneath her. With feline quickness, she dove at his arm, grabbing hold with her teeth while white hot tongues of pain lanced into his wrist, as her fangs pierced his skin. He screamed then, the noise distracting his attacker and for the briefest moment, she released him. Her eyes flashed and eyebrows furrowed with a look of madness, as she lunged forward again, searching for a better grip on his arm with those razor sharp fangs. He almost lost it, then, as he felt her tear into him for a second time. He even stopped fighting for a few seconds, lost in shock, as his mind tried to grasp what was going on; grasped the incredible fact that she was biting and tearing viciously at his arm. He saw images then...his mother, father and most especially, his brother. Deep within, he wondered if this wasn't a sign and recalled reading that sometimes you saw your loved ones, in your final moments. With a panicked jolt of clarity, Christian realized that he might die if he didn't do something drastic, and soon! "Let me go!" he shouted, as he gathered every ounce of strength he could muster. Bringing his left fist around, he struck her jaw as hard as he could, once and then twice, trying his best to knock her loose. For a moment, nothing seemed to happen, as she brushed off his punches, barely registering his futile attempt to break free. Turning her head, her eyes blazed bright green as she abruptly released her grip on his arm, tiny rivulets of blood flowing from the corners of her bright red lips, contrasting sharply with the white of her fangs. Their eyes met briefly and he had the craziest, fragmented thought. One that was totally irrational and lacking any hint of reason, considering the nightmare in which he found himself. An errant thought that broke free in uttered amazement. "My God, you're beautiful!" he whispered to her, as she suddenly froze. He tried to grab her shoulder with his left hand again, trying to push her away, but it was like trying to shove a boulder loose. She simply wouldn't budge. That was when the really crazy thing happened. Her eyes cleared the tiniest bit and her fangs began to retract, while something akin to a measure of sanity slowly appeared in her eyes. As he continued to stare at her in shocked, astonished amazement, she began to speak to him in the sweetest, gentlest tones he had ever heard.

"Anon, forgive me! What have I done? Please, forgive me."

Then, unbelievably, she reached out and gently stroked his cheek with a light caress.

"Please, forgive me," she said again and added, "I'm so very sorry if I hurt you." Quickly she rose up, turned and ran off.

As fast as he could manage, Christian rolled onto his knees and then rose unsteadily to his feet. He tried to shout out to her, as he watched her duck into cover and disappear. All the while he was trying, unsuccessfully, to tell her not to go until, as shock and the sight of his bloody wrist registered, he lost consciousness, falling to the ground in a limp heap.

It was sometime later when he felt himself come back to consciousness. He was in an ambulance and he could feel that someone was tending to him. "Where am I?" he asked, in a hoarse voice. He wondered if they had given him something, since he felt all woozy.

"Hey there, buddy," said a warm voice. "Just taking you to Pine Tree General. Need to let the good folks there check you out."

"What's going on?" he asked, as he tried his best to recall what had happened. Crazy images bounced around in his head. He'd been riding his bike when somehow he'd been knocked off it and maybe even been in some kind of a fight.

"You were attacked by something, out in the forest near your house. I guess your brother found you out there. You're going to be okay, though. We gave you something for the pain and I'm sure they will want to keep you overnight for observation. But I'm sure you will be fine."

Christian thought about things for a moment and then asked groggily, "What happened to the girl?"

"What girl?"

"There was a pretty girl, with white hair and red lips. Did anyone else see her? She was out there, where I was."

The paramedic chuckled. "Calm down there, pal. You must have had a dream, is all. There was no girl anywhere around there that I know of."

Christian nodded. He didn't expect them to understand. Probably thought he was a little bit off his rocker. And considering what he could remember, maybe he was. Maybe he was a bit nuts.

Big John Walkerman walked into the kitchen and grabbed a cup of coffee. He had been up awhile and had even endured an unexpected visit from the local Sheriff, Walter Drawbridge, this morning.

"So what did Walt want?" asked Sara, who was sitting and nursing a cup of coffee at the kitchen table.

"Told me that the older Miles boy was attacked yesterday. Wants us to keep an eye out for anything strange."

"Oh, you mean Christian."

"Yep. Boy was riding his dirt bike with his brother out in the sticks, not far from here, and apparently he was attacked by something. Tore his arm up pretty good, from what Walter said."

"Is he going to be all right?"

"Yep. Sheriff said they gave him a rabies shot and some antibiotics, in case of infection. Other than that, he's gonna be fine."

Sara looked concerned. "So, what attacked him, John?"

John shook his head. "Walter said he spoke to the boy last night and the lad told him it was a wild dog, but I don't think he really believes that, for some reason. Anyway, he was on his way up to the Miles house. Going to have the younger boy take him out to the spot where they found his brother. Guess he wants to look around a bit."

Sara nodded. "Probably a good idea. Better tell the kids to stay close to the house for a few days. In case there is something dangerous running around out there."

"I think that's probably wise. Where are the two of them?"

Sara frowned. "Aaron's out in the barn, fooling about. Danielle's still in bed. Same place she's been for the past two days."

Big John muttered angrily, frustration showing in his face. "Damn it, all! She's right back where she was, isn't she, Sara?"

Sara nodded. "It certainly appears that way, John. She went up to her room after she and Dharalyn had that fight, and has been there ever since. I've looked in on her every few hours, and I have to say, I'm really worried. She's either been crying or laying in her bed, wrapped in her covers and not wanting to talk to anyone."

John shook his head. "What the hell happened between them? I've never even remotely gotten a clear explanation of what caused all this. And even Aaron seems to have been affected by this situation. I asked him if he knew what was bothering his sister, and do you know what he said to me?"

Sara looked blankly at her brother. She hadn't told John anything about what had really happened. Hadn't dared to. Truth was, she wasn't entirely sure they had responded in the right way. They knew Dharalyn was different! And the way Danielle was acting now, it was plain as the nose on her face that the girl missed Dharalyn terribly. Besides, there was the other thing. The thing about Gran that no one else in the family knew about, yet. That alone had made her rethink her own position on things. Sara blinked and answered her brother, who was looking at her with a queer expression on his face. "Oh, sorry! Lost it there for a bit. Um, no, what was it he said to you?"

John pursed his lips. "He said that he didn't care if something was bothering her and that she was a big, fat, stupid, narrow-minded brat." John shook his head and ran a hand worriedly across his forehead. "And that's the nicer version of what he said. I'm telling you, Jay, I just don't know what to do here. I was tempted to haul off and give it to him for talking like that about his sister, but he seems so very upset about all this, I just couldn't bear the thought of laying into him."

"Yeah, he's pretty upset. That's for sure."

John grimaced. "I can't believe I'm saying this, but I think the best thing for this family right now, would be to find Dharalyn and bring her home. God knows I've been worried about her, too."

Sara looked surprised. "You're kidding. You, worried about our little visitor? I thought you didn't like her."

"She was in our care, Sara. And she made Danielle happy. In fact, for the little time she was here, she seemed to heal our family in many subtle ways. Did you see the expression on Gran's face, when she sang to her? I knew then that I had been unfairly hard on her. She really is a sweet kid and deserves our help."

Sara's jaw dropped open. "Am I hearing this right? Big John Walkerman, showing his sensitive side. I should call the papers. Have the mayor announce a special holiday to commemorate this rare event." Sara's attempt to joke fell on deaf ears, as John glared at her.

"I'm going to go up and try and talk to Danielle," he said, as he placed his coffee mug in the sink.

Sara stood. "Good. And if you catch her awake, I've been trying for over a day now, to tell her that Gran needs to see her. Needs to see her, bad. Made me promise to get her down there today."

John nodded and then walked away with a purposeful step.

Moments later, John stood outside his daughter's bedroom door. Gently he knocked, and hearing no response, he knocked again. Finally, he heard his daughter's muffled voice.

"Come in."

John walked into Danielle's room and noticed the general disarray. She was on her bed and wrapped like a cocoon, in all of her covers. There was a pile of dark-blue clothing at the end of the bed, which looked strangely familiar. Seeing his gaze, Danielle threw a part of her bedspread over it, in an obvious attempt to hide it from him. "We need to talk, Danielle," he said, as he moved close to her and then stood, looking down at his daughter, his face rigid with concern. Her face was red and her cheeks were puffy, and it was plain to see that she was very distressed. "Look, honey, I'm sorry, but we're not going to do this anymore. I know you are upset with Dharalyn about something and that you two had a really bad fight. But, you need to get up and deal with it head on, sweetheart." He paused, as Danielle gazed up at him with a stubborn, defiant look that was so reminiscent of her mother. "I know you think your Dad is out of the loop, and in this particular instance, I suppose I am, a bit. I don't have any idea what happened between you and Dharalyn, but I can tell you this..."

Danielle gazed at her father expectantly. His tones were so gentle and not the least bit condescending. Usually, he would have come in and started shouting orders. Get up, Danielle! Get a life, Danielle. Stop feeling sorry for yourself! But he wasn't. He was being kind. The very idea of her father talking to her like a person, like an equal, made her take heed of what he was saying.

John knelt down and smiled warmly at his daughter. Years ago, he had read that when you were big and tall, like he was, it was very easy to come across as threatening when you towered over the person to whom you were speaking. And so, he got down to her level, so that he could talk to her from the heart. "It's quite obvious that you miss your friend. It's even more obvious to me that you need to do something about it. This problem will not go away by itself. You need to deal with it. I think if you are honest with yourself, you know that I am right."

"But Dad," she said, and then paused. She did not want to tell him what had happened, for some reason. Couldn't think of a way to tell her father what Dharalyn was.

John reached out and took his daughter's hand in his. "Listen, get yourself a shower and come downstairs to the kitchen. You and I will work this thing out, together. I promise. Between the two of us, what is there that we can't resolve?"

Danielle looked thoughtful for a moment. Her father was right. She needed to come to terms with this. Probably tell him the truth, for starters. "Okay, Daddy. I'll be down in about ten minutes."

John nodded and smiled. "That's my girl," he said, and kissed her hand. "I'll see you in the kitchen, then."

Danielle nodded and watched as her father walked over to the bedroom door. Suddenly, he turned back toward her. "Oh, and by the way, stick your head in real quick and see your Gran, when you come down. Sara says she needs to see you desperately, or right away...or something like that."

Fifteen minutes later Danielle finished brushing out her wet hair and made her way down the stairs. Taking a hard right, she passed into the short hallway that led to her Gran's room and knocked lightly on the door, so as not to alarm. "Gran, you in there?"

"Come in, Danielle. I've been waiting to see you."

Danielle opened the door with more than a little surprise registering on her face. Ever since the stroke, Gran had had great difficulty speaking clearly. Her words tended to be clipped and unclear, forcing you to listen very closely to her words. Unfortunately, this made many people uncomfortable when attempting to speak to her and Danielle had watched as friends, who'd once been very close, began to avoid her and even stop coming around, altogether. The voice that had called out to her just then, however, had been clear and strong with almost no hint of anything out of the norm. Confused, Danielle moved slowly into the room, staring in wonder as her Gran smiled at her, her face showing very little indication of the right-side palsy that had marred her once perfect smile. Suddenly, she halted, her surprise turning to complete and utter astonishment, as her Gran raised her right arm and waved her over with her hand. *Her right arm and hand that she hasn't been able to move in years!* thought Danielle, *not since the stroke, anyway.*

Danielle's voice quavered with incredulity. "Gran, what's going on? How in God's name are you doing that?"

Her Gran smiled. "I know, dear. Believe you me; I know just how you feel. I'm really quite flummoxed about it all, myself."

Danielle walked over and knelt by her Gran's side. Carefully, she reached out and gently caressed her grandmother's face. "My God, Gran," she said in a half whisper, as she stared at her dear grandmother, who seemed to have been transformed somehow, and much more animated than should have been possible. There was almost no sign of the half-frozen features that had once deformed her beautiful, elderly face. "This is an absolute miracle. How did this happen to you?"

"Our dear Dharalyn happened, Danielle. This has all been happening since the other day. Little by little, I've been feeling better and regaining some of my movement. Ever since I let her, well...since I let her feed from me. I suspect there may have been some positive side effect from her bite that's causing it."

"But she attacked you, Gran. I saw her!" said Danielle, her voice beginning to shake as some of the distress she'd felt returned to her.

"No, honey. You jumped to a wrong, and quite understandably so, very wrong conclusion. You see, dearest, we had discussed it, Dharalyn and I. We spoke in that very special, mind-link way in which she is able to communicate."

Danielle nodded her head angrily. "Yeah, I know all about her special communication skills. All designed to fool the unwary. Get them to trust her and then, pow!... She drinks you dry."

Gran chuckled. A sound Danielle hadn't heard her make in a long, long time. "Sara told me about how she moved that heavy old television of yours, by herself. It sounds to me like she doesn't need to fool anyone. If she was the kind of person who would feed off someone against their will, I don't believe there would be much they, or anyone else, could do about it."

Danielle nodded slowly, as she stubbornly realized that her Gran was probably right.

"You know her, Danielle. You've gotten close enough to sense much of her true character. Can you honestly tell me that there is an evil bone in her entire body?"

Danielle shook her head with indignation and folded her arms resentfully, as she fumed about that one thing that was at the heart of all of this. The thing that truly bothered her the most. That Dharalyn hadn't confided in her about any of this. Marshaling her thoughts, she continued her argument. "But she drinks blood, Gran. Only evil vampires drink human blood. If she was good, she would drink the blood of animals or get it from a blood bank, everyone knows that."

Gran nodded. "Well, yes. In books, in a fictional setting. But in Dharalyn's world, the drinking of blood by her people is no more an act of evil than someone here drinking a glass of water. Although, I'm certain it has a much stronger connotation in her society, than water does in ours. They honor blood in their society as the giver and sustainer of life. The people in her world who provide them their sustenance are greatly honored and from what she has shown me, the honor is one that is highly sought after by them."

Danielle frowned. She was having a hard time coming to terms with all of this. The idea of someone drinking blood for real, as a means of sustenance. Blech! What a gruesome idea! Still, she had to admit, she missed Dharalyn terribly. She had gone over all the things they had shared, recalled all the talks they had had. She'd even gone through the small pile of costume jewelry Dhara had left behind, as well as her old clothing. The thought of that clothing made Danielle suddenly recall the previous night's confusion, as she had puzzled over the blouse Dharalyn had been wearing when she'd come here. Not really all that different from modern, shiny, silk tops you would find in almost anyone's closet, except for one thing. Danielle couldn't for the life of her figure out what the two slits she'd found on the back of the shirt were for. They clung together unless you pulled at them, and then they formed two parallel slits about six inches long, just beneath the shoulder on either side. *Weird...I wonder what the heck that is all about,* she thought to herself, while turning her attention back to her Gran, who was speaking again.

Gran took Danielle's hand. "I want you to do something for me, honey. I need you to do something very, very important and I want you to trust me, and promise me that you will."

Danielle squeezed her grandmother's hand gently. "Of course, Gran. I would do almost anything for you, you know that. What is it?"

Gran looked seriously at her granddaughter, then; "I want you to go and find Dharalyn. I want you to go and bring her home to us. She is in a very bad way, and she needs you."

"But Gran, we don't even know where she is. She could be any-where, right now."

"I know exactly where she is," stated Gran, with utter certainty.

"What! How do you know where she is?"

"How do you think I know?" said Gran, with a wink and a know-ing look.

Danielle gasped. "You've been following her. You've been doing that out-of-body thing you do."

Gran smiled. "Not at first. At first, our Sara had me so drugged up I was unable to go out. But, finally I did. And after a long search, I found her."

Danielle shook her head. "Do you think that's wise, Gran? I mean, maybe we should just mind our own business. Maybe we should just leave her be."

Suddenly Danielle blanched as Gran's voice turned angry. "Danielle Frances Walkerman! If your mother heard you say something so cold and callous! Where is your heart, Danielle? This girl is very special, in so many ways. Special to us and more importantly, to you, whether you realize it or not. How can you even say such an unkind and heartless thing? You, who have always had such a strong love in your heart for your family and the people you care about. And she is family, Danielle, make no mistake about it. If you turn your back on her in this time of her greatest need, I believe you will regret it forever."

Tears filled Danielle's eyes. "I'm sorry, Gran. I do love her and I do miss Dharalyn, but...."

Gran took Danielle's teary face in her hands. "But what, honey? Why are you being so obstinate, so darned insensitive about this matter?"

Danielle shook her head and then blurted out, "I'm really frightened, Gran. When I saw her in here the other day, it scared the bejesus outa me. I've been having such terrible nightmares about what she is, ever since. I'm sorry, but that part of Dharalyn scares me to death."

Gran sighed. "Well then, I guess you have a decision to make. You have to decide either to face your fear, or ignore it. If you choose to ignore it, it will all be resolved on its own, soon enough."

Danielle looked bewildered. "What do you mean, Gran? What do you mean, it will be resolved?"

Gran shook her head sadly. "She is at the cabin by the pond. She's gone there to die, honey. If you wait much longer, you won't have to worry anymore about your fears. She will be gone from this world, and if that happens, then may God have mercy on all of us: for forsaking that beautiful child, for allowing that kind spirit to pass away. What kind of people are we, if we turn our backs on the ones we love, in the hour of their greatest need?"

Danielle was frozen, as her thoughts churned. Dharalyn gone, dead. And all because of her. Her fear and her hang-ups at the very root of things. "Some friend you are, Danielle," she whispered quietly, to herself. Suddenly, she pursed her lips together and clenched her hands as newfound resolve flooded her mind and body. Her lithe figure tensed and coming to an abrupt decision, she stood and moved purposefully toward the door.

Mabel gazed after her granddaughter, who she could see was somehow willing herself to overcome her fear, and her eyes filled with hope. *Come on honey*, she thought. *You can do this. I have all the faith in the world in you.* As her granddaughter reached the exit, she called out hopefully, "Where are you going, dearest?"

Danielle's answer rang with determination as she ran out into the hall. "I'm going to get her!" she exclaimed.

Gran smiled and nodded as she closed her eyes. She calmed herself and with practiced ease she felt herself channel downward, and then with a sudden release, her spirit floated free. Within moments, she was in the barn and noticed at almost the same time as Danielle did that Aaron's horse was gone. *Oh no,* she thought, and sent herself flying down the old trail in her spiritual state, unseen and unknown, but seeing all around her. About a mile from the ranch, she saw what she was looking for: Aaron, on his horse and obviously headed for the cabin, himself. *Oh, Aaron. What are you doing?* she thought again, and then to herself, *Hurry, Danielle! Oh, please hurry.*

CHAPTER 11

SUSPICION AND REGRET

Sheriff Walter Drawbridge got off the four-wheeler he'd been riding for the past hour and followed young Blake Miles to the spot where the boy had found his brother, the day before. "Son, do me a kindness and go stand over there, for now," he said, while motioning to the boy and then moved carefully around the perimeter of the area the lad had just pointed out to him. Walter Drawbridge, or "Walt" as most of the folks around here called him, had been Sheriff of this county for nearly twenty-five years. He'd been doing it for so long that he had acquired, over time, what he referred to as his bullcrap sensor. When people told him a story that just didn't ring true, his left eyelid would begin to twitch, convulsively. Most folks thought it was a nervous condition he had, and he'd let people go on thinking that, but Walt had learned to respect the twitch over the years and it had served him well. Yesterday evening, he had spoken at length to one of the paramedics who had brought the older Miles boy to the Pine Tree General facility. The friendly fellow had relayed some interesting bits of information, not the least being a bizarre story of a white haired girl the boy had been asking about. It was probably just a bit of confused imagination the boy had dreamed up, and the paramedic had chuckled when recalling it. But Walt gave the info its due and filed it away as an interesting anecdote, for now, at least. Walt was a curious guy, and usually hung on to little bits of things that most people would hear and then discard, never to think of them again. His own mind was filled with lots of those little bits, and sometimes those odd bits came together and let Walt form interesting theories, some of which had helped him solve cases that had stymied even the feds. And so, after finishing up with the medic, he had allowed his curiosity to slowly percolate, while making his way with practiced ease through the several doors and hallways of the emergency ward. There he'd dealt with the queries of the attending hospital staff and because of his official status, was quickly supplied with the location of the boy's room and even more importantly, the details concerning his current physical condition. With a soft knock, he'd introduced himself to the lad, Christopher, and had then spoken to him at length about what had happened to him out where he'd been hurt. The boy had proceeded to weave him an incredible tale about trail riding and being knocked off his bike by a wolf, or wild dog of some kind. Some of the details of the ensuing story had been kind of sketchy and the description had grown and changed a few times, as the boy had tried to recall the details of the animal that he claimed had attacked him. While Walt had listened and asked a few pointed questions, he'd made mental note of a few particulars and had watched the lad grow more and more uneasy, as he tried to relate to the sheriff exactly what it was that had happened. Finally, Walt had stopped him, telling him that he had enough to go on, for now. There was no sense in listening to any more of Christopher's obvious hogwash description of the encounter. It was clearly apparent that for some misguided reason the boy had decided to cover up the truth. It hadn't worked, though. Walt's left eye had twitched the entire time.

Walter scanned the area and cautiously moved forward, widening his circular sweep while discounting the booted footprints of his deputy who had been out here on site, helping to retrieve the lad, to the myriad of tire tracks from the bikes and the four-wheeler the deputy had used the day before. As he walked, his eyes scrutinizing the ground and surrounding area, he recalled another "bit" of info he'd nearly cast off as unimportant. He remembered a call from Big John Walkerman nearly a week ago, asking if there were any reports in the area of runaways or anyone missing. There hadn't been, and the two of them had talked about a few other things, before the big man had thanked him and hung up. It had been odd, but Walt hadn't given it much thought, at the time. Now, though, he decided to put the info in the new "interesting bits" file he was just beginning to put together in his mind. He didn't really think it was all that relevant, but he had learned from past experience that it was the non-significant things that often ended up becoming very important, when collecting data involving a mystery. And there was, most certainly, the beginning of a mystery here, of that he had no doubt. Just the simple fact that the Miles boy had tried so hard to deceive him, had piqued his interest way more than if the kid had simply told the damn truth. Suddenly, Walt paused and he peered intently at the ground. "Now that's an odd one," he said, and pulled his camera from the utility bag he had fastened around his waist. In the loose dirt, there was a single footprint that had caught his attention. For one thing, it was small, as if made by a young boy or a girl. But more importantly, its obvious distinctiveness simply stood out. Over the years, he had had more than ample opportunity to view and peruse hundreds of photos and casts of footprints. They were usually made by sneakers, cowboy boots, work boots, sandals, or even smooth soled shoes. But, he had gotten pretty good at telling at a glance what shoe family the footprint came from. You could tell from the tread patterns exactly what make of shoe it was by using an online, forensics database where law enforcement types could search every conceivable tread pattern in existence. This was different, though. This imprint had been made by someone who was wearing a shoe with a tread pattern unlike anything he'd ever seen before. The impression in the dirt plainly showed that the tread was actually made up of rows of gracefully designed, intricate characters, like writing of some kind, patterned across the bottom of the shoe, but still designed to give traction to the wearer. He took several pictures and then followed in the direction of the heel, to see if there were any more prints. *There...by the bush!* He knelt and saw two more imprints, in the softer loam beside the bush. Walt nodded to himself with easy excitement, as he realized that he really had something here. This person, whoever it was, had been running. Running hard and directly toward...Walter turned and looked back about thirty feet to where the other Miles boy was standing. "Right toward the exact spot where your brother was hurt, yesterday," he said softly, and pursed his lips thoughtfully. Yep, there was something going on here that definitely warranted further attention. Walt nodded to himself as he began to formulate how to proceed. He would give it a few days and then talk to the older Miles boy again. Hell, he might even stop in and have a chat with Big John. He was certain as he could be that the boy and perhaps, even the man were holding out on him. Well, he would see. His eye was as reliable as any electronic device and he would just have to see what it could help him learn. There was something weird going on here, and he would find out what it was, no matter how long it took. Eventually, his persistence always paid off.

Danielle rode as hard as she dared, considering she had a good two hour ride ahead of her and the fact that Biscuit, as terrific a mare as she was, was getting on in years and wasn't able to trot for as long or as far as she used to. In her mind, she tried not to think too much about what might happen if Aaron got there before her. She didn't really believe that Dharalyn would hurt him, even though she was a blood-sucking fiend, but she still had plenty of reservations about all of this. No matter what anyone else thought, who was to say that Dharalyn wasn't playing them for fools and simpletons. Her own years of reading every piece of fiction she could find about vampires, werewolves and other evil beasts of more or less that same ilk, hadn't really prepared her for dealing with the reality of there being a real, live vampire in her family's midst. For the past few days, she'd gone back and forth in her mind as to whether she had done the right thing, throwing Dharalyn out. After all, wasn't it better to be safe than sorry? What if one morning she'd awakened, only to find everyone in her house dead from blood loss, and Dharalyn sitting in the kitchen licking her lips at the conclusion of the wonderful family feast.

"Oh, I'm sorry about all this, Danielle. You see, I was having a really bad day. You know how it is when you're PMSing," she said out loud, in a cavalier mimicry of Dhara's voice. Her horse Biscuit picked up her ears, as if she understood everything Danielle was saying and nickered in response. "I just couldn't help myself. Oh, I know you're probably upset, but you do know I'm a blood-sucking vampire, right? What did you expect from someone like me? I mean, this is how we roll."

Danielle shook her head silently as she clucked at Biscuit and lightly kicked her heels to take the mare from a trot to a canter, which was slightly faster, yet wouldn't leave the horse winded like an all-out gallop. Coming over a rise in the land, Danielle gazed ahead, trying to see if she could catch sight of Aaron anywhere. She wasn't certain, but she thought she saw his head and shoulders disappear far in the distance. *Damn it,* she thought, *there's no way I'm going to catch him.* Aaron's horse was a good five years younger than Biscuit, who had turned eighteen this year, and had a lot more speed and stamina. Clucking at the mare again, Danielle brought Biscuit to a gallop, which she held for as long as she dared and then brought her all the way back down to a trot and then to a walk, so that the horse's hard breathing would slow.

"It's okay, girl," she said, and patted Biscuit's neck in affection. "I know you're doing the best you can." Danielle shaded her eyes, and peered ahead again. The trail was twisting and turning now, through a dense area of trees and try as she might, she could catch no further glimpse of her younger brother. She hoped her Gran was right and that Dharalyn was at the cabin. If she wasn't there, then Danielle would have to return home, since she just wasn't prepared for an extended search. She carried enough water in her canteen for a single afternoon, and that was about it.

Her thoughts began to dwell on Gran, then. Her increased dexterity and the ability to move limbs, that a couple of days ago had been paralyzed and immobile, was nothing short of miraculous. Gran apparently seemed to think that Dharalyn had something to do with that. Danielle wasn't quite sure if she believed it, but was certainly willing to give it some consideration, since the vampire's disturbing interaction with her Gran a few days before had been the only recent anomaly in her existence. Gran thought that Dharalyn must have injected her with something that had partially healed her. Danielle didn't know about that. It sounded too much like the stuff of fairy tales. And even though Danielle had seen it with her own eyes, deep down, she didn't really believe that there was some kind of magic healing potion in Dharalyn's bite. Rather, that there was another more plausible reason for her incredible recovery. Problem was, Danielle couldn't come up with any ideas or explanations for what else that might be.

Dharalyn opened her bleary eyes and looked toward the cabin doorway. She was wrapped in an old, moldy blanket she had found in a closet in the bathroom. She felt terrible and as weak as a cobbelcat. The little bit of blood she'd taken from the boy the day before had barely helped her situation at all, and now she was worse off than ever. She doubted that she would be able to defend herself anymore, or even raise herself into a standing position. She was terrified inside that she might revert to that awful half-mad state of mind she'd been in when she'd attacked that poor innocent boy yesterday, and was determined to stay sane, stay herself until her life simply ended. The intense feelings had pressed in on her awareness a few times, though. She had felt the deep, inner call to hunt and feed, no matter the cost to her principles. She was near death and her body was screaming for her to fight, but she was still Dharalyn Xhikaterina Malakovani and a Sedai Novi, heir to the seat of the Khan-Tessera, Empress of the Amalgamation Worlds and she would not disgrace herself again. So, by pure force of will, she had resisted and finally quieted the impulses that had literally beaten on the very walls of her sanity, overcoming their incessant prodding and she hoped, remaining dormant for good.

What was that! she thought, and raised her head expectantly, as she again heard a muffled noise coming from outside. The same noise, she now realized, that had interrupted her solitude before. Gazing at the door, she saw a medium sized shadow fall across the opening, and then someone was there. *Oh Anon, please don't let this be!* she thought, as her anxiety peaked. It was Aaron...! Danielle's younger brother, and he was standing there staring at her with a shocked expression, as if she were some kind of ghost. She sniffed and even without the help of Kquwaya-Set, she could smell him. Smell the subtle hint of the sweet aroma of his life-blood. She could see his pulse pounding rhythmically in his neck, and then the most passionate wave of need Dharalyn had ever experienced swept through her body with a powerful vengeance. She convulsed and inside, the very fibers of her being screamed and cried out to her.

Feed!

Feed!

FEED!

There was prey here! Young and incapable of defending itself against her, even in her weakened state. She felt her mind respond with a kind of internal strife. Equal parts longing, a presaging of the oldest desire, and fear, for the life of one who meant so much to someone she loved. "Danielle," she whispered beseechingly, and tried to take heart, to find strength in the speaking of that name. Again, she nearly swooned as dire need and reason warred within. One part called for her to save herself. Eat or be eaten. It was an analogy that was true across both worlds, this and her own. And where her life was concerned, it was the only choice, imprinted deep within from the dawn of her people's history. As she fought the sweeping, powerful urges, she mentally clambered over the rising tide of emotion and took hold of herself. Either she was a good and honorable person and truly worthy of Anon's blessing and his canon to her people, or she was at heart a ruthless predator. At the very center of things, there was her mind, heart and soul, no matter the urging of primal instincts called into play by the compelling demands of survival. The choice of how she lived, of who she would be, was ultimately hers, and so, Dharalyn made it.

"Aaron, get out of here!" she said, in as stern a tone as she could muster. She was having trouble breathing. The call of his blood took her breath away and her heart was pounding, her body trembling with her need.

"But Dharalyn," he said, cautiously. He could see her face and though he was loath to admit it, he was more than a little scared. "I want to help you."

Suddenly, Dharalyn's face turned ferocious, her teeth extended as she screamed at him with all of her might.

"Aaron, get out!"

"GET OUT!"

"GET OUT OF HERE, NOW!"

Aaron turned and ran. He ran as fast as he could, directly away from the cabin, past his grazing horse and toward the path that had brought him here. As he reached the line of trees that marked the forest edge, he saw his sister galloping toward him and waved. Soon she was at his side, her horse blowing as she jumped off and grabbed his shoulder.

"Are you okay?" she asked him, plainly seeing the look of terror that still marked his face.

He nodded and then said shakily, "I just wanted to help her."

Danielle nodded and tousled his messy hair. "Of course you did. Is she in the cabin?"

Aaron nodded briskly. "Don't go in there, Danielle! She's gone crazy, I think. Please, don't go in there! Let's go back...right now, let's go back together. Really fast!"

Danielle looked at his stricken face. Something had shocked the childlike innocence right out of him. Thinking carefully, she considered her options and then, shaking her head with what she figured was probably equal parts stubbornness and her own foolish resolve, she handed Aaron her reins. "Cool Biscuit down for me. I've been riding her hard. Too hard.... I've got to go and take care of this."

Aaron took the reins and argued plaintively, "Danielle, no! Please, I don't think you should go. You're my only sister and I...."

Danielle gave him a quick hug. "I know, buddy. I love you, too. But, I have to do this. Now, I want you to do exactly what I say. I should be back out in a little while, ten minutes or so, but, if I'm not, or if I don't give you the all clear, I want you to get on your horse and go straight back to the house. Do not," Danielle said emphatically, "come inside the cabin looking for me! Just get on your horse and ride. Okay?"

"Okay," he said, hesitantly.

"Tell Dad what happened and he will know what to do," Danielle added, and then strode cautiously toward the cabin. She felt a little like one of those actors in a horror movie, where one of the main characters is walking into dire trouble and everyone in the theatre is thinking, *No, don't go into that dark room, or old, creepy house. Are you completely stupid? You are gonna be killed or eaten.* And then, the ultra-dumb character does what no normal, thinking person would ever do, and gets wasted. That's what she felt like, now. She felt like she was walking into her own version of a B-horror movie mistake. She just hoped someone wasn't up there in heaven somewhere, eating popcorn and watching her blow it.

Danielle reached the cabin, and moved through the door and into the interior of the room. As her eyes slowly grew accustomed to the dark after being out in the bright sunlight, she spied a small form hunched in the back corner, wrapped in a dirty old blanket. Two green eyes were staring at her with obvious hostility. Softly she said, "Dharalyn, it's me, Danielle."

"Get out of here, Danielle," croaked a voice that sounded as if it was spoken by death-warmed-over.

Danielle ignored the warning and slowly approached the pitiful figure, moving carefully so as not to alarm her. As she reached her side, she knelt down and looked directly at Dharalyn's face. Green eyes glared, as she gazed into twin pools of fiercely feral light.

"You look bad."

"I said, get out of here," said Dharalyn, and then she screamed hoarsely, "GET OUT!"

"Stop your damn yelling," responded Danielle firmly, her own temper bursting forth. "And stop telling me to get out! I'm not going anywhere, you stupid vampire!" She had tried to put a teasing note into that last statement, but could tell she had failed miserably.

"What do you want?" Dharalyn asked. Danielle could see that she was trembling and that she seemed to be struggling to breathe, as if she couldn't get enough oxygen.

"I came here to help you. What the heck do you think I want?"

"Why? After all, I'm a God-Damn, freaking vampire. Those were your words, remember?"

Danielle nodded, ashamed with herself. Especially since hearing her own colorful choice of words thrown back at her, caused her to feel mortified. She never used words like that! Her mother would have scolded her harshly, no matter what the excuse. Suddenly, all of the deepest things she had been feeling over the past few days broke loose. She cast aside her preconceptions, cast off her shackles of prejudice and said with a cavalier attitude that was part of her very nature, "Well, Dharalyn my dear, you may be a freaking vampire. But, you're my freaking vampire! Gran explained everything to me and I know I reacted very badly. You are my best friend, my bond sister from another world," she said, and felt the trueness of it resounding deep within like a bell chime as Dharalyn's glaring eyes softened, "and I should have listened to you, rather than screaming like a lunatic. We are meant to be together, you and I, of that I am certain. I've been completely miserable without you. I know it's taken me awhile, but I'm here now. And I promise I will never leave you again."

Tears began to roll down Dharalyn's cheeks as Danielle's heartfelt words reached into her, touching her in a very profoundly, personal way. Suddenly, she didn't feel quite so alone. She didn't feel so very far from home. The burning need that had a short while ago screamed within, fell away to the surge of a much stronger emotion. Slowly, she raised her hands, leaned forward and then the two of them were hugging, tears falling from both of their faces.

"I love you, Dharalyn," Danielle muttered.

"I love you, too, Danielle."

"Uh, Dhara," spluttered Danielle, as she tried to take a breath. "Could you please ease up? You have the grip of a lion."

Dharalyn released her hold and looked at Danielle's face, which was bedecked with a playful smirk.

"And, I gotta tell you, you could really use a bath!"

Dharalyn responded by pulling back her lips and showing Danielle her glistening fangs. She too, could make a sarcastic point, though admittedly, her response smacked of bad taste.

"Okay, okay," Danielle laughed, uneasily. "Guess it's a bad time for jokes and teasing. Anyway, I guess it's up to us in the family to take care of your, you know...*special needs*. And, as bad off as you appear to be, I think we'd better not wait until we get home." Saying it out loud finally broke down her last, needling doubts. Her mind made up, Danielle pulled her hair back and then leaned her neck to the side. "So, let's do this thing, then. Go ahead, Dhara, I'm ready!"

Dharalyn stared, perplexed for a moment. *What was this that Danielle was offering? Was she asking to be her...;* and then, her sluggish mind prompted her with a sudden realization. Danielle's books! The vampire fiction of this world held the answer. Even as weak as she felt, Dharalyn was unable to withhold a solid laugh. Danielle glanced at her in confusion, her neck still bent to the side in offering.

"What? Are you gonna do this, or not? I'm not gonna sit here like this all damn day!"

Something about Danielle's pose sparked a remembrance deep within her consciousness and a chill ran up Dharalyn's spine, as a dim memory she had completely, utterly forgotten blossomed suddenly within her awareness. *That night, not far from here,* she thought with dismay and felt her cheeks redden in response. *When Danielle held me by the stream!* The thought was too much for her current state and she pushed it down, way down deep, ignoring it as if it didn't exist. Focusing herself, she gazed at her friend who was making this remarkable offer, an offering that crushed societal moralities set forth by her beliefs, and overcame so many fundamental differences between them. Dharalyn felt a rush of genuine affection for her friend, as she reached out a trembling hand and took her gently by the arm. "Oh, Danielle, in my world, only lovers share blood that way, and only if they are bonded in holy union. This is the proper way to give blood," she said, tapping Danielle's wrist.

While Danielle flushed with obvious embarrassment, Dharalyn began to raise her wrist and then paused. As famished and as in need as she was, she simply could not go on without making certain that Danielle knew exactly what it was she was getting into.

"Danielle, if you do this, are you aware that it will need to be a regular thing between us, from here on out? I will have to feed every day, otherwise in a day or two we will be right back in this same situation, again."

Danielle pulled her arm back, realizing suddenly what this would mean. She would be giving a vampire regular feedings, and the very thought of that made her queasy inside. In most of the books she'd read, those that gave blood were meant to be pitied, or worse, people whose lives were given completely over to serving their vampire masters. She shook her head; Dharalyn had said, in her world, those that gave blood were honored and the position was highly sought after. "I guess how you perceive this thing all depends on your own personal point of view, and has a lot to do with the way you were raised, along with the social values you're taught from the time you were born," she said, and stared at Dharalyn, whose eyes were inexplicably focused on her own fingers. Danielle instinctively knew what she was doing. She was trying to hide from her the signs of pleading in her eyes. And that was the absolute crux of who and what kind of person she was. Dharalyn would never force her to do this against her will. Or even allow herself to unintentionally coerce Danielle's decision, here. That was why she wouldn't look at her, right now. She was giving her the space to make up her own mind; call it female intuition, but she could sense it. Surrendering to the wave of affection that surged through her, she realized that she'd been a fool about all of this. This was her dearest friend, and sure, she was a vampire and had things about her that made one check their own sanity at the door, but when you loved someone, you did what you had to do, especially when that thing had to do with saving their life. This young woman had, for some inexplicable reason, been given over to their care. Her Gran understood that, and now in the very depths of her heart, Danielle finally understood it too. With a whisper she said what she needed so badly to say. "I will give you what you need from here on out, from this day forward and for every day hereafter. I will share my life's blood with you, you whom I love like a sister, and I willingly make your well-being my own. This is my promise to you." The statement was a bit prosaic, she knew, but for some reason, it seemed to fit with the solemnness of the occasion.

Dharalyn gave Danielle a look of profound relief and then said in a deep voice, rich with fervor, "Danielle, my need is very great."

Danielle nodded understandingly and then slowly proffered her arm to Dharalyn. "Will it hurt?"

Dharalyn shook her head. "Only the tiniest bit," she commented, and then pressed her lips against the back of Danielle's wrist. Incisors extended with practiced ease, as she pierced the girl's skin and found her veins. Danielle yelped with the initial sharp prick of pain, which felt like a doctor's needle being inserted. Her body stiffened with anxiety and then slowly relaxed, as a feeling of bliss began stealing over her. *This isn't actually all that bad,* she thought, as she watched Dharalyn feed. She noticed, almost immediately, that Dharalyn wasn't taking her blood by swallowing it, like most of the Hollywood vampires seemed to do, but rather, her fangs appeared to be hollow and were pulling the blood from her like two thin straws. As Dharalyn pulled her wrist in tighter, Danielle noticed that there were two teeth that entered her arm from below as well, from Dharalyn's lower jaw. *Hmmm...twice as fast, no waiting,* she thought to herself, amazed at her own relaxed demeanor to all of this. She should be freaking out, but she wasn't. Part of it was likely the warm, languorous feeling that had filled her. She felt wonderful. Like she wouldn't mind doing this all day long! It wasn't long before Dharalyn paused and took Danielle's wrist from her mouth.

"We better stop there. I don't want to take too much, since we don't know how much you can safely give, yet."

"Aunt Sara will know," said Danielle. "We'll ask her when we get back. Did you get enough?"

Dharalyn shook her head. "Not really. I've been so long without a good feeding that I really need quite a bit."

"I can help," said a timid voice coming from the doorway. The girls both looked around and saw Aaron walking slowly toward them. "She's my friend too, you know. I'm part of the family and she's my responsibility, too."

Danielle blanched. "Aaron.... Dad would kill me if I let you do this."

"What Dad doesn't know won't hurt him, Danielle," he said, as his sister looked at him with surprise. He was getting older and he could handle this. "And you know you can't ever tell him about Dharalyn. He would never get it."

Danielle nodded in agreement. "That's an understatement." Then, looking at her brother, she said, "If I let you do this, Aaron, it has to be a complete secret. The best secret you've ever kept. You can't ever tell your friends, or brag about it online. You can't ever say a word about it to anyone but me, Aunt Sara or Gran. Understand?"

Aaron nodded sagely. He understood why his sister was saying this. But she should know better. Nobody kept a secret like he did. *Nobody!*

Danielle turned back toward Dharalyn. "Well, looks like we have another volunteer."

Dharalyn looked unsure. "I don't know, Danielle. He's so young. In my world, we don't feed from anyone under fourteen and even then, only rarely."

"Look, after we get back and get things better squared away, then you can argue with me. For now, considering he's pretty solid for his age, heck, he weighs as much as I do, go ahead and take some blood from him. You still look pretty pale and I can tell you really need it."

Dharalyn seemed to consider carefully for a minute, and then gave in. "All right, but I will only take half of what I took from you, Danielle, and only this one time."

Danielle nodded. "Sounds good to me," she said, and watched as Dharalyn took blood from her little brother's wrist. She reached out and patted him on the back as his face displayed how nervous he was. "Hey," she said in a teasing tone, "look at it this way. Now you can call yourself her blood-brother."

Aaron looked at his sister and smiled at the thought. "Cool!" he said, and laughed with her.

CHAPTER 12

SOLVING AN OLD PROBLEM

It had been over a week since Danielle had brought Dharalyn back home, and things were beginning to settle down and feel comfortable. In fact, they were better than comfortable, they were absolutely great. Aunt Sara had come up with a workable feeding schedule between herself, Gran and Danielle, and so far they had had no problems keeping up with Dhara's needs, which were surprisingly light. Sara had been keeping a close eye on their blood pressure and as far as she could tell, none of them were showing any of the signs that could occur when a person is low on blood, like being anemic or having discoloration under the fingernails. When asked, Dharalyn had explained that in her home world, as few as two people could sustain her, indefinitely. She further explained that a restorative, which was injected when she fed, enhanced their body's ability to reproduce blood and heal at a miraculous pace (*all signs of her bite marks would disappear in about ten minutes*). Danielle had then asked Dharalyn the burning question that was uppermost in all of their minds. Had she ever seen people from her home react in the positive manner that they were all experiencing? She had replied that she, too, was amazed by it all. She had never heard of anything remotely like it happening to any of her people, and she herself could barely believe the changes they were seeing. First of all, Gran was looking and feeling better every day. But that was not what had Danielle feeling so good. No, it was the simple, wondrous fact that almost all visible signs of the terrible acne that had plagued her teen years was nearly gone. That one little fact had her feeling happier than she could remember being in a long time. She had stared at herself in the mirror this morning for fifteen minutes, at least, in disbelief. There were still a few small pimples, but not a single blotchy red mark to be seen. Her skin was tan, smooth and nearly flawless, except for a small amount of scarring. In fact, everywhere she had broken out on her body was almost clear, and she was ecstatic! Aunt Jay had informed them that since helping with the feeding, she'd found that she didn't need to wear her contacts anymore. It seemed that nearly everyone involved had noticed marked improvements to their health. All in all, Danielle was happy and everyone seemed to be doing well. That happy feeling lasted until she walked into the kitchen and saw her father sitting at the kitchen table, nursing a cup of coffee and staring blankly at the wall. "Dad, what's wrong?" she asked, worriedly. She could tell by the distraught look on his face and from his awkward demeanor, that something was troubling him greatly. He had been really supportive over the past week, not looking all that surprised when he'd come home from work and seen that Dharalyn was back. In fact, he had shocked them all when he'd welcomed her with a big hug and told her that he was glad to see her back home where she belonged. And from the affectionate tone of his voice, Danielle knew he had meant it. Danielle had teared up a bit when he'd said that and had noticed out of the corner of her misty eyes that Aunt Sara had, too. It had reminded her how really decent and kind-hearted he could be, when he wanted. Oh, he could be very gruff, and he wasn't exactly what you would call open-minded about a lot of things. But, Big John Walkerman loved his family and protected them with an energy and ferocity that would humble someone looking in from the outside. His family had always been able to depend on him to handle even the toughest situations with aplomb and dignity, and an inner strength that burst from him, at times, backed by a powerful voice and manner. "Dad," Danielle said again, focusing all of her attention on her father, while putting her hands comfortingly on his shoulders, "is everything all right?"

"Sit on down here for a minute, honey," he replied, motioning to the chair next to him. "I guess maybe it's time we talk."

Danielle sat down, a feeling of uneasiness pervading her being. Her father's serious tone had put her nerves on edge. *Something was up...something bad!* She looked at his face and could tell he was having a hard time marshaling his thoughts, as if he knew that what he was about to say was going to hurt her in some very personal way. "Tell me, Dad," she said, with an air of finality and an edge of dread. She had been aware for some time now that they were having some problems, catching bits and pieces of the hushed subject matter between him and her aunt, that often abruptly ended mid-sentence whenever she walked into a room. But, being who she was, she had put a lot of the clues together and had a pretty good idea what this was concerning. "Is it...a money thing?"

Big John nodded. "Looks like the bank's going to go ahead and foreclose on us. I can put them off for a little bit longer, but we're going to have to make some very painful choices." John looked into his daughter's face and saw the glint of fearful apprehension reflected there. She had always been so smart, and he knew she suspected what he was going to say. "I've been offered a pretty good price for the horses. The fellow I sold them to is going to pick them up in a few days. I'm sorry, honey," he said, as he saw Danielle's face suddenly go from shock to one of utter anguish. "I'm really so very sorry!"

"No, Daddy, please no! Not my Biscuit," she said plaintively, as twin, glistening trails of moisture began to slide down her cheeks.

John took his daughter's hands in his large, ham-handed paws. He hated this, hated what it was doing to her. Hated most of all the feeling in his own heart that he had let her down: she who was, and always would be, the jewel of his life. "Their upkeep runs us about five hundred a month and we just don't have it anymore, sweetheart. Besides, I had a chance to get them a really good home. The guy who is buying them has a nice, big family and a beautiful spread up north. He even has a daughter just a little younger than you. He tells me that they all plan to go riding together, and that they will take wonderful care of them."

Danielle shook her head. The idea of Biscuit being ridden by another girl, being brushed and cared for by someone else, the whole idea reeked. "Daddy, what if I get a job? I can work and take care of their upkeep myself. I can do this, you know I can."

John shook his head. "Honey, that won't help. We need the money now. If I don't do this, we'll lose this place within the week. The bank will have us out of here by the time school starts. I'm sorry, but at this point, we have no other choice."

As hard as she tried to stop it, Danielle felt herself choke up and begin to cry in earnest. She knew her father wouldn't do this if he had any other choice, but the voice of reason was drowned out by her own sense of the unjustness, the bitter unfairness of it all. Biscuit was hers.... *Hers!* And no one should have the right to take her away. Standing, Danielle pushed her father's hands away and ran out of the room, her cascading tears coming in an uncontrollable rush.

Big John watched with rueful sadness as his Danielle left the kitchen. He had never felt so low, so less like a man. In fact, he felt like a complete and utter failure to her and to all of the family. How could it have come to this? How could he have let them down, let her down, so badly? Lowering his face into his arms, his own powerfully broad shoulders began to shake with the undeniable outpouring of his troubled heart.

Gran chuckled brightly; she and Sara were staring at Dharalyn's hair, which was currently a bright shade of glowing pink! They had been talking about the problem of Dhara's distinctive hair color, when Gran had mentioned that Dharalyn should try and use her inner power, which the girl referred to as Ayowei, to change its appearance to a more common shade. Dharalyn had given it some real thought and had told them that, as far as she knew, none of her people had ever tried to change the color of their hair using Ayowei, although it should be possible. And so, for the past thirty minutes, she had been concentrating and trying different things with mixed results. The first attempt had been awful. A bright blue coif had been the initial result, which had then transformed with the next try to a fiery red mane, laced with streaks of gold. "I'm sorry, dear," Gran announced with a broad grin, "but it only seems to be getting worse with each attempt."

Sara smiled and nodded. "Yes, I'm afraid all of these would probably attract even more attention than your beautiful white hair would. It's too bad you couldn't just use your magic to copy the color of someone else's hair."

Dharalyn looked abruptly thoughtful and then said, "That's a really good idea, Jay. Let's try that!"

Sara looked surprised. "What! I was just kidding."

"I know, but it's still a really good idea." Dharalyn walked over to the chair where Sara was sitting and held out her hands. "May I?" she asked, cheerfully.

"Oh, honey, you don't want to copy my old hair. It used to be a pretty shade of black when I was younger, but now it's got too much grey in it."

"Still, I'd like your permission to try."

Sara looked up at the pretty girl who was turning out to be such a blessing to them all, besides the fact that her general sweetness and wonderful disposition had won them all over, in such a big way. And Danielle...why, her niece was happier than she could ever remember her being, since her mom had died. That, in itself, had caused Sara to fall in love with this new addition to their little family, with all of her heart. "Okay, if you want to try and copy my ugly old-lady hair, you go right ahead."

Dharalyn smiled at Jay's self-deprecating statement. Danielle had told her that Aunt Sara always, "tells it like it is," meaning that she always told the truth, even if that truth was not self-flattering. Dharalyn let a miniscule bit of Ayowei flow into Sara's hair and used it to sense the tiniest bits of what made it what it was. There was more of a certain substance in her darker strands than in her lighter ones. She relayed the information to Sara, who responded:

"That would most likely be what we call melanin. The amount of it in each hair affects the shade. More melanin makes your hair darker, less makes it lighter. The near lack of it leaves your hair gray or white. There are different types of melanin as well, that affect the color of the hair."

"I see," said Dharalyn, who smiled as she used her Ayowei to copy the melanin, and then....

"Oh, my good gracious!" exclaimed Gran, who then said, "Jay, go look in the mirror. Hurry!"

Sara stood, walked quickly to a full length mirror that was situated in one corner of the room and then stood transfixed, gazing at the flawlessly black coloring of her hair, which had absolutely no sign of her previous gray and which now exuded a lustrous sheen that she hadn't seen in about twenty-five years. "Oh, my goodness!" she stated, as she touched her hair with her fingers, as if making sure it was actually hers.

"Do you like it?" asked Dharalyn, who had come up to stand beside her. "I can change it back, if you like."

"Don't even think about it, sister!" scowled Sara, giving Dharalyn a look of mock warning that was half teasing and half serious. "As far as I'm concerned, you can consider this an early Christmas present."

Gran laughed from her wheelchair. It was plainly evident from the wonder in Sara's face that she meant it. "Just leave her be, honey. Our dear Jay is as vain as anyone, don't you let her tell you different. You try and change it back now, and she'll bite your arm off."

Dharalyn gave Gran a bewildered look and Gran chuckled. "It's just a figure of speech, honey. She won't really bite your arm off," she said, and then added playfully, "at least, I don't think she would."

Sara turned to Dharalyn. "Well?"

"What?"

"Well, what about you? Did you learn anything from changing my hair color? Will it work for you?"

Dharalyn responded by looking at her fingertips. She still had the tiniest bit of the melanin she had copied there.... Raising her fingers to her own hair, she let her Ayowei flow and then Sara shouted with glee, clapping her hands together in excitement. "Oh my God Dhara, you're doing it...that's it!"

Dharalyn turned back toward the mirror and saw that now, her hair was nearly an exact match in shade to Aunt Sara's.

"It's just perfect, Dhara!" exclaimed Sara, gleefully. "It's even prettier than mine. That color looks gorgeous on your long, curly locks."

Dharalyn had been wearing her hair loose since living here, rather than the structured, straightened, honeycombed coif interlaced with a special silver thread that she had worn when she'd first arrived. Danielle had told her to let her hair fall naturally, because it fit better, given the current hair styles here. She still recalled when Danielle and Aunt Sara had made her wear that awful wig, a travesty of a hairpiece that Dhara had utterly refused to wear ever since, under threat of dire retaliation if anyone tried to force her. This, however, had made it necessary for the two girls to pretty much stay indoors ever since, with no possibility of going out to shop, or anything else. Now, with her hair colored a nice shade of black, Dharalyn smiled as she studied her reflection in the mirror. Her tresses fell in easy curls and had grown practically to her waist. She looked like nearly any other girl her age, she supposed, and should fit in well from here on out.

Suddenly, the bedroom door slammed open and Danielle burst into the room, obviously upset and looking red-faced and teary eyed.

Sara quickly turned, and seeing her niece's distressed and highly overwrought appearance, walked hurriedly over to her with Dharalyn a close step behind. "Sweetie, what's wrong?" she asked, her voice filled with concern. She waited patiently for Danielle to respond and then realized that her niece was staring back at her, with a look of open-mouthed disbelief. "Oh, yes. Um, your Gran, Dharalyn and I solved the hair color problem."

Danielle stared with a dumbfounded expression at her aunt, turned briefly toward Dharalyn, and then turned back. "I guess so!" she stated, her voice filled with wonder.

Gran spoke up. "To be fair here, it was, of course, mostly Dharalyn's doing. She's a tricky little thing, that one."

Sara added, as she gazed at Danielle's still surprised visage, "She uh, fixed my hair up pretty good, huh?"

Danielle nodded, pursing her lips and saying nothing.

"So, honey," said Sara, realizing from her entrance a moment ago that there was another matter here to be dealt with, "besides the matter of our hair, what else is going on? You came in here as if someone or something was on fire."

Danielle seemed to catch herself then, and shifted her focus. "Did you know about this?" she blurted. "About Daddy selling the horses, about the bank wanting to take our house?"

Sara nodded slowly. "Yes, baby, I knew. But your Dad insisted that he wanted you to hear it from him. He's a very proud man, your father, and he felt that it was his responsibility to tell you."

"But why, why has it come to this? There must be something we can do!"

"I wish there was, sweetie. But it's been a long time coming. I know you, and I know you've been aware that we've been having some financial problems for some time now."

Danielle nodded her head. "I didn't know it was this bad, though...that we could lose everything."

Sara put her arms around Danielle in an attempt to console her. "It's been slowly snowballing for a long time. First, your Dad lost his business. He had taken out a second mortgage trying to save it. Then we got behind on the taxes, he was out of work for a while and then, of course, we lost your mom and there was a lot of expense there. I tried as best as I could to help, but by then, it was all downhill."

Danielle felt her Gran's supportive touch on her leg, and then Dhara's arms went around her, too. She reveled quietly in the outpouring of love that surrounded her for a few long moments, until her stubborn nature suddenly kicked in. "No, I'm sorry...but I can't believe it. There has to be something we can do. Something we haven't thought of yet. We're a good family, a smart family. I know if we all pull together, we can come up with something...."

A long minute passed silently, all of them lost in their own private thoughts, and then Dharalyn spoke.

"Danielle," she said, hesitantly.

"Yes, Dhara."

"What about my jewelry? I remember when we went to the mall shopping, there was a store there that sold things like that. I remember when I looked at the tags, that they sold for a lot of money."

Danielle nodded thoughtfully, and pulling back a bit from the mutual hug they were all still sharing, she explained, "Yes, Dhara, you're right. I remember that place. It was called Pierre Renoir Jewelry, and it's a very high-end jewelry store in that mall. Only very well-off people shop there. Their jewelry is extremely expensive and they supposedly specialize in nearly flawless diamonds and rare gemstones. I'm afraid that the jewelry that you were wearing is commonly referred to here in this world as costume jewelry. The stones are glass or some other synthetic, made to look like diamonds, but aren't worth very much. I even have a few pieces of it myself, that I got from my mother."

"Dharalyn has some jewelry?" asked Sara, curiously. "I wasn't aware of that."

Danielle nodded, as the group pulled apart. "Yeah, she was wearing it when we first found her. It's all up in our bedroom. I keep it in a bowl, next to the wooden box where I keep my rings and my necklace that Momma made me."

"What kind of jewelry is it, Danielle?" asked Gran. "I know a little bit about gemstones. I was always partial to a pretty emerald, or a beautiful diamond."

"Well, there was a necklace of blue and clear stones, with a large blue stone in the center, and two costume jewelry bracelets with large clear stones, probably glass," said Danielle. "And some strange looking palm thing. Her earrings, I think, she's still wearing."

Sara stepped next to Dharalyn and pulled her hair back, so that she could clearly see the three exquisite blue-hued stones she was wearing in her right ear, set in silvery three-pronged studs. "Those are beautiful, Dhara, and so pristine and dainty. So, tell me Danielle, what makes you so sure that all of her jewelry is fake? How do you know that the stones aren't the real thing?"

Danielle shrugged. "Well, I don't know about those. But in the necklace and the two bracelets, most of the stones are too big to be real. They have to be fake, don't they?" she asked, her look suggestive of someone who lacks complete certainty.

Everyone looked at Dharalyn, then. She shrugged and answered, "The jewelry was made for me by the Gunta artisans and were a special gift from them, when they visited us, once. The stones are mined from deep within their mountains. They shape them and polish them into jewelry. As far as I know, they do not make the stones from glass or anything artificial."

Sara and Gran looked thoughtfully at one another and then Gran spoke in an oddly tempered voice, her face beaming with curiosity. "I think maybe we better have a look at those items, Danielle."

Without a word, Danielle turned and ran from the room. She soon returned, with a small plastic bowl that contained a folded blue hand towel, which held the jewelry wrapped within. She knelt beside Gran's wheelchair and opened the cloth. Both Gran and Sara gasped as the three gorgeous pieces were revealed. Gran took one of the bracelets, which gleamed brilliantly, from the double row of large crystalline gems set within a silver band of exquisite workmanship.

"What do you think, Gran?" asked Danielle. "Could they be real?"

Gran shook her head. "Well, they are certainly large enough and they look real to me, but I just don't know for certain. If they are, they must be worth an absolute fortune. I suppose, though, we should try to look at this situation calmly and with reason, and not let ourselves get too excited. First, let's consider exactly who these belong to and even more importantly, who Dharalyn is. Tell me Danielle, Sara, would someone of her caliber and her social station be wearing fake jewelry? She is, after all, a princess and heir to the Malakovani Sakatherian Regency." Gran's voice took on an exultant tone. "Would someone of her stature wear fakes? I think not!"

Aunt Sara nodded in agreement and then lifted up the necklace. The chain was made up of what appeared to be blue sapphires, but the teardrop stone in the center of a diamond encrusted oval held a large clear stone of a bluish hue. Gran gasped, "Now that is likely real."

"What would it be worth, Gran, do you have any idea?" asked Sara.

Gran sputtered. "Well, this is way outside my scope. I would have to say, probably in the millions. Maybe even priceless, when you consider its source."

"What!" said Danielle. "That's crazy! There's just no way this stuff can be real. What would Dharalyn be doing wearing a necklace worth that much? It would be locked away somewhere, wouldn't it? I mean, something like this must be extremely rare." She looked at Dharalyn with a question in her eyes.

Dharalyn smiled. "We don't lock away our pretty things, Danielle. No one in my home would ever think of taking this from me. I have many beautiful items like these, given as gifts to me and to my family. Many of them are much fancier, and with many more gems of varying color. I like this one, because it was given to me as a gift by my father, when I was very young."

Danielle looked disheartened. "Well, then, even if they are real, I don't see how any of this helps. I mean, we can't sell them. After all, they don't belong to us. They belong to Dharalyn and her family, and we have no right to even consider selling them."

Sara nodded serenely. "Thank you, Danielle, for saying exactly what I've been thinking for the past few minutes. These don't belong to us, ladies. They belong to Dharalyn. Especially the necklace, which, you all heard, is a special gift from her father."

"No, Sara," said Dharalyn, breaking through the cloud of melancholy that had suddenly sprung up. "I am part of this family now, am I not?"

Danielle nodded. "Yes, but...."

"But nothing! Am I not your vampire, Danielle?" she said teasingly, "Didn't you tell me not long ago that I am your sister? And aren't you mine, as well? And Gran and Sara, who give freely of themselves to help take care of me. And dear Aaron, who bravely came to find me and save me. And your father, Big John Walkerman, who hugged me and welcomed me into his home.

Isn't the responsibility of this family's well-being shared by all of us, me included, from here on out?"

Danielle shook her head. "But you are new here, Dharalyn. We don't have the right to dump all of our troubles on you. This has been building for a long time, and we need to solve it without bringing you into it and taking away your only belongings, the few items you have left to remind you of your past, your home and your family." Danielle took the jewelry pieces and wrapped them carefully back up in the blue cloth. "I'm putting these back. We aren't going to talk about it again," she said, her voice trembling, yet firm with resolution.

Dharalyn reached out and grabbed the cloth from Danielle. "It's not up to you. It's up to me. We will sell this jewelry and save this family from the callous insensitivity of the evil bank."

Danielle grabbed Dharalyn's hands. "No, Dhara, I won't allow it! You are not selling your things. It's almost all you have left to remind you of your loved ones. And especially that necklace, which was given to you by your father...." Danielle paused her rant then, her shoulders shaking, as tears rolled down her cheeks. It was plain that the day's events were taking a heavy emotional toll on her. "We can't sell your father's gift to save ourselves. It's just not morally right and we're not going to argue about it anymore!"

Dharalyn clasped Danielle's hands with her own. "I am certain my father would feel great shame and chastise my sensibilities, if I put the value of these pretty ornaments above the welfare of the people I love. You and your family are my responsibility now, Danielle, just as I am yours. And so, if these pretty stones can save us and my new home, then they will do just that. That is my decision, one that by your own admission is mine to make and so you are right, my dearest friend, we aren't going to argue about it anymore," she said firmly, mimicking some of Danielle's own words back to her. "We are going to sell these things and save our home!"

Danielle's obstinate visage slowly changed then, partially relinquishing her stubborn stance before her friend's equally stern posture. "Very well, Dhara, but only the bracelets, okay? Not your father's gift to you."

Gran tugged at Sara's slacks and whispered when the woman leaned down to her. "Seems our stubborn little girl has met her match."

Sara smirked, nodded and stood back up, only to see Dharalyn handing Danielle the cloth, sans the beautiful necklace. "Do you have a way to sell these, or find out where we can?" she asked, as she gazed at Sara.

Aunt Sara looked thoughtful. "Well, I have a good friend who has been in the business for a long time. I will give him a call and see what he suggests we do. I have a feeling we may need to go through discreet channels to get rid of jewelry like this, otherwise we will need to explain exactly where we got it."

Danielle chuckled impishly. "Yeah, that shouldn't be too hard. We'll just tell him the truth. That a beautiful vampire princess from another world was wearing them when she came here through a space-time portal thingy, and since she's part of our family now, she wants to sell them, so that we can pay off the evil bank and save our home. That should do the trick."

Everyone smiled....

CHAPTER 13

TO THE CITY WE GO

"Jay!" hollered Danielle. It was early and she had come into her aunt's bedroom looking for her. *She must be in the shower,* she thought to herself. She heard the water running and realized that her aunt must be getting ready to go to work. While she waited, she cast her gaze about the room and smiled at the many pictures of her and the family that adorned the walls, and nearly every conceivable dresser top and table. On Aunt Sara's desk, she saw an old photo of her mother that she hadn't seen before, and as she stepped in front of the furniture to look more closely at it, her eyes spied a small spiral notebook her aunt had been writing on, next to the phone. Silently, she read the name and address there along with a note that said: *Broker, Samuel Remy, 125 Roosevelt Ave, Jersey City, NJ. Charles Mason's acquaintance who discreetly purchases jewelry and other valuable items.* Realizing what she was looking at, Danielle quickly tore a page from the back of Sara's notebook and copied the contents of the note. Just as she finished up and had folded the paper, slipping it into her jeans, she heard the sound of someone clearing their throat, behind her. Danielle jumped!

"Whoa, you startled me," she said to her aunt, who was eyeing her suspiciously while wrapping her wet head in a towel.

"Danielle, what are you doing in here so early?"

Danielle fidgeted a little and then forced herself to calm down, fearing that her aunt would become even more suspicious. "Uh, I was just wondering if you found out where we can pawn the jewelry."

Sara walked casually over to her desk, took the notebook and slipped it into a side drawer. "As a matter of fact, I spoke at length last night with a dear friend, who said he knew of someone who could probably handle this whole thing for us, and quietly."

Danielle nodded vigorously. "Good! That's what we want, right? So, when are we going?"

"Well, considering I have to work today and tomorrow...."

Danielle interrupted, before her aunt had time to finish her statement. "But Jay, are you kidding me? Those people are coming for the horses on Saturday. We can't wait until Friday to go. What if something goes wrong, or he wants us to come back in a day or two?"

"I'm sorry dear," said Aunt Sara, in a firm voice that smacked of annoyance. "Are things not to your complete satisfaction?" Walking to her dresser, Sara picked up a brush and after removing the towel, began fervently brushing out her wet hair as she continued, "And I don't appreciate you using that insolent tone of voice with me! I've been working very hard to make this happen and spent most of my evening on the phone, trying to find someone who could help us. I even tried to swap my shift last night, but we have one person out right now on vacation, so unless I want to lose my job, we will simply have to wait."

Danielle crossed her arms stubbornly. "Well, what if Dharalyn and I go?" she said hesitantly, and then, from the perturbed look on her aunt's face, regretted even asking.

"Are you out of your mind? Do you really expect me to allow two sixteen-year-olds with a bag of diamonds, to go down into the city and let them deal with some disreputable, back street diamond broker, without me? You must think I'm a complete idiot!"

Danielle nodded meekly. "Sorry, I was just asking."

"Well, you can forget it! You will under no circumstances attempt to do this yourselves. I absolutely forbid it!" exclaimed her aunt, who, after giving Danielle a very stern admonitory look, turned away and then, after a moment, turned back with a sudden thought. "By the way, Danielle, where are the bracelets now?"

"Dharalyn and I were working on taking all of the diamonds out of them, last night. We still have quite a few left to go."

Aunt Sara nodded thoughtfully, while staring at her niece. "Well, just so that I don't have to worry, I want you to go and bring them to me."

"What?" stammered Danielle. "Why? I told you, we're not done yet."

"I don't care. I wasn't born yesterday, my darling. I will keep them in my possession until Friday, when I will take them to the broker." Danielle started to argue further, but seeing the obstinate look in her aunt's eyes, she instead stormed out of the room, grumbling the whole way and making certain her aunt knew of her disapproval.

Danielle burst into her bedroom and glanced at Dharalyn, who was sprawled quietly on her bed, leafing through one of her many books. "Come on," she whispered, urgently. "We've got to go!" Immediately, she went to her nightstand and pulled out the old bank bag, which held the thirty-two diamonds that she and Dhara had finished removing from the bracelets, the night before.

"Where are we going?" asked Dharalyn, looking slightly bewildered.

"We're going to Jersey," she said, as she grabbed her purse and her last ninety dollars, which was all the money she had to her name.

"Danielle," said Dharalyn, as the brown haired girl looked at her with anxious eyes. "Is there any possibility that this will be dangerous?"

Danielle paused for a moment, considering whether to lie. Then she remembered who it was she was dealing with. *She's got some kinda built in lie detector,* Danielle thought to herself, and knew it was pointless. "Yeah, we have to go meet with someone today, and he may not be the nicest person and it may not be the safest environment, where we're going."

Dharalyn nodded and dove into the drawer that Danielle had given to her. She grabbed a couple of things out of it, and shoved them into the knapsack which Danielle was filling with the bank bag and a few other items.

"Why are you bringing those?" Danielle asked quizzically, eyeing the shirt and the strange metallic object that Dharalyn had stuffed into her bag.

"We may need them," she answered. "Trust me."

Danielle shrugged her shoulders in tacit approval, grabbed the knapsack and taking Dhara by the hand, hurriedly pulled her from the room.

Danielle made her way through the kitchen with Dharalyn in tow and found her father and brother there, eating breakfast. "Wow, you're up early," stated Big John, giving her a funny look. "Usually, we don't see you much before noon."

Danielle nodded and grabbed a couple of juice boxes from the fridge, along with some water and several oranges. "Yeah, I'm taking Dharalyn on a little tour of the area. Dad, can I take your GPS?" she asked, sweetly.

"Why in the world do you need that?" he asked. "You going anywhere you haven't been before?"

"Yeah, up by West Point. I don't know the area around there that well and I don't want to get lost."

"Sure, honey," he said. "No problem. Just grab it out of my truck."

"Can I go?" Aaron piped in, his face looking hopeful.

"Sorry, buddy," said Danielle, a pang of guilt running through her. She was gonna burn for sure with all of the lies and baloney she was hurling today. "This is a girl's only day."

Quickly, she kissed her dad on his cheek and was surprised when Dharalyn copied her example. She watched as Dharalyn then kissed Aaron on his cheek, and smiled inwardly as he turned bright red from embarrassment. "See you guys," she shouted, as she grabbed Dharalyn and raced out of the kitchen door.

After filling the car up with gas in Pine Tree, Danielle headed straight for highway seventeen, which she planned to take to the

Thruway and then on to Jersey City. "Dharalyn," she said, cautiously, "I need to tell you something."

"Yes, Dani."

"I've kinda been lying my butt off to everyone, this morning."

"I know," replied Dharalyn, with a slight tone of disapproval. "I could tell."

"It's just that we have to do something and quick, or we're gonna lose the horses. Aunt Sara wants me to wait until Friday, so that she can go, but I'm afraid we'll be cutting it too close. That's why you and I are going, today."

Dharalyn nodded silently.

"Do you think what I'm doing is wrong?"

"Are you doing this for your own personal benefit, or to help others?"

"Well, it's mainly for my family, and a little bit for me, too." She then added, "Dharalyn, I can't lose Biscuit. I've had her for years. Momma picked her out for me, when I was ten."

"Is this hurting anyone else?" Dharalyn asked.

Danielle shook her head. "No, except my aunt and father may have a tough time trusting me again, after today."

"Danielle, I've gotten to know you pretty well and I believe that you are a selfless person," Dharalyn said, softly. "I've seen firsthand how you put others ahead of yourself, even going so far as to put yourself in danger. Though this thing today does help you, ultimately it will save your family from a lot of grief and heartache. What does your heart tell you about what you are doing?"

"It tells me to do whatever I can to protect those I love, both people and animals."

"Then, if your heart is clear, allow nothing to deter you from your goal."

Danielle nodded; her eyes felt suddenly wet. "I don't know how this will play out today. I may need you to be...persuasive," she said, not sure how far she should go.

"Danielle, we are not ruffians. I will not commit an act of unwarranted offense against another. But, if anyone tries to lie, hurt or take unfair advantage of you, then I will bring to bear all that I have to defend and protect you. Remember, though; try primarily to use tact and persuasion in all things. Violence should only be used as a last resort, and only if it is premeditated by the other party."

"Will you know if anyone lies to us?"

Dharalyn smiled. "I will know. Ayowei serves me well in that way."

Danielle glanced at Dharalyn. "I've heard you use that term before. What is Ayowei?"

Dharalyn pursed her lips. "For eons, Sedai have used Ayowei, which we refer to as the lesser power, to complete simple tasks, though it is primarily used in helping us control the greater power, which we call Kamanah. Let me see, how to explain," she said, as she gathered her thoughts. "Ayowei is an energy source that exists deep within the Sedai; we store it there, and it is recharged through the medium of the spirit. In my world, Ayowei is very plentiful and I have never experienced any limit, or shortages. Here, however, for some reason, it recharges very slowly. When I am depleted, it takes nearly a full day for me to renew it."

"What do you use it for?" Danielle asked, her curiosity distracting her from her earlier thoughts.

"A lot of things. For example, I used it to color my hair. Um, I use it to quickly enter Kquwaya, which is referred to as battle-mode, by my people. While in this mode, it enhances my senses, strength and reflexes. I can use it to anchor me in a fight and to flash-move from one point to another."

"Anchor you. What's that?"

Dharalyn laughed. "I have read in your books, how some of these fictional characters fight. They run, punch and do things with no regard for the laws of physics. If I were to hit something, for instance, that contains more mass, or is carrying more momentum than I am, like for instance, a charging bear...."

Danielle smiled. "A charging bear. Where did you come up with that example?"

Dharalyn shrugged noncommittally. "Well, sometimes it happens."

Danielle giggled at the idea. "Rather unlikely, though...but, you were saying?"

"Well, if I were to, let's say, hit a large, heavy bear that was running at me, it would be me that would go flying, and not the animal. Do you see?"

Danielle shrugged. "Kinda, I guess."

"By anchoring myself into the surrounding firmament using Ayowei, I would be able to complete any task within the range of my strength. By anchoring, that which I am anchored into would absorb the energy of the charge and the bear would be knocked away, while I would remain where I was."

"So, you would be like an immovable boulder, anchored into the ground."

"Yeah, sorta. I am, of course, leaving a whole lot out. But you get the basic idea."

Danielle nodded. It all sounded pretty cool. As she turned the car onto highway 17, which was a four lane road and merged into the light traffic, she quizzed Dharalyn further. "So, what else can you do?"

Dharalyn smiled. "Well, what do you mean?"

"You know, the Ayowei power. What else does it let you do?"

Dharalyn continued, "Well, not all of us, but some of us, can do unique and unusual things with it."

"Like?"

"Well, for example, I've got two unique things I can do with it. One of them, which I discovered quite by accident, I call speed-flashing. It's a line of sight ability that lets me move, almost instantaneously, between two points. And then, there's something really extraordinary which the ancient texts refer to as Shonyemaya."

"What's that?"

"It's a talent that's an extremely rare occurrence among my people. In fact, there have only been two recorded accounts in the entire history of the Sedai, of people that have been able to do it."

"Well, what is it?"

Dharalyn thought carefully how best to explain. "It allows the individual to affect the flow of time. To see what is coming, to slow it and exist outside of it for a brief spell, and to even reverse it for a short period."

"Reverse it," said Danielle, in complete amazement. "You mean, like go back in time?"

"Yes, but only a very short distance, five minutes or so. It depends on a number of factors. Each minute of time requires an incrementally greater outflow of power, and so you are limited to the capacity of your Ayowei."

Danielle smiled, excited at the very idea. "And can you do this?" she asked, glancing at her friend's face.

Dharalyn paused, then. She had been explicitly warned by her mother and her aunt, never to divulge this information to anyone. But, they had not known Danielle, known the kind of person she was and the depth of her character. Slowly, she said, "Danielle, this is something that stays between us, and only us, okay?"

Danielle nodded; she could tell from the tone of Dharalyn's voice that she was very serious about this. She glanced over at her friend. "You can do it, can't you, Dharalyn?" said Danielle, with obvious pride in her voice. "That time reversal thing."

Dharalyn lowered her head and smiled. "Since I was very young, even before I knew how to control Ayowei properly. My mother said I would mention things to her, just before they happened. She called my aunt in on it and after the two of them conferred, they decided that it would be best to keep it secret. For now, anyway."

"I could see why that would be important. People might abuse it if they thought you could redo events, change the outcome of things."

Dharalyn grinned and patted Danielle's arm affectionately. "You are wise beyond your years, Danielle Walkerman."

Danielle laughed. "Why, thank you, Obi-wan." Danielle continued giggling at the perplexed look on Dharalyn's face, as she realized the girl hadn't the basic familiarity with contemporary media that would even begin to allow her to understand the humor in what she had just said. "Or, should I say, thank you, my instructor of mysterious, otherworldly concepts."

The rest of the trip passed quietly, each of the girls lost in their own introspective thoughts. As Danielle took the exit off highway 280 to highway 19, she felt her body tense up as they began crossing a bridge that spanned a small tributary, filled with muddy water. "I hate going over these old bridges," she said, nervously. "Most of them look so decrepit and rusty, like they're about to collapse." She'd only had her license for about six months and was still very uncomfortable navigating through heavy traffic, or driving in areas as confusing as New Jersey and New York City. After a few more minutes, she asked Dharalyn to help keep an eye out for their turnoff. Suddenly, realizing she was about to pass it, she careened crazily across two lanes of traffic, earning a din of angry horns and catcalls as she aimed directly for the exit. "God, I hate it down here," she said, with an edge of hysteria to her voice, as she made her way down a side street and then followed the GPS's instructions to a district full of old buildings and dingy streets. Looking on both sides of the road they were traveling, she soon spied what she was looking for. "Okay, here we go...we might as well go ahead and park, since I'm pretty sure the place we want is near here," she said, and dove into an open air parking lot, where she paid an attendant fifteen of her dwindling dollars for parking. Soon, she was gathering up her things and was about to exit the car, when Dharalyn grabbed her by the arm.

"Hold up," Dhara said, with an air of earnest intent. Taking Danielle's knapsack, she dug within it and pulled out the silver palm ornament, which she had been wearing on that first night. She then slipped two rings of the adornment over the second and fourth fingers of Danielle's right hand. A round talisman covered with strange markings pressed against her palm and then was attached to her wrist, while on the reverse side of her hand, a triangular shaped metallic piece fastened on the wide side, to the two rings and on the pointed side again, to a silver wristlet, which clasped about her wrist. When it was fastened in place, Dharalyn inspected it and then twisted something on the palm side of the unit. *It's some kind of device,* Danielle realized, as she felt a tingling sensation travel all over her body. "What is it?" she asked, with amazement.

"It acts as a body shield, against projectile and sharp edged weaponry. It will last for a full day, as long as it's charged up and I charged it myself, only a few days ago. It runs on Ayowei."

"Of course it does," laughed Danielle, and then said jokingly, "what doesn't." She paused then, with a sudden realization. "What about you, Dharalyn? Shouldn't you be wearing this?"

"I have Shonyemaya. If I have to avoid a weapon of some kind, I simply won't be there," she teased, and then added in a much more serious tone, "I have an intuitive feeling, Danielle, that we may be dealing with very unsavory people, today. I will feel much better knowing that you are safe."

"But, what about you!" said Danielle, becoming much more worried, now that they were actually here. "I mean, if we get into a situation, how do I know you will really be all right?"

Dharalyn smiled reassuringly. "Trust me, Danielle. I have trained all my life to deal with situations much more grave than we are likely to encounter today. If we do find ourselves in bad trouble, remember that I am your best friend and that I would never harm you. So if it should come down to it, do not be frightened by what you see me do."

Danielle nodded, not sure if that statement, which was apparently meant to reassure her, actually did. It sounded like Dharalyn possibly had a seriously badass side to her that, should Danielle see it in action, she might find it more than a little alarming. She thought back to the cabin, and how surreal and utterly scary Dharalyn had been, then. Danielle, to be honest, had been fearful for her life, at one point. She figured that the Jersey toughs had likely never encountered anyone with the capacity for violence that she strongly suspected was within Dharalyn's ability to provide, and should it come down to it, they would probably get their butts handed to them. Feeling better, Danielle nodded and opened her car door. "Okay, partner," she said, with an edge of tense nervousness. "Let's do this."

"One more second," said Dharalyn, as she quickly changed out of her top and put her dark blue one on, which had been part of the original outfit she'd worn when she first arrived here.

"I never realized how pretty that top is," said Danielle. "It looks really nice on you."

They walked along the sidewalk that paralleled Roosevelt, as Danielle gazed at the faded numbers on several boarded-up store fronts. "We're getting close," she said, and then heard someone whistle from across the street. She was wearing fairly new jeans and a faded burgundy top, nothing special. Certainly not whistle worthy, by any means. Dharalyn, on the other hand, was wearing one of her new sport-skirts, along with the dark blue top which accentuated her long black locks. Danielle realized that she probably should have made her change into some old jeans before they'd come down here, because, Danielle thought regretfully, she looked *sexy as hell*. Not the best way to dress when trying to remain inconspicuous in the city. "Don't pay them any attention," she said quietly, as a few bold comments were shouted in their general direction.

"Hey Baby, you need some help? You lost?"

"Mami chula!"

"Valla mami, que Buena tu estas!"

Some laughter followed, but Danielle paid them no mind. She had no time for idiots! Suddenly, she saw the building number they were looking for and made her way to the door, with Dhara in tow. The building looked like it had, at one time, been a retail shop of some kind and it still had the bars and shutters over all the ground floor windows. As she pushed open a heavy metal door, Danielle found herself inside a small, badly lit lobby, with squares of cracked blue and white linoleum on the floor, a few chairs and a single metal table against the right side wall. Along the back wall was another metal door, beside a wide countertop, which was studded every six inches with metal bars. This was backed by thick Plexiglas, that looked as if it was bulletproof and a slot in the very center, where transactions of an unknown kind took place. Behind the counter sat an old man of about sixty, in a white shirt, wearing a faded gray hat, smoking a cigar and reading the racing highlights. Danielle sized him up and then approached him, trying hard to sound confident. "Excuse me," she said, sounding a bit more timid than she liked, "but are you Samuel Remy?"

"Nope," he said, in a gravelly voice that sounded as if it had been worn down by sandpaper and the daily grind of a hard-scrabble life.

Danielle waited for the fellow to say something else, and after a moment, grumbled to herself. "Typical," she said, and then added in a voice she hoped was more forceful, "is he here?"

"Yep," answered the man as he turned a page and continued reading.

Danielle fumed. "Would you please get him for me?" she said, with all the firmness she could muster.

The man looked up from his paper, gave the two girls an appraising stare, one that to Danielle's consternation, lingered a little too long in Dharalyn's direction, and then turned and shouted into the back, "Sam, couple a young honeys out here want to see you!"

A voice called up from the back. "What the hell do they want?"

"What do you want?" the old man asked coldly, while staring again at Dharalyn in an unsettling manner.

"Charles Mason gave us his name, said he might be able to take some jewelry off our hands."

The man turned and shouted toward the back. "Charlie sent them. Got some jewelry for ya to look at."

"Send 'em back!" came the glib response. The guy then pointed toward the metal door and pushed a button.

Danielle went to the door and grabbed it as a buzzer sounded. *Must be some kind of remote lock,* she thought. Soon, the two were inside, as the man motioned for them to head on back.

"Second office to your right. Don't touch nothing!"

Danielle nodded and started walking back, with Dharalyn beside her. Once only, she glanced back to see that the old man was studying them intensely while they walked away. "Dirty old geezer," she mumbled, as she turned and made her way toward the second office. Soon, she was at the door and knocked on the doorjamb. "Come in," came a surly response, as she grabbed Dhara's right hand and walked inside. What met her eyes was a disheveled nightmare of an office. Stacks of sports magazines, half empty bottles of booze, girlie magazines that would have made her blush if she'd looked at them closer, and an assortment of other junk lay everywhere. Behind a large wooden desk sat an exorbitantly fat man, wearing, of all things, a colorful Hawaiian shirt and a straw hat. Behind him sat an enormous black metal safe that looked as if it was over a hundred years old and solid as the day it was made.

"Well, what a nice surprise this is!" he said, his tone lightening considerably. "I'll have to thank old Charlie, for brightening my day, with such a lovely pair of young ladies. Do sit down," he said, as he motioned toward a puffy chair, which was the only one on their side that was not covered with heaps of paraphernalia.

Danielle sat uncomfortably on one of the armrests, while Dharalyn took the other. "You Samuel Remy?" she asked, trying to sound mature and unruffled.

"I am," he said, with a friendly air. "Can I get you two gorgeous ladies a drink?"

"That's okay," said Danielle, "We don't usually drink this early in the day." She noticed Dharalyn's piercing glance, but chose to ignore it as she continued. "We're kind of in a hurry, so I'd like to get to the point."

"Please do," said Samuel, all amiable and as pleasant as he could be.

Danielle tried returning his smile, as she ordered her thoughts. "We are in the possession of some diamonds that we need to sell," she said, her voice trembling and nervous, rather than the confident and mature tone she'd been trying for. Now that she was actually here and talking to someone, she found that her heart was in her throat and her palms were sweating profusely. "They aren't stolen, or anything like that. It's just that we might have a hard time explaining how we have come by them, if asked by those in more official channels."

Samuel chuckled. "That's what I'm here for, honey. To help those in need, with these sorts of minor difficulties. Can I see the items in question?"

Danielle handed him a small felt tie-bag, in which she had received some cheap earrings, a few years back. Inside were two of the smallest stones. She had brought the bag for just this purpose, since she did not want to hand over their entire stash of thirty-two stones to anyone, until she was comfortable with the idea.

Samuel opened the bag and dropped the two stones into his hand.

Danielle noticed his eyes getting noticeably wider as he gazed at them, and wondered if they were worth more than she had first thought.

Reaching into a drawer, he quickly pulled out a loupe, which was a hand magnifier that jewelers used to look for clarity and inclusions. As he looked through the hand held lens, his expression got increasingly strange as he perused the stones, his eyes squinting and becoming almost feral. He glanced up at the two of them for a brief moment, with a thoughtful look on his face, and then returned to his inspection. After a few minutes had passed, he carefully put the stones back into the bag and placed it on the desk in front of him. "These are," he paused, as if searching for the exact words to use, "very high quality stones. I can find no inclusions with my hand loupe, though a more powerful magnifier may, under proper lighting conditions." He brushed a handkerchief across his forehead and dropped it over the bag. "I'm not gonna ask you where you got these, but I need to know. Are these all you have?"

Danielle shook her head. "No sir, we have thirty-two in all."

"Thirty-two!" Samuel mused, his eyes wide with surprise. "Thirty-two such stones. Well, I've gotta tell ya, sweet thing, as much as I'd like to, I can't help you with these."

Danielle felt her heart drop. "What! Why not? If you can't, do you know someone who can?"

Samuel thought for only a moment. "I have a business partner who'll take them, I'm sure of it. I'll write down his address and call to let him know that you're coming." He quickly wrote down an address and handed it to Danielle.

"Oh God, it's in Brooklyn," she said, with obvious dismay.

"It's easy to get to," said Samuel. "Just take the Holland Tunnel to Canal Street and you're practically there.

Danielle stood up. "Okay then, thanks for all your help," she said, as she reached out and, removing the cloth that Samuel Remy had laid across it, picked up the small bag and began to put it into her pocket.

"Here, I'll take. that, Danielle," said Dharalyn, suddenly. She sounded a bit on edge, like a circular saw that was idling, and just waiting to rev up and rip through a pile of lumber.

"What!" said Danielle, sensing that something was amiss.

"Go on outside the door and wait for me. I'll join you in just a minute."

Danielle hesitated for only a moment, and then walked to the door, opened it, and closed it behind her, when Dharalyn motioned for her to do so.

"So, what's on your mind, sweetheart?" asked Samuel, his tone filled with vinegar, rather than the honey he'd employed earlier.

"You palmed the two stones and slipped two pieces of metal into the bag. I want our stones back, right now."

Samuel grinned. The hot little piece of trim was right, of course, though he was surprised to have gotten caught, especially by one like her. No one had ever caught him pulling the old switcheroo, before. He was tempted to reach into the drawer for his thirty-eight special, but then, he realized, he didn't need a gun to scare the panties off this little bit of fluff. Samuel glared at her, in the manner he used when bullying his underlings. "You know, I don't much like your smart-ass attitude there, little lady. You come down here to my place looking to score a deal and you have the nerve to talk to me like that!" he snarled, beginning to get angry now. "Far as the stones go...why, we're just gonna call them a finder's fee, and if you have a problem with that, I got me a couple of fellows in the back, that will be glad to explain exactly how things work down here in the Boroughs. They'll bust a few of them pretty fingers a yours, with a piece of heavy lead pipe and when you're hurting so bad you want to die, and begging them to stop, well, then maybe, just maybe...I'll let you go, provided I'm feeling charitable. Or hell, we might just decide to go ahead, and get real down and nasty with the two of you. Get you pretty young things pumped up on some junk, that'll make you all nice and passive. Then, I'll let some of the boys spend a few days teaching you how to be real wimmen, doing what your kind are meant to do," he said, his eyes glinting with an oddly visceral glee, as he got more and more into his foul rant.

"You like to hurt people, don't you, Samuel," she said calmly, and to Samuel's consternation, seemed eerily composed as she walked around his desk to his chair. "You enjoy making them uncomfortable and threatening them with harm. You actually relish any opportunity to frighten those you perceive as weaker than you, and you like to inflict pain, whenever possible. Am I correct in this assumption?"

His eyes got bright with delight, as his smile widened. "Well, now that you mention it...it is one of my own, personal pleasures," he said, as he began to feel a sense of eager anticipation course through him. "Does pretty little kitty want to play rough with ol' Sam?"

"You know, Samuel, where I come from, my people are by the grace of Anon, referred to as the Arbiters of Justice. And my mother, by her birthright, was the Ultimate Arbiter of the people of the Amalgamation Worlds. What this means is, as the Khan-Tessera of the Sedai Novi, hers was the absolute right to stamp out evil, or right any wrong, as she saw fit. Though she is no longer with us, I am her heir, and while this is not the world I come from, I believe that Anon's influence holds sway here, just as it does where I come from, and with that presumption, so would his precepts. And so, though none of this may make much sense to you, there is one thing you need to understand."

Dharalyn's voice became deeply aggressive, like the guttural growl of the lone tigress warning the foolish hunter who stalks her cubs, "Though I am still uncertain as to my exact place in this world, and for that reason must and should show restraint, be aware, I will not allow you to continue on with your evil ways, unchecked. Or to put it more simply, in terms you should understand, give me my stones you rotten little thief, or you will suffer my wrath!"

Samuel was dumbstruck for only a moment, and then laughed heartily, as he stared at the girl with wide-eyed disbelief. Reaching out his left hand, he grabbed her roughly by the arm and pulled her close, while reaching for the phone with his right. "You're a crazy little bitch, aren't you? Completely out of your friggin, lunatic mind. Tell you what I've decided to do...I'm gonna call for my boys, to come and take you for a little walk. You go on ahead and show me some a your wrath, while we wait, sweetheart," he said, and grinned widely. This was going to be fun.

Danielle stood outside the office, gazing around the poorly-lit hallway, while trying hard to relax. "What the heck is taking her so long?" she said, after a few minutes had passed. She was beginning to get bored and didn't like not knowing what was going on. She was just about to knock on the door, when she heard a yelp of sheer terror coming from inside the office, followed by what sounded like something heavy being smashed hard against the wall. This was quickly followed by a lot of blubbering and wailing, mixed with a lot of intensely profuse begging. Mystified, she stood her ground, knowing full well that Samuel had tried to pull something in there and suspecting, also, that Dharalyn was probably making him an offer he couldn't refuse. A moment later, Dharalyn came calmly out of the office door and handed the small felt bag to Danielle, while waving her hand in front of her face.

"Okay, we're good now. Let's get out of here, before I choke to death. On to the next place."

"Is he all right in there?" asked Danielle, a bit of mirth playing across her features and then added, "What the heck is that awful smell?"

"He's okay. He just soiled himself, is all."

"Did he switch the stones on us?"

Dharalyn smiled and nodded. "You saw that? Good girl."

Danielle beamed. "Daddy didn't raise no fool. I just didn't know what to do about it."

"Well, I did," said Dharalyn. "He just needed me to explain that he needs to stop being such a bad person and if he doesn't see the error of his ways, he will be punished harshly."

Danielle chuckled loudly, as they made their way out of the building and back out to the street. "God, Dharalyn, having you around is just like having my own personal Terminator," she said, and then giving her best Schwarzeneggery impression, she added, "don't mess with me human, or else, I'll be back!" Danielle grinned widely at the extremely confused expression that appeared on Dharalyn's face, and spent the entire trek back to the car explaining to Dharalyn who the Terminator was, and what the significance of her statement had been.

"So, you think I'm a human, cyborg robot?" asked Dharalyn in a perfectly casual tone, still not getting the comparison.

"God, kill me now!" Danielle exclaimed, as she silently promised herself to never, ever again use any movie analogies in Dharalyn's presence.

CHAPTER 14

BROOKLYN OR BUST

The girls stood before the steel and glass building in the heart of Brooklyn that matched the address which Samuel Remy had given them. It was a fairly modern building, about fifteen stories tall, with a gray marble facade and several marble columns, framing the main lobby.

"It kind of looks like a bank," said Danielle, gazing at the huge, twenty-foot windows that graced the small plaza along the front. She wouldn't admit it out loud, but she was a little afraid to go in. This was not some sleazy, backstreet pawn broker. This was the building of a powerful corporation, full of movers and shakers, who were used to dealing with consummate professionals, not a couple of naïve young girls from a small, backwater town. It was becoming pretty clear to her that they would be at the charitable mercy of whoever they were supposed to meet with here, and she was certain it would be someone who was used to getting his way.

"You ready?" asked Dharalyn, noticing the apprehensive look on Danielle's face.

"I guess so," she said, and then turned. "I just realized something. What if Samuel didn't call ahead, like he said he would? If he didn't, we're screwed."

"Oh, he called. I'm certain of it."

"How can you be so sure?" Danielle said. She was plainly trying to talk herself out of doing this.

Dharalyn grabbed her hand to reassure. "Because, I told him that if he didn't do like he promised, I would be back to see him."

"So, I take it you used the old, drill them and fill them with dread technique, which is a subset of the shock and awe methodology of proactive persuasion."

"The...what?"

Danielle shook her head and smiled to herself. "Nothing...just something my uncle told me about, once or twice." She could only imagine what Dharalyn had done to Samuel Remy during her little talk, though from the sounds that she had heard, it had been intense. "You show him your teeth?" she asked, curious, in spite of herself.

Dharalyn laughed at Danielle's tone. "Maybe," was all she would say.

"Okay, then, I guess we should have no problem." Moments later, they were standing in the main foyer, in front of the security desk, talking to a well-muscled tank of a man, dressed in what looked like a tailored suit. "Excuse me," Danielle said, her voice sounding, even to her, kind of small and meek. "We were sent here by Samuel Remy, to see someone about a...jewel transaction."

The hulking form nodded, picked up a phone and spoke into it for a moment. After hanging up, he came out from behind the station and motioned for the two girls to follow him. "I will take you up," he said, in a deep voice that sounded as if it were used to getting exactly what it wanted. Once inside the security elevator, the man ran a keycard through a slot and then pushed the button for the fifteenth floor.

Looks like we are going to see the top guy, thought Danielle, who knew from watching television, that all the company CEOs had their offices on the top floors, because that was the most prestigious location in any building.

After the elevator reached the top floor, the security guard took them to the end of a luxuriously paneled hallway, where a beautiful woman wearing a dark blue business dress suit, sat at an all glass desk in a very tasteful, yet chic, front office. This was plainly the administrative assistant's alcove for a top executive and a few moments later, the woman motioned for them to go on in. The guard opened the double wide doors, letting them inside and then closed them, while staying outside in the alcove.

"Hello," came a friendly and charming voice, from across a very wide and expansive office. A middle-aged man dressed in a tailored and obviously very expensive black suit walked over to the two girls and extended a hand. "I am Antonello Michael Moretti, but everyone here calls me Michael."

From the strong Italian accent, Danielle had little doubt as to the fellow's nationality. *Oh God, we're in it deep now,* she thought, as she wished fervently that she could start the day over and never undertake this bad idea, which was quickly turning into an absolute fiasco. Gathering her wits about her, she decided to give it her best, even though they would likely end up in a pair of cement shoes by the day's end. "Hello, Michael," she said, with a confidence she did not feel. "I am Danielle and this is Dhara. We have come to you with a little business proposition."

"Very good," he said, as he motioned them over to a small coffee table, which was surrounded by several cushioned chairs. "Please, ladies, do sit down. First, let me offer you some wine, or perhaps just some coffee."

Danielle considered quickly and then decided to play it up, lest he take them as scared and nervous young girls, which, of course, they were! Danielle looked at Dharalyn and saw that she was surprisingly calm, and appeared to be completely at ease. *Okay, so it's just me who's terrified,* she thought, and then said, "Yes, I will have a glass of wine, thank you."

"Excellent. Bruno, get these ladies a glass of wine. Pour us some of that Chianti, from the old country."

Danielle glanced behind her and saw a large, powerful man, striding over to a fully stocked wet bar, at the same time noticing another man, as well, standing guard by the double doors they had just come through.

Michael Moretti sat across from his two young guests, his mind racing as he wondered exactly what their game was. He knew about the diamonds. And he knew, too, that Samuel wouldn't waste his time and send them to him, unless they were on the level. But, he'd been in this business for a long time, and he had learned to be careful. Things were not always what they seemed, at first glance. Here he was, talking to two very young ladies, probably seventeen, eighteen years of age and something about it chafed. The one that had been doing all the talking was quite attractive, in a plainer sense of the word. But the other was an angel in the making, as beautiful as the loveliest of sonnets had ever sought to describe. These two were a mystery, and that was what had him concerned. First, Samuel Remy hadn't owned up to it, but something had left him very rattled. His voice had possessed a nervous edge to it, and he had pushed very hard for Michael to see these two today, in fact, he had almost insisted, which was strange in and of itself. Secondly, there was the extreme youth of these two and the fact that they seemed to be so very forthright, and downright unafraid. Not so much the talkative one, perhaps, but the other one. The little dark haired beauty; she had eyes that bore right through you and bespoke something he'd rarely seen in his presence, and certainly never from a woman. *Fearlessness!* And lastly, where did girls like these two come by the remarkable stones, which Samuel had sworn to him that they had in their possession? He was intrigued by these two, though he would certainly pass up this opportunity if he sensed, for even a moment that he was, indeed, being played for a fool by one of his enemies or some other, unknown entity. He wouldn't bat an eye at the stones, even though diamonds were a secret passion of his and he usually went to great lengths and utilized any means necessary to acquire the very finest specimens. He would leave these be if he harbored any uncertainty as to the soundness of this matter. His unfaltering conviction shattered however, ten minutes later, as he pored over the stones with a loupe he kept close at hand. He couldn't be entirely sure without his gemologist taking a closer look, but he was fairly certain he was looking at the finest specimens of diamonds he had ever personally seen. The cut, the clarity, the brilliance, the color, all were magnificent! Trying desperately to control his excitement, Michael Moretti took the bag of thirty-two stones and promised the girls he would make them an offer which would make them happy. He stayed away from telling them that he would make them an offer *they could not refuse,* only because the statement was a little too trite for his sensibilities to handle. Although, when it came right down to it, that was exactly what he would do. Make them an offer that they would simply accept, or else.

Danielle and Dharalyn found themselves escorted outside, after Michael promised them that he would make them a fair offer and have their money in about an hour. "Go and grab yourselves a bit of lunch," he had said, with complete equanimity, "while my diamond expert gives me a fair appraisal, and I can make you an offer for the stones." Dharalyn had nodded her approval to Danielle, sensing his sincerity, and the fact that, at the moment, he meant to follow through and make good on this deal.

It was only after the girls left and he had spoken to his expert that Michael reconsidered. He'd rather not part with such a large sum of money, and in fact, was beginning to realize, with an inward laugh, that he had no real reason to deal with them at all, anymore. He, after all, had the stones in his possession and they had as much as said they had no proof where they had gotten them. It was plain they had no one who could force him to make good; after all, you didn't send a couple of young girls to deal with a person of his caliber, if you had someone tougher in the wings. These two were on their own in this, he was certain of it. Still, they were a pretty pair and it was obvious that they needed the money. He wasn't feeling guilty, for he had no compunction about getting over on them. Taking advantage of people was basically what he did for a living, pretty much on a daily basis. But, he was feeling the tiniest bit bad that they would come away from all this with nothing at all. Feeling oddly generous, Michael went to his wall safe, opened it and counted out ten one-hundred dollar bills. Stuffing them into an envelope, he sent Bruno down to the security desk with instructions to give the money to the girls when they returned. Smiling, he felt better that he had done at least that much. Going back to his desk, he poured the diamonds out on the glass top and began to look at them again with his loupe. Fantastic, just absolutely marvelous!

Jack Harold Walkerman had worked for the FBI for nearly twenty years, and had seen it all. Right now, he and his team had the Quest Financial Plaza under surveillance, from a leased office in an adjacent building. It was a thankless task at best, but one that was necessary, to build up a list of known associates of the Moretti family, which was under investigation for suspicion of federal racketeering and money laundering. He had sent most of his team out on other resource gathering tasks, and was manning the bank of monitors and computers with which they were keeping the building and grounds under surveillance, with the help of several dozen strategically planted cameras and a few dozen high powered microphones. He was rarely surprised by anything life threw at him anymore, and he was a bit of a loner, no wife, no kids of his own. His primary source of familial ties came when he would visit his brother John's family, which he tried to do on major holidays, and on rare occasions when he was able to squeeze out a little vacation time. Though he would be loath to admit it openly, everyone in the family knew that the main reason he visited as much as he did, was because he positively doted on his niece, Danielle. In fact, John's dear, departed Marilyn had liked to kid him about it sometimes. "You wouldn't come here half as much if not for her, would you, Jack?" she had teased, and he had grinned back, the truth on his face for anyone to see. In his heart, he liked to think there was a part of him that yearned for what John had, but that really wasn't accurate, at all. He just wasn't cut from domestic cloth, and needed the excitement his work usually provided, in spades. Yet, whenever he was there, one thing was abundantly clear to the whole family; he absolutely adored his little Danielle, though if asked, he would have found the exact reasons hard to explain. It was in part, he supposed, because she always surprised him and had a peculiar way of looking at things, that he admired. And then, there was the fact that she was smart, whip-smart he had called her, and quicker than anyone when it came to learning a self-defense move he'd showed her, or simply remembering a piece of sound advice. He could teach her basic or sometimes even advanced FBI training techniques, such as, tactical examples of how to disarm an attacker, or how to quickly and efficiently quarter and search a dangerous building, and days later she would demonstrate the moves perfectly, or recite the verbal lesson back to him, word for word. Jack shook his head; he loved...absolutely loved that little girl, so very much. They had so many characteristics in common, he thought wistfully, same wild spirit, same inexorable curiosity for the unexplainable and mysterious side of life. After all, look at all those bizarre books she read. Though much of it was complete nonsense, it had made her much more open minded and keenly aware of things other people would never question. For this and other reasons, he thought that someday, she might even make a first rate agent. The thought made him smile; it would be nice to be able to share with her some of the things he knew. Things that would outright shock most folks and make them question their own sensibilities. Jack placed his hands behind his head and stretched out his legs with a yawn of pure tedium, while once again scanning the displays. *This task is about as mundane as it gets,* he thought, and then sighed, as he wondered where Danielle was today and what she might be doing, right now. He really needed to get down to his brother's house and see her soon. He had heard from Sara that she was really having a tough time, poor kid, and regretted not being there for her, more than he had been. Lost in his personal thoughts, he began to wonder why he had even agreed to take this nothing case. *After all,* he thought, *not a damn thing is likely to happen on this stakeout.* He'd be lucky if he even managed to stay awake for the rest of his shift. Which was probably why, he had decided later on when recalling this exact moment, the universe had decided it was time to give him a good jolt. A nice piece of an enigma wrapped in a bit of a cosmic prank, of sorts. How else did you define it, when the object of your recent thoughts and concerns appeared precisely at that moment on the video screens in front of you, with another girl her age and walked into the building he and his team had under surveillance?

And not just any building, but one that was full of people who were known underworld types and currently on the FBI's hot-watch list! The fires of his concern were suddenly stoked to a new high, as he watched the bank of monitors, closely. Then, a little over an hour later, Danielle nonchalantly exited the building and walked off with her young friend in tow. As surprised as he had been by this, he was even more startled when less than an hour later, she returned, went back into the building and then exited again about ten minutes later, plainly very upset and disgruntled about something. He grabbed the headphones and twirled the controls that moved one of the remote microphones, located on the roof of this building, to pick up what they were saying. The mics were calibrated to pick up reflected waves from the windows of the Moretti building, but with a little fiddling, he managed to eavesdrop on the girls, standing on the ground, although the sound was somewhat muffled.

"I can't believe it, Dharalyn. That lousy, thieving bastard! A thousand dollars.... Is he kidding us? What a major slap in the face. I'd love to shove this money right up his damn...."

"Danielle!" exclaimed Dharalyn, cutting her foul expletive off, before she could finish. "Be careful...besides, we're not done, yet."

"What do you mean, we're not done? We are done, Dharalyn! There is no way we are going to be able to get up that security elevator, without one of those security cards, and, oh yeah, without ticking off the half dozen armed guards standing around in the foyer."

Dharalyn, meanwhile, was glancing overhead. She studied the building off to their right and then grabbed Danielle by the hand. "Come on...I have an idea!"

Danielle spluttered angrily, "Idea, I have an idea, too. I say we wait for him to come out and then...."

"Danielle!" said Dharalyn, sharply. "That isn't being helpful. I think, perhaps, it's time to try some shock and awe. You remember shock and awe, don't you?"

Danielle nodded silently and followed Dharalyn like a docile puppy. She was depressed and completely without hope, at a loss as to how this day could get worse. The spiritual puppet masters that oversaw life had apparently seen her coming and had rubbed their hands together with glee. *Oh look, here comes that fool, Danielle! Let's screw her over again, it's easy to do.* She kept up a steady, running commentary in her mind, until finally, she simply ran out of steam. *Where the heck are we going?* she thought to herself, as she followed Dhara into another building that was just across the plaza from the one that the hated Michael Moretti inhabited.

"Wait here a second," Dharalyn said, and then approached a tired looking guard, who immediately perked up when Dharalyn walked up to him. They talked for a little while and then she saw Dharalyn smile, thank him and come back over to where she was standing. "Follow me," she instructed, and headed for the elevators. After the doors opened, the two girls got in and then Dharalyn punched in the top floor.

Danielle shook her head and muttered, "Where are we going?"

"It's a surprise," Dharalyn said, and smiled.

"I don't like surprises much, Dhara," said Danielle, in a tone that exuded childlike petulance.

Dharalyn grinned. Soon, the elevator doors opened and she turned toward the right, hurriedly leading Danielle to a heavy, steel door at the end of a hall. The door was labeled 'Roof Access' and was locked. Dharalyn took hold of the door handle and concentrated. Suddenly, Danielle heard a pronounced click and within seconds, Dharalyn was off again, climbing a steeply inclined set of steel stairs with Danielle following silently behind.

"You know, I don't know what you think this is gonna do for us," said Danielle, her voice tinged with sardonic ire. "In case you haven't realized, this is the wrong building."

"I know what building this is, Danielle," replied Dharalyn calmly, as she opened another locked door which led out onto the roof. Danielle had never cared much for heights and so, she timidly followed Dhara out onto the rooftop, staying far back from the edge. She paused, as she gazed all around her. She could see a huge mound of what was apparently air conditioning equipment behind them, as well as a myriad of pipes and air ducts. Dharalyn had made her way fairly close to the edge of the roof, and she motioned for Danielle to come and join her. At first, Danielle shook her head vehemently back and forth in the negative, letting Dhara know that there was absolutely no way she was moving from her current spot, but then, Dharalyn called to her:

"Please, Danielle, trust me. I think I have a way for us to get over to the other building."

Danielle glared briefly at her friend, in way of response, and battling nearly catatonic fear, she slowly and with great care, placed one tentative foot in front of the other until, after almost a minute passed, she managed to reach Dhara's side. The other building's roof looked to be about two stories lower than the one they were on, and there was a gap of at least a hundred and fifty feet, if not more, between the two buildings. "Well, there's no way we're gonna jump that," she said, nervously. She was feeling a bit light-headed and was extremely uncomfortable this close to the brink of the building, especially since the parapet around the edge of the roof only appeared to be about three feet high. "Can we please go back down, now?" she asked, hopefully, her voice trembling.

"Not yet, Danielle! We have a meeting to keep with a very bad man."

"Yeah, sure, but I don't see how that's gonna work, from way over here!" Danielle hollered, over a loud gust of wind.

"Just remember that I love you, Danielle, and I would never allow you to come to harm," stated Dharalyn, succinctly.

"That's good to know," replied Danielle, as she turned to go back down. Suddenly, she stopped, her eyes growing wide with amazement and disbelief. Dharalyn's eyes had changed and were now like shining green emeralds, her hair was bright white and broad silvery wings sprouted out behind her, a strong, thin frame-work, unfolding and glistening in shiny translucence. *"Oh...My... God.... Freaking Wings!"* she gasped, her body frozen and dumb-struck with awe. Just then, Danielle recalled the two slits she had discovered on the back of Dharalyn's blouse, and now all the mystery of their current location came sharply into focus. *Wings, she has to have the slits to allow her wings to unfold.* She stood there, grinning like an idiot, as she took it all in. *This was amazing!* She had never dreamed Dharalyn could do something like this, that she had wings that would probably allow her to fly. "OH, CRAP!"

she said aloud. "Don't tell me you plan to fly across?" The sudden realization of what that fact meant to her personally, slammed into her like a battering ram, just as Dharalyn picked her up in a cradle hold and quickly took the last few steps towards the edge of the building. The piercing shriek within her built and let loose as Dharalyn launched herself from the top of the parapet. "DHARAAAAAAA!!!!!!!!" she screamed, at the top of her lungs, and watched helplessly as they launched into empty air, and then raced across the broad expanse to the other building's roof. Even when they touched down, Danielle was still making a loud, shrieking, breathy noise, her arms wrapped tightly around Dharalyn's neck.

"Danielle, my dear friend, it's okay!" yelled Dharalyn, as Danielle fought to stop hyperventilating and tried to calm down. "We made it; you don't have to yell, anymore."

Danielle took a couple of deep breaths as she released her hold. Her throat hurt and she was still a trifle winded from all the screaming. After a few more minutes, she realized that they were, indeed, on top of the other building. She glanced at Dharalyn and was surprised to see that the vampire was back to her old self, no wings and black hair. "So, what now?" she asked, with a shaky voice, still terribly unsettled.

"Shock and awe, I suppose," said Dharalyn.

Danielle pointed an accusing finger at her friend. "Remind me to kill you tomorrow, after I've recovered from having near heart failure."

Dharalyn nodded and grinned widely, while waiting patiently for Danielle to pull herself together.

Suddenly, Danielle got very still, as an incredible idea swept through her, an idea so buoyant, so thick with details, that it took a few moments for her to sift through it all and put the pieces in their proper order. Finally, she had it. For it to work, though, she would have to be utterly and completely convincing, an actress of the first magnitude, and that meant she could show no doubt, no fear, no lack of confidence. An hour ago, she couldn't have done it, but she had just flown between two buildings, carried across by a vampire. Not a fictional creature, but the real thing. The

fundamental truth of what that meant, in this Hollywood era society, carried within it a lot of power. A lot of mysticism, which had
its own *je ne sais quoi*, as the French said, that something special
which could make this all work, if she could sell it. "Dhara," said
Danielle, her voice tinged with growing enthusiasm. "Are you sure
this thing works, and will stop bullets?" she asked, holding out her
palm. Dhara checked the device, making certain it was still on.

"I am positive, Danielle," she stated, sincerely. "No projectile of
this world can harm you while you wear a Pametra."

"I have an idea," said Danielle, gravely. "I need you to follow
my lead, when we go down to see our friend, Michael." She then
explained her idea, carefully, and with increasing passion, as the
details slowly unfolded.

Dharalyn nodded and smiled her approval as she listened,
impressed with her friend's imaginative plan. They would need to
sell this with complete conviction, and she told Danielle so. There
would be no room for mistakes or bad judgment calls. *This just
might work, though,* Dhara thought hopefully.

Michael Moretti smiled with satisfaction, as he placed the diamonds back into the bag he had stored them in and prepared to
place them in his vault. A sudden commotion outside his office
door startled him and he heard his secretary's shrill voice, saying,
"You can't go in there!" Turning, he glanced toward the entrance
and his jaw hit the ground, figuratively speaking, as two people he
had never expected to see again, walked boldly into his office.

"How the hell did you two get in here?" he asked, as the
two young girls from earlier strode forward like they owned the
damn place. "Get them outa here!" he shouted, at his two guards.
Immediately, Carlos walked over to the brown haired girl and
grabbed her from behind, only to be flipped over and sent sprawl-
ing some ten feet away from her. Bruno grabbed at the black
haired beauty and Michael stared as the two hundred and fifty
pound gorilla was sent flying backward, the loud smacking report
of her punch reverberating off the walls of his office. He stared
in shock at the crumpled form of one of his toughest men, taken
down by a single punch from a petite girl. *A girl!*

"You're in way over your head here, Michael. Call off your bully boys or we're gonna start getting serious," said Danielle, her voice pitched in a seriously threatening tone. She was utterly shocked at the fact that she had somehow taken down the hefty guard who had grabbed her, but she tried not to let it show. She thought, then, of how a two-hundred-year-old, arrogant and physically superior vampire would feel and act in this type of situation. She tried to wear the sense of it about her like a cloak, allowing it to fill her and looking with disdain upon the mere mortal who had offended her being. Basically, she was self-hypnotizing herself, with as much crap as she could stomach.

Antonello Michael Moretti didn't get where he was by being a fool. There was something strange going on here and it puzzled him, and he was determined to discover what, exactly, it was, before making his next move. He would see what these babes had to say for themselves and then take them out, the hard way. It would also give the rest of his men time to get up here to his office from the security area. Once the numbers were on his side, these two would think twice about playing rough.

Danielle eyed Michael with a glaring stare. "You disappoint me, Michael.... We give you a chance to enter the threshold of a new world and you treat us with this...disrespect!"

Michael shrugged; he had no idea what the little bitch was talking about and to be honest, he really didn't care. It would all be over soon, anyway.

"I know what you are probably thinking, Michael, and I can assure you, you're perception about this matter is grossly incor-:ect, so let's cut to the chase, shall we?"

Michael nodded and folded his arms in a power posture, still not impressed. "What do you have in mind?" was all he said.

"Do either of your boys have a pistol, preferably one with a silencer?"

Michael nodded again, although the request did surprise him. "Certainly...I keep one over there, in my right hand desk drawer."

"Have one of your men go and get it, would you, please?"

Happy to oblige, Michael motioned for Bruno, who was now up on his legs again, to go and get the gun. He didn't let his guys carry personal pieces in his presence. You couldn't be too careful, these days.

A moment later, Bruno had the HK forty-five, which was fitted with a silencer, in his hand and stood waiting for his boss's instructions.

"Have him fire it at me, if you would be so kind. Go for a kill shot," said Danielle, praying that Dharalyn knew what she was doing.

Michael frowned; crazy little bitch wanted to die. Well, okay then, he had wanted to put new carpet in the office, anyway. He nodded and watched, as Bruno fired off four quick rounds in succession, at her chest. Pop, pop, pop, pop went the pistol, as the silencer muffled the reports of the firing bullets. Then, Michael felt a distinct wave of nausea and dizziness sweep over him as the girl, who was obviously and unbelievably not dead, knelt down and picked something up off the floor. He watched, spellbound, as she walked over to him and dropped the four silver slugs into his hand. They were flattened from the impact and still very hot to the touch.

"Want to talk, now?"

Michael nodded, as the main doors opened and five more of his guys piled into the room. He paused for a brief moment, thinking fast and then shouted, sternly, "Hold up, I want all of you guys to step outside this office. Get out of here, now!" he added hoarsely, when they stood, milling around confusedly. He watched as slowly, the dumbfounded looking men left the room. Bruno looked at him, the expression on his face plainly disturbed. Bruno had never been scared before, that Michael could ever remember, but he was definitely on edge, now. Michael motioned for him to leave as well, and waited until the guard closed the outer doors. "Okay, you got my attention, girlie. What gives?"

Danielle folded her arms. "What gives is this. I represent a very old and royal vampire family that wishes to expand its holdings, here in the states. We are known as the Vulkiri and we are headed by a very old and powerful vampire prince, known as the Walker Man."

Michael chuckled uneasily. "Sweetheart, you pull a mean trick there, with the bullets and all, but there ain't no frigging way I'm gonna believe in some vampire bullcrap. You need to come up with a whole lot better story than that."

Danielle walked up to Michael and stared angrily into his eyes. "I am over one hundred years old. My sister, there, is over three hundred. I am becoming increasingly offended by your poor attitude, Michael. Maybe I will take my diamonds and go to one of the other families. Perhaps they would be more appreciative of our gesture of friendship."

"Say what you will, I say it's all crap. You say you're a vampire, well then, prove it!"

"Dhara," said Danielle, calmly, giving Michael as unflinching a stare as she could muster. "Show him your true form, please."

A moment later, Michael felt the color drain from his face as he gazed at the green-eyed, winged vamp goddess, that was the stuff of legends and nightmares. She had transformed right in front of him and when she'd smiled at him, revealing her fangs, he could not help the streak of icy fear that raced up his spine. A long moment passed, as his brain desperately worked to process this stunning revelation. "My apologies, my lady," stammered Michael, as he quickly backpedaled from his previous conviction. "I meant no disrespect. I'm with you, all the way. You can count on me, from here on out. We can definitely do business, your family and mine. Oh," he paused, as he tried to figure how best to repair the damage done in their original meeting, "and about our earlier misunderstanding. I will be glad to advance you, uh, sixty percent of the value of your gems."

"Eighty percent," said Dharalyn, firmly, and as she moved closer to Michael, gave him a wickedly fanged grin.

"Eighty percent, yes...absolutely! Fair as fair can be. I hope that your family and mine can have a long and beneficial relationship."

"I don't see why not. We do not bear you any grudge, as to your previous insult to our integrity and trust. We will of course expect you to deal with us fairly from here on out, though."

"Of course, of course," said Michael. "Let me get you your money right now. Will cash be all right?"

"That will be fine," said Dharalyn. "And Michael...."

"Yes," he replied, as amiable as he could be, desperately wanting to get back on good terms with the vampires.

"Our anonymity is extremely vital to us. Not one word of our connection or dealings with you from here on, will be tolerated. As head of your family, we will hold you ultimately responsible for the discretion of your people."

"Absolutely," said Michael, as he moved to a large corner safe that was open and began to count out thick stacks of money, placing them into a duffel bag he had on hand. He would have to have a talk with a couple of his guys, and if they didn't understand, then they would have to disappear. He wasn't about to take any chances. He knew a fair bit about vampire mystique and an interesting thought had made its way into the forefront of his mind. Most people might fear a situation like this, but he saw only the advantages. Vampires were apparently not fictional at all, but quite real, in every sense of the word. This singular fact spoke to a profoundly basic level of his psyche, a deeper, darker yearning, that excited him. Immortality was calling him. If he did a really good job for them, perhaps they would welcome him into their family. He would make a fine vampire.

FBI agent Jack Walkerman nearly jumped out of his skin, as he saw Danielle and her friend exiting from the front doors of the Quest Financial Plaza. His mind raced furiously, as he contemplated the situation that currently presented itself. *Where had the girls come from? The problem was, he hadn't a damn clue!* He checked the computers which monitored all of the access points to the building and kept video logs within the software, any time someone went in or out of one of the service doors, or side doors of the building. *There was nothing there!* This place was locked down tight. Everyone came and went from the front foyer. He shook his head, as perplexed as he was annoyed. There was something strange going on here, something that made absolutely no sense. Jack thought for a while and looked at his watch. His replacement would be coming in just a little while. Jack perused the monitoring equipment for a bit more, his uncertainty growing, and then did something he had never done, in all his years in the agency. He reached out with a mouse pointer and copied all of the files that showed his beloved Danielle's comings and goings from the building to a personal flash drive, deleting the originals when he'd finished. He didn't know exactly what was going on, but he would get to the bottom of this himself, preferably without the agency's interference.

CHAPTER 15

AN UNEXPECTED SURPRISE

Danielle knew she was in for it when they walked in through the kitchen door. Aunt Sara stood by the sink with her arms folded, her face a mask of barely contained fury. "Dad home yet?" she asked meekly, while placing the heavy duffle bag on the floor next to the door. She had hoped, all the way back, that they would beat him home, since dealing with him tonight with all they'd been through today would have been too much for her to process. Danielle was mentally and emotionally exhausted, which was why the two girls had hardly spoken on the drive home.

"No, he left work a little while ago. He got off at nine and is probably on the road, right now." Her words were clipped and laden with heavy overtones. "You need to feed, sweetie?" she asked Dharalyn, who nodded. Sara softened her tone a bit; she was not mad at their guest, and knew full well where the blame for this entire fiasco dwelled.

"Look, Aunt Sara, I'm...." Danielle began.

"Save it, Danielle! I'm way too pissed, right now, to reason with and will probably say something I'll regret. Best this wait until the morning, when you can talk to both me and your father at the same time. He doesn't know where you went today, but I'm sure you will figure out how to explain it all to him. Especially, if you have what I think you do in that bag." Her eyes had glanced quickly at the duffle bag Danielle had carried in, and now, were glaring back at her with a distinct look of reproach.

Danielle nodded once in affirmation, afraid to say anything out loud.

Sara nodded and reached out, taking Dharalyn by the hand. "Come on, honey. Let's take care of this so you two can get on to bed. I can tell by your faces that this has been a tough day."

Dharalyn followed Sara out of the room, glancing at Danielle with heartfelt concern. She looked extremely apprehensive, and Dharalyn told herself that she would do this quickly and get back to her friend. She needed her, right now. She could see it in the bleakness of her eyes.

While lying in bed, Danielle thought back to the day's events. Something had happened, earlier, that she couldn't explain, and now that it was quiet, she couldn't stop thinking about it. When they had gone back into Michael Moretti's office, one of his guards had grabbed her, and without thinking, she had twisted and pushed him away; only to see him go flying from her and end up sprawled on the ground, as if he'd weighed thirty pounds, rather than two-thirty, which, from the size of him, was probably a good guess as to his actual weight. She'd thought at the time, that it might possibly have been an adrenalin rush, but now, thinking back, she doubted it. She had been full of nervous energy, sure, but the kind that made her sick to her stomach, not the kind that gave superhuman strength. In the silent darkness, an errant thought suddenly came to her. Maybe, it was a Dharalyn thing. Look at Gran, for example. Gran could move her right hand and had regained a tremendous amount of dexterity on her right side, the once completely paralyzed side of her body. Aunt Sara had said that she, herself, no longer needed to wear her contacts anymore, and then there was her own, personal discovery, that the terrible acne that had plagued her for the past few years, was suddenly and completely gone. Not a spot or a sign of it anywhere on her body. What if the acne wasn't the only change taking place in her? The thought scared her a little and she worried what it all could mean. Maybe they were all slowly turning into some kind of vampiric creatures, themselves. The thought made her smile nervously, to herself. Dharalyn would laugh, if she knew Danielle had thought that. Like she had explained, other than a need for blood, she had very little in common with the fictional vampires of Danielle's world. Danielle knew that there were plenty of people in Dharalyn's world that were not blood drinkers, though they supplied blood to the Sedai. She wondered if they ever experienced any changes from the exchange. The thought made her sit up and call out in a soft voice, "Dhara!"

"Yes, Danielle," came a muffled reply.

"I was just wondering something."

A moment passed and then Danielle felt her mattress bounce, as Dharalyn jumped into bed, beside her.

"What?"

Danielle turned on her side and faced her best friend. "Were you awake?"

Dharalyn grunted in agreement. "Umm Hmm. I'm still too energized from today."

"Me, too...listen, I was wondering, if you could tell me something? You know, how, since you've been feeding, there've been some changes with Gran, Sara and myself?"

Dharalyn raised her head and propped it on her right arm. "You've seen something else change, with you?"

"Yes, my acne has totally disappeared, including the pock mark scars on my back and face."

"Oh yeah, I noticed that you looked really nice the past few days. I thought maybe it had just gone away on its own."

"No, I think this is still all part of the blood thing," she said, and then paused, as a thought hit her. She had first given Dharalyn blood in the cabin, but in actuality, she had noticed a reduction in her acne days before that. Deciding that it was just a coincidence, and that it had just cleared up a little on its own, as it did on rare occasions, she continued, "It's been my personal nightmare for years now, something that, in trying to treat it, I've tried nearly every remedy under the sun with little or no effect, and then, as soon as I began giving you my blood, poof, it goes completely away, just like that. So I was wondering, are you completely sure that none of the people in your world receive any positive effect from supplying blood to the Sedai?"

Dharalyn looked thoughtful for a moment. "No, Danielle, nothing has ever been mentioned, or written about it, amongst any of the races that inhabit the Amalgamation worlds. Other than being considered a great honor to be rewarded with Tha-Notoo, which is to say, becoming a blessed blood giver and enjoying the elevated privileges of such, no physical changes have ever been evident."

"Haven't you been wondering about us, about the way it's helped Gran and Sara and me?"

Dharalyn smiled and nodded. "I think it's truly a wonderful thing, Danielle. I like knowing that by helping me, you, yourselves, are receiving a benefit. Especially dear Gran, who is so very happy now. But, truthfully, I am as mystified by all this as you are. So, tell me, what has made you bring this up, now?"

Danielle then told her about the situation with the guard, and how she had thrown him off her. "And I don't know how I did that. Do you think, maybe, it has something to do with you? That somehow, I'm changing in other ways?"

Dharalyn mused, "I don't know, Danielle. Like I said, this is all very new to me, too. I know you will be experiencing change in a spiritual sense, but that is due to something else entirely, and it will be much more gradual. But these physical manifestations, these are new to my experience. I guess we will just have to wait and see what happens."

"Should I be scared?" Danielle asked, her voice troubled.

"I don't believe so. Everything we've seen, so far, has been very beneficial. Let's not look for darkness where there has been only light. As far as what happened to you today, tomorrow we will put it to the test and see if you have indeed manifested some physical change, or if it was just a matter of happenstance, due to the intensely stressful situation in which you were involved."

Danielle grimaced. "Okay, then, I guess I shouldn't worry until there is something to worry about."

Dharalyn nodded. "Exactly. Now, we should get some sleep." She began to roll out of the bed, when Danielle reached out and grabbed her arm.

"Dhara, please stay. I'm feeling really anxious and I feel better when you're close by."

Dharalyn lay back down and closed her eyes. She, too, liked the feeling of serenity and the comfortable intimacy of friendship she felt, when she was close to Danielle.

"Dhara?"

"Yes."

"What did you mean by, I will be experiencing other gradual changes on a spiritual level?"

Dharalyn giggled softly. "Go to sleep, Danielle. We cannot solve all of the mysteries of our bond in one night."

Danielle blew some air out through her nose, signaling her displeasure. "You're not gonna snack on me, in the middle of the night, are you?" she said, in a blatant taunt, obviously designed to engender a response.

"Good night, Danielle!" said Dhara, refusing to rise to the evident goad.

"Blood sucking vampire," she teased, provokingly, and nudged Dharalyn in the back with her knuckle.

"Scared of heights, baby!"

"Fanged, winged menace!"

"Needy, complaining human!"

"Three-hundred-year-old-hag!"

"World class liar!"

It was never clear to Danielle who swung the first pillow, but for the next few minutes, amidst raucous laughter and thudding projectiles of cushion, the two girls forgot their problems, and reveled in the pure release of trivial teenage ambivalence and frivolity. It was, in a very real sense, just what they both needed.

The next morning seemed to come pretty quickly. Danielle awoke with a feeling of distinct dread. She had an awful lot to explain to her father today, and it didn't help that Aunt Sara was so angry with her. Usually, her aunt was on her side, giving her emotional and verbal support. Today, she suspected, she was pretty much on her own. It was going to be interesting, and if she knew her father, LOUD.... Quickly, she jumped into the shower, planning to get downstairs early. Her father was a morning person, and she figured she'd talk to him before they had an audience. Seconds later, she had an uneasy moment, when the door unexpectedly opened and Dharalyn stepped inside with her. The shower was a modern, walk in type, easily able to accommodate two people; however, showering with another person was something Danielle wasn't used to, outside of the school locker-room shower, that is. And, to be honest, she'd never been at ease with that scenario, either. "Uh, Dhara," she said, a bit embarrassed and not sure how to proceed with what was, to her, a delicate subject.

"Yes, Danielle. Good morning," Dharalyn responded in a cheery tone, as she began to wet herself down.

Danielle stuttered, "Do you always take showers together, where you come from?"

Dharalyn looked at her, perplexed. "Of course, my Shovanei always shower with me, otherwise, how could they assist me with my hair and cleaning?"

"Shovanei...are those like, your servants?"

Dharalyn nodded, still looking uncertain. "Yes, they were my handlers and my personal Tha-Notoo, those responsible for my care. Is this not okay, Danielle?" she asked, suddenly picking up on Danielle's distress. "Does my being in here bother you?" Suddenly she turned as if to leave. "I'm sorry, my dear friend. I've offended you in some way."

Danielle grabbed her arm. "No, that's okay. It's just that I'm not used to having servants and all, and, well, usually I don't shower with anyone...at least, not here."

"I can leave, if this makes you unhappy, Danielle."

Again, Danielle shook her head. "No, this is fine. We have many cultures in our world where this is common. There is no reason why you have to change to suit my narrow social prejudices."

"Still, I can tell you are uncomfortable."

Danielle shrugged her shoulders and grinned. "I will get over it, although, Dhara...."

"Yes."

"Please don't ever jump in a shower with my brother, Aaron. Though I'm sure it would absolutely make his day, it would not go over well with the rest of the family."

Dharalyn laughed. "Danielle! My Shovanei were all female, like me. I would never shower with someone of the opposite sex."

Danielle giggled. "Just making sure. You have a way of shocking people, sometimes. I'd rather my brother, or God forbid, my father, didn't receive the surprise of a lifetime." As the thought of such a startlingly awkward scenario actually occurring, hit them, both girls began to laugh uncontrollably.

After finishing her shower, Danielle dressed and quickly headed down to the kitchen. *Please, be there by yourself,* she thought repeatedly, only to have that hope dashed to pieces, as she walked into the kitchen and saw her aunt and father sharing coffee at the kitchen table.

"Well, hey! You're up early, again," said Big John, in a teasing voice. "That's two days in a row. What are you up to today? You two girls off on another adventure?"

From the pleasant tone, Danielle could tell he had no idea what was coming. She saw Aunt Sara glance at her, but couldn't tell if her mood had improved, or if she was just waiting for the condemnation and yelling to begin. Danielle grabbed herself a cup of coffee. *There is only one good way to do this,* she thought. *Start at the beginning and bring him up to date on everything. Just let it all out, every gory detail.* She cleared her throat, gathering her resolve. Just as she opened her mouth, prepared to start her grand oratory of revelation and information, Aaron popped into the kitchen, with Dharalyn just a few steps behind. *Great! The gang's all here,* she thought, morosely. Danielle waited, as for the next several moments, greetings and a generalized morning hubbub filled the kitchen with its familial hum. After Aaron got his cereal, and Dharalyn looked at her with a tight-lipped supportive gaze, Danielle started up again. "Uh, Dad," she said, tentatively, squeezing his shoulder to get his attention, "I really need to talk to you this morning." Her father gazed at her with a puzzled look, which quickly changed to one of guilty self-loathing.

"Danielle, if it's about the horses, there is really nothing we can do. And it won't help to get yourself and everyone here all upset, talking about it. This is what has to be."

"No, Dad, it's not that. Dharalyn and I have resolved the family's money problems. That's what I want to talk to you about."

Big John looked bewildered. "Solved our money problems. What in the world do you mean, Danielle? You rob a bank or something, honey?" His tone was teasing, with a hint of curiosity. It was plain he thought she was putting him on.

"No.... Dad, please listen to me. You are really out of the loop on some things around here, and I think it's about time I bring you up to speed. Some of this stuff you kind of know, and some of it's gonna be brand new information. At first, you are going to have a hard time accepting it, but I want you to really listen, okay? I want you to try and understand what I'm going to tell you, and to realize that everyone else in this house is already aware of these things. Well, most of them, anyway" she amended, realizing Aaron knew nothing about the city trip. "But please know that some of what I did, I did for all of us. I hope you don't get too angry with me, and will try to be as understanding as you can." She was becoming flustered, and knew it. No matter how she phrased all of this, he was going to blow his top during certain parts of it.

Big John recognized the angst in his daughter's face and suspected that he might not like what he was about to hear, but he realized, too, that whatever it was she had to say, whatever had been going on in this house, it was largely responsible for her dramatic emotional recovery, and the new passion and zest for life that shone from her eyes. He was grateful for whatever had forced that change, and was determined to give this his careful consideration. "Danielle," he said, calmly. "Honey, say what you need to say. I will sit here and try to listen and not interrupt you until you are done."

"Great, Dad, that's all I ask. Just hear me out, before you judge me too harshly." Danielle paused to gather her thoughts. She felt a tinge of surprise, when her aunt gave her a tight-lipped smile and nodded, as if to say, *go ahead and do this. I am with you.*

"Okay, then," Danielle said, "where to start. Well, Dad, you know how and where we found Dharalyn, up near the campsite, and I know you don't really believe she is from somewhere else. But, since she has lived here, Gran, Sara, Aaron and I, well, we've gotten to know her very well. In fact, she's become like family to us, and we all love her dearly. But, there is something you don't know about her Dad, something that the rest of us have known, for some time. It's why I got mad at her last week, and threw her out of the house. You see, I also had to grow to understand and accept that which makes her different from us. But, you need to understand this, Dad, Dharalyn is good. Very good! We all love her so much and the difference in her that caused us so much consternation back then, is one of the things that binds her to us, now. You see," she paused, as she tried to decide how best to proceed, "in Dharalyn's world, her people are much like us. They live together peaceably, love one another, have families and share their lives with those closest to them. Where they differ is in the area of sustenance. Where we need water to live, her people need regular provisions of blood to survive. She doesn't subsist on only blood, she can eat fruit and some vegetables, like we do, but she needs a regular intake of blood, which allows her to digest her food, just like we need water to do so. Now, keep in mind, Dad, even though Dharalyn is a kind of vampire, she is not a vampire like we read about in the books of this world. She is not evil, doesn't turn into a bat. She doesn't feed on a person's neck, like the Dracula tales in the old movies. She's a regular person, just like you and me, just a little different. Oh," she then added, as she had another thought, "and the cool thing about her is, when she feeds from us, it causes good things to happen to us. Like me, my acne has cleared up, and Aunt Sara, Dhara fixed her hair and she doesn't need to wear her contacts, anymore. And then there's...."

Big John couldn't take anymore. Here he was, thinking his little girl had made some miraculous recovery, regained her common sense and left behind the terrible depressive state she had been in, when instead, what was becoming all too clear to Big John was, she had, without his realizing it, gone stark raving mad. Somehow, the events of her life had impacted her in such a negative way, that she had apparently begun hallucinating and was having a massive mental breakdown, including the inability to tell the difference between what was real and what was fictional, and part of the make-believe world of her books. He turned to Sara, angry that she had not warned him about Danielle's obviously deteriorating state of mind. "Oh my God, Sara! Did you know about this? Did you know my little Dani has lost her grip on reality? When were you going to tell me about this?"

Danielle paused; she hadn't expected this reaction. Apparently her old man thought she had gone insane. "Dad!" she said, "I am not crazy."

Big John stood up, running his hand nervously though his hair. "Honey, you need help, in a big way! Don't you worry though, Daddy is going to take care of everything. I will get you the help you need and no matter what it takes, we will make you well again." Turning to Sara, he asked, "Sara, do you still have that number for that psychiatrist? I think we need to give her a call, right now. See if maybe we can get Danielle in to see her, today."

"John, please sit down!" came a clearly recognizable, elderly voice from the kitchen doorway. "Your daughter is not crazy, so stop making an ass of yourself." He knew that voice. What he didn't expect, was that the person who was talking to him so clearly, would also be standing.

Standing on her own two legs! Mabel Frances Walkerman, his mother, who should be in a wheelchair, suffering from partial paralysis, was standing in the doorway, leaning on a cane!

Slowly, she ambled into the room, as Sara, who had stood up, pulled out a chair for her next to Dharalyn. "Thank you, dear," Mabel chortled, "still getting my strength back. Getting better every day, though." She seated herself, turned toward John and peered fiercely into his eyes. "Listen to me, my son, your darling daughter has not lost her mind. Now, why don't you sit down and let her finish explaining everything. And please, try and keep an open mind."

"But Mother," he sputtered, "how is this possible?" Big John was shocked to his core. There were a few certainties in his life. One was that he loved his family dearly, loved his mother. Two, was that she was paralyzed and would only have limited use of her limbs, for the rest of her life. He had realized, long ago, that she would never recover, especially to the extent where she would ever walk again. And yet, here she was, *walking!*

"Well, it's all thanks to our little miracle, here," she said, patting Dharalyn's hand and holding it firmly in hers. "Like Danielle told you, she comes from another world. Turns out, one of the side effects of us taking care of her, is that we also receive some incredible, therapeutic benefits. And if you have any doubts, then ask yourself, what else could be responsible for my returning health? Ever since I started giving Dharalyn my blood, I've experienced a miraculous change in my condition. Now, Danielle, go ahead and finish your story, sweetheart. Your father needs to hear everything."

John slowly sat back down at the table and gazed at Dharalyn, with both wonder and trepidation in his eyes. "So, she's really...."

"Yes, Dad, she's a vampire," said Danielle, "although, a very good one."

"Okay, I think I've got it so far, honey," said Big John. "Don't know quite what I think about all this yet, but, go ahead on with your story. I'll try and deal with it the best I can."

Danielle was taken aback for a moment. Where was the big explosion? Where were the shouted expletives and waving of arms? This was a new Big John, one that had her momentarily baffled. Then she saw the look in his eyes as he gazed at Gran, and realized he was stunned. Revelations he had never expected to see were appearing in front of him, and for the moment, anyway, he was transfixed with the wonder of it all. "Well, okay, where was I before my father decided to have me committed to the loony bin, oh yeah...anyway, as you know, the family is having some financial difficulties. So, Gran, Sara and I were talking to Dharalyn the other night, when the subject of the jewelry she was wearing when she arrived here, came up. I, myself, had never given it much thought since I assumed it was all just costume jewelry, but it turns out that it wasn't costume jewelry at all, but the real thing. A side note, Dad, Dharalyn's family, where she comes from, is really powerful and really, really rich. Anyway, we decided that the thing to do, and Dharalyn agreed, since she says we are her family here and she insists that this is a one-for-all, all-for-one kind of scenario, that we sell the diamonds from her two bracelets. So, Aunt Sara called a jeweler friend of hers and got the name of a guy down in New Jersey who purchases jewelry and anything else of value that has a questionable history as to its origin. You know, because we can't really tell anyone where the stuff came from, or we're all liable to end up in Dad's loony bin, together. So, Aunt Sara got the information and yesterday morning...," she paused, and took a deep breath, "okay, Dad, here's the part where you might get a tad upset, but keep in mind that we were never in any real danger, and it all turned out all right, in the end." Danielle saw her father give a bewildered glance toward Aunt Sara and saw her shake her head, as if to say, *you know your daughter, when she gets an idea in her head.* Danielle hesitated then, her heart beginning to hammer a bit. "Um, I need a bottle of water, real quick," she said, suddenly. She made her way to the fridge and grabbed a bottle of water, while out of the corner of her eye, she saw everyone looking at each other as if they were having some sort of silent conversation. Weirdly, no one said a single word, though.

Danielle returned to her spot, took a mouthful of water and then said, "Okay, now, where was I?"

"You were about to explain how you deceived and lied to your aunt, and went to the city without her," quipped Aunt Sara.

Danielle saw her father's eyes sharpen and deep lines form in his forehead, a sure sign that he was about to lose it. Quickly, she tried some verbal damage control and continued, "Right, um, well, I knew that with the people coming this weekend for the horses, that we couldn't wait a few days, so I took the initiative to handle the matter myself, with Dharalyn's help. And Dad, just so you know, Dharalyn is really strong and fast, just like in the vampire stories, so I knew we wouldn't have anything to worry about. So, yesterday morning, we took the diamonds and headed down into New Jersey."

Big John interrupted, "This was yesterday morning, when you asked to borrow my GPS?"

Danielle gulped and nodded glumly, knowing where this was going.

"And told me that you needed it to navigate around West Point?"

"Yes, sir," she said, meekly, her voice losing its edge.

There was a long silence that was finally broken by Aunt Sara's rejoinder. "Well, don't stop now, dearest. I'm dying to know how your day went. There's plenty of time to discuss, afterwards, the consequences of lying to both your aunt and to your father." Sara glanced knowingly at John, who grimly nodded his head. It was plain from the look he gave her, that he was using all of his self-control to keep himself from saying a word.

Danielle took another drink of water. At least Gran was still looking at her kindly, and Aaron. Dharalyn didn't look very happy, but that was probably because she was feeling guilty about being part of their great deception. *Well*, she thought, *nothing to lose now, so I might as well jump in with both feet. Things certainly can't get much worse.* As fate would have it, that was the precise moment that the doorbell rang.

CHAPTER 16

AN UNEXPECTED VISIT

Danielle didn't know what to say when she crossed to the kitchen door that led outside, opened it and saw her Uncle Jack standing there. Normally, a visit from her favorite uncle was a cause for celebration. But, considering the highly problematic conversation that she was having right then, his timing couldn't have been worse. Still, she knew he expected a big welcome and so obligingly, she wrapped her arms around his neck and gave him a big hug and kiss, which was her typical greeting. "Uncle Jack, it's so good to see you," she fibbed. "What has you up in this neck of the woods?"

"Well, mostly I miss my favorite niece and nephew," he said, and then added, "My God, Danielle, look at you! You've gotten as pretty as a peach." He stepped back, gave her a once-over and nodded. "Yep, you definitely inherited your mother's good looks. Thank goodness you didn't get any of your father's bad qualities," he said, jokingly.

Danielle blushed furiously; other than her mother and her father, no one had ever called her pretty. The compliment affected her more than she liked to admit.

"Hey there, Pal!" Uncle Jack exclaimed, as Aaron rushed up and gave him a big hug as well. Jack pounded him on his back and said, "Wow, you're getting solid. You been working out there, buddy?"

"So what brings you up here, Jack?" Sara asked, as she walked up for her own hug.

Jack began to answer and then froze. Everyone in the family saw his gaze falter and turn to astonishment, as he looked toward his mother, who was standing and making her way carefully toward him. "What the hell!" was all he could say. His chest suddenly tightened with emotion, his breath came hard and his wide eyes began to well up with tears. Up until that moment, Jack would have described himself as a pragmatist, recognizing the truth in all things and never subject to whims, or flights of fancy. There was a methodical and logical sequence to the patterns and paths that defined their existence. Things in life were subject to a very narrow set of rules and obvious principles, a premise of simple cause and effect. He didn't believe that there was a magical person in the sky, looking after them, didn't believe in miracles, never had much faith in prayer, or use for mysticism, or this New Age way of thinking. He'd seen it all, been in all manner of tough situations, seen things that most people could never imagine, and he'd never seen anything that could make him question the code of fundamentals by which he lived his life. Which was why, for the first time in his life, he was completely and utterly dumbstruck....

"How is this possible?" he choked out, and then he was at a loss for further words. He was holding her, tears streaming down his cheeks as his mother, who should be confined to a wheelchair, hugged him fiercely and whispered in his ear, "Surprise!"

It was a long while before things settled down and they were able to all sit back around the table, which to Danielle, had always been a kind of unofficial family center for meetings and what-not. Her father, Big John, had phoned in to his job and taken the day off, and so had her Aunt Sara. It seemed that everyone there knew that there was too much on the table, an awful lot to be discussed, within their family, and it was apparent no one wanted to be left out of any of it. Danielle herself, though pleased to see her uncle, was also brooding over the fact that apparently, he would now be present for the humiliation that still awaited her once their earlier discussion resumed. After things had settled down a bit, she pulled Uncle Jack by his hand and introduced him to Dharalyn.

"Hello," he said, in a friendly tone, "how nice to see you again."

"Oh no, Jack," she said, correcting his obvious mistake. "You've never met her, before. She's new here...a new addition to the Walkerman family."

Jack nodded. "Oh, I know, dear heart," he said, using the endearing term he always used toward her. "This is the first time for me to meet her in person, but not, actually, the first time I've seen her."

Danielle paused, not quite grasping what her uncle was saying. Then, seeing the strange look in his gaze, she suddenly felt cold inside. *Oh No! No, no, no, no, no, no, no*...she thought to herself, a bit of hysteria taking hold of her. *There was no way, no possible way her luck was this bad!* Forcing herself to gather her wits about her, she made herself smile, in what she hoped was a casual way. "Whatever do you mean, Uncle Jack?"

Suddenly, her aunt stepped up. "Jack, before you showed up, Danielle was about to tell us about her trip to the city, yesterday. Would your untimely visit have anything to do with that?"

Jack grinned crookedly at his sister. "Really, well, it appears, then, that I arrived exactly at the right time. That's kind of what I wanted to talk to her about. I guess now we can all hear this together."

Danielle blanched at the knowing look that Jack gave her. There was a little hint of a playful tease in his words, but not much. She sensed that behind his words was something more: concern, maybe a touch of ire....

Uncle Jack raised his voice, so that everyone in the kitchen could hear him. "Everyone," he said, "though there are many questions I would like to ask you all, especially you, Mom," he added, and squeezed her shoulder affectionately, "I think, maybe, we should all take our seats and allow my dear niece to tell us of her adventure, yesterday."

Big John glanced at his brother, who gave him a serious, knowing look in return. He knew something, and John suspected that maybe his brother's visit today was not just by chance, after all. Nodding his agreement, he helped orchestrate everyone into their seats, and then, took his own. "Okay, my dear daughter," he said, irritably, and folded his arms. "I think we're all ready to hear the rest of this, now."

Aunt Sara jumped in then. "Wait just a moment, Danielle," she said, and then leaned over to her brother, Jack, and explained, "There is going to be a lot of information here that you are not going to understand. Some of it is even going to shock you, much like the change in Mom, here. Just trust me when I say, you have a lot of catching up to do, brother dear, with what's been going on here within our family. Just follow as best as you can and I will fill in the blanks later, when we have a chance to talk by ourselves."

Jack nodded slowly, his pursed lips showing he was confused, though his eyes seemed to burn with curiosity. "All right," he said, simply. "Go ahead, Dani."

Danielle looked at the room full of faces that were staring at her. Though a couple of them were friendly and supportive, most reminded her of what it might feel like to stand in front of a firing squad. "Well, I guess I left off at the point where we went to New Jersey." Danielle then proceeded to explain how they had met up with Samuel Remy, to try and sell the diamonds, and how the pawn broker had said that he couldn't help them and then sent them on into the city to meet with Michael Moretti. At that point, her Uncle Jack interrupted her.

"Excuse me...did you say you had a personal meeting with Antonello Michael Moretti, head of the Moretti crime syndicate?"

Danielle nodded succinctly, ignoring the glaring look from her father. "Uh, yes," she answered, softly.

"Was this the first or second time you entered the building?"

Danielle was stricken silent, as her worst fear was suddenly realized. *He had seen them! How was that even possible?*

"Jack," said Sara, who was as confused as most of the people sitting at the kitchen table, "you saw Danielle in the city, yesterday?"

"More specifically," he answered, "I saw her and this little lady," he pointed toward Dharalyn, "enter the Quest Financial

Plaza yesterday, just before noon. My office has had them under surveillance for weeks and I was there, manning the computers and other support equipment when I see these two go inside at around eleven, come out approximately an hour later, go back in at about one o'clock and come back out, about ten minutes later. And then," he paused, wondering how to explain what he'd been unable to understand, himself, since the day before, "and then, I saw these two come back out of the building again, about three hours later. Which, I have to say, has me absolutely baffled, since dozens of cameras, aimed at every single building access point, did not catch them going back into the building through any entrance we had covered. That's why I am here, today...to find out why they were there, in the first place, and to find out how the heck they got back in without my knowing about it." Jack's voice had turned very serious and had a sharp edge to it, not the least because he was very concerned for the future welfare of his niece. "This is very bad, Danielle! Do you even know who these people are? How incredibly dangerous it is to have any dealings with them! Especially this particular syndicate boss, Michael Moretti." His angry countenance faltered, then, and quickly softened, as regret for his sharp words took over. He was a tough son-of-a-bitch when he had to be, but there was and always had been, one great weakness in his armor, one thing that broke him into pieces. *Danielle's tears, which were currently flowing freely.* Abruptly, he stood up, walked over to her and knelt down on one knee while grabbing her arms, stroking them and then giving her a quick kiss on the backs of her hands, as he tried to comfort her. "Honey, I don't mean to yell and upset you. It's just that, don't you know what you mean to me? Mean to all of us? When you went back in there that second time, I was about to call in the troops to get you out. When you came back out so quickly, I was so relieved; especially after I saw the two of you walk off. I figured that was the end of it, at least for the day. I planned to come up here and make sure you didn't ever do anything like that, again. Imagine how I felt, when hours later, after my gut had finally unclenched, I saw the light of my life come back out of that building, which was filled with only the worst kinds of people. I couldn't help but wonder what the hell you were doing in there!"

Danielle nodded, her tears slowing as she began to sniffle. She had tried to be strong, but the looks she'd been getting from her dad, on top of Uncle Jack hollering at her, had broken through her resolve. She was only sixteen, after all, and a girl could only handle so much.

Jack looked at her and smiled warmly, and was relieved to see it returned. "Now...what were you doing in there, Danielle? I need to know."

Danielle plucked up her courage and began to explain. "Well, Michael Moretti had tried to steal the diamonds from us, I mean, he gave us a lousy thousand dollars for them," she said, and glanced toward Aunt Sara, who looked bewildered. "I was so mad! What kind of fools did he think we were? So Dharalyn and I decided to go back in and force him into making it right. Make him give us what we deserved. After all, they were Dharalyn's diamonds, from her bracelets. We didn't steal them or anything, and he was wrong to try and rob us, just because he thought we were a couple of naive little girls."

Jack chuckled. "Heh, no one who knows you like I do, sweetheart, would ever make the mistake of thinking that about you."

Danielle grinned just a little, then, emboldened by her uncle's praise. "So, Dharalyn and I snuck back into the building...." she continued, and then was interrupted.

"How, exactly, did you sneak back into that building? I was watching the whole time, from every angle, even went back and checked the logs. How the heck did you get in there, Danielle?" asked Jack, his eyes peering at her intently.

She hesitated and noticed, at the same time, that the kitchen had gotten very quiet, as if every one of them was waiting to hear the mystery explained. This was a particularly delicate part of the story, which she really didn't especially want to enlighten them on, for a number of reasons. She glanced toward Dharalyn, who she could see looked fairly uncomfortable, herself. Finally though, she relented, realizing there was no way around this. She was going to have to confess another one of Dharalyn's little secrets. "Well, to put it quite simply, we went over to the next building, went up to the rooftop, and then Dharalyn flew us across to the roof of the

Moretti building." Silence reigned, then, as everyone looked at her with various expressions, which were pretty easy to read. Her uncle thought she was straight-up lying, her father thought she was being a wise-ass, her aunt looked stunned, her grandmother looked amazed and kept glancing toward Dharalyn, who had her head down and looked rather sheepish, and Aaron...well, Aaron was simply smiling with delight.

"Danielle Frances!" said Jack, sharply. He had never scolded her before, but she was going too far, now. "You may think this is all very funny, but I promise you, it is not. This is very serious business, young lady!"

"Jack," said Gran, as both he and Danielle glanced at her. "Leave my granddaughter alone, please. If she said they flew across, then darn-it-all, that's precisely what they did!"

"Mother," said Jack, who had stood and was folding his arms, like he always did, when he was absolutely determined to stand his ground, "that statement is utterly preposterous!"

"You're a little out of the loop around here, dear, and I want you to just trust me, for now. Now, please come here and sit next to me, and let Danielle finish her story. I'm getting a bit tired of all the interruptions that, I'm afraid to tell you, are based on some false and inaccurate presumptions."

Jack looked at his mother for a moment, deciding whether to argue the point, and then relented; for now, at least. Just the fact that his mother was walking made him a little uncertain about things that, heretofore, he'd always accepted as unequivocal truths. *Perhaps, for now,* he thought, *I might be better off suspending any doubts I have about all of this and take more of a wait and see attitude.* "All right, Mother, perhaps you are right. Maybe I should just wait and see how this all plays out. If nothing else, it should all make for a very entertaining morning."

Once again, Danielle found herself standing alone and at the very center of attention. Taking a deep breath, she forged ahead, realizing that no matter what she said, a lot of this was going to be hard for most of them to swallow. She took heart, as she looked into her grandmother's smiling, supportive gaze and silently thanked her dear gran, who had always been the most open-minded person she'd ever known. "Well, anyway, like I said before, Dharalyn flew us across to the roof of the Quest building. That was when I came up with a plan, to help us get the upper hand on things, after which we went down and burst into Michael Moretti's office," she said, and then thought, *what the heck, throw it all out there and let them swallow what they can.* "While in there, I told him we were an old, aristocratic vampire family and I let one of his guards shoot me with a pistol, twice," she said, not daring to look at her father. "I was fine, because Dhara had given me a Pametra device, which shielded me from harm from projectiles. After that, I picked the bullets up and handed them to Michael. He was pretty impressed, but still didn't really believe me, so I had Dharalyn go Kquwaya-Maxx on him, which is third-level battle mode. So, she went ahead and turned all winged-fanged-vampire-goddessy on him, at which time he freaked out and believed us, then. He told us he was really sorry, went to his vault and gave us our money, and then we took it and left. The end!" she said, flippantly and walked a couple of steps to the corner cabinets, where the duffle still sat where she had tossed it on the floor, the night before. She picked it up, carried it over to her father, plopped it down in front of him on the table, and opened it, so that he could see the dozens upon dozens of wrapped stacks of one-hundred dollar bills, which filled the bag to the brim. "And there you go, all the money we need to keep our family solvent," she said, matter-of-factly. She then, without any further tolerance, or patience for the feelings of the others, strode from the kitchen and went to her room. She'd had enough for today, and right now, she wanted to be alone for a while. Even her father's shouted demand that she come back didn't slow her down. She was tired of the looks, the obvious skepticism concerning her remarks, and the seeming attack against her character. It was a highly personal affront to her self-esteem and even more, to her self-image. Danielle's patience, her stamina and her ability to deal with any more bull-crap, was simply at the limit of her endurance. Let them decide what they would do, without her. They'd done what they had to and she wasn't going to apologize to anyone about what she and Dhara had accomplished.

Big John stood. "Sara, would you mind going and bringing her back here, immediately? I still have a few dozen questions I want answered."

"Leave the poor girl be, John!" said Gran, firmly, waving him back into his seat. "She needs some time, alone."

"Well, I need some damn answers," he said, heatedly. He was angry, and to be honest, more than a little alarmed. It was pretty plain to him and probably to everyone here, that she and Dharalyn had risked their very lives yesterday, and on more than one occasion.

"You will get your answers, John, but not now. You try and push her anymore, at this time, and all you will get is a bunch of obstinate, teenage backtalk. And you know that won't solve a thing."

"But, mother," Jack chipped in, as he pushed his chair back and began to pace about the kitchen area, waving his arms to accentuate what he was saying, "you don't really expect us to believe all that nonsense about flying vampires, deflecting bullets and facing down a mob boss. As much as I hate to admit it, I think our sweet little Danielle has lost her dear little mind. I don't know, maybe she's experiencing some sort of mental collapse, a delayed reaction, due to the overwhelming depression she's been burying, deep within. I just know that everything she's said to us is simply damned impossible and moreover, sounds downright nuts and completely and utterly delusional."

Big John stood. "I'm sorry, mother, but I'm afraid I have to agree with Jack, here. I can't go along with any of this either." He was about to say more, but Sara stood and barked at the both of them.

"John, Jack, sit the heck down!" she glared at the two of them, until they did as she said. "I know she deceived us, yesterday and I'm still angry about that, but what Danielle is NOT, is a bold-faced liar! Dharalyn, honey, I'm sorry. But, I think maybe it's time we show these two imbeciles that life still holds more than a few surprises, and that one of those surprises is a lot closer than they think." She held out her hand and led Dhara to the clear area, where Danielle had spent the last hour trying to explain everything. "Okay, honey, I think it's time you do your thing. Show these two boys who you really are!"

Dharalyn looked at Gran, who nodded her support. *Okay,* she thought silently, *but I hope I don't get kicked out of the house again. I really like it here.* She paused, then, realizing what she was wearing. "Sara, do you mind if I go change my shirt, real quick? This is one of the two that Danielle bought me and I don't want to destroy it."

"Sure, honey, you go on ahead and change. We will wait here for you."

Dharalyn ran from the room and made her way through the den, foyer, living room and up the stairs, to her and Danielle's room. Inside, she quickly changed into the dark-blue satiny top with black borders she'd worn yesterday in the city, when she'd done her transformation, the same blouse that she had worn when she'd first come here. It was the only top she had that supported her third-level change, without tearing in the back. Danielle gazed at her, quizzically, from where she was lying, brooding, on her bed.

"No way!" she said, as she suddenly realized what was going on. "Who's making you do this?"

"Sara thinks it would be best, that it will help your uncle and your father to understand."

Danielle jumped up. "Then I'm coming with you, to help handle what will probably be two grown men freaking out!"

Dharalyn smiled, warmly. "That would be great, Danielle."

Moments later, Dharalyn returned to the kitchen with Danielle in tow. They both received many mixed glances, though Dhara could tell that both Sara and Gran were pleased that Danielle was with her. Dharalyn turned once toward Danielle, for emotional support. "Well, should I do this?"

Danielle was grinning with a mischievous edge to her features and a strange twinkle in her eyes. "Wait Dhara, before you do this, I've been kind of thinking. Before we showcase this particular little pageantry of yours, I think we should coin a catch-phrase, you know, to help commemorate the event."

"A what?" asked Aunt Sara, plainly confused.

"A transformation catchphrase: Like, Shazam, or, By the power of Grayskull. You know, it's what some superheroes say, just before they change into their alter egos."

"Oh yeah, you're right, Danielle," said Aaron, enthusiastically, and then added, "how about something that has to do with her change? I mean, what's it called, where you come from, Dhara?" he asked, with a smile. He was thrilled, and loved this kind of stuff. Dharalyn was a kind of real-life superhero, he supposed, and he thought a catchphrase was a really good idea.

"The process of my transformation has three parts, actually, but in my world, the descriptive word for that change of state is Khala Mordia, which means: Change of Being."

"That's it, Dhara," Aaron said eagerly, "that's what you should say, when you change."

"Enough!" said John Walkerman, in a voice that was both gruff and annoyed. "You kids seem to think this is all a joke of some kind. Well, I'm here to tell you, it's not funny. Danielle, if you and Dharalyn have something to show us, then do it now. I'm about all out of patience here, with this ridiculous nonsense!"

Danielle nodded at her father, her face a mixture of embarrassment and stubbornness. "Okay, Dad," she said simply, and then added, "Dharalyn, let the power of shock and awe begin."

Dharalyn looked around the room at the many faces, some staring in marked skepticism, some with open curiosity, one plainly still feeling the effect of her chastisement, and one of pure, innocent joy. The last one, of course, was Aaron, who was grinning with delight. Dharalyn smiled back at him and felt a sense of playfulness fill her. If Aaron wanted her to mimic one of these superhero people, then, for him, she would deliver. Raising her arms in the air, she clapped her hands together and shouted:

"Khala Mordia!"

Dharalyn then brought forth the full power of her Ayowei, to speed up the transition and a distinctive glow, from the force of that power, surrounded her. First came Kquwaya-Set, where the main visible change was that her eyes glowed brightly, her fangs became more pronounced and her hair shone glistening white, then Kquwaya-Shira, where her skin became infused with graceful lines of silvery patterns, which signified increased toughness, speed and strength, and last, Kquwaya-Maxx, where her wings decompressed and expanded with shimmering translucence, until they spread nearly two-thirds the width of the kitchen. Through each change, Dharalyn heard cries and gasps of exclamation and exultation from nearly all parties, until the last change, where John and Jack both stood and jumped back, shocked expressions notwithstanding, each of the men voicing loud expletives.

"Holy smokes!" yelled Jack.

"Dammit, will you look at that!" pronounced John.

"Holy mother above, may the saints preserve us," said Sara, who thought she'd been prepared for the transformation, but found, instead, that she was sadly mistaken.

"Absolutely glorious!" laughed Gran, with giddy surprise.

"Totally awesome!" shouted Aaron, and then added, "she's like a super angel!"

Danielle stood to the side, smiling proudly and thinking to herself, *she did look a little like an angel, if that angel was equal parts goddess and total badass.*

For the rest of the morning and partway into the afternoon, Dharalyn and Danielle talked and fielded questions about who Dhara was, how they had first met, and so on. Most of it was for Uncle Jack's sake, but Danielle didn't mind. What really surprised her the most, though, was her father's and uncle's general attitude and demeanor about everything. Her father seemed to have calmed down dramatically, and her uncle seemed almost like a kid in a candy store. The wonder of this whole thing had gotten to him; almost as if it had awakened something deep inside that he'd forgotten about. After a while, her father put a casual hand on her shoulder and gently guided her outside.

"Well, you two certainly had quite an adventure yesterday, didn't you?"

"You're really mad, huh Dad?" asked Danielle, waiting for the hammer to fall.

"Not as mad as I should be," Big John replied, shaking his head slowly from side to side. "To tell the truth, I'm more relieved than mad, relieved we're not going to lose the house and everything else. Our financial problems have weighed very heavily on me for some time, Danielle, and now to have that terrible worry go away...well, it buys you some forgiveness. Not a lot, mind you, but some.... You should never have gone to the city and done such a foolhardy thing. But I guess that's part of your nature and in the past, now, and I just can't find it in my heart to be too hard on the both of you."

"Really!" exclaimed Danielle, whose heart leaped at the news.

Big John forced a glaring look at his only daughter. "Which is not to say you are going to get away with this scot-free, my dear. Nope, you will be turning your car keys over to me, today, and your aunt is making up a long list of projects that need to be done around here. That should keep you two busy and out of trouble until school starts."

Danielle frowned, her face the very image of a reprimanded teen. "What about Dharalyn, will she be going to school with me?"

"I spoke to Jack some about that and he and I will be talking more, later. He has some contacts that can get her what we need, so that it looks like she has a past, and belongs to us. He knows how to handle the money, too, so that it doesn't send up any red flags. Leave it to me, honey, I will try and see to it that you don't lose your new best friend, anytime soon."

"Thank you, Dad!" she said, with a relieved smile, and grabbed him in a big hug. They held each other for a long while and then parted. "So, you're okay with Dharalyn's uniqueness?"

Big John harrumphed. "Well, I still have a little way to go on all that. Don't know if I will ever be able to handle the whole blood thing. Sara tells me you three have it all under control, though, so if you don't mind, I'm going to try and not think about that part, too much. Make it a kind of a need to know thing. If it's something I don't need to know, then leave me out of the loop. Although, honey," he then said, with added concern, "I want you to leave Aaron out of all of this blood giving stuff. He's too young and imma-ture yet to handle something like this with any kind of delicacy."

Danielle nodded, not daring to mention Aaron's one experi-ence with the blood giving. She heard the door open and watched her uncle walk up. "Mind if I talk to my niece a little bit?" he asked, casually.

John nodded. "Go ahead, but you and I need to talk more, later," he said, then patted his brother's shoulder and went back into the house.

Jack waited for him to leave and then gazed at his niece with a thoughtful expression. "That girl Dharalyn, she's a real surprise. Got a good head on her shoulders," he said, as he placed an affectionate arm about Danielle's shoulder. "And I have to say, she's very pretty, too."

"Uncle Jack!" she said, disdainfully, "Eww...you're old enough to be her father."

Jack chuckled. "Hey now, don't go taking that statement the wrong way. I'm not being creepy, I'm just saying that she is a very attractive girl, and women, even very young women with that kind of beauty, can sometimes be very deceiving. You're so taken in by their appearance, that you miss other, important details about them that you should be noticing. Besides, Dani, it's never bothered you before, when I mentioned that I thought some girl was good looking."

"Yeah, but she's my age, Uncle Jack. Sixteen...."

"Yeah, you're right, I suppose. I probably should have explained what I was getting at, in a better way. Anyway, I want to talk to you about something very important," he said, giving her a serious look.

Danielle nodded, wondering what was up.

"About this girl, Danielle, I want you to do me a big favor. I want you to try and remain objective, where this girl is concerned, and stay alert. I know you two have become close, but you are a smart girl. I want you to keep your ears open for any inconsistencies in her story. Look for anything that may make you question if she's really who and what she says she is."

"Uncle Jack, what are you saying? You think she's some kind of spy or something?"

"Honey, listen...you have always been a real sharp cookie, smarter than most others your age and in my line of work, it pays to be extra careful. I've met a lot of people, in my day, who were not at all who or what they appeared to be. I just don't want you to be taken in, is all. Watch her, and don't take anything she says as gospel. Use that intellect of yours, be perceptive, ask questions and above all, be vigilant. I know you think this girl is from some other world, or, like you stated, another dimension or possibly a parallel universe of some kind. But, the real truth is probably a whole lot simpler and much closer to home."

Danielle thought he sounded a bit like a throwback, some kind of paranoid, cold-war-era spook. But she knew it was best to humor him, especially if he was going to help Dharalyn get valid ID and papers.

"I think it is a good idea that she is staying here, with you. It will let me keep a close eye on her, and with your help, we will make sure she doesn't have any hidden agenda."

"Okay, Uncle Jack, you can count on me," was what she said, but inside, she was seething. The most important encounter anyone's possibly ever had, and all her uncle saw was a possible Russian plant. Maybe a genetic mutation of some kind, here to bring down the country in some manner that no one had realized, yet. Danielle began to wonder if maybe Uncle Jack was losing it. Well, she would keep an eye on him, too.

Later that day, as she stood out behind the shed, Danielle found herself in a contemplative mood. She kept thinking back, to when they'd been in Michael Moretti's office; she had tossed that guard like he'd been thirty pounds, instead of two-thirty. As foolish as it sounded, even to her, she wanted a bit of quiet time to test herself in that regard and this was the first time since then, that she'd been able to get some alone time. *Oh well, no guts no glory; here goes nothing*, she thought, to herself. Walking to the edge of the trash hole and trying hard to not feel incredibly stupid that she was even out here doing this, she climbed down into the fairly deep hole, being careful not to step on anything sharp until she was stand-ing next to the old television set Dharalyn had tossed in there. Grabbing it with two hands and trying not to lose her balance, she tried to lift it and found, unsurprisingly, that it wouldn't budge at all; she couldn't even move it a little. Danielle stood and looked at it for a moment and then had a humorous thought, *I know, I forgot to use my Ayowei, like Dharalyn does.* Laughing at herself for even imagining she could do something like this, and feeling more fool-ish than ever, she concentrated and said out loud, "Ayowei come to me, help anchor me, so that I can throw this TV set out of this huge hole." Focusing her mind on the heavy set lying in front of her, she then picked up the TV in one smooth motion and threw it five feet straight up out of the hole, over her head and far out over the edge. She stood, stricken in wide-eyed amazement and heard it crash and break, as it landed heavily, somewhere far out of sight. "Okay," she said out loud, talking to herself, "what the freaking heck was that?" The simple fact of the matter was, though she had given this thing a try, she had never in a million years actually thought it would work, and had maintained a cavalier attitude about it all. She had expected to fail, had been certain that the city thing had been a fluke, a onetime, adrenaline sourced, freak occurrence. And now that she had done the impossible, she found herself clueless as to how to proceed. "How the heck do I explain this one to my father? Hi Dad, thought you should know that I just picked up a three hundred pound television set and threw it about thirty feet, without breaking a sweat. Yeah, that should do it. He's already on the edge of his sanity, about all of this Dharalyn's a vampire stuff and could really use another shock, or two. I should just walk in there right now and tell him that I'm experiencing some serious side effects from the vampire bites." Danielle continued her fantasy dialog, knowing full well she could never tell her father about this, or Uncle Jack, either. "Nope, nothing strange going on with you, Danielle...in fact, I've gotta say, that's just par for the course when your best friend is a vampire and her bite is known to have a few weird side effects. Yep, just another normal day, here, at the old Walkerman house."

CHAPTER 17

NEW AND OLD ACQUAINTANCES

The last few weeks before school started passed slowly, but as the girls would attest, they were not days filled with merriment. Danielle and Dharalyn painted walls, cleaned out the basement, worked in the yard and generally, or so Danielle called it, performed many useful tasks like any good slaves would. Her father had been true to his word and taken her keys, making sure she didn't go anywhere without either himself or Aunt Sara along. Dharalyn worked industriously by her side and had been surprisingly uncomplaining, considering her upbringing and previous station. The nights were spent talking in their room, as Danielle's and Dharalyn's friendship grew stronger and more comfortable. One night, just a few days before school started, Big John surprised the girls in their bedroom with a couple of bank cards.

"For school clothes and other necessities," he told them. "Not for buying useless junk." He then explained to both of them, that Uncle Jack had come through on Dharalyn's ID and papers, and that she was registered to start school as a junior, along with

Danielle. "She's your distant cousin," he said, with a knowing wink and a smile, "from your mother's side of the family."

"Thanks, Dad," Danielle said happily, as the two girls made plans to go shopping the very next day. "Maybe we can get Aunt Sara to take us before she goes in to work." After he left the room, Danielle watched as Dharalyn closed another book and opened a new one, from the stack Aunt Sara had brought upstairs. The two of them were involved in a crash course of 'get Dhara prepped for High School 101'. Danielle, at first, had thought it would be nearly impossible to bring Dhara up-to-date on years of history, math and the sciences, but the girl had been sitting on her bed for the past few weeks, every evening, going through about a book a night. And now, she could see, Dhara was reading the history textbook she herself had read only last year. "I can't believe how fast you are learning this stuff. Do you really comprehend everything you're reading in all of these books?"

Dharalyn nodded, giving Danielle a quick smile and returning her attention to the book in her lap, which she was reading at about a page every six or seven seconds.

Feeling a bit jaded at watching Dhara turn page after boring page, Danielle had a thought. "You know, I've been meaning to ask you about something."

"What's that?" said Dharalyn, her eyes busily scanning lines of text.

"Well, I was just wondering...how exactly does that Shon-ya, Um, Shony-miya, Shon-yu-may thing work? That reverse time thing you do. When you use it, does everything in the whole world go back?"

Dharalyn smirked and peered at Danielle with a penetrating look. "It's pronounced Shonyemaya, Dani. What in the world made you ask that, and why are you interested in this, all of a sudden?"

"I've just been thinking about that kind of stuff a lot, lately. For instance, you said that you can only reverse time for about five minutes. How does it work, exactly?"

Dharalyn placed a bookmark in the book she was reading and set it down. She could tell from the curious look on Danielle's face that this was going to be a long and involved question and answer session. "Well, it works a bit differently, depending on how I'm going to use it. If I'm slowing or reversing time, then when I call upon it a globe of pure Ayowei forms around me, about sixty feet in diameter. So to answer your question, the effect is localized. It only affects that which is within the periphery of the globe of energy."

"What happens if you shrink the globe, make it smaller? Does it last longer, then?"

Dharalyn paused, in thought. Danielle had a way of seeing directly into things, in ways that had never even occurred to her. "I honestly don't know, Danielle. It's possible, I suppose. I've never tried to do that particular thing before."

"I see, well, that's interesting. And what about the other thing you told me? Preconception; how does that work?"

"Well, for that, I focus on something and then I use Ayowei to glance forward, into the time stream. That's the only way I can think to describe it. A lot of what I should know about all of this, Danielle, I would have learned, had I gone on to the Sedai Novi University of Synda Majoris Laureal, after passing the Probost, which, of course you know, that I failed. It is there that I would have studied the finer details and minutiae, concerning the control of both Ayowei and, more importantly, the use and control of Kamanah. Also, I would have studied many of the deeper mysteries of our Arts and learned much about the rarer gifts that occur sometimes, like Shonyemaya."

Danielle nodded, as she gave Dharalyn a wicked little grin. "I see. So, what you're saying is, you really don't know what the heck you are doing, for the most part."

Dharalyn laughed at that. "Yes, you could say that. Whatever I know about Shonyemaya, I've pretty much figured out on my own."

Danielle giggled a bit more and then, in a blink, turned immediately serious. "Dharalyn, listen, I have been thinking. I think you should try and reach out for your Egana again, and find the source of your Kamanah."

Dharalyn's smile vanished and was replaced by a look of unease. "What...why would you say that?"

Danielle got up and walked over to Dharalyn, sitting next to her on her bed. "Look, I've given this a lot of careful thought over the past few weeks. I think, to resolve the guilt you feel about your past, you need to face your fear. I think maybe, all that happened to you the last time was that you freaked out, because of all the pressure put on you. I'm willing to bet that if you try it with me helping, you could possibly succeed where you failed, before."

Dharalyn shook her head in firm denial. "You don't know what you are talking about," she said, reproachfully. "You have no idea what it was like the first time I tried it. I hope you never have to face such fear Dani, such complete, overwhelming despair. It was the worst thing I've ever experienced."

Danielle pursed her lips, her eyes narrowing, like they did when she was adamant about something. "I know you haven't gotten over it though, not at all. You talk about it in your sleep, did you know that?"

Dharalyn felt a surge of annoyance at what she felt was Danielle's cavalier attitude toward her feelings, as well as what she was certain was a completely false statement. "I do not talk about it!"

"Oh, yes you do! You keep saying the same thing, over and over. You keep calling your mother's name and telling her that you are sorry, sorry that you failed her. And sometimes, you cry. I've seen the tears traveling down your cheeks in the middle of the night while you're asleep. And I've heard you, time and time again, ask for her forgiveness. This thing is eating you up inside, and you need to do something about it. You need to face your fears, Dharalyn. I think you need to try again."

Dharalyn got angry then. "That's what I get for sleeping next to you all the time. You, listening in on something very personal that is none of your business."

Danielle folded her arms and said forcefully, "None of my business! I'm Sho-Notoo, remember? Your little soul bond buddy. I don't know exactly what that means yet, but I'm pretty sure it means that anything having to do with your well-being is my darn business!"

Dharalyn stood up with an indignant glare and walked toward the door. As she reached the opening, she turned and faced Danielle. "You know, Dani, until you know a little more about my responsibilities and about the power I wield, until you've experienced a little of what I know and have been through, you should just stay out of it!"

Danielle sat still, feeling a bit crestfallen; she was not used to being chastised by Dharalyn. She knew what had initiated this entire conversation, the thoughts that had been on her mind for weeks, and suddenly, she blurted out, "I picked up the heavy TV set and I threw it a really long ways."

Dharalyn looked shocked and then came slowly back into the room, her eyes suddenly curious. "What TV are you talking about?"

"The big one, out in the trash hole. The one nobody could move, but you. I called on Ayowei and threw it about thirty feet, up and out of the hole."

"Danielle!" she said, in an astonished voice. "That's pretty incredible and actually, it's kind of hard to believe! Why didn't you tell me about this, sooner? Why keep this from me?" There was a strained bit of joy in her countenance.

Danielle laughed half-heartedly. "Because, I haven't been able to do it again. It's still lying on the ground where it landed, a good twenty-five feet from the edge of the hole. I've been trying to make it work again, but I can't. I wanted to figure it out, so that I could surprise you with what I could do."

Dharalyn came all the way back into the room then, and sat beside Danielle. "Oh, Dani...it took me a long time to learn how to call on and use my Ayowei properly, if that's what you did. And if so, you must have done it by accident, somehow. This is so amazing!" she said suddenly, and grabbed Danielle in a hug. "I've expected some changes in you, but didn't want to raise your expectations. Since Sho-Notoo is so extremely rare, what comes out of it is still somewhat of a mystery." She paused then, and seemed to have another thought. "And as far as I know, it has never, ever resulted in a non-Sedai gaining the use of Ayowei.

Danielle smiled happily. "So you're not mad at me anymore?"

Dharalyn smiled broadly and shook her head. "I don't know why I even bother. No one can ever stay mad at you. Not even your Aunt Sara."

Danielle glanced out a window and then at the clock on her desk. "It's getting late. If we're going to go school shopping in the morning, we'd better call it a night."

A short while later as Danielle lay in her bed, she saw Dharalyn come into the room from her visit downstairs. "You feed tonight?"

"Yes, it was Gran's turn." Dhara explained, as she got into her own bed in the alcove.

"I've got you in the morning," said Danielle, "so we can get an early start."

"You talk to Jay?"

"Yep, she said she'd take us early, before work."

"Good."

Danielle looked over at the other bed. "Why do you bother getting in your own bed, when you know you'll be in mine in less than an hour?"

"I don't know. Habit, I guess."

"It's stupid. You should just come lay down by me, right from the start."

Moments later, a patter of feet heralded Dharalyn's arrival. "You're right, move over."

"I'm already over," said Danielle, in mock irritation.

Dharalyn got into the bed and then turned her back toward Danielle. "Good night."

Danielle turned on her side facing Dhara and then reaching out, she began exploring her friend's back with her fingertips.

"Danielle!"

"Yes."

"What the heck are you doing?"

"Tracing your ridges."

"What?"

"The tiny ridges on your back, where your wings come from."

Dharalyn sighed loudly. "Do you think you could do that sometime when I'm not exhausted?" she asked, impatiently.

"Okay, sorry."

A few quiet moments went by and then, "Danielle!"

"Yes."

"Maybe you are right. Perhaps I should try it again, with just the two of us."

"Okay, good," said Danielle, as she grinned silently to herself.

"Stop grinning, you idiot."

"I'm not," said Danielle, with a petulantly defensive tone, wondering for the hundredth time how the heck Dharalyn always seemed to know what she was doing or thinking.

The next morning, as Danielle entered the kitchen and read the note that her father had left on the table for her, she squealed loudly with glee, "Dharalyn!"

"What," said Dhara, as she walked in and spied Danielle's radiant visage.

For an answer, Danielle held up a ring of car keys, which she shook noisily. *Danielle's own car keys!* "Daddy left a note saying I can use my car to take us shopping. He says our punishment is at a provisional end."

Dharalyn raised her eyebrows. "Provisional?"

Danielle smirked as Aaron walked into the kitchen, whistling. "That's father-speak for, I'll be watching you, so you'd better behave."

"Where you guys going?" he asked, as he opened the refrigerator and pulled out the milk.

"Shopping at the mall for school clothes," replied Danielle, warily.

"Can I come?" he asked suddenly, his face buoyant with hope.

Danielle was about to smash his hopes, wanting another girls only day out, when Dharalyn answered for her.

"Of course you can," said Dhara, cheerily. "I'll bet you could use a bunch of new school clothes, too."

"Sure can," he said happily, and then smirked at his sister as he poured cereal into a bowl. "Thanks, Darlin'," he said, using the nickname the whole family had adopted, except for Danielle.

"The kids at school will tease you unmercifully if they hear anyone call you that," she had informed Dharalyn privately.

Dharalyn did not mind in the least though, and gave Aaron a bright smile as he smiled back. He was as happy as a lark.

Three hours later found them at the Centertown Mall, walking through the spacious galleries lined with shops of every description. Danielle had just sent Aaron back out to her car with an armful of bags for the second time. "He's actually turning out to be quite a big help," she said, her eyes shining from the exuberance of shopping for the first time in her life, without having to pinch pennies. So far, she and Dharalyn had spent more on new clothes than she even wanted to think about. "Dad is going to flip, when he sees how much we've spent. Come on, I told Aaron to meet us over at Starbucks. I need a cup of coffee." As they made their way toward the coffee vendor, which was at the very front of the entrance to the food court, Dharalyn suddenly moved over to Danielle's right side, causing her friend to give her a quizzical look. "What's up?"

"I just saw someone that we kind of need to avoid," said Dharalyn, with a hint of anxiety.

"Avoid? You don't know anyone, outside of the immediate family. Who do you need to avoid?"

"Danielle," said Dharalyn, in a panicked voice, "did I ever tell you about the boy I attacked in the woods that time, after you threw me out of the house?"

"What boy? Oh wait," she said, remembering something she'd overheard her father talking to Aunt Sara about. "You mean the Miles boy? I heard he was attacked by a wolf or a wild dog, at least that's the story, from what my Dad said. Nooooooo!" she exclaimed, in astonished denial, putting Dhara's statement together with her father's in a sudden epiphany, "You didn't!"

"Yes...it was me," Dharalyn said, matter-of-factly.

"Holy shh...sugar! Do you think that he might recognize you?"

"I don't know. It all happened really fast, although he did say something."

"What did he say?" asked Danielle, only half listening; she had stopped now, and was gazing off in the distance, trying to see if she could spot Christian, anywhere.

"Well, first he swore at me."

"Yes."

"Then he hollered for me to let him go."

"Okay."

"Then he got really weird and said, *my God, you're beautiful.*"

Danielle turned and looked at Dharalyn, her eyes as wide as saucers. "He said, my God, you're beautiful...are you sure?"

"Yes, I'm sure."

"Well, then we're totally screwed," she said, her small hope fading.

"Maybe he won't remember. Maybe, now that my hair is black, he won't recognize me."

"Yeah, and maybe the moon will fall from the sky and crush us, so that we won't have to deal with this. Dhara, when a guy says something that profound, you can bet your face is burned indelibly into his brain. Oh, he'll recognize you all right! Besides, there's the little fact that he lied about what happened to him. This could be bad."

"So what do we do if he sees me?"

"Simple, you deny, deny, deny and deny again. You have no idea who he is. You've never seen him before, and you have no idea what he is talking about. You've got to make him doubt himself, utterly. That's your only recourse."

"Wow, you sound like you've had some experience with this type of thing!"

Danielle looked sharply at Dhara. "Was that a dig? Cause it sounded an awful lot like a casual statement, swaddled in an insult."

"Danielle, would I do that to you, my dearest, sweetest friend in the whole world?"

"Nearly your only friend too, better not forget that," she teased back. "Come on, let's get to the Starbucks, before Aaron can't find us and freaks out." Suddenly she paused, stricken, as a tall boy with blond, curly hair and profoundly blue eyes stepped directly in front of her. He didn't even glance in her direction, but she knew immediately who he was. Tommy Wheeler.... Danielle had a huge crush on him, and he was very often the object of her most secret thoughts and fantasies when she was alone. For a moment she forgot to breathe, lost deep within her own thoughts and then jumped, as someone touched her arm.

"Danielle, are you okay?" asked Dharalyn.

Danielle's face flushed with embarrassment. "Sure, of course I am. I was just thinking, or had a sudden thought about something, I think."

"What?"

"Oh, nothing," she said, curtly. "Come on, let's get that coffee."

Dharalyn gazed at her friend, perplexed, as Danielle suddenly walked off, and with an odd feeling that somehow she was missing something, she followed slowly. Soon, the two girls found themselves at the coffee shop, and Danielle placed an order with the girl behind the counter for an espresso. As she paid for her order, she blanched as she heard a familiar, sickly sweet voice coming from behind her.

"Well, if it isn't Danielle Walkerman. Why, how in the world have you been?"

Danielle turned around and her face fell as she saw standing before her, Melissa Wellington, a strikingly blond, blue-eyed high school princess, who was head of the PTHS Cheering squad and the one girl whom she hated most in the entire world. An individual who over the past few years, had apparently made it her life's ambition to make Danielle feel disliked, unwelcome and socially insignificant. Before Danielle could utter a single word, Melissa continued her rhetoric as if she were bestowing a generous gift, just by noticing her.

"Wow, why look at you! You've really gone and changed a whole lot over the summer, hasn't she, Kaylee?" she said, with a patronizing tone to the girl who was with her. "Why, you almost look presentable now, without all those horrible red spots all over your face."

"Hello, Melissa," said Danielle, timidly, *"still dressing like a slut I see,"* she mumbled quietly, so that only Dharalyn could hear, or so she hoped.

"So, who's your new friend?" Melissa said, crinkling her nose as if detecting a bad smell and giving Dhara a once over that made her feel uncomfortable.

"This is my cousin Dharalyn, who is staying with us now. Dhara, this is Melissa Wellington and her best friend Kaylee Young," she said, all politeness and forced civility.

"So, where exactly do you hail from, Dhara?"

"She's from a small town near Chicago," said Danielle, wishing that they would go away.

"Does Dharalyn talk at all, or do you plan to answer all of her questions for her?" asked Melissa, her voice turning querulous and dripping with sarcasm.

"Oh, I can speak for myself, I assure you," answered Dharalyn, pleasantly. "I don't think Danielle meant to be discourteous, Melissa. She was just being a little protective, since I don't know anyone."

"Yeah, well, isn't that just peachy. So, I certainly hope you two are out doing a little shopping? I mean, you can both certainly do with a wardrobe upgrade. And, by the way, Danielle, please don't take this wrong, but, I really need to say, it wouldn't hurt you to try wearing a little makeup sometime. It'll help you look less like a farmhand and maybe help soften those harsh features of yours. Who knows, with a lot of luck, a little cover-up and some mascara, you might actually find yourself a boyfriend this year."

"Yeah, I'm sure some of the computer geeks or Goth weirdoes would be interested," interjected Kaylee, and then added, "the hopelessly ugly ones, anyway."

"But, they're all ugly," stated Melissa. The two girls giggled at each other as if sharing a private joke, and then walked away, noses held high and acting as if they owned the mall and everything in it.

"God, how I hate her!" fumed Danielle, watching her leave. "All she does is look for ways to torture me."

Dharalyn placed a consoling hand on Danielle's shoulder. "I think that at heart, she's just a very unhappy person, Danielle. She strikes out verbally to keep people at bay, especially those who engender feelings of jealousy, or who she thinks of as superior to her in some way. I mean, try and take it as a compliment that you bring out strong feelings in her."

Danielle peered at Dharalyn with raised eyebrows, taken aback by what her friend was saying. "Why are you defending that rude bitch of a girl? She manipulates and controls people like they are her personal slaves, and always with that phony smile, sugar-coated words and casual disregard for any decency."

Dharalyn smiled. "Dani, I'm not taking her side. But we, as good and kind people, need to try to be understanding of the shortcomings of others. You need to look deeper for the reasons for their misbehavior."

"Try telling that to her!" Danielle said, and stalked off, a bit upset with Dharalyn. Melissa Wellington had a way of bringing out the worst in her and try as she might, she just couldn't see what Dhara meant, or, to be honest with herself, didn't want to see Dharalyn's point at all. What she wanted, at the moment, was very simply to bask in her hatred toward Melissa Wellington. Turning, she faced her friend again and added, "Look, I understand that you feel it necessary to see the good in all people. But I'm telling you, there is no good in her. She is an evil, manipulative little troll. She is followed around by her group of sycophantic admirers, who pander to her every wish. If she hates you or picks on you, then they all do. Over the past years she has made my school life a veritable hell and I, for one, am not interested in finding out what makes her so unhappy. In fact, I'd like to be the one who makes her even unhappier, maybe by giving her my old acne problem. I'd love to see her deal with something like that, the way I had to."

Dharalyn nodded and smiled supportively. "Okay Dani, I can see you're very upset, so let's leave this subject alone, for now. Come on, we were having a really nice time today, so let's not let her spoil it for us."

Just then, Aaron came up to where they were standing. "Hey, you guys, I'm starved. Could we get something to eat?" He grinned widely at Dharalyn. "They have a salad bar here with a good selection of fruits. Want me to get you your favorites, pineapple and strawberries?"

"Good idea, Aaron," said Dharalyn, with a light laugh. "And yes, I would love some strawberries, right now."

Happily, Aaron bounced away on his errand. Danielle chuckled a little as she watched his happy antics and then grabbed Dhara by her arm. "Sorry about all that," she said, appealingly. "I can be a bit of a grouch when she is around."

"Just try and kill her with kindness, Dani. You didn't see her expression when she saw you turn around. She feels threatened by you for some reason, and it might behoove us to try and find out why."

"Oh, I can tell you why," stated Danielle.

"And no more disparaging comments at her expense. You lower yourself to her level when you do that. I want you to be nice."

"Well then, we need to not discuss Melissa Wellington in any way, shape or form. It just isn't within the range of my willpower, to be nice to her."

Soon, the three of them were sitting at a food court table and eating. The mood had shifted and the conversation was, for the most part, cheerful and about the day's events. Danielle had gotten some Chinese food, Aaron a burger and fries and Dharalyn was eating some sliced pineapple, which as it had turned out, was one of the several fruits from this world that she absolutely loved. She had just begun to cut into a fat strawberry, when someone slid into the seat directly across from her, next to Danielle.

"Hello Danielle, Aaron," said Christian Miles, as he stared straight at Dharalyn with a crooked grin. "Who's your new friend?"

"Christian, hey!" choked Danielle. Christian was dark-haired, had dark brown eyes, looked to be about five foot ten or eleven and had a thin, muscular build. He was wearing pleasant smelling cologne and was peering intently at Dharalyn in a way that made Danielle nervous. They had never really been close friends, although he had always spoken nicely to her and never treated her like a leper, or someone unworthy of his attention. "Uh, this is my cousin Dharalyn. Dhara, Christian lives a mile or two up the road from us. He's a junior this year, like we are. So, how are you, Christian?" she added, trying to get his attention off Dharalyn.

"Oh, great!" he said, gaily. "Say, don't I know you from somewhere?" he asked Dharalyn, as he studied her face.

Dhara shook her head slowly and answered in a measured, perfectly controlled voice, "I don't believe we have formally met, Christian. I haven't been living here for very long, or been introduced to many people yet, I'm afraid."

"Funny, you look a lot like someone I met once." He then turned in his seat and faced Danielle. "I saw you two earlier, walking around and I have to say, Danielle, you've really changed over this past summer. I mean, you really look a lot different."

Danielle felt her face turning red as she began to choke on her food. "Uh, okay Chris," she blurted, when she could finally get it out. She had no idea what, exactly, he was trying to say to her and decided it was just his way of attempting to be nice.

"You know, I've been working on a couple of special art pieces this summer. One, in particular, I'd really like you two girls to see. It's a pencil drawing and probably my best work, ever. Why don't you and Dharalyn drop by sometime, so that I can show it to you?"

Danielle nodded. "Sure, I think we can do that."

"Great!" he said. "Well, I can see you guys are plenty busy shopping and all, so I won't take up much of your time. I've got to go and buy some sneakers myself and maybe some jeans. My parents have been giving me grief about the ones I've been wearing, saying they're too dirty for school and all. I figure I'll get some of those new jeans, with the holes and the worn out look. That ought to shake them up, a bit."

Danielle laughed a little at that. She was really nervous, and wasn't sure why. Christian stood up then, said goodbye to all of them and then began to walk off. Suddenly he paused, turned and leaned down next to Dharalyn's ear and whispered something. Whatever it was, it made Dharalyn's face go pale and Danielle could tell she was a trifle uneasy, which was not like her. Aaron had not noticed anything out of the ordinary and so Danielle kept quiet, only glancing toward Dharalyn when the girl gave her a deeply troubled look.

That night, back in their bedroom, Danielle brought up the Christian meeting. "What did he say to you?" she asked, and then was surprised when Dharalyn got really quiet. For a moment, she thought her friend wasn't going to tell her, but then she began to explain.

"That day in the woods, when I attacked him, I fortunately came to my senses before I hurt him much. I told him I was sorry and asked him to please forgive me."

Danielle's mouth dropped open. Here was another revelation from that time, that she'd known nothing about. "So, what did he say to you?"

Dharalyn gazed intently at Danielle with a knowing look. "He whispered to me three simple words...."

"Yes."

"He said, '*I forgive you*'."

"Oh crap," Danielle said, her expletive underscoring the intensity of her feelings. "Well, I guess we can forget all about the deny-till-you-drop idea. You know, I just had another thought."

"What's that?"

"You know that picture he wants to show us?"

"Yes."

"I'll bet anything that I can tell you what and who it is about, right now!"

"No...." said Dharalyn slowly, afraid to even ask.

"Oh yeah, I'll bet that somewhere in his house there is a picture of your face, my dearest Dharalyn, hanging on his wall."

"You think anyone will be able to tell it's me? Is he any good?"

Danielle chuckled. "God, yes. He's freaking awesome! Won all kinds of awards, over the years, for his work. His portraits look exactly like whoever they are about. Make no mistake, anyone who knows you who sees it, is going to know it's you."

"So, we should go and take a look at it, then?"

Danielle nodded. "Oh, more than that Dhara. Not only do we need to see it, if it's what I think it is, then you my dear, need to talk him into giving it to you. Can you imagine the gossip if it ends up in the next art show, and he explains to someone where he got the inspiration for it?"

"Hmmm, I see your point."

"Thank you. I knew you would."

Dharalyn stretched her arms. "It's been a long day. Ready for bed?"

Danielle peered at her clock. "No, it's still too early yet. This is the perfect time to try something else I've been wanting us to do."

Dharalyn looked stricken, sensing the meaning from both the words and her tone. "No!"

"Yes! You said you would try it again. So, come on. As your Sho-Notoo, I really want you to do this with me."

"Danielle, being Sho-Notoo does not give you any right to pressure me into something I don't want to do."

"Stop being a big baby. Besides, you told me you would and someone of your station should never lie to her best friend."

Danielle glanced at Dharalyn's face and paused; the look she was getting was not friendly, in the least.

"A friend would not ask me to do this, Danielle. You have no idea what it was like, the first time."

"True," Danielle said, and then added in her most persuasive tone, "But I know in my heart that you need to do this. That whatever hope you have of ever returning to your home is connected with you overcoming your fear and reaching your Egana. I feel the truth of it deep within me." She did, too, though to be honest, she wasn't actually sure if it was a deep-rooted certainty, or just her own stubborn nature that was making her press this point.

"Fine!" said Dharalyn, in a voice that was both angry and exasperated. "But, if I do this and it doesn't work, you're not allowed to ever ask me to try it again.... Promise?"

Danielle nodded slowly, surprised at Dhara's vehement tone. "Okay, I promise," she said, reluctantly.

Dharalyn sat cross-legged on Danielle's bed and motioned for her to join her. As Danielle faced Dhara, she leaned forward and they clasped their arms together.

"Okay, now I don't know how much of this you are going to be able to see or sense. When I enter the state of Memordei, I will release my Ayowei and I will begin to fall into my center, in an attempt to reach my Egana. Should I get there, I will see an artifact, represented by a serene garden of grass, bushes, flowers and ferns, surrounding a beautiful pond filled with a kind of liquid energy. This is my mind's interpretation of Anon's blessing and the representation of Kamanah. It is here that we Sedai have revealed to us the quality and magnitude of our gift."

Danielle nodded; she had heard this all explained, before. "Will I see it, too?"

"No. I know very little about what happens when a Sho-NoToo is involved, but according to all I have read about it, I am pretty sure you will see nothing. It is possible you may sense what I'm going through, but you will see very little else. Are you sure you want to do this?" asked Dharalyn, hoping Danielle was having a change of heart.

"I'm ready. Let's do it," said Danielle, adamantly, her determination unwavering.

Dharalyn frowned and then resigned herself to moving forward. "Okay. Here I go," she said, nervously.

She slipped into a relaxed state, as she had been trained. With barely an effort, she entered Memordei and felt the world around her fading away. When she was completely relaxed and tranquil, she essayed a thought, "*You there, Dani?*"

"*Yes!*" she replied.

Surprised, but not completely so, by the strength and clarity of Danielle's answer, Dharalyn released her Ayowei with practiced ease and sensed in the far, far distance the spark of her Egana. Slowly and carefully she began her descent, sensing the *other* that was with her this time. As she fell and dropped deeper and deeper into her awareness, she began to hope that this time might be different. Perhaps the increased confidence she was feeling due to Danielle being with her would do the trick. Maybe this time it would go smoothly.

The sudden and brutal awareness of a titanic force crashed against her senses, then. Much worse than before, Dharalyn felt herself falling helplessly into a maelstrom of unspeakable power and ferocity. She felt herself scream, but couldn't hear her own voice within the tumult that raged all about her. It was as if all the mighty power and force of the universe was lashing out at her, angry for the impudence, the effrontery, of daring to seek out that which was denied her the first time. Her fear grew and swelled within her breast, until she thought she would burst from the palpable terror that infused her. She had no control over her surroundings, nothing to hold to as she was tossed about like an insignificant bug and pitched helter-skelter by rampaging, livid forces of unspeakable torment. That she was evidently unworthy was made patently clear, by the overwhelmingly negative response to her very presence here. All about and below her was blue, lightning-filled emptiness that stretched outward in a vast expanse on all sides of her. Fearing to go farther and with all of her might and power, she reached and clawed at the ether, trying to pull herself up and out of the frantic turmoil. She cried and begged for someone to hear, someone to come and rescue her. Her begging turned to whimpering, then to pleading, crying for the soothing touch of a loving hand, for something, anything to reach down and pull her up and out of the terror that enveloped her in every direction. She could hear a mewling sound, not unlike that of an infant terrified beyond the capacity of a young mind's ability to grasp the horror of its circumstances, and somewhere deep within her own mind, she sensed that the pitiful sound she perceived was in actuality, her own. It was all hopelessness...all about her...a sense of utter futility and then.... *Then, suddenly, it was over.* Somehow, she wasn't sure exactly how, she was back in the bedroom, covered in beads of sweat and shaking uncontrollably. Danielle was with her, holding her tightly and her face was pale white, like a death mask. It was obvious to Dharalyn that whatever she had felt, whatever it was she had just gone through, Danielle had experienced some or possibly all of it, herself.

Danielle held her and pulled her into her protective, encircling arms even tighter. "Never again," she whispered, hoarsely. "Never, ever do that again. I'm so, so sorry! You shouldn't have listened to me." The two of them grasped each other tightly for a long time, each of them sobbing and shaking with relief, from the lingering effect of the trauma they'd been through together.

"Never again," Dharalyn agreed, her voice cold and frightfully bitter. "She should have had them kill me, when I failed it the first time!"

CHAPTER 18

NEVER MESS WITH THE MOB

Antonello Michael Moretti was sitting at his desk, rolling a pen back and forth across the glass top, while four of his top guys stood patiently watching him. They knew from experience that the big man was mulling something over, something that was really eating him up and when he was good and ready, he would tell them precisely what it was.

"Okay men, here's what we are going to do," he said, his voice cold and determined. "Bruno, I want you to go get the security tapes for the building and find a couple of really good pictures of those two little babes that were here, a few weeks back. Then, I want you and the rest of your guys, to take the rest of the crew and canvass the local parking garages. They can't have parked more than two or three blocks away. Take the pictures and show them to every person from every garage, until you find someone who remembers them. When you find that, get the surveillance footage from the garage and get me a license plate number."

"But boss, what if no one remembers them?" said Carlos, one of the guys that had been present at the scene of his humiliation.

"Hell, Carlos, I know damn well you remember that fine little black haired girl, and you only saw her once. One of those depraved ass-wipes that works at those parking garages is gonna remember seeing that sweet piece of tail, I guarantee it. Offer a little green for information, while you are at it. That always helps jog a few memories. Now, get going and don't come back until you have something for me. Bruno!" he added sharply, giving the man a look that would make lesser men quake, "I want hourly updates. You find me something, dammit! We're going to find those two, if we have to comb the entire city. Also, have someone go and look up our old friend, Samuel Remy; I'm willing to bet he'll remember something useful about those two that will give us a lead, and make certain you press him until he does."

"You got it, boss. Remy will probably be our best shot. I'll go see him, myself." Bruno knew this was a hot item and knew, too, that they'd better have some results by day's end. Moretti had been stewing over this for weeks and something had finally caused him to blow.

Michael Moretti waved his hand dismissively for them to leave. He did not smile or say anything as his men filed out of his office. After they'd left, he turned his chair toward the window overlooking the city and contemplated, in detail, what he would do when his men found the two girls. He had a contact overseas that would give him a pretty penny for them if they were both virgins. Take them and make them disappear, for good. Sell them on the skin market, as it was referred to in certain circles. It was a white slavery trading ring and not anything he himself would have dirtied his hands with, but it would be a fitting conclusion to this little matter. *But then, would it really be enough,* he thought, as he began to bite his nails, a bad habit that he had kicked years ago and one that only surfaced when he was very anxious and unsettled. Those two had made a jackass out of him, right here in his own office, the center of his authority and the very heart of what was a much respected organization, in his line of work. It had taken him a long while to recognize this situation for what it was, but his determination to see the absolute truth in things, his natural ability to discern any hint of subterfuge, along with a keen pair of eyes and a considerable intellect, which helped him perceive the evidence of this fraudulent undertaking, had finally forced him to see reason. Everything those two girls had done could be easily explained. He'd spoken at some length to an arms expert, talked to a master magician and quick change artist, and pieced together exactly how he had been duped. The talkative one, she'd called herself Danielle, had been wearing a new lightweight bullet proof undergarment that the arms guy had said was thinner and lighter than anything previously available. He wasn't sure where she could have gotten her hands on something like that, but time would tell. When he got hold of her, he would find out. He had ways of getting information from her without too much bruising, which would result in lowering her value. And then, there was the other girl: the magician had assured him that he could duplicate the remarkable illusion Michael had described and which she had put on with practiced ease, including the display of fake wings, and had offered to prove it in person, for a considerable fee. There was no need, though; he knew in his heart that there had been something out of kilter with the whole business. And as far as knocking old Bruno around, hell, so the girl knew some Martial Arts! Could possibly have been on some PCP-based drug, as well. That would have done it. He fumed as he recalled how some of his men had borne witness to his humiliation. Respect for his leadership abilities was paramount, in this business. He could little afford for rumors to circulate among the other families, of how he had been deceived. Better they learned, instead, that some foolish individuals only tried to put one over on him and had, as a result, been caught, tortured and humiliated to such an extreme that no one would ever consider screwing him over again. True, it had actually taken awhile for him to see it, though he had honestly had doubts, from the beginning. His suspicions over the weeks had quietly simmered, though truthfully, what had finally tipped him over the proverbial edge, was recalling the name of the vampire clan they were supposedly from. *The Vulkiri.* He had learned, in speaking to his youngest daughter, who had an interest in vampire books, that it was a derivative of the term Volturi, which apparently was some kind of coven in a favorite series of vampire books, among the younger generation. It had come up one evening during a family dinner as she'd been talking about some movie that she'd seen. He had gotten so angry, that he had hurled his meal against the wall and raged at his family for over an hour. That had occurred just a few days ago. Since then, he'd been working out the details of how they had pulled it off. He had it now, and it was time for some payback. He didn't know where they were yet, but when he found them, he was going to enjoy showing them what happens when you mess with someone of his stature and influence. *In fact,* he thought with a self-satisfied grin, *to hell with selling them to the slavers.* It wasn't as if he needed the money, and when it came right down to it, selling them wasn't going to make him feel any sense of real satisfaction. More importantly, he needed to send a strong message, as well as set an example for his business partners. He had a private estate up in Maine, where he liked to go when he needed peace and quiet. It was an extremely remote location and allowed him to do pretty much as he pleased, without any neighbors sticking their noses in his business. He would take them up there, he suddenly decided. Michael smiled to himself with satisfaction and nodded his head with the delicious thought. *He knew what to do with them!*

The first few days as a high school Junior were pretty hectic and kept Danielle in a constant state of high anxiety. Feeling protective about her and worried she might have trouble dealing with all of the new things coming at her, as well as finding her classes, Danielle tried to be with Dharalyn every moment she could, but after the third warning in as many days for being late to her own class, Dhara put a stop to it.

"You're going to get yourself in a lot of trouble, so stop babying me. I will be just fine."

Danielle grumbled about it, but did as she was told. She wished they had more classes together, or all of them in fact, but Dharalyn's late enrollment had caused her to get a much different schedule than she had. Besides two classes, science and English, the only other things they shared on their schedules were lunch and twice a week, gym class. The period before lunch she had a ceramics art class, and to her surprise, Christian sat next to her, while they attempted to make something meaningful out of a lump of earthenware clay.

"So, when are you and your cousin going to stop in and see me?" he asked, casually, as if idly curious and not the least concerned about when they would come.

Danielle, not taken in by his seemingly innocent question, answered, "Oh, I don't know. One of these days, soon. I can't promise anything, but I will talk to her about it. Maybe over the weekend we will stop over."

Christian smiled. "Excellent! I really hope you will make it. Say, Danielle, what are you two doing Friday evening, after school? Do you have any plans?"

"That's tomorrow, right? I don't think so."

"Good, because I was wondering, a friend of mine, Melissa Wellington, is having a little celebration at her house tomorrow night, kind of a back-to-school hullabaloo."

Danielle felt herself tighten up inside. She didn't like at all where this conversation was going.

"Anyway," he continued, unaware that anything was amiss with her, "I saw Dharalyn in the hall earlier and when I mentioned it to her, she said it sounded like fun and she would talk to you about going. So, I thought I'd mention it to you now, so that you don't feel like you're being blindsided."

"Uh, Christian," Danielle started slowly, unsure exactly how to proceed, "that's very nice of you and all, but Melissa and I have never been very friendly. There is no way she is going to invite me to this get-together of hers."

"Doesn't matter. It was actually mine and Tommy's idea," he said, referring to his friend Tommy Wheeler, who was Melissa's on again, off again boyfriend, depending on her mood, "and even though it's at her house, the guest list is totally up to us. So, will you two come?"

Danielle balked at his question. "I don't know.... This kind of social gathering is not really my type of thing. And trust me, when Melissa finds out you invited us, she won't be very happy about it. Not at all."

Christian looked crestfallen and his voice took on a pleading timbre. "Come on, Danielle, help me out here. Look, to be perfectly honest with you, I really like your cousin and I know there's no way she will come unless you do, too. Listen, I promise to keep Melissa off your back. And you will have a good time, I'm sure of it. You know," he then said, his voice dropping in volume as if sharing a secret, "I probably shouldn't tell you this, but there's been a lot of talk about you among some of the guys here at school."

Danielle felt her stomach drop at that thought. "What kinds of things?" she asked, sullenly, prepared for the worst. For years, she had strolled the halls of this school, knowing full well what the boys thought of her. Plain old boring, homely, unremarkable Danielle. There had never been any guy interested in her, she hated to admit it, and didn't expect that to change, anytime soon. It was Dharalyn the guys were going gaga for. The evidence had been all around them, ever since they'd walked into the school together that first day. Everywhere they went guys stopped talking, stopped walking, turned and just about slobbered themselves silly, acting like a bunch of apes in heat. She heard the whispering, though admittedly, she hadn't made out exactly what they'd been saying. But she'd caught enough hushed, half heard comments to get the gist of it, all right. Dharalyn was a hot topic around here; she didn't need Christian to tell her that.

"Well," Christian continued on in guarded tones, unaware of the turmoil going through Danielle's head, "for one thing, most of them can't get over how really good looking you've gotten over the summer. I believe the term I've heard used most by everyone is, totally hot!"

Danielle made a sound that she was fairly sure was her jaw hitting the floor. Of all the things she'd been prepared for Christian to say, that particular statement was so far down the list as to not even be visible by electron microscope. *Hot!* If there was one thing she definitely was not, it was THAT word. She'd often had trouble keeping a tight rein on her temper, although in school she had always worked hard to maintain it. This from him, however, went beyond bad taste and his misguided attempt at humor had backfired, totally. When she'd seen him at the mall, he'd told her she'd changed a lot and that hadn't been too bad. But now, here he was making up a bunch of crap and telling her she was good looking, and that some guys thought she was hot! That, she simply could not bear! "You know, Chris, I've always thought you were a pretty nice guy. But I have to say, that is about the most insensitive thing I've ever heard you or anyone else say to me. If you are going to make up ridiculous stories at my expense, please make sure you actually have a point, besides trying to make me feel bad."

"But, Danielle," he said, raising his hands in protest.

"But, Danielle nothing! If you really like Dharalyn, then you should know she doesn't like people who make hurtful comments at the expense of others, or who try to manipulate people's emotions by buttering them up or by outright lying, just so they can achieve their own selfish, self-serving agenda. She's much smarter than that, Chris! A whole lot smarter and you really should know better." Unable to contain herself any longer, Danielle got up, grabbed her book bag and began walking out of the room, ignoring the stunned looks she was getting from the other students. As she reached the door, Miss Moore, the art teacher, called out to her.

"Danielle Walkerman, please get back to your seat this instant! Whatever it is you feel the need to do, it can wait until class is over and I have properly dismissed you."

Danielle acknowledged the teacher with a scathing glance followed by a third fingered salute and then walked out of the room, the class exploding behind her in an uproar.

Dharalyn had gone to the school library between classes to get a copy of a physics book she had accidentally left at home, and had gotten turned around. By the time she'd found the book, realized she had gone to the wrong end of school and had headed in the right direction, she was a good ten minutes late for class. As she reached the first floor hallway, a hall guard called out to her for her hall pass. This was something that she had a really hard time getting used to. Guards in a school! And on top of that, guards that expected her to answer to them, rather than the other way around. To her way of thinking, their whole manner was inexcusable and utterly lacking in the proper decorum that was her due. So, when the hall guard called out to her while she was deep in thought and wondering if she was going the right way, she dismissed him with a simple hand gesture that any of the Atrova Guardians in her world would have understood and with the gravest humility, would have begged her pardon. That was not to be the case here, however, and after being chased down and unable to present a hall pass, something else she was having trouble comprehending, *a slip of paper that means it's okay to walk down a hall,* Dharalyn found herself standing in front of the assistant principal along with, to her consternation, *Danielle.* After being read what Danielle later referred to as the riot act, she found out that the two of them would be spending the afternoon after school let out, at something called detention. It was, apparently, a place where miscreants and troublesome types were sent to be punished. *My Aunt Olmerelda would get a huge laugh out of this,* Dharalyn thought to herself. She had remarked on more than one occasion that Dharalyn was entirely too strait-laced for her own good and needed to raise a little heck now and then. *Olmé would be so proud of me if she could see me now,* thought Dhara, with a self-deprecating shake of her head.

Michael Moretti smiled and rubbed his hands together with glee. They had gotten the girl's license plate number at the very first parking garage the boys had checked. One of the workers there had recognized the dark-haired girl's picture immediately and had, according to Bruno, gone on for nearly ten minutes about what a looker the girl was, before Bruno had gotten annoyed and slapped the guy's ears back. Impatient to know more, Michael then had his secretary Bianca, who'd worked for him for fifteen years and was trusted with these types of tasks, phone their contact at the motor vehicle bureau and get the girl's personal information. Within an hour he had a complete workup of the damn girl sitting on his desk including address, phone number, birth date, social security info, hell, everything he needed to know about Danielle Walkerman. For a moment he nearly lost it again, slamming his fist repeatedly on his desk, as he recalled the Walker-Man reference the girl had used on him. His men looked at him anxiously, as he pulled it quickly together. Now was the time to remain calm, use this as an example of what would happen should any of them ever contemplate doing him wrong. Again, he tasked Bianca and had her call the girl's house to find out the exact whereabouts of the young ladies he so desired to see back in his presence. Within ten minutes, she was back and said to Michael:

"I spoke to a woman named Sara, who is apparently this girl Danielle's aunt. I told her that I was with Hollister, which is a very popular girl's clothing store, that something Danielle had ordered was missing some sizing information and that I needed to speak to her. She informed me that the girls would be coming in early this evening, because they are both staying late at Pine Tree High School for detention. She doesn't expect them to be home before six or seven o'clock."

"Excellent!" shouted Michael Moretti, his exuberance overwhelming his composure. "Bruno, take four guys you can trust and go to that school and get me those two little bitches. After you have them secured, I want you to call me and then bring them to our private terminal, in Newark. From there, we will fly the whole party to my place up in Maine, where we will get to know these two young ladies very well. Very well, indeed," he chuckled, as a wicked sneer transformed his features, giving him a predatory look. He was practically giddy with joy from imagining the looks that would appear on their young faces when they saw him; when they realized he had found them out and that it was he, Michael, who had kidnapped them and that their fate now rested with him. That's when things would really get deliciously interesting. First, of course, would be the commencement of all the begging and the pleading, oh, and of course, the abundance of tears. The fear from the two of them would be so thick, it would be palpable. He practically grinned from ear to ear as his imagination churned with the thoughts of how gratifying he would find the groveling of the two girls, before him. But none of it would have any effect on him, not in the least! He would revel in their terror and when it reached the pinnacle of madness, then he and his boys would really start in on them. Yes, they were going to have a really good time in Maine and, truthfully, he couldn't wait for the party to start.

Bruno turned and selected four men he knew he could count on to follow his orders without question. Carlos, Bernardo,

Giovanni and Marco. He sent the first two to get the hardware they would need. Shotguns would be best for this kind of work. Then, he sent Giovanni and Marco to get a van along with plenty of plastic ties and duct tape. Since they would be going to a school, he was pretty certain that there would be other kids there, who would need to be subdued and kept quiet. A few heavy plastic ties on the ankles and wrists, some duct tape across the mouth, and they would be out of harm's way for the duration, while Bruno and his boys collected the two girls in question, per Michael's orders. This needed to go well, and he didn't want anything to go wrong. Hopefully, they wouldn't need to kill anyone, but if someone got heroic, then he would do whatever he deemed to be necessary. He had one purpose and that was to get the two babes in their custody, and be in and out of there, fast. The last thing he wanted to have to do was to call Michael Moretti and tell him that things hadn't gone well, and that they didn't have the babes in hand. He'd seen the look in his boss's eyes and knew he was really looking forward to having them in his clutches. Bruno grimaced to himself, just a little bit. He was a hard man and not prone to feeling overwhelming sentiment toward anyone. But these two were so young, and he knew what was likely in store for them. *It would almost be better for them, if they try something and we end up having to take them out,* he thought. These, of course, were private contemplations that he would never dare speak aloud in Moretti's presence. But, honestly, it would be a much more merciful ending than what the boss had in mind. As far as Michael's plans for the girls went, well, he didn't know everything, but what he did know...it made him queasy just to think about it.

CHAPTER 19

HIGH SCHOOL HORROR

If there was anything Danielle hated more than detention, she didn't know what it was. Mr. Banks, who was by day a math teacher, took great pleasure in making the entire detention scene one of ultimate boredom. He didn't allow you to read, listen to music or even do your homework. All you were allowed to do was sit quietly and stare at the walls. Danielle suspected that in a past life he had likely been a mole or maybe a weevil; certainly not a human being of any kind. A person of any decency, whatsoever, would at least let them be productive in some way during this three hour stretch of time. *God, kill me now,* she thought to herself, and not for the last time. She gazed around the room, surprised to see that there were only three people here. Herself, Dharalyn and some Goth chick whose name Danielle could not remember. *Oh well, still early in the year. I'm sure it will fill up much more, before long.*

Mr. Banks stepped out of the room and almost immediately, Dharalyn heard a "Pssst," coming from beside her.

"Hi, you're new here, aren't you?" asked a girl who was dressed entirely in black, and who sported blue-frosted hair and black lipstick.

She was the oddest looking person that Dharalyn had ever seen before. "Yes, I'm Danielle's cousin from out west. My name's Dharalyn," she said, in a tone louder than a whisper, yet softer than a regular speaking voice.

"Hi, I'm Varvara Petralia, or as my friends and family call me, Vee."

"Nice to meet you, Vee," replied Dharalyn, as she peered anxiously out the door, waiting for the teacher's return.

"Oh, don't worry about old Banksee. He's slipped out for a smoke. He'll be gone fifteen minutes, at least. You can pretty much count on him to slip out about once an hour, whenever he has to be here."

"You sound like you spend a lot of time here in detention."

"Yeah," she said, chuckling, "I guess you could say it's almost a hobby of mine."

Dharalyn glanced over at Danielle and was surprised to see that her chin had fallen to her chest and her eyes were fluttering closed. Apparently, she was really tired and seemed about ready to fall asleep.

"You know, I've been wanting to talk to you," whispered Vee, in a conspiratorial voice. "I've been watching you ever since you came here. Not creepy like or anything. I'm just the curious type is all.... There's something about you, something different. Like, you don't exactly fit in with the mundane majority."

With a shake of her head, Dharalyn grinned at the girl. "I'm not sure what to think about that.... So, I'm not mundane, you say?"

Vee smirked. "Don't take it personal. I'm just really intuitive and tend to speak my mind. I think it's because of my affinity for the dark and the mysterious side of life. The world is full of strange things, and I consider myself a student of the bizarre and misunderstood things, that most people don't even care about."

"What do you mean? What kind of things are you interested in?"

"Oh, you know. Things that defy explanation. Things that go bump in the night. Stuff that rattles the mind. Like psychic stuff, for instance, you know, powers of the mind. I've been reading a lot about Eastern philosophy and how to channel your Chi, and such."

"Sounds pretty interesting."

"It is. So tell me, what is your deal, Dharalyn? Besides having a rather odd name, like me, you have a real deep mystery about you. It shows up in your aura, which blazes like the dickens. I've never seen anything like it before in my life."

Dharalyn sat stunned. Up until this second, she'd had this girl classified as nice but kind of nutty in a harmless way. Now, she wasn't so sure. "Are you saying you can see my aura?"

"Oh, sure. All the women in my family have always been a little, off, you know. I think my great-grandmother was a gypsy fortune teller, or something. I saw an old picture of her dressed up like one, but whenever I ask my mother about it, she gets really quiet and shushes me. That's the way my Mom handles the weird stuff, even though she can see people's auras, just like I can. She pretends they aren't there though, and won't even let me talk about them. Anyway, everyone here at school pretty much considers me a nut job, but I still kinda hope we can be friends."

Dharalyn smiled warmly. "I don't see a problem with that. I kind of like strange things, too. So does Danielle."

Vee nodded. "Yeah, your cousin has always been on my not a total cretin list. She's always seemed pretty genuine to me, and not all contrived and fake, like most of the mundys."

"No," said Dharalyn, "she's certainly not fake, or, a mundys did you say?"

"You know, a mundainer. They who lack imagination and are doomed to live and work in a boring, dull existence. The mundane. So, let me ask you, and don't take this the wrong way. Do you believe there are things in our world that defy description? Things that actually exist, that most people think are fictional or the stuff of legends and fairy tales?"

"I don't know," said Dhara, suddenly feeling a trifle uncomfortable. "Why do you ask that?"

"Well, I know it sounds funny, but I just get these feelings sometimes. And the first time I saw you, the first time I saw your incredible aura and looked into your eyes, I thought to myself, there is a girl whose eyes have seen things that others have never dreamed of. There is someone who understands the real reality behind the curtain that eludes most of us."

Dhara nodded slowly, again not sure what to say.

"So, tell me, Dharalyn, as a simple matter of curiosity. Do you believe that it is possible that something that is considered to be fictional like, well, let's say ghosts, or demons, or even vampires could possibly walk the earth?" asked Vee. "That they are not just imaginary, but that they actually exist, for real?"

Dhara nearly choked and felt herself go pale. *Who in the world is this girl,* she thought, as her emotions gyrated madly. "I don't know," she said, a little too forcibly, trying her best to maintain her composure. No one had ever caught her so off guard before, or caused her to feel quite so distraught.

"Because, I have to tell you, I think it is entirely possible. I've always believed that some of the myths and folklore of our society are based in reality. And vampires absolutely intrigue me."

"Why do you believe that?" asked Dharalyn, as she turned toward the sound of a clearing throat.

"You there, chatty girl," said Mr. Banks, who had walked in while she'd been talking. "Come on up here, please."

Dharalyn stood and with a strange feeling of dread, unlike anything she'd ever experienced before in her life, approached the teacher's desk.

"Do me a little favor, will you, since keeping quiet is something you apparently haven't mastered yet? I forgot my keys for the front doors to the school. Go to the gym and take this note to Ms. Forester, the Cheer Squad coach. Tell her I need to borrow her set of keys and since the Cheer Squad is nearly done for the night, she'll be leaving way before we do. And please try and hurry. I don't want you to miss her."

Dharalyn nodded and glanced once toward Danielle, who she could see was now wide awake, and Vee, who was trying hard not to laugh. "I'll be back soon," she said to the two girls, and left the room. Getting her bearings, she headed down the hallway and soon passed the main foyer, where the guard desks sat empty and glanced out of the double set of swinging front doors that marked the main entrance to the school. She had just crossed the wide empty area and had entered the adjoining hallway that led past several empty classrooms, when she saw someone she recognized walking toward her.

"Hello, Melissa," said Dharalyn, cheerily, as she walked another twenty feet or so and then stopped. "I'm looking for Ms. Forester; can you tell me if she's still in the gym?"

"Yes, she should still be there. If not, then you will find her in the girls' locker room, closing up."

"Thanks," she said, and began to walk away.

"Uh, Dharalyn," said Melissa, hesitantly. "It is Dharalyn, right?"

Dhara stopped and turned back around. "Yes, that's correct."

"Listen, some of my friends and I are having a sort of back-to-school party at my house, tomorrow night. I just want to invite you and tell you that it would be nice, if you came. I think you would probably fit in well with the crowd I hang out with. And, there will be quite a few guys there and probably even a couple of college types," she said, giving her a knowing wink. "Anyway, there are a few people who have expressed an interest in meeting you and I think it would be a really good opportunity for you. So, do you think you might come?"

Dharalyn nodded thoughtfully. "I think we might. Danielle told me that she had spoken with Christian about it earlier today and I'm pretty sure I can talk her into coming."

Melissa looked momentarily taken aback. "Christian Miles invited Danielle to come to my get-together?"

Dharalyn smiled. "Yes, he told her he wanted both of us to come. She didn't seem too eager at first, but I told her it would be good for the both of us to get out and meet a few people, in a more casual setting. I think I should be able to talk her into it by tomorrow."

"Uh, Dharalyn, I'm very sorry," Melissa said, melodramatically, "but Christian is mistaken. This little soirée is only for a certain kind of people. Your cousin, I'm afraid, is part of a socially inept group that, for the most part, my friends and I try to avoid. Trust me; she wouldn't have a good time or fit in well with my friends. She would be much better off going to something like a Harry

Potter reunion, or possibly a poetry reading. The people who will be at this party are trendy, interesting and know how to carry on an intelligent conversation. This party is not for someone like her, and to put it more directly, she is just not invited."

Dharalyn gave Melissa a steely look. "I'm sorry you think that way, but you should know, Melissa, Danielle is my very best and dearest friend. If she is not welcome at your party, then you will not see me there, either."

Melissa's eyes were bright as she smiled sweetly. "That's okay! I just thought that you might want to raise your social standing a bit. I mean, if you're comfortable hanging out with a social leper, then who am I to care?" Without a further word, she turned her back on Dharalyn and walked off.

Dharalyn shook her head with disbelief at Melissa's arrogance and watched her walk into the wide, central foyer, headed toward the hallway Dhara had just left. She was just about to turn and head toward the gym, when she paused. She could see that Melissa had stopped behind the guard desks and was looking toward the front doors, in a queer way. Feeling an odd sense of foreboding steal over her, Dharalyn stepped backward into the partially hidden doorway of the nearest classroom, and then stood quietly and listened. There were people, men she could hear now, coming in through the front doors. There was a strange clinking of what sounded like something metallic and then a snapping, ratcheting noise that she didn't recognize. Dharalyn tensed as Melissa, who'd been standing utterly still, suddenly cried out in terror and began running into the far hallway. Reaching back with her hand, Dharalyn grabbed and twisted the door handle of the heavy door and found it was locked. Drawing on Ayowei to allow her to quickly transition into Kquwaya-Set and then Kquwaya-Shira, which gave her increased strength, she forced the handle downward and heard it snap. Soon she was inside the dark room, and watched through the cracked opening of the door, as several men dressed all in black came hurriedly into view. With her enhanced senses, she could now hear the shouted commands and see the guns in their hands. Something was going on, something bad. Quickly, she closed the door and mentally prepared herself to call on Shonyemaya precognition. She needed to see what was coming.

"Marco, you got him trussed up yet?" asked Bruno. They had arrived at the Pine Tree High School and grabbed a grounds guy, who had been working outside of the school changing trashcan liners. Right now, he was lying on the floor of the van after being roughed up a bit by his guys.

"Yeah, he's not going anywhere."

"So, what did you find out?"

Marco grinned. "Not many people here, tonight; just a bunch of cheerleaders down at the gym, doing their thing with their coach, and a detention class where our two girls should be. Gym is all the way down the right hall, off the front foyer and detention class is down the left hall. Supposed to be the second classroom on the right."

"Good," said Bruno, succinctly. "Carlos, you Marco and Giovanni head down to the gym and bring them all up to the detention room. We'll lock them down in there, take the two girls Michael wants and be out of here in twenty minutes. With any luck, it will be hours before anyone knows that something is up. Boys, stay in touch on the two-way radios. I want to know if you see anything suspicious, or hear immediately, if anything goes wrong."

"No problem, boss," said Carlos, knowing how important it was that things went down fast and smooth. "We'll have the whole bunch from the gym back to your location in about ten to fifteen."

"Good," said Bruno. "Bernardo, you're with me. Since you're the youngest and the fastest, I want you to walk around and keep an eye out for any stragglers that might be roaming the hallways. If you see anyone wandering around, you get them and bring them to me."

Bernardo nodded. He was excited at the prospect of violence. He loved slapping people around and he hoped he would have the chance to play rough.

"We'll leave the van parked here," Bruno explained, and then added, "That was a good idea, Marco, hotwiring this old Hostess panel van. Anyone that sees it will think we're here filling the vending machines and won't think anything of it. Okay, boys, keep your guns hidden beneath your overcoats. Let's not tip anyone off, early. Move fast and don't be afraid to set an example, or two. Try not to kill anyone, though if a situation arises, don't be afraid to shed some blood. A little splash of Johnnie Red always helps to keep the little sheep scared and in line."

Bruno jumped out of the driver's seat and covered his shotgun with his long black trench coat. Quickly, he moved to the other side of the van and headed for the front doors, with the rest of his guys following close behind him. As they made their way up the few steps and pushed their way into the front foyer, Bruno saw the youthful form of a pretty blond cheerleader who'd been crossing the foyer, stop and stare curiously at them. Next to him, Bernardo cocked his shotgun menacingly, sending a cartridge into the chamber with a sharp, metallic click. Bruno watched the girl's eyes widen in shock, as she registered what the idiot next to him had just done. She let out a yelp of alarm mixed with fear and then took off running. Like a shot, Bernardo (the idiot) took off after her, as Bruno yelled for him to get her. He then told the second group to get a move on, hoping that no one had heard the frigging girl's squealing. They needed to get this done quickly and quietly. Let just one student with a damn cell phone get loose for a bit and this whole thing could turn into a circus act. Hoping that Bernardo was as fast as he seemed, Bruno headed quickly for the detention room. He needed to get the two girls they were here for under his control, fast. That way, if in a pinch he needed to make a fast exit, he could scram and leave the others to fend for themselves.

Melissa dove into the corridor that turned toward the right, past a school trophy case and then left again. She paused for a quick second, uncertain of what to do. Except for the light coming from the door of a single classroom, the hallway beyond was dark, since the lights on that far end of the building had been shut off. Making a decision, she quickly ducked into the girls' bathroom that was right in front of her. Swiftly, she made her way to the farthest stall and went inside, locking the stall door and then standing on the seat like she'd seen people do in the movies. That way if someone came inside, and looked underneath the stalls, they wouldn't see any feet and hopefully, they might think no one was in here. She tried to recall if it had ever actually worked in the movies, but couldn't remember. She hoped so. Her heart pounded and she began to sweat profusely. What the hell were those men doing in her school, and why were they carrying guns? She tried to come up with a reason they would be here, but she couldn't begin to fathom what that purpose might be. *Maybe they're terrorists planning to kidnap us all*, she thought. Why else would five men with shotguns come into the school, like they just did? She looked at her watch and stared bleakly as a minute and then another, slowly ticked by. She was surprised no one had followed her in here and she rose up a bit, trying to relieve the nervous strain and tension in her leg muscles that were tight as a drum, from the overwhelming fear coursing through her body. She was sure that one guy, the younger looking one, had come after her. But, surprisingly, there was no sign of him and all was quiet. She had just about decided to take a peek out of the bathroom door and see if she could see anything, when she heard the bathroom door suddenly slam open with a loud "BANG".

"Come out, come out wherever you are," a sneering voice with a strong Italian accent, said. "I've been looking for you, my pretty little lady."

Nervous and growing increasingly scared, her legs began to shake with the strain of standing motionless in a crouch. Her heart began to thud so loudly, she knew it must be audible to the man. As she saw a shadow appear between the cracks of the metal stall, she began, against her will, to whimper with fear.

Danielle had let her head fall forward again, fighting the urge to close her eyes since Mr. Banks would yell at her if he caught her sleeping, when a strange voice that hinted of familiarity brought her instantly awake.

"You, where is your little dark-haired friend?" said a deep voice, that was filled with derisive tension.

Danielle's eyes focused and her mind froze, unable to accept what she was seeing.

"I said, where the hell is she?" Bruno shouted, smacking his hand down on Danielle's desk, to get her attention.

"Excuse me," said Mr. Banks, who had made his way up behind the brutal stranger, "you can't just come in here...."

Bruno turned and whipped the shotgun barrel around in an arc, which intersected with a satisfying "crack" against the side of the teacher's head. The man fell like a limp sack of potatoes, as one of the girls shrieked in surprise.

"Shut up!" Bruno shouted, at the weirdo with the blue streaked hair. "Now I'm only going to ask you once more, and then I'm going to start hurting you. Do you understand me?"

Danielle nodded her head as tears clouded her eyes. She didn't know what this man was doing here, but she had a pretty good idea who had sent him and she was badly scared. "She went," her voice broke and she nearly gagged, as surging emotion and stress welled up inside her. "She went to the gym," she said, her voice shaking, afraid to lie and even more, unable to think of anything else to do. "She went to the gym, to take a note to the Cheer coach."

Bruno pulled a radio from his pocket and said, "Carlos, you there?"

"Yep," came the short, but distinct answer.

"Dark-haired girl went to the gym with some kind of note. Keep an eye out for her and let me know when you have her."

"Roger that."

Bruno placed the radio back in his coat and pulled out some plastic ties. "You there," he motioned toward the weirdo and growled forcefully, "get over here."

Vee came forward slowly and fearfully. As the man held out the plastic ties, she took them and then proceeded to drop a few.

"Pick those up!" he ordered. "You," he then said, pointing at Danielle, "move all of these desks out of the way. Clear the front of the room."

Danielle did as she was told, while the human equivalent of a gorilla, Bruno, she remembered his name was, pulled Mr. Banks around and used the heavy plastic ties to bind his wrists and his ankles. She sobbed once or twice, as she spied the dark smears of blood on the floor, which had obviously come from the bad cut she could see on the teacher's head. She hoped desperately that he would be all right, and silently prayed that wherever Dharalyn was, she would see these men coming and avoid being taken. She wasn't sure what she could do about them, but knew they were in for a very bad time if her friend didn't manage to get the upper hand on them, somehow.

Bernardo or Bernard, as his friends called him, had taken off after the little blond as soon as she'd ducked into the hallway. He ran to the front desks and turned into the left hallway, just as the girl ducked out of sight to the right. He ran quickly down the twenty-foot section, which jogged right at some displays, turned right for another ten feet or so and then turned left at the beginning of a long hallway. Putting on a burst of speed, he ran forward and then thought to check the doors of the darkened classrooms he was passing. As fast as he could, he checked first one locked door then another, skipping the lighted one where Bruno was headed, until he reached the far end that was considerably darker. It was then that he realized the girl couldn't have gotten this far, without his seeing her. *Must have missed something*, he thought, angrily. He'd been really pleased when he found out he was going on this little excursion. It was a chance to prove his worth to Mr. Moretti and to Bruno. But, more importantly, it had sounded like he was going to be able to have a bit of fun. Bernard liked roughing people up and even more, he liked terrorizing and mentally torturing them, whenever he got the chance. When he found that they were going to be scaring a bunch of high school kids, well that thought had given him great pleasure. Also, included as a bonus, there was the fact that no one here would be able to defend themselves, or give him and his bunch the slightest bit of a fight, which made the whole thing just about perfect. Not like dealing with some gang members from down in the city, or some of the other, tougher hoods that ran in his circles. No, this would be cake, absolute frosty sweet cake. He passed the lighted room where he heard Bruno inside, shouting and had a momentary qualm at the thought of having to explain to his squad boss that he couldn't find the missing girl. Worried and wondering what he could have missed, he suddenly spied the door to the girls' bathroom that he had overlooked, his first time through. Smiling with renewed confidence, he walked up to the door and kicked it open, hard. "Come out, come out wherever you are," he said, feeling the excitement build within. "I've been looking for you, my pretty little lady." Although he couldn't know for sure, he felt certain she was here. In fact, he would have bet his life on it. As he moved slowly forward, he could hear a slight whimpering noise coming from the last of the five stalls and grinned hugely. Reaching the stall, he tried the door and found that it was locked. *No matter,* he thought. He tapped his shotgun barrel against the metal door frame and said, "I know you're in there. Open the door and come out, or at the count of five, I'm gonna start blowing holes in the door with this shotgun. One," he said, resisting the urge to go quickly. He wanted to make this last. This type of thing was gloriously delicious to his nature, and he loved to draw it out, so as to engender as much fear as possible. "Two...three...four...." When he was about to say five, he heard the door unlock and he pushed it open. Standing inside was a beautiful blond haired girl, dressed in an adorably sexy cheerleading outfit. He'd only gotten a quick glimpse of her before, but now that he could see her, his pulse quickened and he smiled. She was a peach, a veritable sweet juicy peach and this was going to be even better than he had thought. He grabbed her wrist and pulled her roughly out of the stall, pushing her against the wall. "So, how do you want to die?" he asked her. "Quickly, or slow like?" He wasn't actually going to shoot and kill her, but she didn't need to know that.

"Please," she pleaded, in a tiny voice that was shaking so bad she was barely intelligible, "please don't hurt me."

"Well, I don't know for sure, but I might be willing to let you go," he said slowly, allowing the hidden meaning behind his words to seep into her awareness. "I could just tie you up, for instance, and leave you here till morning. If I do that, if I let you live when so many others tonight are going to die, what are you willing to do for me?" he asked, leering at her, his eyes gleaming bright as his pulse quickened even more. The girl said nothing; her eyes were as wide as saucers and tears were streaming silently down her cheeks. "Hmmm, tell you what. You behave like a good girl and as a reward, if you don't try anything funny or try and get away, I'll let you live. You have my word on it." He carefully set his shotgun down on a sink off to his right and then placing his hands on her waist, he leaned forward and kissed her roughly on her neck. *God, she smells good,* he thought, and impulsively, as he often did in the heat of the moment, he revised his plan on how far he would take this. Looking into her eyes, he could tell she was getting ready to bolt. They always thought they could get away, if they caught him off guard. "Uh, uh...don't you dare test me," he growled, menacingly. "I know you think you might make it to the door, but you won't, and then you'll regret it, princess." She whimpered then, causing his overall excitement to escalate even more.

"Please, please, I beg you, don't do this," she said, beginning to plead in a choking, crying voice, "Please...."

Bernard grabbed her shoulders roughly in both hands and squeezed hard, to make sure he had her full attention. "You do what I say or I promise I'll hurt you bad. You understand me, bitch?" he said, with a snarl, and peered directly into her eyes with a vicious look designed to intimidate. "Do you?" he said again, shaking her hard and then slamming her back against the wall, to better make his point. Finally, as all hope seemed to drain from her features, she gave him a fearful little nod of acquiescence and he grinned with satisfaction. Grabbing her waist again, he slid his hands around her back and then slipped them slowly up underneath the colorful top of her cheerleading outfit, enjoying the sensation of her soft skin, until he reached the fastening to her bra. She was scared out of her mind, and he knew from other, similar situations he'd been in, that she would comply to his will from here on out. *What a sweet treat this will be!* he thought, as he unhooked her bra, feeling the muscles in her back quivering with fear beneath his hands. He watched as she closed her eyes, listened to her whispered, half-heard desperate prayer and smiled as a tear fell from her lashes. From directly behind him, as his mind spiraled upward with growing passion, he heard the swooshing sound of someone opening the heavy wooden bathroom door and with a flash of annoyance at being interrupted, he began to turn around, ready to tell whichever of his guys it was, to get the hell out. Before he could finish the turn, Bernard felt himself yanked violently backwards and then flung sideways, as if he were a ten-pound sack of flour. His reflexes kicked in as he reached out with his arms defensively, trying vainly to stave off serious harm as his body smashed hard against the row of sinks there. He felt one of his wrists slam painfully against a large mirror, and saw his shotgun which had been lying there, fly out of sight as the air gushed out of his lungs in a loud whoosh. In the broken reflection in front of him, he caught a momentary glimpse of white hair and gleaming emerald eyes, eyes of a strange, alien nature that would have terrified him if he'd had even a moment to think about it, but then he was grabbed again and with an involuntary yelp, he felt himself tossed hard in the opposite direction, against one of the stall doors. He thought he heard some bones in his arm snap and possibly some in his ribcage, as he slammed straight on through the metal door, coming to a crashing halt against an immovable cement wall. The astonishment he felt barely had time to register, as the shock to his system and massive pain coursing through his body caused him to pass out.

Dharalyn gazed at Melissa, who was looking terribly disheveled and saw that she was eyeing her nervously. "You okay, Melissa?" she asked, walking slowly toward the girl, who seemed frozen in place, her body language markedly apprehensive. "It's all right. It's just me, your friend, Dharalyn." Slowly she reached out and took Melissa's hand, pressing her palm in a gentle, reassuring manner, with her fingers.

Melissa looked at her with wild eyes. "He was going...he was going...." she huffed wildly, seemingly unable to catch her breath, or marshal her thoughts. There were tears streaming down her face as she tried to pull herself together.

"It's okay," said Dharalyn, in a calm, reassuring voice. "I won't let him or anyone else hurt you." She spun about and dragged the unconscious gangster from where he was lying, and set him up against the broken stall. Using Ayowei to help bend the metal, she curled one of the stall support bars that had broken loose on one end, around his neck, effectively locking him in place.

"Dharalyn," said Melissa, apprehensively, while wiping the wetness from her eyes and cheeks, "there are some more of them. I think they went to the gym."

"I know.... And I'll do something about them as well, but I'm going to need your help to do it safely. Are you up to it?"

Melissa looked down at Bernard, who moments ago had made her feel completely helpless. She hated feeling that way, and knew somehow that this was going to bother her badly for a long time, unless she redeemed herself, somehow. She shrugged her shoulders in response. "I don't know if I can," she said, uncertainly, but then slowly nodded. "I will try though," she then added, her confidence lacking, but finding renewal in Dharalyn's actions. "Dharalyn," she said, staring at her with a look of wide-eyed apprehension, "why do you look like that, and what's with your teeth?"

Dharalyn gave her a long, appraising look. "It's a rather long story, too long to tell you right now and kind of a secret, Melissa. I will tell you later, when we have the time and if you promise to keep my secret. Right now, though, I need very badly for you to trust me. Can you do that for me?"

Melissa hesitated for a moment, then nodded, as her roiling emotions began to well up inside. Suddenly, she began to sob in a stuttering, choking manner that seemed to be only seconds from breaking loose in an uncontrollable torrent of emotion.

"Melissa, please! Stay with me, here! I need you to get control of yourself. I know you; what kind of person you are. You're a strong woman, a leader. I need you to reach down, deep within and find that inner strength I know you have. Draw it from the anger I know you must be feeling. If we are going to help the others, we need to go now and more importantly, I really can't do this without you. Wouldn't you like to get a little payback on these creeps?"

Melissa willed herself to calm down and in so doing, found a kind of stubborn fortitude she hadn't known she had. Forcing herself to breathe deeply, she wiped again at her tear streaked cheeks. "Are you sure you can handle them, Dhara?"

Dharalyn smiled and nodded. "Definitely! You just be your charming self and I will handle all the rough stuff. I promise!"

Melissa gave a half chuckling sob and began to follow Dharalyn out of the door. Suddenly, she stopped, turned, and with a fierce expression on her face she took three quick steps, lashed out with her right foot and kicked the man who'd just attacked her square in the face. Blood sprayed from his nose and there was a new, bright red bruise on the side of his cheek that hadn't been there, before. Melissa turned and faced Dhara with a steely look of determination on her features. "Okay, now I'm ready," she said, with surprising conviction, as she reached out and took the other girl's hand. "Let's go get them!"

CHAPTER 20

NEVER MESS WITH A VAMPIRE

Danielle sat on the floor next to Vee and carefully watched Bruno, who she could see was in a heightened state of anxiety. The big man had stepped close to the door and seemed to be watching for someone. Next to her, Vee was crying softly and kept rubbing her eyes with the backs of her fingers, while glancing periodically at Mr. Banks, who was at the very back of the room on the floor, trussed and tied securely. Reaching out a consoling hand, Danielle grasped her right hand in her left. "Shhhh, it will be all right."

"No it won't," sobbed the girl, her heavy black mascara and eyeliner mixing with her tears to form black streaks and rivulets, all down her cheeks. "I always knew it would end badly for me. This guy is going to shoot us all, you just watch and see. I can see some of his intent from the color of his aura. It's very dark, and it shows that he completely lacks the slightest compassion or sensitivity. I don't want to die," she then added, her sobbing increasing and her tears falling more frequently.

They were sitting on the floor, against a row of tightly packed desks. Danielle had been surprised that Bruno hadn't fastened those plastic ties on their ankles and wrists like he had their teacher, and as she thought about it, she surmised that it was probably because he planned to take herself and Dharalyn with him, and so needed her free. Though he'd left Vee loose too, she thought he would probably tie her up when they were joined by the others. She knew from hearing his radio conversations that they were out rounding up everyone else at the school, which she believed only amounted to members of the Cheer Squad. She knew they were here both because Mr. Banks had sent Dhara to the gym and because she had seen Melissa herself earlier, on her way to the gym with some of the other cheerleaders in tow. Melissa had seen her too, but had acted as if she hadn't even noticed her, which was pretty much normal behavior for her, and typical prima donna behavior for all of her best friends. Danielle glanced at Vee once more and came to a sudden decision. Grabbing her small handbag, she reached inside and found the Pametra device, zipped safely in an interior pocket. Bruno had searched both hers and Vee's bags earlier, and taken the other girl's cell phone, smashing it on the floor. She, of course, didn't own one, a sore spot between her and her father, and even felt a little embarrassed when she'd had to explain it to the thug. Taking Vee's right hand, she slipped the fully charged device (Dhara had recharged it weeks ago) over the girl's second and fourth fingers, and then clasped it about her wrist. "Now, this is going to tingle a bit, but don't be scared," she whispered, as she twisted the circular center on the palm a quarter turn to the right.

"Oh," said Vee quietly, "that feels really weird. What the heck is it?"

"It's something I got from a friend and it will protect you from projectiles. You know, gunfire and such. Nothing can hurt you now," she said, seeing the disbelief registering in the girl's face. "I know it's hard to believe, but watch." Danielle slipped a pen from her bag and holding it like a knife, she jabbed it with a quick downward thrust at the girl's exposed wrist. Vee reflexively pulled her hand back, though not until after the violent pen jab and then said in wonder, "Wow, I didn't even feel that. I should have an ink-pen hole in my hand, at least."

Suddenly, they heard someone holler. "What the hell are you two up to?" shouted Bruno, who was striding toward them and looking as mad as an angry bull. He seemed ready to yell at them some more, when suddenly his radio squawked noisily. "Boss, we're down here at the gym and we've got the kids and their teacher bound and gagged, but that girl you want never showed up, and she wasn't already here when we grabbed this bunch either, far as we can tell."

Something isn't going well, thought Danielle, optimistically. *I'd be willing to bet that pretty soon, they're gonna start having a little vampire problem, if I know Dhara.*

"What do you mean she's not there? Rough up some of those damn kids or their frigging teacher. Someone there must know where she is. Find her now, dammit!" he shouted into his handheld radio and then clicked it off. A thought seemed to come to him and he raised the radio to his mouth again. "Bernard, report.... Bernard, this is Bruno, answer the damn radio, immediately!" He had a sneaking suspicion he knew what the young SOB was probably up to and he was getting angrier by the minute. When they left here, he was going to break the young idiot's nose, for good measure. Damn hormone driven punk was just about useless. Only the bleak sound of white noise answered his radio challenge. Pissed, Bruno looked down and then reached out and grabbed Danielle by her wrist. Pulling her roughly to her feet, he marched her over to the entrance of the classroom and turned her to face him. He then grabbed her throat with his right hand and pushed her hard against the cement block wall next to the doorway, smiling at the resounding "whack" as the back of her head met the wall. "Where the hell is your little dark-haired friend at? I'm not screwing around with you, missy!" he said, gruffly.

"I told you," she said, gasping meekly, trying to ignore the painful throbbing of her head, "Mr. Banks sent her to the gym. Maybe she had to use the restroom and hasn't gotten there, yet," she added, in an attempt to waylay his doubts. She didn't actually believe that, but she hoped to give Dharalyn time to find a creative way to take care of those guys and get back. *Before this big brute loses it,* she thought, disconsolately.

"Maybe," Bruno looked thoughtful, then added, "if she isn't there within the next five minutes, though, I'm going to start breaking things, like...pretty little fingers. Maybe the sound of your screaming will bring her running. Or, if nothing else, help to jog your frigging memory." He reached under his jacket and pulled his .38 loose from its shoulder holster. "I can see you're not wearing your body armor now," he said, patting her down on her waist and stomach. "I bet you would feel these bullets now, if I decide to shoot you." His confidence increased as he saw the fearful look appear on her face. Much different from the little performance she and her friend had put on for Michael, in his office. He had to admit, even though Michael was sure, he himself hadn't been entirely certain these two girls had been faking things that day. The aura of fear coming from her now, though, was substantial. This little lady was badly scared and knew she wasn't going to be deflecting any bullets today. The certainty of it was all over her face. One more time, Bruno raised the radio to his mouth. "Bernard, come in. Answer me, immediately!" Nothing.... He hoped the guy was having a good time, because he was going to kill him.

Dharalyn and Melissa stood back from the entrance to the girls' locker room and whispered.

"Do you think they're all in there?" asked Dhara.

"I'm sure of it. Ms. Forester always likes to end up the Cheer practice session with a group discussion. I would be in there now, except I was running to my locker to get something out of it. That's why I was down on the other side of the school."

"Listen, Melissa, there are three of those mob guys in there. We need to somehow single them out. You have any ideas on how we can do that?"

"Well, what if I go to the door, open it and then act scared and run back past here? Can you handle them if one or two of them follow me?"

Dharalyn gazed all around as if searching for something, then walking swiftly down the hall, she stopped in front of a wall case with a glass panel, which held a fire extinguisher. Opening the small door, she hastily removed the heavy metal canister. She saw it had a thick metal ring around the top and tested its strength by swinging it around in a circle. *This will do!* she thought. Quickly, she walked back to where Melissa was watching her. "Ready. Get them to follow you and run past me, here. Way past," she added, "I don't want you getting hit by any flying bodies."

Melissa couldn't help herself and grinned. "You certainly have a lot of self-confidence. I'm almost looking forward to this," she said, trying to rein in her nerves. "Batter up, Dharalyn, I'm about to send you a curveball." Melissa took a deep breath and then walked into the small alcove that was about ten feet wide and ten feet deep, which marked the heavy wooden door that was the entrance to the girls' locker room and shower area. Giving Dharalyn a backward glance, she marveled at the girl's green eyes, white hair and, oh those teeth! Strangely, rather than being scared, she felt self-assured and even a sense of smugness at what she knew the girl could do. After all, she had seen it herself, up close and personal. Shaking her head and brushing her fingers though her hair, Melissa began to whistle purposely and opened the door into the room beyond. In front of her, all of the girls and the four boys that made up the Cheer Squad were sitting on the floor, with their wrists tied together with some kind of plastic straps. Ms. Forester, who was also on the floor, looked up at her with despairing eyes and a blood spattered face. Two of the hoods flanked the group, only about fifteen feet away from where she was standing by the door, which was pretty close. Too close, in fact! "Oops," she said, in a sweet, nonsensical voice that was completely contrary to her actual feelings in this moment, "wrong room. I was looking for someplace else." Quickly, she turned and ran back out of the door allowing it to swing shut behind her, as she heard a savage voice behind her bark hurried commands. She sprinted out of the little alcove, slowing a bit so that the thugs didn't completely lose sight of her and then ran into the left hallway, as two of them came bursting out of the locker room door. She saw Dhara out of the corner of her left eye, crouching down on the floor near the alcove entrance and then she ran for all she was worth, down the hall toward the boys' side of the school hall. She didn't stop until she heard the sounds of men being hit by the heavy metal fire extinguisher, followed by bodies thwacking hard against the walls. She turned and made her way quickly back toward Dhara, who was checking on the two men, who were now lying face down on the floor.

"They out of it?"

"Yes, we need to move them away from here and tie them up."

"These will help," Melissa said assertively, starting to sound more like her old self, as she grabbed up a bunch of long plastic ties that had half fallen from one of the hood's pockets.

Dhara motioned to Melissa and the two of them grabbed the first man by his feet and pulled him down the hall, depositing him in the boys' locker room alcove. "Tie him up securely," said Dhara. "I'll go get the other one."

Melissa nodded and proceeded to fasten several straps around the guy's wrists and ankles, made easier by the fact that he was still face down. Soon, Dharalyn was back with the second man and within moments, he was strapped up tight, as well. The second man moaned a bit as Dharalyn looked at Melissa. "Got any idea how we get the last guy to come out?"

Melissa nodded. "I have an idea that could work, if we knew his name."

Dharalyn lost no time in turning the moaning man over. He opened his eyes slowly and she leaned down over him, showing her fangs and trying her best to look every inch a hungry, blood-thirsty beast of modern fiction. "The man still inside the girls' locker room. Tell me his name, or I will drink you dry."

The man stared in horror at the sight before him. A sight that before this moment, he would have sworn couldn't possibly be real. Still, he hesitated.

"Tell me now!" she said, pitching her voice in a low growl, just like she imagined an evil and malevolent vampire would. She shook him a little and he said, his voice quaking with fear,

"Carlos, his name is Carlos."

Dharalyn dropped him back on the floor and stood. "Come on," she said, "we don't have much time."

"Wait," said Melissa, as she looked down with disgust at the puddle of wetness growing beneath the man Dharalyn had just... persuaded. Pulling off the man's shoes, she yanked off one of his socks and stuffed it into his mouth. Glancing up at Dharalyn with a look of seriousness, she said, "We don't want him hollering out and warning his buddy."

Dharalyn couldn't help herself and smiled warmly. The girl was empowered now, and ready to do what needed to be done. She was thinking clearly, and had come a long way from the terrified victim she had been, only ten short minutes ago. "Awesome...good thinking, Mel."

Melissa gave a grim nod of her head as she followed Dharalyn back to the girls' locker room entrance. Suddenly she said, looking a bit uneasy, "Um, I know that was just an act and all, but I was wondering. When this is over, you're not going to do like, some kind of a vampire, blood drinking thing on me, are you? I kinda like being human, is all."

Dharalyn looked at her, seeing the touch of apprehension in her features and hearing it in her tone. "Melissa, please, I'm not an evil, scary thing. That's not who I am at all and I would hope after what we've been through already, that you would know that. I'm just trying to save everyone and keep them from being hurt by these men, okay? Besides," she added seriously, "you and I are friends, aren't we?"

Melissa nodded, feeling a little foolish, though to be fair, she still wasn't entirely comfortable with the fangs or the unnaturally bright eyes. The white hair and the graceful silvery lines running through her skin, she could deal with. In fact, she thought Dharalyn kinda had a cool, modern art nouveau look going on.

"Okay, Melissa, so far your ideas have been pretty good, so what's your plan now?"

"This," she said, grinning broadly as she walked up to the door. She was definitely feeling a lot better, and had no lack of faith in Dharalyn's ability to handle things. "Be ready," she said, in a loud whisper. Slowly she cracked the door and then, pitching her voice gruff and low, she said, "Hey, Carlos, come out here quick and give us a hand with this bitch."

"You can't handle one little girl?" yelled an answering voice, from inside.

"We got the other one, too. Come on out here, for a second." Melissa let go of the door and quickly moved past where Dharalyn stood, out of sight. No sooner had she gotten around the edge of the locker room alcove, when the door slammed open.

"What in the...! Where the hell are you guys?" he said, warily.

"Over here," said Melissa, her man's voice imitation cracking a bit under the strain.

Carlos moved slowly forward, bringing up his shotgun. As he turned the corner, he saw the two girls standing together and he swung his gun barrel around to cover them. Suddenly, the white-haired girl blurred, and then she was beside him. Quicker than he could believe, she reached down, grabbed the gun out of his hand and then swung it butt first at his head. The last thing he remembered, as blackness closed in all around him were the bright green eyes, glaring at him with pure fury.

"I don't believe it," said Melissa. "You did it!"

"We did it!" Dharalyn corrected her. "There is, however, one more thug to deal with. I have to go and get the guy that's still down in detention, with Danielle and Vee."

"Come on, then," said Melissa, with a rush of confidence and zeal. "I'll help you."

"No, Mel, help me get this guy tied up and then go and help all of the people in there," she said, motioning toward the locker room. "They're your responsibility, now. You need to get them loose and out of here to safety."

"But I want to help you," she said, obstinately.

"You already have, Melissa. I couldn't have done any of this without you. You know that, don't you?"

Melissa nodded, reservedly. She felt pretty good about the fact that when it had counted, at the end, she had proved she had the right stuff. "Okay, I'll do what you say. And when I get them out, we'll call the police, right?"

"Yes! Get the authorities here, as quick as possible."

"Dharalyn," said Melissa, as she grabbed Dharalyn's hands in what for her was a very uncharacteristic show of sentiment, "be very careful."

Bruno fumed as he hollered into the radio. No one was answering him now, and it didn't take a genius to figure out that something had gone wrong. Horribly wrong. He began to doubt, once again, the mob boss's assumptions. He hadn't been in there at the very end, when Michael had met with the two girls that last time, but he had seen the boss directly afterwards and the man had been badly spooked. He remembered how shocked he himself had been, when they had showed up at Michael's office again, and he also remembered thinking that even though the little girl he had here with him now had done most of the talking, it had been the other one he sensed was the one to watch. She had been strangely cool and quietly reserved, and he also remembered that he had felt a chill when she had looked at him with those piercing green eyes. He knew that look, had seen it before in the Moretti family's most seriously badass members. It was a "don't screw with me" look, that made you realize that here was a person who knew, KNEW they could take you down in seconds. Yes, he had felt a chill with her, and he'd never gotten that feeling from a damn woman before, let alone a young girl. In his heart, he knew now that Moretti had figured this situation all wrong. That chick was frigging bad news and was probably taking his crew apart, even now. His gut told him she was the reason none of his guys were answering their radios, and that it wouldn't be long before she showed up to finish the job with him. He glanced momentarily at the brown-haired figure, who was back sitting quietly on the floor after he'd finished threatening and knocking her around earlier. She was kind of cute, he thought, and as he turned away, he saw from the corner of his eye that the little scamp was watching him carefully. He couldn't help himself and he turned and sneered at her, with a look that said that he got it now. This one was as sweet and innocent as they came. And that forced bravado she had shown them that day in Moretti's office had been magnificent, but it had all just been part of an incredible act. There was no badass in her. She was as soft and sweet as they came. The real badass was likely on her way here right now, and Bruno needed to move fast if he was going to come out of this on top. The way he saw it, if things had gone like he believed, he had only one card left to play in this game gone wrong and he would be as ruthless and as cruel as the situation called for, in order to extricate himself from what he now considered to be Michael's newest and worst fiasco. He wasn't going to die or go to prison, just because Moretti had sent them all into a dangerous situation without proper preparation. This whole thing had been poorly planned and thought out. Mostly, because Moretti himself tended to be reckless, stubborn and perverse when he felt he'd been wronged somehow. This wouldn't be the first time men had died because his boss tended to dwell upon his regrets and overthink a situation that would have been better left alone. Bruno walked over to Danielle and pulled her roughly to her feet, squeezing her wrists tightly and smiling at the yelp of pain he elicited from her. He then grabbed the front of her blouse and dragged her across the room, only pausing for a brief second to turn and pump two bullets from his thirty-eight snub nose revolver into the weird girl with the streaky blue hair. The shots rang out loudly in the confines of the cement block classroom and Bruno turned away, not needing to check to see if she was dead. He was a crack shot and both bullets had hit her squarely in the chest. *No big loss there*, he thought, as she slumped over onto the floor. *Probably would end up a frigging drug addict or a damn derelict, anyway.* Besides, with what was coming, he didn't want to deal with someone being on his blind side. Even though she'd been a scared little sheep, even sheep could sometimes find the source of their courage and against all reason, would charge the wolves.

Dharalyn heard the echoing shots ring out and "speed-flashed" the entire length of the first hallway, to the front foyer. She then rushed to the beginning of the second hallway and "flashed" (a mode of instantaneous travel) to just outside of the lighted classroom door. She would need to be careful here, the door was ajar and she didn't know what she would find inside. She was scared, yes, but she also knew Danielle had the fully charged Pametra device in her possession and hoped with all of her heart that the girl was wearing it. She did a quick check of her Ayowei reserve, which was down to about a third, plenty to do what she needed to when she stepped inside. Carefully peering around the door, her heart leaped into her throat and her pulse quickened mark-edly as she spied the nightmarish tableau laid out in front of her. Vee's poor body was lying crumpled on the floor toward the back of the room, leaving Dhara to believe that the girl had been shot. Further back yet, against the rear wall was the motion-less body of Mr. Banks, who was also obviously hurt very badly. And then there was Danielle, who was standing in front of Bruno like a human shield, with a pistol pointed at the back of her head.

"So are any of my men left alive, or are they all out of commis-sion?" he asked, fairly certain what the answer would be, but need-ing to ask it, anyway.

"They're alive, but currently unable to assist you in any way," said Dharalyn, in a calm and unruffled voice, assessing the situation and looking for the best course of action. She had let Melissa do the planning before, mostly because the girl needed to prove her own worth to herself, so that she would get through this night with as few scars as possible. Now though, Dharalyn put her own consid-erable mental faculties onto the problem, watching carefully for an opening, readying herself to react in a split second, if the bal-ance of chance swung in her favor. She could see that Danielle was not wearing the Pametra, and tried not to dwell too long on that disturbing and discouraging fact. She needed to focus and stay sharp, waiting for her chance, should it come. Listening carefully, her Ayowei enhanced senses coming to their peak, her improved hearing told her something else of importance. The girl Vee, who was lying so still on the floor, was apparently playing dead. Her breath was slow but even and her heartbeat was strong, though it was racing at a much higher rate than normal. Dharalyn was quietly exultant. *The girl was faking!* A stolen glance and Dharalyn saw the reason for her well-being: Danielle's Pametra was in use, after all and was on the girl's right hand. Danielle must have put it on the other girl to protect her from harm. Despite the dire circumstances, Dhara felt her pride toward her friend swell within her breast, as the realization of what she'd done and why filled her heart. *There is no greater or more selfless act than placing the welfare of another ahead of your own,* she thought, as her determination to save her friend grew even stronger. She gazed piercingly at Bruno. *Your move, creep,* she thought.

Bruno wasn't fooled. From the moment he'd seen the girl appear at the door, he knew his suspicions had been right. This one was one tough mother of a little lady and something in her dangerous demeanor told him he'd better play this very carefully, or his fate would end up the same as whatever had befallen the others. He knew what this one was capable of. He had been hit by her once in Michael's office and had gone flying as if he'd been hit by a wrecking ball, something he had never quite gotten over. Michael had said it had been PCP or some other drug, but Bruno had never really believed that. And he certainly didn't now. The girl's hair was bright white and her eyes blazed with a fiery, green intensity that shone like some deranged, feral beast out of a science fiction movie. There was a graceful, silvery cast to her skin that if you looked close, seemed to be a design of some kind. No, this was going to come out bad for him, unless he played it hard and aggressive. There was only one thing he could do that would get this chick off his back. It was obvious that she cared very much for this girl, Dani, at whose head he was currently pointing his gun. The best play here was to give her something much more important to worry about than chasing after him. "So, what is your name?" he asked the green-eyed demoness, a term he had decided was fitting, under the circumstances.

"I am the Ultimate Arbiter of Justice; I am Dharalyn Xhikaterina Malakovani, of the Sakatherian Regency of Asreod and your fate is at hand."

Bruno felt his jaw drop. He didn't know exactly what all that mess she had just said meant, but it sounded significantly bad ass. He knew now, with utter certainty, that he'd better be cautious. "Well, Dharalyn, then I want you to move slowly toward the back of this classroom. Do it now, or I will shoot a nice big hole in your little friend here. Somewhere that won't kill her, but it will hurt like a son-of-a-bitch." He watched as the girl slowly relocated herself toward the back of the room, moving in a sinuously slinky fashion that reminded him of a jungle panther, circling its prey. She showed him a glimpse of white fangs, as she snarled silently at him and his confidence nearly wavered, as her eyes never left his. He knew she was only waiting for him to drop his guard for an instant, and then she would pounce on him. He envisioned having his throat torn out by this girl, and his imagination began to pummel him with fearful images of what might be. Bruno hated to admit it and his self-respect was taking a major hit with this realization, but he was scared out of his freaking mind. He carefully edged himself over toward the classroom door, keeping Danielle between him and his nemesis. As he reached the opening, he stopped. This was it! This was where he made his play and gambled that her little friend here meant more to the vampire bitch than catching him did.

Dharalyn moved slowly to the very back of the room, past the spot where Vee was still lying, motionless. She'd been hoping he would slip, but even the "Arbiter of Justice" comment or the show of her teeth, which she knew freaked these people out, hadn't rattled him much. This guy was cool and resourceful, and was evidently used to intense situations. She could only hope that when he went out into the hallway, he would take his eyes off her for just a split second. That was all she needed to allow her to *speed-flash* to his side in an instant and disable him. Up until now, the opportunity to move hadn't yet appeared. She paused suddenly, sensing something in his demeanor change. She saw a cold, malevolent look fill his eyes as he stood still at the door, and then watched in horror and disbelief as he discharged his gun through Danielle's shoulder, and then a second time into her side. Blood spurted in a red shower from two places on Danielle's body, as a scream surged up from deep within Dharalyn's breast. Her body a blur, she flashed towards Danielle's side, just catching her as she began to fall face forward toward the floor, from the impact of the bullets slamming into her little frame. She sensed Bruno running off, but his whereabouts were no longer of any concern to her. Dharalyn turned Danielle over and saw the wounds on her dear friend's body. There was one in her shoulder and one in her side. A voice inside told her he had meant only to wound and not to kill too quickly, to give him the time to get away, while Dhara tried to save her. Though Danielle had not been killed instantly, Dharalyn knew that from the amount of blood near her body, it would probably be only a matter of minutes before her friend was dead from blood loss. She hollered for Vee to get over to her and was relieved to see the girl arrive quickly at her side. "Do you have any towels or shirts of any kind?"

"Oh Jesus, oh Jesus," said Vee, "is she going to die?"

"Vee!" shouted Dharalyn, "please, focus! Do you have any cloth, towels or something I can use to slow this bleeding?"

"Yes," said Vee, who immediately stood and ran to retrieve her large shoulder bag. Digging frantically inside, she hastily pulled out a white t-shirt and a towel. "My gym stuff," she said simply, when she returned.

Carefully, Dhara tore the towel in half and placed the pieces on the front and back of the waist wound, which was now bleeding steadily, although thankfully, slowly. "Hold these in place!" she said, and getting no response, looked up to see the girl staring at her in wide eyed amazement.

"So you're a...you're a..." she said, haltingly.

"Yes, I'm a vampire, Vee. Now, help me with this, or I swear I will kick your ass!"

Forcing herself to take her eyes away from Dharalyn's face, she pressed down on the top cloth on Danielle's waist, while Dharalyn began to work on her shoulder. She placed half of the rolled up t-shirt underneath the shoulder and then pressed down on top with a firm hand. This wouldn't hold for long, but Dhara just needed to buy a little time so that she could think of what to do. "Vee, I'm going to try to do something, to save Danielle. Whatever you do, do not let go of the cloth. You may feel something weird, or see something you do not understand. Don't let it freak you out. I need you to watch over her, while I try to use a power I have, to save her. Okay?"

Vee nodded, sensing that Dharalyn was sincere and not likely to harm her. "I told you, I'm into weird stuff. I knew something strange was up, the second that guy shot me and the bullets didn't hurt me. It was this, wasn't it?" Vee raised one of her hands from the bloody cloth and showed Dharalyn the Pametra.

"Yes, that device was mine. It protects the wearer."

"Danielle saved me. She should have put it on herself, but she put it on me, instead."

Dharalyn gritted her teeth as her emotions surged. "That's why we have to save her, Vee. There are too few people like her in this world. We can't lose her."

Vee nodded vehemently. "What do you want me to do?"

"Just watch her closely, and put your other hand over here, on her shoulder. Keep a firm pressure on these, okay? I've got to concentrate and won't be able to help you."

"What are you going to do?"

"I'm going to try and reverse time," replied Dharalyn, ignoring the shocked look on Vee's face, as she brought her hands together and summoned her Ayowei to begin Shonyemaya, the rare ability she had been born with that allowed her to influence the flow of time. Immediately, she sensed with her inner sight that there would not be sufficient energy to take them back, far enough. Her Ayowei reserve was down too low, about twenty percent. The initial creation of the sixty-foot diameter time globe would use up three quarters of that. She would only be able to go back about thirty seconds. Not nearly enough. Dharalyn panicked for a moment and began to pray. "Anon, guide me in my hour of need. Don't allow this darling girl, one of your most precious daughters to fade away from this world, because of my shortcomings. Please help me save her, Anon." Suddenly, a memory of Danielle in their bedroom, laughing and teasing came into her mind. She was always so inquisitive and curious, and that morning while they'd been discussing Shonyemaya, amongst other things, she had asked what Dhara now recalled had been kind of a silly question.

"What happens if you shrink the globe, make it smaller? Does it last longer, then?"

Why not, thought Dharalyn impulsively, *maybe it was worth a shot!* Dharalyn concentrated and released Ayowei, calling on and forming it into a globe of pure energy, which signified the commencement of Shonyemaya. This time though, unlike the previous times when the globe had formed into its default diameter of sixty feet, Dharalyn focused and refined it downward, into a much smaller orb. She felt immediately encouraged, as she realized that the smaller globe was taking significantly less energy to form. Soon she had it, a glistening sphere of energy, sparkling beautifully all about them. Dharalyn had to give Vee credit. Though her eyes were filled with gleaming astonishment, she never released her pressure on the bandages and kept her cool, in what must have been a stressful and anxiety laden situation for her. Quickly, Dharalyn looked back and saw the point that she needed to take them to, to reverse the hurt to Danielle, and then compared it to her Ayowei reserve. She was still short, by about thirty seconds. And every second that ticked away was adding to the distance. She felt a surge of frustration build up inside her. She couldn't let Danielle fade away, could not let her die! She pulled the globe in even tighter and looked again into the time line. No good, every passing second was lengthening the span she needed to reverse, and she clenched her fists and shook with despair. *NO!* She thought desperately, and then shouted out loud, as if shouting her defiance against the will of Anon himself. *"No, this will not be! I will not allow this to be!"* She needed to do something immediately, or minutes from now Danielle would be dead, and no amount of Ayowei would bring her back. Once the spirit left the body on its final journey, no amount of time reversal could undo the final separation of body and soul. It was an irrevocable underpinning of life that was subject to the indissoluble laws, and the unfathomable workings and limitations of the lesser power. Dharalyn's body began to shake with mounting fury. *Not this time! She would not lose someone she loved, again!*

CHAPTER 21

LOVE, FRIENDSHIP AND A VAMPIRE'S BITE

There was only one small chance that came to her mind, and in truth, it was hardly a chance at all. At the very best, she would simply fail again. And at the worst, well, she could die in the attempt. Of course, as far as she was concerned at this moment, so depressed and emotionally bankrupt did she feel in her current state of mind, a universe that allowed the death of Danielle didn't need her in it, either. Dying itself didn't scare her anymore. In fact, the only emotion Dharalyn was feeling at the moment, was growing anger; anger toward the mob, anger toward an unsympathetic universe, anger against a seemingly indifferent God, but most of all, anger against herself. The simple fact was that she was completely inept, too unworthy to even call herself a Sedai. At twelve, she had scored very poorly when she'd tested her Ayowei ability against the Obelisk of Ovarious, and then, even worse, failed that which no one in her family had ever failed before...the Probost, and was a source of extreme embarrassment and humility to her family's legacy. Her mother had died while trying to protect her and Dharalyn had often wondered if that had somehow been at the root of what had happened to her: if she, Dharalyn, had ultimately been responsible, in some way, for her mother's death. Keeping her alive after failing the trial of the Probost was considered a capital offense against tradition, as well as accepted Sedai doctrine and, furthermore, it was against the will of Anon himself, no matter what her Aunt Olmerelda believed. Dharalyn reached out a hand toward Vee and squeezed her arm. "The idea I was relying on is not going to work. There is only one thing left to me, so I need you to be steadfast in your resolve. Don't let anything you see or feel scare you away from her. I need you, Vee. Can I count on you to stick by her side?"

Vee nodded solemnly. "It didn't work? The thing you were going to do to reverse time. Can't you do it, now?"

"I tried, but there just isn't enough power left to me. I must try something much more dangerous. It won't affect you, but you may sense something powerful, because of your special sensitivity with auras. I need you to promise me that you won't give up on Dani, or run off during the course of this perilous task that I am about to attempt."

Vee glanced at her with a look of extreme intensity. She wasn't sure what the vampire was babbling about, but Danielle had put herself in this position because of her. She would never forsake her, now. "I will be faithful and not give up, *if you don't!*" She spoke the last few words with as much intensity as she could muster, not sure why it mattered so much. She just felt deep inside that it did. "Do what you have to. I will still be here, I promise! But please, for God's sake hurry! I don't think she will last very much longer."

With the critical seriousness of their situation driving her, Dharalyn released her Ayowei and began to enter the state of Memordei, the spiritual commencement of a Sedai's journey toward her Egana, the center point of her spirit's essence and her soul. She felt the familiar detachment of her mind from the outside world, felt the sights and sounds of her physical surroundings fade into non-existence. Saw the beginning of the swirling vortex that marked the entrance to her own personal odyssey, one that was supposed to take her deep within and connect her to a place outside of normal time and space. A place deep within that was unique unto herself and only known to her. She allowed herself to be drawn in, pushing back the cloud of apprehension and fear that was already starting to impinge on her thoughts. Far below, she saw the tiny spark of light beckoning to her, but knew how terribly misleading it was. It looked as if it would be the easiest of things to travel toward. But she knew better now, after having failed on two completely separate occasions, before. The last time, with Danielle, had been an absolutely horrible experience. It had affected both of them deeply and had left her gasping and filled with mind-numbing fear, when it was over. They had made promises to each other that day; Danielle, that she would never ask and Dharalyn, that she would never again violate herself in this manner. But of course, that was before Danielle had been shot by a maniac. That was before Dharalyn had lowered the ravaged body of her darling friend to the floor, her life a temporary thing now, only minutes or perhaps even less, from being gone forever. There was very little time, and Dharalyn knew that this was her one last chance. Her last chance to save Danielle who was, literally, the most precious person to her in this, or any world. Feeling a wave of anger and raw determination sweep through her body, Dhara cast away the negative feelings in her mind and threw herself with all the power of her Ayowei into the awaiting maelstrom, below. Once again it slammed her about, howling and thrusting against her with its unabated ferocity. Dharalyn snarled and shouted out a blinding scream of utmost defiance. "Not this time!" she yelled. "Kill me if you want, but I will overcome or die in the trying!"

And at that, the lightning filled emptiness redoubled its attack on her awareness. She could hardly believe the sense of utter, limitless power she faced and felt the fading strength of her remaining Ayowei dwindle, like the pouring of a cup of water beside the roar of a mighty waterfall. Her consciousness was battered and she felt her resolve waver, while her hopes began to crack and weaken. She could not do this! It was too much! There was no way for a physical being to battle such a monstrous, obliterating force of wildness and ferocity. She thought for a brief moment of turning back, of giving up. But then, Danielle would be lost. She would die and the only excuse Dharalyn would be able to give was that it had been too hard, that in the end it had proved too difficult to achieve her goal. And so, as a result, her beloved friend would die....

Danielle would die....

Gone forever....

She would pass over to another existence, gone from those who loved her...gone from those who cherished and needed her.

Her best friend ever, the best person she'd ever known, dead and gone because she had given up with yet another pitiful, lame attempt.... Once again, Dharalyn would be a disappointment, a contemptuous failure, her weakness leaving another lifeless body behind. And once again, she would be all alone.

Completely and utterly alone....

"DAMN YOU!" she screamed over and over again at the very top of her lungs, each shout of profanity more colorful and descriptive than the last, until her throat was raw and hoarse. She gazed defiantly, angrily into the roaring tumult that would dwarf even the mightiest tornado with its sheer size and power. It had been nothing though, for what came then had no worldly description, as the wild tempest hit her again with a violence that diminished in comparison all that had come before. There was no answer to this, no God here to protect her, and she knew that she was nearly at the end of both her physical and her spiritual strength. Her determination and refusal to quit surged as Dharalyn drew every erg, every last scrap, every last scintilla of Ayowei from deep within and then with the mightiest of final efforts, she cast herself downward. Racing like a dart before the wind, she tore through the vast obliterating force and explosive cacophony of sound that tried to deny her, tried and tried and then...suddenly...failed....

Everything was absolutely quiet and still as a caught breath, held lightly within. Dharalyn was shivering and shaking almost uncontrollably, while standing silently on a green, grassy knoll, surrounded by a broad swath of yellow and red flowers. In the distance the flat expanse of grass and colorful petals curved gracefully upward, where it was bordered high above by strange trees with broad, high-topped leaves. For a second she felt a surge of anxiety, as she realized she couldn't hear anything, so utterly quiet was it in comparison to the deafening tumult she had just survived. Finally, tiny, twittering, melodic sounds reached her, as the rushing noise in her ears subsided. Birds...thank god, she could hear and see a myriad of colorful birds as they chirped gaily. In front of her, she watched as hundreds of them flew all around a small glade, filled with beautiful trees covered with pink blossoms and bushes with broad leaves of white and green stripes. Fat, flowering bushes of white blooms occupied nearly all of the empty spaces between, fanning out in a gardener's loosely planned, chaotic pattern of riotous growth. The ringing in Dharalyn's ears subsided even more and she nervously jumped, as a sound from behind abruptly startled her.

"What is this place?" asked Danielle.

"Dani!" screamed Dharalyn, her voice rough and raw sounding. She reached out and pulled her friend into her arms, squeezing her as tightly as the comparative weakness in her arms would allow.

"Wow, you sound bad. And by the way, I never heard you swear like that before, ever. I didn't think you even knew those kinds of words."

Dharalyn's resultant laugh sounded strange even to her own ears, as she released Danielle and let her arms fall limply to her side. "I know them because you do, dummy. I got my entire language skills right out of your head."

Danielle grinned and then looked suddenly nauseated. "Oh, I don't feel so well. That trip down was a rough one."

"I don't think that is the only reason you feel bad, Dani. You were shot, remember?"

Danielle looked momentarily confused and then said, "Oh, yeah. With all of that terrible stuff you just went through, I almost forgot."

Dharalyn paused with a sudden realization then, as incredulity filled her eyes. "What the heck are you doing here? How in the world are you even here, at all? As far as I know, no Sedai has ever seen another person when they reached their Egana. In fact, I'm fairly certain nothing like this has ever been recorded in any of the Sedai manuscripts I've ever read."

"If you don't know, I certainly don't. I just remember you going down into the vortex and I was with you, somehow. I don't have a clue how."

"Me either, Dani," said Dharalyn with a dazed expression to her features, "me either."

"So where exactly are we and why are we here?"

Dharalyn smiled serenely. "Well, if I'm right, we are here in my spiritual center, my Egana. And through that glade over there, we should find Anon's Blessing, the visual representation of my gift."

"Oh, yeah, you mean that pool of water thing."

"Well, it's not really water, Dani. It's actually my reserve of Kamanah, the Greater Power. I came here in the hope that I could use it somehow, to save you."

Danielle stepped forward. "Well let's go then. I certainly don't want to die while you stand here yapping. Let's go see this pool of not-water."

Smiling, Dharalyn took her hand and moved forward with a small bounce to her step, glancing right and left through the small openings and paths that lay between larger clumps of greenery. After walking for a minute or two through the center of a group of larger trees, Dharalyn noticed that the surrounding greenery was getting smaller and less dense until suddenly, they walked out into the open again.

"I don't get it," said Danielle, "where's the pool thingy?"

"I don't know," replied Dharalyn, who was beginning to feel awfully anxious and a bit lightheaded. "Maybe we passed by it somewhere inside the glade."

"Dhara, I was looking to either side as we walked through. This little oasis of yours isn't that big. There is no pool of water anywhere in there."

Dharalyn's eyes began to smart as tears welled up behind her eyelids. This just couldn't be. Could the reason she had had such a tough time getting here to her Egana be that there was, in actuality, no blessing from Anon to see, no peaceful, serene little pool to show the level of her gift? No connection to Kamanah awaiting her discovery? Could it be that the purpose of the maelstrom was to keep her from discovering that very simple fact? Of all of the people of her proud lineage, of all the entire line of the Malakovani family, was she the first to have no link to Kamanah, whatsoever? Dharalyn felt herself waver and become increasingly dizzy, kneeling down onto the ground, before she lost her balance and fell. Suddenly and without warning she began to cry, violent wracking sobs shaking her whole body. Her tears fell in a torrent, as everything she'd been holding back hit her at once. She was not blessed by Anon, which was why there was no pool. She was in fact, a complete and utter failure to all who had loved and cared about her. But most of all, she could not save Danielle, the one person she would give everything she had, everything she was, to save. The problem, she finally understood, and it had taken all of this for her to ultimately recognize it, was that her worth was zero, nothing.... In the history of her people, she was the most worthless excuse of a Sedai Novi to have ever been born. Dharalyn knew she was wrong to be so full of self-pity and remorse, at this moment. But, she just couldn't help herself; the disappointment cut her oh, so deeply. She had always believed deep down, that someday she would overcome her fear. And now that she had, she had received as a result the ultimate betrayal to her humility, a soulfully devastating answer to her prayers: the simple fact of her complete and utter unworthiness to receive Anon's blessing.

Danielle felt terrible, not just because in the real world she knew she was dying, but that after all her friend had been through, all she had overcome, Dharalyn had received the absolute worst shock and greatest disappointment of her life. Danielle felt her obstinate nature rise up within her, like a smoldering volcano. She knew Dharalyn's true worth and knew that the lack of Kamanah didn't have a darn thing to do with her real value to those who loved her, but she could also understand how terribly let down her dearest friend must feel. "What a freaking slap in the face," she said out loud, to nobody in particular. As she watched her friend's crying form and wished fruitlessly that she could have a personal word with Anon himself right now, she gazed around the surrounding area, her mind detached and wandering, like she often did when she found herself in an uncomfortable position, where there seemed to be nothing she could do to help. As she studied their beautifully serene surroundings and marveled at its basic simplicity, she noticed curiously that all around them, the land curved upward toward a high ridge and it was only in the approximate center that there was really any heavy growth. Everything else was just green grass and loads of colorful flowers, except for the tall, pale-barked trees she could see growing up on the nearby ledge. Staring at the trees, which looked oddly familiar in a half-remembered way, Danielle frowned and turned in a circle. They were fairly close, right now, to one side, but she could still see that all around the two of them the land appeared to slope upward in every direction: *that was weird.* It was almost as if they were inside of a great big....

"Wait here," said Danielle abruptly, as she squeezed Dharalyn's shoulder. It was only about a hundred yards or so to where the ground began to swell upward and soon, Danielle had jogged to a place where the ground began to quickly rise. Pressing forward, she shortly found herself climbing up a pretty steep incline and she paused mid-point, studying the landscape from what was now a much higher vantage point. "Awesome," she said softly, to herself, "just what I thought." Giving Dharalyn a quick glance to make certain she was all right, Danielle turned her attention back to the task in front of her. The ground was getting steeper now, not too sheer but enough that if she slipped, she could end up rolling a good way back down, into what she had seen, was a valley of sorts. *Yep,* she thought to herself, *this whole place is just one big crater.* Another minute passed and soon she was just below what she now recognized as a wide, growth-filled plateau. She could hear an oddly familiar sound coming from above and as her curiosity grew, she pulled herself up and onto the wide, flat crest of the hill, quickly making her way across the width of the terrain, through a scattering of palm like trees and a thick undergrowth of giant ferns. Suddenly she stopped, as she let out a gasp of surprise. A host of chills swept up through her spine, making her arms and fingers tingle. "Holy crap!" she said, and stared in disbelief. It took a moment more to register what she was seeing and then she turned back around and walked back through the trees, to where she could gaze back down the hill toward Dharalyn, who was looking up at her.

Danielle waved at her madly to come up, and was soon gratified to see that Dharalyn had stood and was now coming toward her. Within a couple of minutes, she reached the bottom of the steep incline and began a careful ascent, to where Danielle was standing. Too impatient to wait, Danielle cupped her hands together and yelled down to where Dharalyn had reached the steepest part of the slope. "I think I found your little pool, Dhara!" she yelled, smiling with unreserved joy.

"What?" hollered Dharalyn, who was getting closer now and was only fifteen feet or so from the top.

"I said I found your pool, in a way, sorta!"

Dharalyn paused in her climb and looked up toward Danielle. "Really?" she asked. "You're not teasing me, are you? You found it?"

"No, I'm not teasing you. I would never joke about something like this, now get up here!" shouted Danielle, the excitement building within her. As Dharalyn arrived at the edge, Danielle reached out and grabbed both of her hands; she then led her through the palms and ferns to the other side of the plateau.

"Holy smokes!" said Dharalyn, in a mixture of shock and exultant joy.

"My words, exactly," said Danielle, as she placed her arm around Dharalyn's waist. "See, you're not a failure, sweetie. Hell, you're a freaking prodigy, is what you are!"

Dharalyn stared in amazement as she looked out over, not a glistening pool or like her mother, a small silvery lake. But wave after cresting wave of surging surf and a vast, blue, seemingly endless oceanic vista, which stretched off into a distant, many hued horizon of pink, red, orange and yellow that continued on as far as the eye could see. So broad and wide was it, that there didn't appear to be signs of it ending in any direction.

"So, there wasn't any pool in the center of the island, only this," said Danielle wonderingly, as she waved her arms outward toward the sea. "Is this your Egana?"

"I don't actually know, Dani. I can't really say if this is it. I've never heard of anything like this, before. It might be just what it looks like, an ocean."

"But what if it is, Dhara?" asked Danielle. "Would it mean that you are now all-powerful and mighty beyond belief?"

Dharalyn shrugged her shoulders in a noncommittal gesture. "I don't know, Danielle. If this is truly my gift, which now that I'm thinking about it, is very unlikely, then this only shows my potential and the magnitude of Anon's blessing. After the gift is revealed, the new Novi Initiate spends the next five years learning to harness and control her connection with her gift of Kamanah. The first thing we learn is how to charge the towers, which is also our final test and how we reveal our exact gift to the council."

"I see. So how were you going to use this, to help me?"

"Well, if this actually is the source of my Kamanah and not just a...well, an ocean surrounding this island, then first, I'm supposed to attune myself to it."

"How do you do that?"

"My mother told me she knelt and put her hand in the water, and then she sang the Song of Carrabrus, which is supposed to make us one with our gift."

"So, do you know the song?"

Dharalyn gave Danielle a sidelong glance, filled with astonishment. "Are you kidding me? Do you know how many years I studied this stuff?"

Danielle walked over to the edge of the wide shelf they were on and looked down the sharp drop off there. She was, essentially, standing on the outer edge of a rocky cliff wall that fell at least a hundred feet, onto shoals that were being steadily pounded by powerful waves. "Well, I'm here to tell you, there is no way you are going to put your hand down into that."

Dharalyn nodded and gave Danielle a half smile. "That's just what she did. Only the words are truly important. I shouldn't need to actually touch the water, itself." Her voice took on a more serious tone. "Now, come closer to me. Time may be slowed in this place, but I don't want to waste any more of it. I have a situation waiting for me, and I need to get to it."

Danielle nodded and joined Dharalyn by her side. "Are you going to sing now?"

Dharalyn nodded and then closed her eyes in preparation.

"Am I going to understand this, or is it gonna be in some weird, alien language of yours?"

Dharalyn expelled a breath full of air in clear annoyance, and then quickly placed her hands on Danielle's forehead. "Here, let me give you a quick language lesson."

Danielle felt a strange sensation, somewhat like a cold cloud being pushed into her head and almost immediately, the understanding of a completely new language filled her mind.

Dharalyn released her hold on Danielle and readied herself again, closing her eyes.

"This is so cool," Danielle said, "I can actually...."

"Danielle!" said Dharalyn sternly. "Please shut up, before I brain you one."

"Oops, sorry," said Danielle, meekly. "Go ahead." For a moment nothing happened, and then a beautiful sweet voice rang out, gaining strength with each passing moment. Danielle gasped silently, as she realized with growing wonder, that she now understood the meaning behind the Sedai words which made up Dharalyn's song. A song which was called Soolah ya Carrabrus, and which in English loosely translated as: Song of Carrabrus.

Sha-ma gayatrool Loora, Pa don digh ya sool.
(Most gracious Lord, for the gift of water.)
Nu-la shi-ya comanay, cann gess darhool.
(My grateful acceptance, your humble daughter.)

Kal grann nu-dah bae, kansee nu-la keeEss.
(Please show me now, attend my need.)
Po shalgot ha ho-ruus, ya javall hweeEss.
(Let signs be shown, of prophecy decreed.)

Progoso neaha, kelay ya phreet.
(Precious gift, heart of fire.)
Lonshoul ya gaessa, kayl nuwalla.
(Soul of passion, sage desire.)

Ta qwallae minnuel, don jhale mon giea.
(A promise given, the time is now.)
Nu-la kelay mon huriss, acca drunen sacra.
(My heart is true, most sacred vow.)

Yashee nu-la drendicass, pic-walle nu-la chilla.
(Accept my burden, cast off my youth.)
Bil ghanna vol whinna, bil kheas don hurissan.
(To serve with wisdom, to seek the truth.)

Nu-day don zhranna, nu hroo don cqies.
(I am the chosen, I have the right.)
Nu-la jhanille hruex, bil ghanna don shard.
(My solemn oath, to serve the light.)

Hum backa lu ghuum, nan jessa ou-bale.
(And so I've come, reborn this hour.)
Nu sola cann thrusae, jac-quay nu-la mon-shale.
(I await your blessing, confirm my power.)

Shal-kali-ha-bil-jarwa, Anon! All praise be to thee, Anon!

As the final word was spoken, titanic columns of water shot high into the sky. Filled with apprehension, Danielle backed up a step and gazing around, she could see ten, twenty, heck, hundreds of them, all around the island and far into the distance. The mighty columns climbed ever higher into the sky above and then amazingly, spread out above them to form a glistening, water-like dome, miles above their heads. Where they met, the individual plumes crashed together and began to glow in undulating waves of power, which lit up in brilliant blues, reds, yellows, pinks and greens. Danielle was reminded of what she'd read about the northern lights, how beautiful they were, though she doubted anyone in her world had ever seen anything as remotely daunting and mind numbingly spectacular as this. After a few minutes passed, Danielle forced herself to look away from the majestic view overhead. She waved her hands, trying to get Dhara's attention, as she saw that her friend was also staring in wonder at the awe-inspiring sight before them. The noise was incredible and she had to shout over the tumult. "This is ludicrous. I mean, talk about being an over achiever. I guess it pretty much answers your question, though. This is your Kamanah pool, alright. When you learn how to use it, you're gonna be a real pisser. So, what do we do now? What's the plan?"

Dharalyn looked thoughtful. "Well, initially I hoped maybe I could use it to recharge my Ayowei, and maybe reverse time, undoing the damage to your body."

"Will it work?"

"I don't know. I actually know very little, almost nothing really, about Kamanah. The teaching of it is prohibited before one becomes an Initiate."

Danielle frowned. "So, you have all this potential, but don't even know where to begin or how to use it...at all?"

Dharalyn nodded. "It would be as if you were given all the tools of a doctor, in your world. All the tools, devices, medicines and everything you could ever need. But you would not know how to use any of it, until you went to medical school."

"I could, however, figure out how to use a Band-Aid without all that," said Danielle, hopefully.

"And that is my hope. That somehow this will help. It was the only thing left I could think of to do."

"It was extremely brave of you, Dhara," said Danielle, knowing full well what it must have taken for her to decide to do this.

Dharalyn nodded again and said, "Enough wasting time. Let's see if I can at least recharge my Ayowei." She closed her eyes and stood with her arms outstretched for a moment, and then spoke in a reverent tone, "Anon, thank you for the gift of your most magnificent blessing. Allow me to connect with it now, for my need is very great. Help me to begin down this new path, with your guidance and the sanctification of your trust." She reached out with her newfound awareness and discovered that there was now a pulsing aura of energy overhead, that seemed to call out to her in a strange manner, which was almost sensuous in its languorous, charged nature. Cautiously, she pulled at it and felt it swell tentatively toward her, as if yearning somehow to be joined with her. Suddenly, without warning, her Kamanah seemed to coil up and then surge forward in a powerful wave, hard and forceful and within a half second, she felt her Ayowei recharge as if a barrel had been upended into a cup. Power heaved and rolled heavily all around her, crashing inward in powerful waves of unrestrained energy, unimaginably vast and overwhelming to her untrained senses. At once, she pushed against it with her mind and felt it back off some, although not nearly enough. The respite was short, as the force of it surged again and just as it began to overpower her senses, she threw up her hands as though to protect herself from being smothered, while urgently trying to gain some control over it with her mind. Little by little, she used every lesson she had learned through controlling Ayowei. Focus, channel, control, and manage the flow, close off the inner vortices of her mind's eye. Little by little her effort seemed to pay off until finally, all but completely exhausted, she felt it thankfully begin to recede and respond to her TelePsiKynesis commands. Shaking a bit from the mental exertion she had somehow just endured, she glanced over at Danielle and could see that her friend looked really bad. *Much worse in fact, than she had only a moment ago.* "You okay, Dani?"

Danielle nodded. She couldn't believe what had just happened. She had felt it, a huge overwhelming force, crashing and pounding all around Dharalyn, and had sensed that her friend was in a panicked state. Danielle didn't quite know how she'd managed it, but somehow she had reached out with her own mind and pushed the energy back away from the two of them, until it had quieted. She looked at the worry on her friend's face. No time to concern her with this, now. She had much more important things on her mind. "Did it work?"

"Yes," said Dharalyn, closing her eyes for a moment, as she replayed the memory of all that had just occurred. It was a bit much, had nearly gotten away from her in fact, but she felt like in time she should be able to gain some measure of control over it. She would just have to be really careful, until she learned what she was doing. As she opened her eyes, she looked around and was shocked to find that Danielle was gone from sight. She turned in a circle, with the thought that her friend might have scampered off like she tended to do, but then had a sobering thought. Maybe she had gone back. Maybe she was at the end of her strength. Dharalyn panicked with the possibility that Danielle might be gone for real, and quickly allowed Ayowei to flow, pulling her swiftly into Memordei, the transitional state that brought her both in and out of her Egana. In what seemed like only seconds, she opened her physical eyes and found that she was back in the classroom, where Vee was eyeing her expectantly.

"You were gone for a long while," she said accusingly. "Did you do it?"

Dharalyn ignored her and sent out her Ayowei, calling Shonyemaya into focus and creating at once the smaller sphere, which would allow her to reverse time in a more localized spot and increase the time she could affect. She pushed her awareness out into the time line and looked back to the point just before Danielle had been shot. She compared it quickly to her now fully recharged reserve of Ayowei, to see if she now had enough to do this thing. Dharalyn felt the breath explode out of her in a rush as she realized with despair, that they had spent too long away. There was still not enough to do it. Even now that she was fully charged, she was still way too short on the power needed. "Nooo!" she cried out in hopeless denial. After all she'd been through, after the incredible striving to reach her Egana, she was still to be deprived of a way to save her beloved Danielle. Dharalyn reached out her hands and placed them lovingly against Danielle's dear, sweet face. She scrutinized her breathing and listened carefully to her heart, which she discovered to her surprise was still beating strongly. Strongly beating without any sign of laboring, or a weakening of her pulse. And her breath, her breathing was strong and regular and Dhara found herself gasping with amazement, as Danielle suddenly inhaled deeply and sighed.

"Ugh, I feel so freaking crappy," said Danielle, as she opened her eyes.

"Holy Mother Mary!" exclaimed Vee, "you should be...dead."

"Really? I don't feel like it, not yet, anyway," Danielle said and then tried to sit up.

"Dani, what are you doing?" said Dharalyn, who could hardly believe her eyes. "You were shot at point blank range...twice. How is it you can move?"

Vee began to hyperventilate. "Maybe she's a vampire, now. Did you turn her, somehow?" she asked Dharalyn.

In answer, Dharalyn ignored her ridiculous statement and pulled one of the bandages away from Danielle's waist wound, noticing immediately the lack of new blood on the floor and the nearly sealed hole in her side. *There should be a lot more blood, all over,* she thought, hiding her amazement, *and she should still be bleeding.*

"Maybe it was your blood thingies. Gran says something you put into us when you feed, heals us. Like it did with Gran and Aunt Sara."

Dharalyn nodded thoughtfully. "Maybe, but that works much slower. This happened very fast. Oh," she said suddenly, as a thought hit her, "It must have something to do with Sho-Notoo, Danielle, the bond between us, which enabled your Ayowei. Even though you can't use it yet, it increases your body's ability to heal itself. Just like me; those two shots would have put me down, but I would have recovered from them, after a bit. Just like you now, my dear sister."

"So she's a vampire, then?" asked Vee, who began slowly sidling away.

"No!" exclaimed both girls in unison.

"Listen Vee, do me a favor," said Danielle, "I will fill you in on everything, but for right now, hold the crazy questions."

Vee nodded. "Okay, it's the least I can do for you since you saved my life, but I just want to be completely clear about this thing. You're telling me you're definitely not a vampire?"

Danielle gave Vee an exasperated look. "Vee, if you ask me that again, I swear I'm going to kill you when I feel better."

"All right, I guess I believe you. But one thing, I want in, okay? I want to be part of the inner circle, with you two."

Danielle and Dharalyn gave each other distinct looks of uncertainty, but then with a sigh of resignation, Danielle answered, "Okay, you're in. But as part of our little group, you have to swear to keep Dharalyn's secret, okay?"

Vee smiled broadly. "Are you kidding? Of course I will. The idea of having a vampire for a friend is just so cool. I won't say a single word to anyone, you have my oath. And speaking of which, you better change back to your human self before someone sees you," she said to Dharalyn. "And, may I suggest you guys get on out of here. I don't think you want to be around when the cops get here. I'll stay and look after Mr. Banks. He stirred a couple of times while you two were out of it, so I think he'll likely be okay. But I wouldn't feel right leaving him here alone, until some help arrives."

Danielle stood weakly, leaning on Dharalyn. "Are you going to know what to say?"

Vee chuckled. "Besides being an admittedly rather strange individual and able to see people's auras, I lie better than practically anybody. What can I say, it's another talent that runs in my family."

Danielle stared at Vee with a confused expression. "Huh, what are you saying?"

"Oh, nothing. It doesn't matter. I'll say you two took off after the gangster dude left and that I don't know what else happened around here."

"Thanks, Vee. I won't forget this," said Dharalyn.

"No worries; besides, you're stuck with me from here on out."

Dhara nodded and headed toward the door. They would be lucky to get out of here before the authorities arrived. "Danielle, I might need to do a bit of flashing, with the two of us. It might make you dizzy, so be prepared."

"Yes, master," Danielle joked, though she didn't feel very funny. She felt weak and the back of her head still hurt a little. All she wanted was her nice, soft, warm comfy bed.

CHAPTER 22

ALL IS WELL THAT ENDS....

Danielle spent most of the next day in bed. Though the scars were nearly healed, she was still pretty sore in the two places she had been shot and she really felt it if she moved wrong. The night before, the two girls had finally come home after speaking to the police, who had unfortunately arrived just as they had exited the school. Between the two of them, they had given both the police as well as everyone here at home a general explanation about what had happened. How the mysterious men had come to the school and apparently tried to kidnap some of the people there. They hadn't mentioned anything specific and for the most part, seemed to have gotten away with explaining details that would have caused the family to worry unnecessarily. To put it simply, they had played dumb as to what exactly had gone down, and had only said that one of the men had held them in their classroom, and then left them when things had seemed to go wrong. Early this morning, they'd gotten a call that the school had been closed for the day, to allow the police a chance to send in a forensics team, and take statements from all of the people who were there the previous night. It wasn't until after her father had left for work that she and

Dharalyn told the whole truth about what had actually happened, to Gran and Aunt Sara. Her father knew absolutely nothing about the shooting and Danielle was busy arguing vehemently with her aunt, to make sure that it stayed that way.

"Auntie!" said Danielle, begging a bit, "this whole thing is already really freaking him out. Let's let him get over the idea of Mob guys coming to the school to achieve some dastardly, unknown scheme...."

"It wasn't unknown," she had said heatedly, "you know darn well why they were there. And he needs to be made aware of the facts, so that we can properly prepare, in case they are not done coming after you two."

"I know," she had replied, "but let's give him time to deal with the story we've already told him right now. When the time is right, I will tell him the whole truth."

"Danielle! You know darn well that you will never be able to explain this to him without him going ballistic, especially if he finds out I let you talk me out of telling him everything."

"But Aunt Sara, I think this all falls under that 'need to know' limitation that he told us, once before."

Aunt Sara shook her head. "No, Danielle. You know what kinds of subject matter he meant by that. This does not fall under that particular edict of his. Keeping this from your father would be wrong, and you know it!"

Danielle had noticed Dharalyn talking quietly to Gran, and then her grandmother had pitched in. "Danielle may be right, Sara, and Dharalyn just brought another possibility to my attention. I think we need to consider this very carefully."

"You do?" said Aunt Sara, as she folded her arms. *She wasn't going to be talked out of this.* "Tell me why you all think so."

Gran pursed her lips. "If we tell John everything right now, with that quick temper of his, he is likely to drive straight into the city tomorrow and confront this Mr. Moretti face to face. And you know very well what a huge mistake that would be."

Sara hesitated. She knew her brother well, and he was afraid of no man. Hearing that these men had come to the school to kidnap his little Danielle and Dharalyn, who he had become quite fond of and would protect like one of his own children, there was no doubt that he would probably do just that. And if he learned too, that Danielle had actually been shot in the process, well, then all bets would be off. Big John Walkerman was likely to try to take on the whole Moretti syndicate by himself, responding with a father's natural instinct to protect his child at all costs, and as a result, get himself killed in the process. "So, what do we do, then? You know this is a real problem, Mother, and it isn't just going to go away. This wicked man won't stop with only this one attempt to get the girls. As soon as he finds out that his men failed, he will just come at this family again from another direction."

"I'm sure you are right, Sara," she said, "but Darlin assures me he won't do anything, right away. And that should give us a chance to figure out how best to handle this matter. Right now, I heard that the authorities have no idea why these men were at the school, and even though John may have some suspicions of his own, I say we let them cool, for now."

Sara chewed on the side of her lip, like she did whenever she was deeply anxious. "And what about what happened to Danielle? What about the fact that this other crazy idiot, who was at the school last night, shot her twice and nearly killed her?"

"Auntie," said Danielle. "I'm fine now, really. In another day, there won't even be any scars. We can't let Daddy be killed over something that almost happened, but then didn't."

Sara shook her head and pursed her lips apprehensively. "I don't know about this, but I'll go with the majority decision, for now. You know, though, that this isn't over. Call it what you will, my woman's intuition tells me that this man, Michael Moretti, isn't through with his vendetta and will eventually come after you girls again."

That was when Dharalyn had taken Aunt Sara by her arm, and escorted her out of the room and had a private talk with her. When they'd come back, her aunt had looked a tiny bit better, but not much. After her aunt and grandmother had left the room to let her rest, Danielle had pressed Dhara on what she'd said to her aunt. Five minutes later, she sat on her bed fuming, as Dharalyn turned her back on her and left the room. Despite Danielle's best arguments and entreaties of persuasion, her dearest friend had told her nothing.

Sheriff Walter Drawbridge had been up all night long. He'd left the school to the state forensics boys and had made his way to the hospital. After speaking to the nurse in charge, he made his way toward a room on the third floor, where one of the men they'd removed from the school earlier was being held. He was still in the hospital instead of the lockup, because he'd been banged up a whole lot more than the others, and after some consideration, Walter decided he wanted to have a personal chat with him. While he walked, his mind dwelled on the bizarre scene at the school. This was one of those strange things you didn't see very often. For one thing, none of the state detectives on the scene had a clue as to why these particular men had come there. They had interviewed all of the kids on site and none of them seemed to have any idea what the men had wanted. They seemed to be looking for someone, or possibly something, was all that they had said, though no one seemed to know who or what they'd been looking for. Even so, there were just so many odd things about this scenario that bugged him. Like how this man he was going to see now had been found with a metal bar wrapped around his neck and the fact that it had taken an acetylene torch to get him out of it. Then there was the report from one of the forensics guys, one of their onsite blood experts, who had found some blood smeared on the floor that he was certain had not come from the teacher, Mr. Banks, who'd had a nasty bump on his head and a small cut that had bled some, but nowhere near the amount needed to make the mystery smear mark. And that mark, according to the scene investigator, they'd only found after using a Luminol based spray. Apparently, someone had cleaned up most of the blood before the investigators had gotten there, though the student they'd found caring for the injured teacher had claimed she knew nothing about that. There were a lot of inconsistencies at this crime scene, the kind that nagged at him with their ill-fitting nature. Like the cheerleader who the State Boys were claiming was a bona fide hero. She had taken out three of the bad guys on her own, using nothing but a fire extinguisher to somehow knock them unconscious. Walt had hefted the thing himself, giving it a practice whirl or two. He was a pretty fit man for his age and weighed twice what this heroic little lady did, and if she had actually swung that thing with the force and precision allowing her to take out three hardened criminals by herself, then he was going to join the circus and call himself a clown. It just didn't fit, and he planned to stop by later and have his own little talk with the supposed hero cheerleader. For now though, he had a more pressing engagement. Sheriff Walter Drawbridge showed his identification to the cop standing outside of the hospital security room, opened the door and walked in. He saw immediately that the man lying in the bed was busted up pretty bad. Casts on his wrist, his left arm, a body cast to protect several shattered ribs, black eyes, contusions over every visible part of his body. Someone had apparently worked this guy over, but good.

Bernard looked at the Sheriff as he came into view. He wouldn't be saying a thing to any cops. If Moretti found out he'd talked to the police about this caper, he'd be dead before he got out of these casts. He groaned in pain, as the throbbing in his arm got worse.

"Hurts, don't it?" said Walter, in a neutral voice. "I've had a few busted bones, in my time. Nothing worse than that kind of pain, when the old narcotics start to wear off. Oh, except of course, for the frigging itching later on. 'Bout a day or two after you've sweated in that stuff a bit, you'll be itching so bad you'll be ready to pull those casts off yourself, 'cept that would be detrimental to your health."

"What do you want?" asked Bernard. "I ain't got nothin to say to no cop."

"Oh, hell son, I'm not a cop. Just a friendly, neighborhood county sheriff. And I have me a pretty good idea who you guys all work for, so I doubt anything I can say to you is going to get you to tell me anything about why you were there at that school. But, I'm here on a different matter son. One that won't cause you any problems, but may shine a light on a little mystery I've been tracking. Tell you what, I'll just ask you a couple of questions that I promise won't cause you to break your professional oath, in any way. You do this little thing for me and answer me truthfully son, and I will speak straightaway to the head nurse on this floor, who is a personal friend of mine and make sure you have no issues at all with pain or any other discomfort. Heck son, she might even give ya a good scratch or two, if you help me out. Sound good to you?"

Bernard considered things for a moment, and then nodded his head a tiny bit, which hurt like hell. What did he have to lose? Especially since he was no fan of pain and the nurses around here didn't seem to care one bit that he was in agony. "Okay," he said, "deal."

"I'm just going to say a couple a words, and then you say whatever words come to your mind, after that. Okay?" Walt paused for a moment, letting this all sink in and then said, "A girl with white hair." A few seconds passed in complete silence and then the felon answered in a nervous tone:

"Bright green eyes, eyes that pierce you to your soul."

"Hmmmm," said Walt, and then said, "Anything else you can add?" Another quiet moment passed, as the two men stared at one another. "Listen, son," said Walt, in a friendly tone, "whatever or whoever did this to you, is still out there. And I'd like to catch it, before it decides to pay you or someone else in your crew a visit." Walt immediately saw a look of dread fill the man's eyes and then, the man added:

"I only caught a brief glimpse. But in the mirror, I think I saw these sharp teeth. Like a wolf or some vicious kinda human predator, like you see in a monster movie or read in a book. Not something you'd ever think you'd see in real life, though."

"'Cept you did see it, didn't you?"

"Yeah."

"That it?" asked Walt. He was pretty sure he had gotten everything, even though it sounded crazy as hell. Funny thing was, he knew the guy was telling the truth as he knew it.

"Yep, that's everything I know."

"Want to tell me who sent you guys to the school, while you are at it?"

Bernard closed his eyes. He had said all he was going to say. When he opened them again after a while, the nosy Sheriff was gone.

Melissa Wellington sat at her desk in her home, eyeing the card that lay in front of her, trying to decide what exactly she wanted to say. Her mind was mush right now, though, since it had been a very trying day, both mentally and physically. The police had been here much of the morning, and then the local paper had showed up, too. After speaking with the police, she'd had to pose for some pictures, which truth be told, she hadn't minded too much. The reporter had kept calling her a local hero, and she guessed that even though she had kept certain facts out of her statement to the cops and her answers to the reporter, the fact was she had played a really big part in what went down. She wasn't a complete glory hog though, and would have been happy to give Dharalyn a little of the credit, but there were obvious reasons why that would not fly. Even though she'd had ample opportunity, she hadn't said a word, or broken confidence with Dharalyn. The girl had saved her life and more, and in Melissa's mind, that simple fact alone had earned her respect and a singularly strange determination to keep the girl's secret. And what a secret it was, too. Before yesterday, Melissa had walked in a world that, for the most part, was easily understood and held no real surprises to someone like herself, who was well-read and worldly. Now, however, all that had changed in a single night's adventure. That girl Dharalyn was a real life, ass-kicking vampire chick. And a good one too, not evil at all, or so Melissa believed. After all, she had saved her from that despicable pervert in the girls' room, and then had helped Melissa save all of her friends. And if she had been a bad, evil vampire, she would never have done any of those things. So Melissa found, in spite of herself, that she was truly intrigued by the possibilities. She wanted to get to know this girl better, maybe even become friends. And if that didn't work out, well, you never knew when having a little bit of leverage on someone like her might come in handy. After all, knowing people's secrets or most private fears had always worked out for her, in the past.

Melissa looked up, as her mother came flouncing into her room. "Hi, honey," her mother said happily, "there's a TV crew downstairs that wants to talk to you. I guess my little hero's work is never done. And you know, your Dad and I were thinking, this won't look bad on your college applications, either: the fact that your entire community owes you such a large debt of gratitude, for saving so many of the other Cheer Squad members from whatever those terrible men had in mind."

"Thanks, Mother, I'll be down in a minute. I want to fix my hair and freshen up, if I'm going to be on television. Oh, by the way, is that annoying old Sheriff gone, yet?"

"Yes, dear," said her mother, who was now rifling through her closet, plainly on a mission to find what she deemed was an appropriate look for her daughter's appearance on TV. "He left a little while ago."

Thank God, he's gone, thought Melissa, the guy positively creeped her out. The whole time he'd asked her questions and listened to her answers, his eye had convulsed and winked like a freak in a carnival show. *He should get that looked at by a doctor,* she thought with a sardonic smile, as she got up to get ready.

Walt stopped by the Walkerman house on Sunday afternoon, to see how John's girl was doing. He knew from a list he had, that she'd been one of the teens up at the school during the mob fiasco, and he'd already made the rounds to most of the others. As he knocked on the door, a booming voice invited him in.

"Walt, you old son-of-a-gun, how are you?" asked Big John, who shook the sheriff's hand with gusto.

"Pretty fair, John, and you?"

"Not too bad. Back's been giving me issues lately, but so far I'm still moving. How are Trish and your little one, Laura?"

"Fine," lied Walt. Trish was his wife and Laura was his twelve-year-old daughter. "They're home, spending the day looking through old photo albums and preparing Sunday dinner. I'll be joining them myself, as soon as I get done with my follow-ups to the High School situation."

"The police were here yesterday taking the girls' statements. There still more you guys need?"

Walt nodded. "Just doing a little digging on my own, John. Those state boys sometimes overlook things, and I like to do my own follow-up in these matters."

"Suit yourself, I'll call the girls down," said John, friendly but a little irritated, as well. He really wanted the girls to have a chance to settle down after all they'd been through and the last thing he wanted was for them to have to relive the entire event again, for the Sheriff. Still, sometimes it paid to be neighborly, and stay on the old boy's good side. "I'll be right back, Walt," said John, as he left the kitchen.

A moment later, Sara Walkerman walked into the kitchen followed close behind by John's boy, Aaron, and then by the grandmother.... Walt stared for a long moment. He couldn't help himself. "Uh, sorry for staring, Ma'am," said Walt. "But I thought you were in a wheelchair, last I heard. I'm glad to see you are up and about."

Mabel Walkerman grinned and thought furiously. They hadn't quite decided as a family, how to explain her miraculous recovery. "Well thank you, Walter. It's hard to explain really, combination of some natural remedies I've been taking and a fair amount of prayer. Little by little I started feeling better, until one day I was back up, again."

"Well that's just terrific, Mabel," said Walter, who was genuinely pleased. He always liked hearing good news when it came to families with medical issues. "It sounds like you've been truly blessed. I'm so very happy to see this, for myself."

Mabel smiled; Walt seemed to be genuinely happy for her recovery. In fact, she didn't ever remember him being quite so animated.

"Here they are," said Big John, as he walked into the now crowded kitchen with both Danielle and Dharalyn in tow. He saw Walt glance at the girls and then look again, with genuine surprise showing on his face and his eyes peering intently.

"Well, heck, John, don't tell me that all this time, you had another daughter hidden away somewhere?"

John laughed, he hoped not too forcefully. "This is Danielle's cousin, Dharalyn. She's from the Midwest and is staying with us, now."

"Oh, okay, now this makes more sense. I had her listed along with Danielle, on this report," he said, showing a report binder he was carrying. "But I thought it was a typo or a mistake, since I knew, or thought I did, that Danielle was the only teenage girl living here. Well, my mistake. Hello there, young lady," he said, by way of introduction. "I'm known in these parts as Sheriff Walter Drawbridge, though most of the folks around here just call me Walt."

"Nice to meet you, Walt," said Dharalyn, a bit timidly.

"Hey there, Walt," said Danielle.

"Danielle," said Walter, "good to see you, too. You girls feel like having a little sit down, with me? Won't take but five or ten minutes, and then I'll be out of your hair."

Danielle and Dharalyn both said they didn't mind, and Walt went through the same few questions he'd asked most of the other students. He knew, from the police report, that Dharalyn hadn't been in the detention room when the one thug, who had first arrived, had taken out their teacher. From the report, one of the perps had made the two girls, Vee and Danielle, sit on the floor until things had gone bad, at which time he'd just up and left. This was where he had a problem. In the report he held, one of the cheerleaders said she remembered one of the thugs in the larger group telling one of the other perps, who at the time was binding their wrists, to make sure to leave their legs free. When the second perp had questioned the first perp about this, the first perp, who was likely the group leader, had said that they were planning to move this group down to the other room. In Walt's mind, some obvious pieces to this puzzle were missing and he suspected that this particular room, the detention room, was where he was missing something.

"So where were you, during all of this?" Walt asked Dharalyn.

"I had found a classroom open, when I saw the men first come in and ducked inside. It was very dark in there and they didn't see me."

"And so, you stayed in there until when?"

Dharalyn paused then, not sure how to proceed, since lying didn't come very easily to her. "Well, after a little while...."

"She saw me walking the halls looking for her and came out of the classroom," interrupted Danielle. "That was when we went to the main entrance, where we saw the police arriving and so we waited by the front doors for them."

Walt was irritated, but tried not to show it. He'd been trying to get a read on Dharalyn's story, which for the most part rang true, but then Danielle had jumped in with her version of the answer, just as his old eye had begun to twitch. He hadn't been focusing on Danielle at the time, and so the whole question had been a throwaway. Probably true, but he couldn't know for sure. Being a patient man, he decided to table the current conversation, for now, and if the opportunity arose, revisit it at another time. "Well, I suppose that's all I need from you two right now. John, Sara, Mabel, it's been a pleasure." Big John then shook his hand and Sara and Mabel gave him a quick, neighborly hug.

A short time later, Walt was outside with only his thoughts for company and thinking he might call it a day, carefully pulled out his cell phone. "Guess I'll give the girls a call, let them know I'm on my way home," he said, to no one in particular. Looking at the phone and seeing only two bars of signal strength, he casually walked across the lawn, away from the gravel drive as he held his phone out, looking for a better signal. "That's better," he mumbled, and held the phone down near his waist so he could see the numbers out of the sun's glare. Suddenly he hesitated, and knelt down on the ground near a spot of bare earth, where the grass only grew in thin tufts. The spot was apparently the site of a small mud puddle whenever it rained, because square in the corner of the dried mud, was a perfect impression of a small shoeprint. The imprint was made up of rows of intricate characters, like writing of some kind, patterned across the bottom of the sole. He knew this print. He had a picture of it that he had taken out in the woods not two or three miles from here. Walt turned and looked back toward the house, with both a thoughtful expression on his face and brown eyes that shone with curiosity. *Yep*, he thought to himself, as his mind whirled, *something more here I need to be considering.*

Dharalyn sat at a lunch table, just outside of the cafeteria double doors that opened to the outside dining area, when she spied Danielle making her way toward her. She opened her container of grapes and pineapple that Gran had made for her this morning and was startled when someone else dropped down beside her.

"Hey there, my new buddies," remarked Vee. "How are you guys doing this fine day?"

"Hello, Vee! Nice to see you," said Dhara, smiling at the plucky girl. She was wearing her hair with red streaks, today.

"Hi, Vee," said Danielle, as she sat on the opposite side of the table. "I see you've changed color on us."

"My hero," Vee said sweetly, grinning at Danielle. "No, really," she said in a very serious tone. "I know I haven't told you yet, but thanks for saving my worthless life."

"Thanks for helping to save mine," said Danielle, giving her a wide grin, "and you are definitely not, in any sense of the word, worthless."

"You're welcome," Vee said brightly, as she plunged a straw into a carton of milk. "By the way, I gave those cops a real good yarn to suck on. Nothing at all about, you know what. I even managed to clean up most of Danielle's blood, before they got there," she whispered. "Oh, and here's your palm thingy back," she added, handing a small plastic bag to Danielle. "I don't think it works, anymore. It doesn't make my hand tingle anymore and when I tried it yesterday, I hurt my hand."

Dharalyn and Danielle both laughed at that. "It just needs to be recharged," said Danielle, putting the plastic bag inside her handbag.

"Hey, ladies," said Christian as he sat down next to Danielle, directly across from Dharalyn. "Shove over some, Danielle," he said, giving her a butt nudge.

"What are you doing here?" said Vee.

"He's a friend, I think," said Dharalyn, as she smiled coyly at Christian, who was giving her the strangest look.

"Don't you usually hang out with the stuck-up crowd?" said Vee, accusingly.

"I hang out with who I want to hang out with," responded Christian, as he gave her a warm smile. "Even rude people, sometimes."

While Vee scowled, Christian gave Dharalyn another wide grin, as he stared at her. "So, you hear the rumors floating around?"

Dharalyn and Danielle looked at one another. "No," they answered in unison.

"You know how everyone says Melissa is this big hero, and all. Well, a little bird whispered to me that there may have been someone else, giving her a hand. Someone who doesn't want any credit for helping all of those people. I've been giving it a bit of thought and wonder who that could possibly have been, if it's true. You have any ideas Danielle?" he suddenly asked, as he turned and glanced at the startled girl.

"I have absolutely no idea what you are talking about," Danielle said flippantly, and began opening the bag lunch Gran had made for her. "You know, Chris," Danielle stated, "you have an infuriating way about you sometimes, anybody ever tell you that?"

"Maybe," he responded. "I think you told me that once, or something close to it."

"No, what I told you was that I find you very insensitive, at times."

"Oh, yeah," he teased, "I believe that was just before you flipped me the bird."

"I didn't flip you the bird. I flipped the teacher the bird. If I was gonna flip off an illiterate like you, I'd just give you these three fingers," she said, holding up her second, third and fourth fingers all together, "and tell you to read between the lines."

"Danielle," warned Dharalyn, "I don't think we need any more detention, thank you."

"Yeah, Danielle," said Christian in a teasing voice, "stop being so crabby and vulgar. Or I'll embarrass you and tell everyone here, how really good looking a certain friend of mine thinks you are."

"Who thinks she's good looking?" asked Vee.

Christian smiled and looked at Danielle, who was ignoring him at the moment. "Don't know if I should say. Last time I talked about this, I got yelled at."

"Please tell us, Christian," said Dharalyn, giving him a warm smile that she could tell, was having a profound effect on him.

Christian looked into her green eyes and felt a nervous twinge in the pit of his stomach. *The way it sounded when she said his name... wow!* Pulling himself together, he quickly said, "Well, a really good friend of mine.... She doesn't want to believe me about this, but he's told me twice now, that he thinks she's really cute."

"Who!" chorused Vee and Dharalyn, at the same time.

"Tommy Wheeler," said Christian, as he observed Danielle's attempt to ignore him. "And he means it!" he added, fervently.

Danielle gave him a murderous look that caused him to laugh out loud, and then raising his hands defensively, he jumped up and walked off.

"Oh, God," said Vee, as she saw who was coming their way, "what now?"

Dharalyn looked up and saw Melissa Wellington walk up to their table. "Hi, Dharalyn," said Melissa, as she handed her a card. "I wanted to give you this. It's personal," she then added, hastily. "Read it when you don't have an audience."

"Okay, Melissa, thanks," Dharalyn said.

"Oh, and by the way, because of the fiasco at the school last Thursday evening, my party had to be rescheduled for this coming Friday night, at eight. I would really like you to come," she said, looking at Dharalyn with a strange expression on her face, "and by all means, bring your little friend, Danielle. I don't suppose you'll come unless she is invited, too."

"And my friend Vee, can she come, as well?"

Melissa raised her hands and then dropped them, while sighing loudly. "Sure, why not. As long as we're being downwardly mobile, we might as well invite the whole, sorry bunch." Melissa glared at Vee and then turned and walked away, her shoulders and head held high.

Danielle grimaced and shook her head. "There is no way I'm stepping foot in that witch's house!"

"Me, either," said Vee. "I wouldn't be caught dead...."

"Oh, yes, you are," said Dharalyn, giving Danielle a hard, firm look. "And so are you," she added, turning and giving Vee a friendly squeeze on her wrist. "We need to be the better people, here. Show her that her arrogance and tendency toward pettiness doesn't scare anyone away."

"Dharalyn," said Danielle, in a complaining tone that suggested she was readying an argument.

"No, Danielle, I'm very serious about this. This type of social gathering provides an excellent opportunity for us all to learn to bridge the gaps between one another. Reach out and befriend even our would-be enemies, until they fold under the pressure of friendship, harmony and love."

"Oh, my God, is she for real?" asked Vee, as she pointed her thumb at Dhara and gave Danielle a bewildered glance.

"Oh, I'm afraid so. Welcome to my world," Danielle said in a tone dripping with exasperation.

Vee gazed between her two newest friends for a moment and then came to an abrupt decision. "Okay, then," she said, with a sullen shrug of her shoulders. "I guess you can count me in." Grumbling to herself, she suddenly added as an afterthought, "Can I get a ride?"

Danielle nodded once, folded her arms and scowled.

Later, at home, Dharalyn opened the card from Melissa and read:

Dear Vampire Girl,

This letter isn't easy for me to write, but I feel the need to personally thank you for what you did for me, and the way you made me face my fears. I've always thought of myself as a strong person, but that guy, the one in the bathroom, he would have taken everything from me, my self-respect, my dignity and most of all, my virtue. There's no doubt in my mind, if he had gone through with his intentions, he would have scarred me for life. I've never felt so utterly helpless, so completely petrified and incapable of moving or even speaking. I was scared and in a very dark place, and there was a moment where I was absolutely certain I was going to die. Then, like an answer to my silent prayer, you suddenly appeared. Like some wild, avenging angel, you had such a frightening look about you and for a second I was afraid of you, but then, when I saw your concerned eyes looking at me after busting that guy up, I knew, deep in my heart of hearts that you were my friend and there to rescue me.

It took a while for me to realize that you did more than physically save me; you empowered me to take my life back. By involving me in taking out the rest of those hoodlums, you helped me face my fears and inner torment so that I don't wake up screaming and having nightmares over this for the rest of my life.

I know most people think I'm kind of a biatch and sometimes I probably am, but I want you to know that I really like and respect you. I have never felt this kind of connection with another person, never really had a true friend, one I could trust not to stab me in the back or talk bullcrap about me. But I know from our short time together that you are not that type of person. I can tell there is no pettiness in you. You don't use other people's pain to make yourself feel superior, or so that you can exploit their fears for your own benefit like some people do. So, I hope this doesn't come across as too mushy, but I sincerely want you to know that with all you've done for me, I will never forget or forsake you. Dharalyn, I consider you my only real friend and I honestly hope that someday, you might feel the same way about me.

Lastly, please know your secret is always safe with me and will die with me.

Love,
Mel

P.S. I know you're very close to Danielle, so, for your sake, I will try and get along with her, even though she really bugs me sometimes.

P.P.S. Oh, who the hell am I trying to kid! I don't know why, but I can't freaking stand that girl. I will, however, like I said, try to be nice.

After Dharalyn read the card, she placed it carefully inside the small box Gran had given her, along with her other treasured possessions. The necklace that her father had given her and a copy of Danielle's lullaby, which her best friend had sung to comfort her that first, lonely night.

That evening as Danielle lay sleeplessly in her bed, her cold feet pushed up under Dhara's warm legs, her mind coursed with a single disturbing, unrelenting thought. Of course, Christian had been making it all up, but then again, he liked Dharalyn a lot, anyone could see that. And so, would he dare get on her bad side by telling Danielle a bold faced lie? One that was at its heart, ultimately hurtful and mean spirited? Deep down, she didn't believe for a moment that what he had said was possible, and had dwelled on it through an interminably long school day. A day when she should have paid more attention to her classes, rather than dissecting every nuance of Christian's facial expression, when he had made that one particular statement. Still though, she was uncertain, she couldn't let go of the completely annoying, nagging, unlikely possibility that there was the tiniest, infinitesimal bit of truth to his unexpected declaration. A simple sentence that had packed a whole lot of scary possibilities within those few, modest words:

Blue-eyed, blond haired, absolutely gorgeous Tommy Wheeler, thought she was good looking.

CHAPTER 23

WELCOME TO THE NSA, JACK

"**G**ood morning Katheryn, so what's the good news today?"
Katheryn Kranshaw, Jack Walkerman's very attractive personal secretary, smiled widely at her boss with teeth so white, Jack often teased that they could use them as a light source, in the event of a power failure. "Well sir, there's a strange, little man waiting for you in your office. He's been in there for about a half hour now."

Jack nodded, opened the door to his office and went inside. The man sitting in the leather chair next to his desk was small in stature and had a very solemn cast to his features. He stood immediately as Jack entered and said, "Agent Jack Harold Walkerman, I presume?"

"That's correct," replied Jack. "Who the hell are you and what are you doing in my office?"

"Marlin J. Smith, special courier for the National Security Agency. I've been directed to hand you this missive and answer any questions you might have."

Jack faltered. "The NSA...what in the world does the NSA want with me?"

"You sent a preliminary report about subject DM16 to your immediate supervisor. Well, he forwarded it to our offices and it has been assigned a priority one escalation by the senior staff there." Marlin Smith raised his right hand and Jack saw that he had a slim, metallic case attached to his wrist. The courier spun a couple of numeric dials, and then turned to Jack. "I need your thumbprint for identification, please."

Jack pressed his thumb against the appropriate black square on the case and saw a green light flash. A moment later, the case opened and the courier handed him a thin folder. Jack's eyes widened at the official designation on the cover, which showed that it had come straight from Washington, D.C. and so immediately opened it. Quietly and with great consternation, he read the document.

NATIONAL SECURITY COUNCIL MEMORANDUM 1078 - ABOVE TOP SECRET

September 15

Special Review Memorandum SUBJECT/DM16
To: Jack Harold Walkerman/FBI
CC: The Secretary of Defense
BCC: The Attorney General
The Chairman Joint Chiefs of Staff

SUBJECT: Agency Reassignment

After receiving your preliminary report on subject DM16, the NSA Director/ Fort Meade in conjunction with FBI Task Force Supervisor/Washington, D.C. hereby grants you temporary transfer to NSA Headquarters, Fort Meade for Blue Team, Special OPS session committee consultation and project assessment.

Per this directive, you are hereby ordered to:

1. Immediate relocation to Fort Meade to determine short-term risk assessment concerning DM16 consistent with U.S. security interests and long-term control/treatment and management of DM16.

2. Proposals for timeline concerning best scenario for the procurement/ confinement and debriefing of DM16.

3. Recommendation for appropriate steps to be taken concerning the disposition of DM16 and as to the possible benefits with all information to be directly forwarded in conjunction with NSA/Director to the current administration heads.

The President has directed that the NSA in conjunction with Agent Jack Harold Walkerman, implement maximum cautionary measures and utilize all available resources in the review of this matter. The review should be forwarded to the Presidential Threat Analysis Committee by November 15th.

(signed)

Salizar W. Brezinski

NATIONAL SECURITY COUNCIL
INTERDEPARTMENTAL GROUP
FOR SPECIAL OPS ASSESSMENT PER PRESIDENTIAL SECURITY
REVIEW MEMORANDUM NSC-1185

Jack wiped the back of his hand across his forehead, as his mind raced. His little memorandum, which he had sent per standard operating procedure, had been given a case designation that should have seen it fast-tracked into the 'unexplainable phenomena' area of the DSR computer system, which stored thousands of new pieces of information on every conceivable threat. Most of the information in this designated class revolved around things like UFO sightings and alien abduction reports and so, went unread and were simply filed away. Jack had submitted the report on what he'd learned, primarily as a precautionary measure in case matters pertaining to Dharalyn came to light in the future. He had never expected it to be reviewed, let alone given what was now a high priority, national security response. He was being transferred to Fort Meade, on loan to the NSA for an unspecified amount of time. And it was very likely that soon they would be bringing Dharalyn in for an intensive debriefing, the likes of which only the NSA could provide. The end result being that Dharalyn would probably end up in a secure, underground facility somewhere and behind locked doors for good.

Jack felt a sudden wave of nausea sweep through him. This was not what he had wanted at all. Though he was suspicious of Dharalyn's true motives for being here, he had figured on keeping a close eye on the vampire girl himself, and only calling in the proverbial cavalry if the situation eventually warranted it. Deep down, he didn't truly believe Dharalyn was an actual threat of any kind, certainly not a national security one. However, something in his report had apparently come to the attention of a much higher authority, and things were liable to escalate quickly, if he couldn't find a way to control it. He wasn't especially concerned about the vampire girl or what would become of her, she wasn't the issue here. In fact, part of him would be more than glad to see her permanently removed from Danielle's presence, except for the fact that he had seen for himself how much better his niece was now. He knew, without a doubt, that Dani would be absolutely crushed if this 'Dharalyn' was taken away. There was an unmistakable bond between them; one Danielle needed more than anything right now, especially with her mother gone. It might even cause her irreparable emotional harm, and could possibly send her back into that dark place, which she might never again escape. Jack fretted, and decided he would try his best to provide damage control over the ensuing situation. He would never even consider bending the rigid guidelines of his integrity, or fail to keep his oath. That was one thing he would never do...except, possibly, where Danielle's wellbeing was an issue. Sometimes in life, an individual could mean so much to you, that you would break that which by its very nature was indissoluble. This line of thought made him pause in retrospect. Was he really ready to put his entire career on the line over this matter? Risk his pension and the respect of his peers, which he had earned for years of exemplary service? After all, he was known to be steadfast in all things and always stayed the course. He was a consummate professional, and his character was as solid and immoveable as the bedrock of the earth. He would do what he had to do, dammit. He was Jack Walkerman, FBI, and he had a responsibility to his post and to his service. *Sorry Dani,* he thought to himself, *but this has to be done.*

He turned and looked morosely out of the window of his office as he reevaluated and took stock of the situation. The unexpected lump that had appeared in his throat was forcing him to consider the fact that he wasn't being honest with himself at all. If this proceeded like he suspected it would, there would be an unavoidable casualty in all of this; a complete loss of faith and trust from someone very near and dear to him. It was something that bothered him deeply, more than he liked to admit to himself, because in fact, it would be seen as a betrayal on his part. Jack snorted and lifted his head high as he tried to fight off the melancholy mood that threatened to undermine his self-confidence. He needed to remember who he was, and what he stood for. Again he found himself vacillating between two important points of view, his professional responsibility versus the guilt that lay within his heart. So what if this situation traumatized her, that was life! Maybe it was about time she grew up a bit. Time she realized the world was a mean, tough place to live and there was very little room for sentimentality when it came to protecting the people and the security of this great country. Though she would hate him at first, he could only hope that eventually she would realize he had done the right thing. Jack placed his hand against his forehead and rubbed his temples, keeping his face turned away from the NSA courier. Incredibly, he felt a dampness appear at the corner of his eyes, though he refused to give credence to that fact by wiping them. When this situation played itself out, they would go in and take Dharalyn away, and send her to a place where she would never be seen or heard from again. A place where she would be poked, prodded and treated in a way that had very little to do with Fidelity, Bravery and Integrity, the proud motto of the FBI. The resulting tragedy of this situation would primarily center around his relationship with Danielle. Because, after the dust settled and those who played for keeps made their bold moves, there was one thing of which he was completely certain.

His precious niece, she who'd brought such unmitigated joy and been a beacon of light, a ward against the shadows of his solitary and lonely existence, was NEVER going to speak to him again!

EPILOGUE

"If it pleases my lady, the priests are here with their results," stated the herald, whose job it was to announce visitors.

"Show them in," said an irritated Heradeth Maximus Gordred, powerful Sedai Novi, Empress of House Gordred, head of the New Order and de facto Khan. All this because those damned Fayeki had failed, weeks ago, to accomplish a very simple task. Soon a group of five Cavalithic priests shambled into her private audience chamber, which was a small, crystal domed building located in the center of an extensive garden, which was kept meticulously groomed by her small army of servants. All along the curved wall of the room there were 32 Cascai Tha-Notoo retainers, kneeling on their Serept-Ti (pads of respect and subservience), blood-sworn to obey her slightest whim or command. Interspersed between every third Cascai was an Atrova Guardian, garbed in the black and red ceremonial robes of The House of Gordred. They stood ready to defend and protect her with their very lives, should the need arise. The priests stopped and made obeisance, by bowing nine times in succession and then kneeling before her, with their foreheads against the floor. After a moment, she waved her hand and her daughter and heir, Sorellia, clucked and signaled for them to stand and come forward.

"What have you discovered about the whereabouts of the Malakovani heir?" asked Heradeth, her haughty voice high and impatient.

The head priest, Calumus Eventi, stepped forward looking extremely apprehensive. "We've gone over the Portal and studied the transport crystals extensively, My Lady, and we can find nothing that gives us any indication of where the malfunctioning Portal may have sent her."

"Do you think it likely that she may have been killed, then?" she asked hopefully.

The priest looked even more crestfallen. "No, My Lady. If she was, then the Caradinian Life Jewel in the throne of the Khan would be extinguished. The fact that the previous Khan is dead, but the jewel still shines brightly, proves that the heir is indeed still alive somewhere. We just have no way of tracking her through the Portal, since it is agreed that the accident that caused the Portal glitch sent the heir somewhere outside of our known spatial continuum."

"So, you have no way to track her, yet you are certain she is still alive?" Heradeth said scowling, her desire to assume the seat of Khan-Tessera and thereby gain complete control of the Sedai council, thwarted by this one frustrating detail.

"Excuse me, My Lady," said a tentative, squeaky voice.

Heradeth saw that one of the Cavalithic novices at the back had spoken, earning him a glowering look from his superior.

"Yes," she said imperiously, giving him a sharp glance, "you have something you wish to add to this discussion?"

"My Lady, please," interrupted Calumus, "this particular novice has been a grave disappointment to our Order, and his speaking out of turn will earn him a severe punishment for his temerity. I beg you to please disregard his insolent outburst!"

Ignoring the head priest completely, Heradeth motioned the novice forward. "You appear to have something to say," she stated coldly, as he knelt before her. "I hope, for your sake, it is worth-while. Present yourself and be heard!"

"Thank you, your most magnanimous and benevolent Heradeth. My name is Cascious Bronavul, first level novice of the Cavalithic Order of House Gordred. Though my superiors think otherwise, I believe I have a possible solution to your problem."

"And what would that be?" she said, curiously. She could see by the look on his face that the head priest was growing absolutely beside himself with anger. It was almost worth the interchange to watch him fume, though this one would pay dearly later, if his gamble fell flat.

"My Lady, I believe the very answer you seek lies in understanding the fundamental characteristics of the Caradinian Life Jewel of the Khan's council seat. You see, it is attuned to the house of Malakovani, and more specifically, the council seat holder and the Malakovani heir. If we employ the proper resources, I am certain that we can track her, using a kind of homing tracer. Once attuned to the same frequency as the Caradinian Jewel, it should lead us, or at the least show us, the current location of the heir."

Heradeth thought furiously, for a moment. It was a stretch, to be sure, but it might possibly work. She stepped down from her dais and stood directly in front of the novice. "And you believe you can do this thing?"

Cascious put on a brave face. "I am certain of it my lady, if no one stands in my way, that is." He glanced back towards Calumus Eventi, who would have his hide if this failed and then added, "If I am given all the support and resources I will require, I am sure that I can get you the information you seek within fifteen days, twenty at the most."

Heradeth studied the young upstart before her. She liked his temerity and his lack of fear. It would drive him to succeed at all costs. "Very well," she said, as a barely suppressed smile appeared on his face. "You do this and besides having my personal recognition for your efforts, your place in the New Order will be a certainty. You have ten days to bring me the results I need. Now go, I will see you have the full support of your priesthood," glancing sharply toward Calumus Eventi, to make certain he understood, "and that you get all the resources you require. The rest, my young novice, is entirely up to you."

"My most humble appreciations, My Lady. I will not fail you, you have my word."

"Very well, then...you may go." With that, she dismissed the group of priests with a wave and then retired to a rear chamber, followed closely by her daughter, Sorellia. "Make certain that buffoon Calumus doesn't undermine the efforts of this young novice, Cascious Bronavul," said Heradeth, brusquely. "I'm certain he would like nothing better than to see him fail, and I wouldn't put it past him to do something underhanded to make certain that the young man does. It is absolutely essential to our plans that he comes through on this matter. Also, prepare a full team of priests, oracles, Fayeki and a few Sedai Novi from within our family, to go out once we find the location of the Malakovani heir. I want this to be entirely aboveboard and done according to the letter of the law. Once she is legally tested and found to be unworthy in the eyes of Anon, I want the Praxillari notified so that they may carry out their honor-bound duty, without any more delays. Afterward, her body is to be returned to Asreod, where the results of her examination, resultant failure and cover-up by her family are to be made public. This will allow us to denounce her family's claim to a council seat, casting them out in dishonor and making me the new Khan-Tessera, by default."

"Yes, mother, it will be as you wish. Once we locate her, are you certain that she will fail the test?"

Heradeth nodded. "Yes, my information is infallible, and from an unequivocally reliable and trustworthy source. She failed the Probost and that fact was then covered up by the Khan-Tessera and Empress of House Malakovani, Pharalyn Sarina Malakovani. When her daughter, the heir, is found and it is confirmed that she is not one with her Egana and linked to her source, this travesty will finally be put right, and the ascension of House Gordred can move forward, with the support of the entire council behind it."

Sorellia Maximus Gordred gave a tight lipped and rueful smile. "I am so proud of you, Mother. Soon the hopes, dreams and aspirations of our house will come to pass, and it will have you to thank for it."

Heradeth caressed her daughter's cheek and said, "It has been a long time coming, my dear one; for within you lies the culmination of all of our families' expectations. Now that you have passed the Probost, you will soon stand before your peers and charge the Crystal Towers, proving once and for all that House Malakovani has been eclipsed, and that House Gordred is now without peer and stands alone as the most blessed of Anon. Now, go and see to all our preparations, as I have bid you. I am tired and need to rest a bit, as well as feed."

After Sorellia left, a tall shape moved out from a dark corner.

"Your daughter is lovely and quite dutiful, if a bit naïve," said Abraxis, stroking his chin thoughtfully, "though I must say, sometimes I get the feeling she is only telling you just what you want to hear."

"Do not ever doubt my daughter's conviction. She is loyal, powerful and completely devoted to furthering the goals of this family, and that is what's important."

Feeling somewhat chastised, Abraxis quickly changed the subject. "Do you think this novice will find the location of the girl?"

"He will, if he values his future."

"And if he finds her, what then?"

"Then she will be tested and when she fails, again, the Praxillari Elite will seal her fate."

"And if somehow she passes?"

"You yourself told me she would not. Are you having second thoughts about this matter?"

"Not at all. I believe exactly as you do, that the girl should have been executed at the conclusion of her Probost, which I know for an absolute fact she failed. It was the greatest sacrilege against the Creator's will that her mother deigned to save her, against accepted doctrine and the conventions of our faith, therefore compromising her position and placing her own life at risk."

"Which is why the majority of the council agreed along with the support of the Praxillarium Nine, to terminate her life."

"So, it wasn't a unanimous vote in the council."

"No, I'm afraid as always, there were a few dissenting opinions. Some wanted to hear her side of things, although that is completely unreasonable. There is only one answer, one way to handle things when Sedai law is broken. Only one manner of justice, when a Sedai has failed the Probost and poor Pharalyn has received her just due for deceiving the Sedai Novi Council, by lying to protect her daughter."

"Not all may see it that way."

"They will, when the girl is tested yet again and fails before the Sedai Oracles."

"And if by some extreme fluke, she doesn't?"

"Then you would likely be found criminally incompetent and ultimately liable for her mother's death," said Heradeth, "which is why, if the girl should somehow pass, you will need to make certain that none of those who are involved with the testing of the girl return. Only the Sedai are sacrosanct in this matter, all others are to be considered expendable and should be silenced, if the cause demands it."

"Even though I am a Guardian and trained in all forms of advanced combat, how do you expect me to stand alone against the Praxillari and the rather large contingent of support staff that will accompany us?"

"All of the Sedai who will accompany you will be completely loyal to me and some of them are nearly as accomplished as I, in both power and ability. Besides, both the Praxillari and the Fayeki that will accompany you are loyal to my house, and I will instruct them to follow your lead in this matter. With them along and the power of the Adepts, you should have no trouble dealing with any unexpected circumstances that may arise. Besides, we both know that it's very unlikely that this particular situation will come to pass. The girl will fail, as before, and the Praxillari will do that for which they are ordained. It is doubtful that you will even need to get your hands dirty in this."

"Then why do I need to go at all?"

"Oh, come now, Abraxis. The girl knows and trusts you. Who better than you, the captain of the Malakovani Guardians, to handle this matter with the least amount of trouble?"

Abraxis nodded. He was faithful and pious, and would do what had to be done in the name of justice, honor and according to the precepts and will of Anon. "Very well," he said, as he turned to go, "all will be as you wish."

GLOSSARY

Danielle's Lullaby:

Go to sleep and good night
Everything will be all right
Don't you fear I am here
I will make it all okay
Try to relax under the stars
I am never very far
So put your trust in me
Then you will see
That no matter where I am
You're always in my heart

(Written for Danielle by: Ciara Clark, Age 13)

Made in the USA
Charleston, SC
29 July 2012